Direct Actions

by
Terry Olson

authorHOUSE™

1663 LIBERTY DRIVE, SUITE 200
BLOOMINGTON, INDIANA 47403
(800) 839-8640
WWW.AUTHORHOUSE.COM

First published by AuthorHouse 09/28/05

ISBN: 1-4208-7475-6 (sc)
ISBN: 1-4208-7476-4 (dj)

Library of Congress Control Number: 2005906866

Printed in the United States of America
Bloomington, Indiana

This book is printed on acid-free paper.

For Bryna, Sierra and Jordan
the patient Muses of East Lansing

Acknowledgments

Thanks to Nicole Appleberry, Courtney Bach, Emily Bach, Gary Byrne, Jo Byrne, Alicia Davis, Jeff Foldie, and Ian Wright for their contributions in bringing this novel to life. Special thanks to my wife and children, for their indulgence and support, without which this book would not have been possible.

1

Jeremy Jefferson hustled along the sidewalk toward the courthouse, checking his watch on the way. He had no time to admire the gorgeous October afternoon. He was five minutes late for the arraignment, and Judge Welch, above all things, was prompt. Jeremy leapt up four marble steps to the entrance and listened to the lonely rhythm his dress shoes tapped out in the sleepy hallway. He leafed through the file as he descended a stained oak stairway to Welch's basement courtroom.

In seconds, Jeremy had absorbed the basics about his client. Zeb Radamacher stood charged with one count of felony arson and one count of malicious destruction. He had already been in jail for a week, unable to post a twenty-five thousand dollar cash bond. Zeb was seventeen, lived with his mother, and together, the two of them could not afford to hire a private attorney to defend the case.

Jeremy shuffled through the police reports in the file, consuming the facts of the alleged crime. Zeb had apparently put sand in the crankcases of three pieces of heavy equipment at a construction site. And as if that wasn't enough, he had thrown a homemade gasoline bomb onto a bulldozer for good measure. Unfortunately for Zeb, a state trooper passing on the interstate had seen the blaze as soon as it started and made it to the scene in time to tackle the fleeing boy.

"Pleased you could join us, Mr. Jefferson," Judge Welch said as Jeremy entered the courtroom. Welch's sarcasm was coated with a good-natured smile and might have passed for sincerity to a casual onlooker.

"Sorry, Your Honor," Jeremy said. "We were just called down on this case this afternoon."

Jeremy was the last player to enter the stage. The judge sat behind a maple-stained bench, raised to reflect his authority, flanked on his left by the court recorder. Deputy Gaylord Short, a good-natured bailiff, stood at the end of the jury box guarding a prisoner – presumably Zeb Radamacher. Ed Gray, Wabeno County's elected prosecutor, was seated at the prosecution desk. An audience of one sat in the pews that made up the courtroom gallery. She was a young blonde woman who Jeremy recognized vaguely as a reporter for *The Milton Beacon*.

"Could I have just a moment with my client, Your Honor?" Jeremy asked.

"Certainly, Mr. Jefferson," Welch said. "Certainly. We're all here to serve you."

Jeremy approached the prisoner. The boy had pale white skin and a shock of tangled blond hair. He looked like he had just awakened. His eyes were a clear blue, and he smiled slightly, somewhat amused, as if the arraignment was staged for his entertainment.

"Zeb?" he whispered, as he laid a hand on the boy's shoulder. "I am Jeremy Jefferson. From Mr. Sage's office. Mr. Sage couldn't be here, so I'm here to get you through this hearing."

The boy nodded without a word.

"We already represent you on this arson and destruction of property case," Jeremy whispered, holding up his file. "But we've been called down for an arraignment on a new charge. Do you understand?"

"Not really," the boy said.

"We've been appointed to represent you on this case, where you've already been charged."

"Uh-huh."

"And now they're filing a new charge – they're accusing you of another crime. We got a call that there'd be an arraignment on the new charge this afternoon. We'll walk you through the arraignment now, and then get appointed to represent you on this new charge, okay?"

"I guess," Zeb said. "What's the new charge?"

"I don't know yet," Jeremy said. "We'll find out together."

"Okay."

"Keep quiet for now. We'll find out what the new charge is, and I'll try to get you some kind of bond you can post. Your bond's at twenty-five thousand on the arson case. Are you going to be able to post that?"

"My mom is trying," Zeb said. "She said she might come up with enough for the bail guy in a week."

"Okay," Jeremy said. "Hang in there. I've got all your info in the file here. So just let me do the talking."

2

Zeb nodded.

"Ready, Your Honor," Jeremy said, walking to the lectern in the center of the courtroom. Jeremy motioned for Zeb to join him as Welch called the case. Welch called Jeremy forward and handed him the amended complaint with the new charge. Jeremy's eyes darted to the middle of the document. Count Three - Terrorism. The war on terror had only been a news story to Jeremy Jefferson. Reading the charge on the complaint seemed slightly unreal.

He whispered to Zeb to inform the boy he was about to become an accused terrorist, pointing out the new charge for his client to read, but it only drew a look of overwhelmed confusion from the boy.

"Counsel," Judge Welch said, "your appearances for the record."

"Jeremy Jefferson on behalf and with Zeb Radamacher, Your Honor."

"Ed Gray on behalf of the People of the State of Michigan, Your Honor."

"You are Zeb Radamacher?" Judge Welch said to the boy.

The boy looked to Jeremy, who nodded in the affirmative, and the boy said, "Yes, sir."

"Mr. Radamacher, I have just handed your attorney a copy of an amended complaint. Do you acknowledge receipt of that document?" Judge Welch said.

"We'd acknowledge receipt of the complaint, Your Honor," Jeremy said. "We'd waive reading and ask the Court to enter a plea of not guilty."

"Very well," Welch said.

"Now, Mr. Radamacher," Welch continued on methodically, "you understand that your attorney has waived reading of the charge against you, and the Court is going to enter a plea of not guilty on your behalf."

"I guess," Zeb said. "Yes, sir."

"You understand that this amended complaint contains an additional charge? You have already been charged with arson and malicious destruction of property, and now the prosecution has added a count of terrorism. That charge carries with it a maximum penalty of up to life in prison."

Zeb looked to Jeremy again. "Yes, sir," he said quietly.

"And you understand that you have a right to an attorney at each and every stage of this proceeding?" Judge Welch said.

"Your Honor," Jeremy said. "Our office has been appointed to represent Mr. Radamacher on the first two counts. He's indigent, and we'd ask that you appoint our office to represent him on this new count as well."

"Very well," Welch said. "Mr. Radamacher, I am going to appoint Mr. Sage's office to represent you on the added count. Do you have any objection to me doing that?"

"No, sir," the boy said.

Welch droned on, informing the boy of his rights. Jeremy nodded as required to guide Zeb through the correct answers, while looking through his file preparing to argue for bond. He had anticipated making a routine bail argument as he would in any case. But, seeing the terrorism charge, and knowing that the local press had been summoned to the courtroom, he doubted Welch would grant a bond low enough to actually get the boy out of jail. At best, Jeremy might get the judge to continue the current bond, and Zeb would have to come up with some cash if he didn't want to sit in jail while the case worked its way through the system.

When finished reading the boy his rights, Judge Welch addressed the prosecutor.

"Any argument on bail," Welch said, "Mr. Gray?"

"Thank you, Your Honor," Ed Gray said, rising from his chair at the prosecutor's table. His short black hair was straight and graying; his voice calm. "As you may be aware, the defendant was charged with arson and MDOP last week. He sabotaged a number of pieces of heavy equipment at the Blue-Mart construction site out on US-27. One bulldozer was burned with a homemade incendiary device – a Molotov cocktail. The defendant was apprehended fleeing the scene.

"Total damage at the site is approaching a hundred-thousand dollars, Your Honor. In addition, it delayed construction for two days, which is going to be very costly to the developer.

"It's fortunate that we're only talking about property damage. Given the size of the blaze, we are very lucky that no one was injured or killed.

"Detective Russell has been working non-stop on this case, looking into the defendant's motive for this crime. What she has found, Your Honor, is frankly chilling.

"The defendant maintained a website in the weeks before this attack. That site is nothing short of an environmental terrorist's manifesto. It plans the terrorizing and take-over of the entire county. In addition, the word 'ELF' was spray-painted on one piece of heavy equipment at the site. Investigators now believe this graffiti is a reference to the Earth Liberation Front, a group well-known for its acts of sabotage.

"It's clear that the defendant's act of sabotage was an act of terrorism, Your Honor. He is as much an enemy of the state as any terrorist. Whether it is radical Muslim terror, or radical eco-terror, the law sees no real distinction.

"Given that he was apprehended at the scene, the likelihood of conviction is high in his case. The defendant has shown himself to be a grave threat to the safety of the community. Also, because the potential penalty is life imprisonment, the risk that this defendant might try to go underground to avoid prosecution is high. The court rules allow you to deny bail completely in cases of treason. The People would submit that the terrorist act for which the defendant is charged is within the term 'treason' as it is used in the court rules. We would respectfully ask that you deny bail in this matter."

"Mr. Jefferson," Welch said, without hesitation.

"First off, I'd object to the court drawing any conclusions based on some unidentified website," Jeremy started. "There is no evidence, other than the prosecutor's representations, that my client is connected to any terrorist ideology or act.

"Second, the notion of presumption of innocence is something the court is surely familiar with, even though that concept may be lost on Mr. Gray. There has been no evidence presented at this point. All we have are charges. Charges my client has denied with his plea of not guilty.

"Third, Your Honor, Zeb Radamacher is only seventeen years old. He is an honor student at Milton High School. He has no criminal record, whatsoever. He lives with his mother, right here in Milton. He has nowhere to run and no intention of running. He already has a twenty-five-thousand dollar cash bond in this case. The factual allegations of the crime have not changed at all, Your Honor," Jeremy said. He could feel the hot color coming up his neck as he spoke. "The only thing that has changed is that the prosecutor now wants to label the conduct as terrorism.

"Mr. Radamacher's mother is getting close to making arrangements on the original bond," he continued. "It would be highly unfair to lock this boy up for the months leading up to a trial in this matter, based on the mere allegation of terrorism. The America I know, Your Honor, is not a place where someone is locked up because a prosecutor utters the word 'terrorism.' And frankly, if that is where we are in America, then I could honestly understand why some people might be out posting websites advocating the overthrow of the government. Because to deny bail in a case like this is not American. It's tyranny.

"Finally, I have not had much opportunity to look at the court rules, as Mr. Gray obviously has. But if memory serves, Your Honor, the court rules only allow denial of bond on the charge of murder or treason. Treason is a specific crime, which has not been charged here, and the rule should be narrowly construed. We'd be asking for the current bond to continue."

Jeremy immediately recognized hostility in the wrinkled face of Judge Welch. The judge sat still for a moment and then said, "Well, Mr. Jefferson, you may find it tyrannical, but my job as a judge is to protect the people of this county, and the state, and this country.

"I find that Mr. Radamacher is a threat to the community and a risk of flight. I also find that the crime of terrorism is within the term 'treason' as it is used in the court rules on bail, and I am going to deny bail in this case."

The judge's recorder set the case down for a preliminary examination in one week, and Jeremy absently jotted the date in his file. Zeb Radamacher's face was slack. Jeremy told him he would come to the jail to talk more about the case, and Deputy Short whisked the boy out the back of the courtroom. Jeremy turned to leave and saw the reporter scribbling feverishly with her head down. From an angle, and with the yellow overhead lighting in the basement courtroom, she reminded him of Hannah. He had deliberately avoided thinking of Hannah in the long months since their break up, but here she was again in the face of a stranger.

"This is fascist," Jeremy half-whispered to Gray, who was gathering his file. The terrorism charge had caught Jeremy off-guard. He had sensed the public mood veering toward a witch-hunt mentality since 9/11, but to have his seventeen-year-old client denied bail on grounds of treason seemed a little unreal.

"Fascist?" Gray sneered at him. "We prosecute a guy for blowing things up and we are fascist? Tell it to a jury."

As Jeremy left the courtroom, he watched the reporter. She approached Gray to get the terrorism briefing for the day. Soon, the good people of Milton would have someone close to home they could hate and fear.

Lost in his thoughts, Jeremy left the courthouse. He was oblivious to the golden sun as it touched the changing autumn leaves on the big oaks that guarded the entrance. Jeremy had felt a sense of unease since the terrorist attacks on 9/11. But he was certain it was not the same sense of unease that he saw in the faces of the citizens of Wabeno County.

He absorbed the public sense of fear, anger and bewilderment from looks and glances; from snippets of conversation overheard; from standing in line at the market watching fellow consumers; from talking with families of the criminals he represented. The general sense of loathing that had settled on people since 9/11 was a narrative that had been spelled out on the evening news and on cable television. It was a narrative played out on network shows, rushed to production, with plots focused on policemen, firemen and CIA agents fervently protecting the security of the homeland.

The entire community was gripped with fear – fear that the world had changed and was now unpredictable. Fear that, at any moment, a bomb might explode in the very center of Milton. Fear that a bacteriological agent might run rampant through the county. Fear that the food and water supply might be contaminated by radiation. A xenophobic fear that made a suspect of anyone whose skin shaded to the color of caramel or olive. A nationalistic fear that saw flags fly, not just on the Fourth of July, but on every day of the year, in a futile effort to make life seem normal again.

Jeremy's own sense of unease was the polar opposite of what he had observed in the public at large. His unrest was caused not by the downing of the Twin Towers, but by the American reaction to the event; by people being warned to watch what they said in times of terror; by the xenophobia and nationalism that was not only rampant, but fashionable; by a first war in Afghanistan that was loved like a child, and a second in Iraq that was approved by a mass suspension of disbelief; by detentions of citizens at foreign prisons without charges or lawyers or even access to courts; and by the willingness of those around him to sacrifice their own liberties to be saved from a threat level of red, orange or amber.

For the two years before the arraignment of Zeb Radamacher, Jeremy's alienation had been palpable. Now, it had taken life. He had a sense that tyranny was nearing some corporal incarnation. As he walked to Charlie Sage's office – an old two-story home that had been converted into a law office – he felt both helpless and angry.

Jeremy entered through the back door and found Charlie reading the *Detroit Free Press* in the law library. He sat across from Charlie, waiting for his boss to finish the sports page. The law library was a converted kitchen. It bore the name "law library" tenably, because a full complement of Michigan case law lined custom-built shelves on every wall. But the cramped room was more social club than library, and, to Jeremy, it had the comfort of home.

"So, how'd it go?" Charlie said, closing his paper.

"Unbelievable," Jeremy launched in with fervor. "They've charged the kid with terrorism. Terrorism has come to Milton."

"I figured as much. Did you see what was spray painted at the scene?"

"E-L-F," Jeremy said.

"The Earth Liberation Front," Charlie said. "They blow up things for a cause. The kid is a terrorist. I'm surprised they didn't charge it the first time. Guess they thought he had a thing for Santa Claus."

"It gets better. They denied him bail completely. Not that twenty-five thousand wasn't doing the trick. But they've just locked him up. Call him a terrorist and lock him up."

"I don't think so," Charlie said, reaching for a copy of the court rules. He thumbed expertly to the appropriate page. "Only for murder, treason, or a violent felony while on probation, it says."

"I know. I told Welch. He found this to be treason. Denied bail. Reporter in the back of the room."

"We'll ask for a review at exam. I'll appeal it if he doesn't come to his senses," Charlie said.

7

"I called Ed a fascist."

"He's not a fascist. A neo-con, maybe, but not a fascist."

"He was going on about a website. Radamacher was apparently plotting the overthrow of the free world in Wabeno County."

"Well," Charlie said, "if he's linked to ELF, he's a radical. Let me see the file."

Charlie splashed pages out of his way and found something.

"Says his dad is Mark Radamacher," Charlie said.

"Who?" Jeremy said.

"Mark Radamacher. He's that Christian Identity preacher up in Watson. A wacko."

"Oh yeah. I remember," Jeremy said. There had been an article about Radamacher in the *Beacon* the previous spring. He was a lifelong resident of Wabeno County. He served a prison stint and then came back and set up a white separatist church – called the Christian Identity Church – in the northern part of the county. It was a very divisive issue for the folks up in Watson. "Kid has fallen a long way from the tree."

"Radical thought is radical thought," Charlie said.

"So, I told Welch that it was un-American to lock people up just because they are accused of terrorism. I said it was no wonder people would advocate revolution in a system like that."

"You didn't say that."

"I did," Jeremy said, smiling.

"Well that was stupid. Lawyers don't advocate revolution. We uphold the law. That doesn't help your client, knucklehead."

"It felt good," Jeremy said.

"Well, I'm glad you feel better, but you're gonna have to keep your own feelings in line if you are gonna defend this kid."

"You're gonna give me this case?" Jeremy said. "It's a life offense."

"You're ready for it," Charlie said. "Just don't ask the jury to overthrow the government, okay?"

Jeremy nodded in agreement, though he did not wholly agree. The post-9/11 world felt fascist to him. He was happy to be representing the young, if misguided, rebel.

Most public defense clients did not rate a visit on Friday afternoon. But, Jeremy had taken a liking to Zeb Radamacher. He wanted to visit the kid and see just how he intended to overthrow the natural political order in Wabeno County.

2

The Wabeno County Jail was a low concrete box the color of sandstone. It was an obvious add-on to the existing building that housed the sheriff's department. The jail was on the south side of M-145, halfway between downtown Milton and the US-27 exit, about one mile from the Sage Law Office. It had taken Jeremy a few months of going inside the jail to get over a minor case of claustrophobia that the structure affected.

Through the jail doors was a small waiting room with metal chairs and tables, and walls lined with lockers. Michelle, the day shift guard, worked the main desk behind an inch of plexiglass.

"Working late on Friday?" Michelle said.

"Yeah," Jeremy said. "I need to see Zeb Radamacher."

Michelle scanned a computer printout. "Here he is, Zebediah Radamacher. You want contact?"

Jeremy had been leery of contact visits with felons in the early days, but like the claustrophobia, it passed. Clients were always more wary if they could not shake your hand. "That's great."

Michelle buzzed Jeremy through a heavy metal door leading back to the contact visiting rooms and the main jail. Another guard came out, patted Jeremy down, and led him to the first room. Jeremy busied himself with a pen and legal pad, writing nothing important, but trying to look engaged for his first private meeting with Radamacher.

The guard led Radamacher into the visiting room and advised Jeremy to ring the buzzer when he was finished.

The boy looked sobered by the afternoon's events. Jeremy launched into a long explanation of the charges, the preliminary examination process that was upcoming, and the denial of bail. He talked until the boy appeared somewhat reassured by his lawyer's knowledge.

"So, do you have any questions?" Jeremy said, finishing his standard spiel.

"Are the things we say in here private?" Zeb asked.

"Yes, they are," Jeremy explained. "As long as you don't include me in conversations conspiring to commit a crime, the things you say are completely confidential."

"So, am I going to get life in prison?" Zeb said.

"That is the maximum possible penalty if you are convicted on the terrorism charge. But the sentence could be any term up to life. I can't promise you anything at this point. But, I will do everything I can to ensure that doesn't happen."

Zeb asked several procedural and technical questions that confirmed Jeremy's belief: he was a pretty sharp kid. Jeremy answered the questions directly as best he could and leafed through the file, taking in the details Zeb had provided in an office questionnaire. When Zeb said he had no other questions, Jeremy started in with his own.

"So, you didn't fill out our intake sheet where it asks you to describe what happened," Jeremy said.

"Yeah," Zeb said. "I wanted to be comfortable with whoever my lawyer was before I said anything."

"Okay. Well, what happened?"

"You have the police reports, right?" Zeb said.

"Yes," Jeremy said. "But I don't believe everything the state police tell me. So why don't you give me your version?"

"Don't I have the right to remain silent or something?" Zeb said.

"Yes," Jeremy said, becoming annoyed. Sometimes smart clients were the worst clients. "But, that is the right to remain silent before the court and in police questioning. I'm your lawyer. I'm trying to help you. And if you don't tell me what happened, it's going to make it very difficult for me to do my job."

"Okay," Zeb said. "Well, like I told the officer that night, I saw the fire and ran to see what was going on. I was just about to go get help when I saw the police car."

"So you're telling me that you have no connection to this fire?" Jeremy said.

"I didn't say no connection. I said I saw the fire."

"Okay, but you didn't have any part in setting the fire," Jeremy said.

Zeb shook his head.

"And you didn't have any part in helping anyone else set the fire," Jeremy said.

"Nope. Wrong place at the wrong time," Zeb said.

This fit with what the boy had told the trooper on the scene, but it didn't nearly explain the truth. Zeb had tried to run from the trooper. And when the trooper finally caught him, Zeb was wearing work gloves and large socks over the top of his tennis shoes. Rather than confront the boy directly right out of the gate, Jeremy decided to move on to other areas of inquiry.

"Okay," Jeremy said. "So what was the prosecutor talking about today with the website?"

Zeb squirmed in his seat and paused before speaking. "I am an anarchist. Do you know what that is?"

Jeremy had the vaguest notion about anarchist philosophy, but he claimed total ignorance to encourage the boy to speak.

"Anarchists believe that hierarchical societies are destructive," Zeb said. "They destroy humanity. They destroy the environment. An anarchist believes that if you remove the hierarchy, things will work better. I believe that. So I am an anarchist."

"So you want no government," Jeremy said.

"No," Zeb said. "I just don't want a hierarchical government. I want a true democracy. Where people decide things. For the good of the community. Anarchists believe in liberty. And freedom. Something we don't really have now."

"I'm not sure I follow," Jeremy said, "but what does this have to do with a website?"

"There aren't many anarchists in Milton, Mr. Jefferson," Zeb smiled. "So I set up a website to share my ideas. To see how alone I was."

"And what kinds of ideas are on the website?"

"Basic anarchist stuff. Explanations. Links. You know."

"What about the environment?" Jeremy said.

"Capitalism is destroying it."

"Uh-huh," Jeremy said. "So, did you say that on the website?"

"Yeah," Zeb said. "I talked about the destruction. It is the biggest threat we face."

"And did you talk about ways of stopping the destruction?"

"I talked about peaceful resistance. And about democratic action," Zeb said.

"What kind of action?" Jeremy said.

"Like getting enough anarchists to move to Wabeno County to take over the government. Dismantle it, basically, from within," Zeb said.

"Where did you come up with that?"

11

"I read about it," Zeb said. "Did you know that the Libertarian Party once set out to take over New Hampshire?"

"Not really."

"They did. They asked their members to move to New Hampshire. The idea was to get enough of them there so that they could take over the state democratically."

Jeremy nodded.

"So I stole that idea," Zeb said, "for Wabeno County. I called the site Milton Anarchy. Did you know that only nine thousand voters from Wabeno County showed up for the last governor's election?"

"No," Jeremy confessed.

"Yeah," Zeb said. "Crazy, isn't it? They were split just about even between Democrats and Republicans, too. About forty-five hundred each. So I was trying to get five thousand anarchists, or people like me, to move to Wabeno. That's Milton Anarchy."

Jeremy was impressed with the boy's intellect and political savvy and was moved by the power of the boy's innocence. Zeb had an honest and unyielding belief that he could change the world to his liking. It was an innocence that Jeremy could scarcely remember in himself at any age. He jotted down the web address and tried to remember if he had believed in anything at seventeen. Perhaps there was some part of him that had once believed in something; a part of himself that was atrophied by disuse.

Jeremy knew that good lawyering required dispassionate thought – a separation of emotion from logic. But, for a moment, he let himself think emotionally. He was moved at some level by Zeb's quest to change the world. Listening to the boy talk of true democracy and freedom, he was almost convinced that Zeb might be best served by someone who shared his utopian dreams.

Jeremy's analytical brain regained control in an instant. He reminded himself that the boy's political thoughts had contributed toward his being charged with a life offense. Jeremy's job was to prevent or lessen the term of imprisonment the boy was likely to receive, if that was possible, regardless of the political future of Wabeno County.

Having satisfied his desire to meet his radical client, he told Zeb he would visit with him before the preliminary examination and excused himself to start another quiet weekend of northern life.

Autumn weekends in northern Michigan offered Jeremy a full menu of activity. He could hike, fish, four-wheel, bow hunt or get drunk and try to stay warm and dry on the couch. A year's acclimation had yet to instill a desire to be an outdoor sportsman, so he wasted Friday and Saturday night with a case of Labatt's and a warm wool blanket. Charlie brought his own case of beer – Old Milwaukee – on Saturday night, and the two discussed the gamut of politics, law and philosophy until Charlie staggered out the door early in the morning.

On Sunday the mid-morning sun caught a gap in his bedroom drapes and woke him. His eyes and mouth were dry, and his temples throbbed with each beat of his heart. He stared at the plaster ceiling for a time and decided to go to the office. Zeb Radamacher had not strayed far from his thoughts over the weekend. It felt invigorating to defend a criminal with a cause, for a change.

He brushed his teeth but skipped a shower and shave. He pulled on old jeans and a Michigan State sweatshirt, slipped his running shoes on bare feet, and left his two-bedroom ranch home for the office.

He stopped across from the Sage Law Office at the Morning Grind, Milton's own addition to the coffeehouse economy that had swept America through the turn of the century. He ordered a tall Ethiopian blend to go. As he waited, the bells at the front entrance rang and the reporter from the *Beacon* walked in. A Cubs baseball cap was pulled low to cover her blonde hair.

Jeremy thought to glance away and escape somehow without exchanging small-town pleasantries but was too late. She looked at him with clear, chocolate eyes and broke into a wide smile that could have stopped traffic. She was beautiful in her own right, but as she turned her head, there was a precise angle where Jeremy could not help but be reminded of Hannah.

"Jeremy Jefferson," she said, offering her hand. "I'm Allie Demming. With the *Beacon*."

"Yes," Jeremy said, taking her hand. Her handshake was warm and soft, but firm. "Hello. I've seen you in court. You have the cops-and-courts beat now?"

"Yeah. I just got it this summer. Interesting case here," she said, holding up her folded copy of the *Beacon* and pointing to the front page headline – "Eco-Terror Charges in Local Arson."

"Yes," Jeremy said. "We live in interesting times."

"Chinese proverb?" she smiled. Jeremy was impressed that she picked up on the reference to the old Chinese curse – "May you live in interesting times." Not everyone in Milton lacked depth, he marveled.

"I liked what you said in court," she said, offering him her copy of the paper. "I used a quote from your speech."

"Well," Jeremy said, taking the paper and glancing at the story, "thanks."

He made small talk and avoided her eyes while he waited for his coffee.

13

"Off to work for the oppressed," he said, when the clerk handed him his order. He tried to hand the paper back to Allie.

"No," Allie said, "you keep it."

"Thanks," he said, leaving.

"This is an interesting story," she said. "You should call me sometime to talk about it. We'd love to have your side of things."

Charlie's standing order was to avoid publicity on cases. But, Jeremy agreed to call her anyway, out of politeness, and left for the office. He regretted his promise to call almost immediately. Though her invitation was business and not personal, he knew that she would be waiting for his call. Her smile had told most of the story, he thought.

It had been more than a year since he had abandoned the partnership track at Barnes & Honeycutt, and with it, his engagement to Hannah Yale. He still ached when he thought of her and her unwillingness, or inability, to understand that he was crushing himself trying to fit in to the large firm. The move to Milton to work for Charlie hadn't fully sated his need to find himself. He felt better in many ways. But Jeremy recognized that he was still way too screwed up to even think about a romantic entanglement with someone new, let alone someone who looked like Hannah's sister.

He zipped his car up the driveway to the rear parking lot of the Sage Law Office. He loved Sundays at the office. It was churchly quiet. No phone calls. No secretaries. No interruptions. Sometimes Charlie would make a Sunday appearance, but even on that rare occurrence, Charlie would be too wrapped up in his own work to be much of a distraction to Jeremy.

Jeremy trotted up the steps to his second-floor office and plopped down in his fabric executive chair. His desk was covered with files, pleadings, legal pads and manuals. Jeremy pushed back the clutter far enough to lay down the *Beacon* and his coffee.

He read Allie's story on the Radamacher case as the computer booted up. Her writing was crisp and clear. She accurately stated the basics of the arraignment, and since Ed Gray was her main source, the article had a prosecution slant. Near the end, she wrote:

> Radamacher's attorney, Jeremy Jefferson, sought the Milton High School senior's release on a cash bond.
>
> If we deny bail based solely on accusations of terror, Jefferson argued, "Then I could honestly understand why some people might be out posting websites advocating the overthrow of the government.
>
> "To deny bail in a case like this is not 'American.' It's tyranny."

It seemed like an accurate quote to Jeremy. But, Charlie wouldn't like it. His words were intemperate and not likely to go down easy with the masses – at least those in the masses who bothered reading the *Beacon*. People in Milton, the county seat for Wabeno County, still backed the war in Iraq by an overwhelming margin, despite being told that all the reasons for the U.S. invasion were false. Milton was a locale that had become very patriotic with the World Trade Center bombings, and few, if any, locals would have any sympathy to anyone labeled a 'terrorist.'

Blunt assertions were a problem Jeremy had struggled with throughout his six years as an attorney. He had spoken what he truly felt and believed in court, but sometimes the uncensored truth was anathema to a client's best interests. Courtrooms had far less to do with truth than they did with theater. It was a fact that Jeremy knew but still failed to integrate into his everyday practice. Sometimes it occurred to him that he might be too honest to be a lawyer. But that bordered on cynicism, and at thirty-three, he was not ready to give in to that particular brand of poison.

Jeremy pulled the Radamacher file from the top of his cluttered in-box and removed his notes from the folder. He typed in the web address Zeb had given him on Friday and waited.

The browser was slow to retrieve the site. After several seconds a white screen appeared with the words:

This site is under construction.

Jeremy retyped the web address with the same result. Either Zeb had given him the wrong web address or the site had been edited.

He thought for a moment and Googled the Earth Liberation Front. Jeremy learned that the ELF site acted as a clearinghouse for information. ELF operated in anonymous cells, much like a terrorist group. Their manifesto was straightforward: Capitalism was ruining the earth's environment, and the most effective way to strike at capitalists was through economic warfare.

Members of ELF were to wage economic warfare on capitalism through direct acts of property destruction. So long as the action took every precaution to avoid harm to humans or animals, the action could be considered an ELF action. Reports of actions were sent in anonymously and posted on the website.

Zeb's exploit had been listed:

ELF Destroys Bulldozer at Michigan Blue-Mart Construction Site

October 11, 2003 -- The ELF press office has been informed of a claim of responsibility for a burned bulldozer at a Blue-Mart development site in Milton, Michigan. A gasoline bomb was used to ignite the bulldozer. The bulldozer should cost the developer $100,000 to replace. The monkey wrenchers left their calling card, spray-painting "ELF" on a nearby backhoe. Let this be a lesson to the capitalists at Blue-Mart -- direct action against your property will continue if you proceed with the development of this location. It will never be cost-effective for you to develop in this community.

Jeremy had been dubious about the terrorism charge against Zeb. The crime required proof of a specific intent to undertake a violent or destructive act for a political motivation. But, if the prosecutor could connect Zeb with this website, then the political motivation needed to prove the crime seemed like a slam dunk.

Jeremy still admired Zeb's commitment in some way. The boy was certainly misguided, but at least he was taking action on issues that moved him. Jeremy could never remember having such conviction and had difficulty imagining the sacrifice of breaking the law to serve a cause.

Jeremy next pulled up the election results for Wabeno County from the elections bureau website. Zeb had been right. A democratic revolution in Wabeno County could be had for as little as five thousand votes. And again he admired the exuberance of his young client. He was not only a dreamer and a radical willing to fight in a revolution, but also a democrat, contemplating a peaceful transition to a world that better suited him. In a different world, Zeb could be cast as George Washington instead of Osama bin Laden.

Jeremy turned off the mind-numbing expanse of his Internet browser and jotted thoughts on a blank legal pad:

Website altered + ELF notified + Zeb in jail = outside accomplice.

The one thing Jeremy had learned to fear as a trial lawyer was the unknown. Getting blasted with unexpected evidence in a courtroom usually left a lawyer stranded like a man hanging on the edge of a cliff. The solid footholds suddenly vanished when confronted with some unknown fact.

The one advantage he had as a defense lawyer was his client. Clients were almost invariably at the scene of the crime and could provide the most helpful description of all that was missing from a police investigation. All that was required was a little trust - enough trust in their lawyer to give up their guilty truths. Zeb, Jeremy surmised, was nowhere near coming clean. His client was not going to make the process an easy one. Jeremy was going to have to continue digging to find out what really happened.

3

Allison Demming was bored writing for a small-town weekly. She had written for a daily college paper and had interned at the *Chicago Tribune*, and the pace of the action at the larger papers was much more her style. She only had one deadline a week for the *Beacon* – Friday at 11:00 p.m. Though she always had a number of stories to write to fill her column inches for the week, the absence of a daily deadline hanging over her head was something that she always missed.

Monday morning brought a squall of activity to her desk that she found refreshing. Most of the action was generated by her lead story of the week – the Radamacher case. Her intuition told her the case would have legs. This was confirmed when she waded through her morning e-mails. A typical feature story might generate anywhere from zero to ten responses from readers. But, she had forty-six e-mails on the Radamacher case.

The readers were split. About two out of three of the responses were grateful that Ed Gray had taken such a hard stance against the eco-terrorist menace. The other third generally supported the environmental movement and called the prosecution unfair and Radamacher a hero. She sent a blanket response to all the readers thanking them for their interest.

She called Jeremy Jefferson's office and left a message. She wanted to get his side of the case for a new story this week. She also wanted to take advantage of the opportunity the story gave her to get to know him better.

By mid-morning she got a call from the AP. They were picking up the story on the wire and wanted to talk to her for background. Then came more background calls from reporters at major papers. The *Free Press*. The *Tribune*.

Later in the morning, she called Jefferson's office again and left a second message. He should really know how much interest the story was generating.

Her patience with life at the *Beacon*, and in Milton in general, had been wearing thin. She had always seen herself in a large city with a major paper, but after college, the job market had been tight. Then her father had been diagnosed with Alzheimer's. So when there had been an opening at the *Beacon*, she jumped at the chance to get some experience at a weekly while staying with her parents.

She constantly reminded herself that the arrangement was temporary. But, three years slipped by like a silent stream, and it was just inertia – and the stranger her father had become – that tied her to the little town. She had yet to start circulating her clips, but she was looking at openings on the Internet, imagining herself in Chicago or St. Louis or Seattle. All the interest in her latest story made her long for a cavernous newsroom, the din of telephones, the cacophony of voices, the anonymous cubicle, and the daily struggle to feed the beast.

Nearing the lunch hour, her thoughts drifted to Jeremy Jefferson again. She considered whether to call him a third time. Now that she had an excuse to talk to him, the idea was almost irresistible.

She had seen him around the courthouse frequently since taking over the cops-and-courts beat. Whispers there said that he had given up a partnership with a large Detroit firm to come and practice law with his friend Charlie Sage. He looked, dressed and talked like a well-heeled attorney, confirming the gossip.

He was tall and graceful. His dark hair had been short and coiffed when she first saw him but had grown increasingly free. He wore expensive suits with designer ties that made him stand out among the other lawyers in the Wabeno County Bar. She bet five dollars with the girls in the clerk's office that he was gay, and was pleased to pay off on the bet when the clerks learned that he had ended an engagement at the same time he left the firm in Detroit.

Allie had never competed for men's attention. She had been aware of the power of her beauty since she was a teenager. Men had always noticed her. She thought that it was Jeremy's failure to notice her that probably most attracted her to him. She had almost decided to take his disinterest as final, until Friday in Judge Welch's court. As she sat in the back of the courtroom that day, writing notes, she had felt his gaze on her. And, then again on Sunday, at the coffee shop. His eyes were dark but warm, and when he had finally started to look at her, she could almost feel the weight of his stare.

His presence in Milton was a mystery to Allie, almost as puzzling as her own. But at least she had an excuse to try to get to know him better.

She dialed his office again and fought through the dutiful secretary.

"This is Jeremy," he said.

"Hi," she said. "This is Allie. At the *Beacon*. How are you?"

"Hello, Allie. Great. Little hectic around here. Sorry I didn't get back to you right away."

"That's okay," Allie said. "I just wanted to let you know that your case is getting lots of attention. It hit the wire, and I've been getting calls all morning. You are going to get your fifteen minutes of fame on this one."

"Really," Jeremy said. "I haven't had a chance to read your article yet."

"Oh. That's okay. I get those papers for free, ya know," she said, hiding her disappointment. "But, I just wanted to give you a heads up. And keep me in mind if you want to get your side out. I'd love to work with you on this."

"I appreciate that," Jeremy said, pausing. "But, we usually don't have any comment on our cases. We don't try them in the press."

"Yeah. That's Charlie's line anyway, right? I thought you might have a different approach."

"Nope. Charlie's the boss," Jeremy said. "So for now, we don't have any comment."

"Okay," Allie said. "Well. Keep me in mind, all right?"

"Okay. I'll do that."

She hung up the phone, her face contorted between a smile and a pout. He hadn't even read her story. He was oblivious to her. No man had ever blown her off. He was definitely a challenge.

She replayed the call in her head. It was awkward, but it was a start. Maybe he was just gun shy, she thought. Perhaps she'd need to break the ice herself. She looked at the calendar on her desk. She had complimentary tickets to *Our Town*, opening at the Milton Playhouse on Saturday. That would make for a nice date. She liked the idea. She'd wear her red dress, with Jeremy Jefferson on her arm as an accessory.

Jeremy hung up the phone in the library and returned to the chessboard.

"The girl from the *Beacon*?" Charlie said.

"Yeah," Jeremy said. "Apparently our friend Zebediah is going to be famous. His story has been picked up on the wire."

"Grand," Charlie said, taking Jeremy's pawn. "Her article made you sound like a lunatic."

"So you read it?"

"I read everything about our cases, lad," Charlie said, resolutely deploying his king-side knight.

"I didn't like it, either," Jeremy said. "You were right, o' wise master. Never talk to the press."

"Well, you can't avoid it on some cases," Charlie said. "You can't stop them from using what you say in court, so just start by trying to not sound like a lunatic on the record, okay?"

"I wasn't shooting for lunatic. If Gray and Welch weren't such fascists, I wouldn't have said those things."

Jeremy fought off Charlie's initial onslaught on the chessboard, but he was hopelessly positioned and struggled to find any move.

"That's mate in seven," Charlie said, with the swagger of an uncrowned grandmaster from Washington Square. "That'll be one dollar."

Jeremy had yet to beat Charlie in their lunchtime chess matches. His best strategy had been to drag the opening game out long enough, so that he wouldn't have to get beat twice in one lunch hour.

"This is one of those cases where you might need to get out there in the press just to stay even," Charlie said. "They already have the kid painted as the shoe-bomber."

Charlie Sage was the smartest man Jeremy had ever known. Charlie's parents were retired professors from the University of Michigan. They sent him to Cranbrook in Bloomfield Hills, and on to Harvard where he studied the classics. He was an average student at Harvard, which, according to Charlie, meant that he spent most of his non-class hours getting stoned and hanging around Harvard Yard or Cambridge pubs.

Charlie had taken some time off after graduation before deciding on law school. He had actually managed to support himself for an entire year in Las Vegas, doing stage magic and playing poker.

When he finally took up his legal calling, Charlie aced his admissions test, graduated *summa cum laude*, and recorded the highest score on the multi-state bar examination since its inception. His credentials gave Charlie wide opportunity. He received a clerkship on the Michigan Supreme Court but turned it down when he saw Wabeno County was looking for a contract public defender. Charlie had been quietly fighting the battle for civil rights ever since, defending the poorest clients the system could dish out.

In the year since Jeremy had joined Charlie's office, Charlie had held fast to a rule of avoiding any media coverage on cases. Jeremy disagreed with his mentor's policy. The media infiltrated the lives of modern jurors like swamp water infiltrating a wetland. Even in a place like Wabeno County, jurors tended to have massive exposure to the most banal of crimes. Television, radio, newspapers, and now, the Internet, let people know who the bad guy was long before any court proceeding, and it was difficult to shake them from their early opinions. Jeremy figured the only antidote was to get his side of the story out quickly and hope to neutralize any early information from the prosecutor or the police. Charlie lifting the ban on talking to the press might help get a fair trial, Jeremy thought.

"I can't believe you are going to give me the green light to talk," Jeremy said. "I was hoping to avoid that new girl from the *Beacon* on this one."

"What?" Charlie said, setting the board for a second game. "I thought you'd love that assignment. Talk to the really hot reporter chick. Sounds rough."

In the months since Hannah chose the firm over his sanity, Jeremy had stopped looking at all women. He was a monk. He could not remember looking any woman in the eyes, even his clients, until he had chanced a look at Allie Demming. He thought, perhaps, it was only the hunger of his eyes that made him think Allie was beautiful. But Charlie, a man of good taste, confirmed her objective beauty.

"She looks just like Hannah when she holds her head a certain way," Jeremy said.

"No, she doesn't. Let me see that picture again."

Jeremy got out his wallet and showed Charlie the picture of Hannah that was front and center.

"No resemblance," Charlie said, now playing white. He opened in a Ruy-Lopez that Jeremy had little idea how to defend. The blistering attack was over quickly. "That's two bucks," Charlie said, packing up the pieces in a worn cigar box.

Jeremy took a single from his wallet and threw it at Charlie. "I'll get you the rest tomorrow," he said. "Only at a certain angle, but she looks just like her."

"Well, I guess you'll just have to tough it out," Charlie said. "Talk to her before the exam and try to get some positives about the kid in the paper. I'm going to court."

Charlie picked up a pile of files from the hallway credenza, grabbed his coat off the rack and headed out the back door. Jeremy wasn't sure just what info Charlie wanted him to put out. It was his first life offense, and his only defense at this point was his client's denial in the face of all reason. He would wait a few days for things to sort themselves out and then call Allie Demming about the case, if Charlie was still insisting.

4

Kurt Bishop dusted off his 2:00 p.m. meeting by 2:15 p.m. He still had a few minutes before the governor would return from lunch. He told his secretary to advise him when the governor returned and fished a copy of the AP wire report off his desk. He wanted to look at the item again before taking it to the governor.

His eyes glided over the passage, soaking up detail and context. It was not the political issue that caught his attention as much as it was the name of the defense lawyer who had made a notorious statement actually favoring terrorism.

Bishop had gone through law school with Jeremy Jefferson. Jefferson's own law school career had been like that of a mechanical rabbit to Bishop's greyhound. When Bishop made the honor roll, Jefferson was there several places above him on the list. When Bishop made law review, Jefferson was selected as editor. When Bishop graduated with honors, Jefferson was *magna cum laude*.

Though Jefferson had scarcely been a passing acquaintance – Jefferson had always been aloof, Bishop thought – Bishop had come to despise him as a nemesis. It was a petty jealousy to be sure, but a full one. Achievement in law school had as much to do with success afterwards as voters' true opinions had to do with selecting candidates at the ballot box. Bishop could have finished in the bottom tenth of his class and would still have far surpassed his classmates. Success after law school was far more about connections to open doors and raw ambition to pile through them once open, he thought.

His father had gotten him a job on the congressional campaign of Roger Howell while he was still finishing his final year of law school. Howell was a bright star in the party. A former veteran and FBI agent, Howell projected a clean-cut image as a no-nonsense, tax-cutting, law-and-order guy.

Bishop saw his opening with Howell. He worked hard, cared about no one, and earned a spot as Howell's top aide in Washington after the election. In two short terms, he had helped Howell hone his natural image. Then they set their sights on, and captured, the governor's office. It was a natural stepping stone if they were going to take a shot at the presidency. Bishop was pleased with his plush office next to the governor, but he often daydreamed of a desk very close to the Oval Office.

Bishop may not have been the editor of the law review, but he had an uncommon political sense that most lawyers never possess. And while it brought a thin smile to his fleshy face to see Jefferson representing such an unpopular cause, and doing a poor job of it at that, Bishop saw an even greater good in the developing story.

His secretary buzzed him on the intercom. "I just saw him go in," she said.

Bishop folded the wire report and stalked to the governor's office. The governor's secretary let him into the suite.

"So, did Fritz cave on the tax cuts?" Bishop asked.

Howell was looking out the velvet-draped windows absently, toward Michigan Avenue.

"Yeah," the governor said. "I told him I was going to pull the plug on the charter schools initiative if he didn't get the package through. You were right. That was the ticket."

Howell smiled and eased into his burgundy leather chair. He looked tired, Bishop thought. Though Howell was only forty-five, age was taking its toll.

"Even with the tax cuts and the welfare bill," Bishop said, "the party still needs one more theme for the mid-term election."

"Death penalty?" the governor said.

"No," Bishop said. "That'll never make it. It's a good issue, but it's constitutional. It'd get bogged down."

Howell nodded. His desk was polished mahogany. It was bare, except for two wooden in-baskets, a quill pen set, and a picture of his wife, children and dog, facing away from his chair.

"I think I may have something," Bishop said, slapping the folded press report in his hand and setting it down before the governor. "Just off the wire today."

He gave Howell five silent minutes to read the news brief before launching in.

"It's not an action issue, really," Bishop said. "You come out with some policy aimed at this problem – maybe a legislative proposal – and whether there is action or not, it lets you take a stand against terrorism at a state level."

"God," Howell said, "I don't want to get stuck on some environmental issue. Have you seen the negatives for us on that stuff?"

"Yeah. I know the numbers are bad on green issues. But, that's the beauty of it. This case will take the edge off those numbers, I think. Make the tree-huggers into terrorists."

"I don't know," Howell said.

"Well, let's release a statement condemning this act of eco-terrorism," said Bishop. "And I'll get Artie to take some numbers on how it goes over."

"All right," Howell said, stifling a yawn. "I guess that can't hurt. But, let me see the release before it goes. Anything I can't bump for today?"

Bishop helped the governor clear his schedule. He was pleased he could stick it to Jeremy Jefferson and carve out a nice wedge issue at the same time. Politics was a wonderfully harmonious game, he thought. He had the press release drafted and approved before the governor left at 3:00 p.m., and Artie Fisher in his office by 3:10 p.m.

Jeremy spent most of Monday afternoon waiting on Judge Parr. He had scheduled a motion to compel discovery on a drug case where the prosecution was refusing to turn over police reports regarding their snitch's history as an informant. The motion was set for 1:30 p.m. But for a public defender before Lawrence Parr, 1:30 p.m. could mean anywhere between 2:00 p.m. and 5:00 p.m.

He had adjusted to the waiting. In his days at Barnes & Honeycutt, time was money. His services as an associate were billed out at two hundred and fifty dollars an hour. His clients in those days, rich corporations and powerful insurance companies, did not like to pay their lawyers to sit around and drink coffee. For that reason, judges mostly granted deference to high-powered lawyers from silk-stocking firms. In the courthouse pecking order, high-priced lawyers were called first and their wait times were minimized. If forced to wait in the old days, Jeremy would have immediately busted out his laptop to catch up on office work, or he would have worked clients over the cell phone. Anything to keep the meter running.

Now, Jeremy enjoyed his delays. He would drink coffee and watch whatever action was taking place in the courtroom. If he was reading a book, he would bring it along and could usually finish a chapter or two. He took a copy of *Post Captain*, by Jack O'Brian, out of his briefcase and settled in for a long wait.

After re-reading the same page three times, Jeremy put the novel away. He was antsy to see Zeb at the jail, and Parr was never going to get to his case.

Circuit Judge Lawrence Parr shuffled into the courtroom at 2:00 p.m. looking ready for a nap. There were only two cases on the docket, and, predictably, he called the civil matter before Jeremy's case.

A young insurance lawyer from Lansing was arguing for dismissal of a case brought by Milton's local ambulance-chaser, Tommy Hughes. The insurance lawyer was green, and even with the ever-accommodating Michigan Supreme Court backing his arguments with decision after decision, he was on the verge of snatching defeat from the jaws of victory.

Hughes got up and obfuscated the facts and law of the case, all the while with a warm voice and gregarious smile. After a half-hour of mind-numbing argument, Hughes had done enough to sway Parr that the case should proceed to a jury trial. Parr then called the civil attorneys to the bench.

"Mr. Jefferson," the judge said, after a short, whispered exchange with the civil lawyers. "Are you ready on your matter?"

"I am, Your Honor," Jeremy said.

"Where's the prosecutor?" Parr said.

"If I could just step out for a moment, I'll get her," Jeremy said.

"Ms. Fitchett is on that file, Judge," said the court recorder. "She asked that I call her down when we're ready."

"I was going to get your case out of the way, Mr. Jefferson, but I have to meet with these gentlemen in chambers for a settlement conference," Judge Parr said, motioning to Hughes and the young insurance lawyer. "We'll be back in a minute." And with that, Judge Parr disappeared until 4:15 p.m.

When he finally came back to the bench to hear the motion, Pamela Fitchett was called down from the prosecutor's office on the second floor. In her opening remarks, Fitchett told the judge that she agreed with Jeremy's brief, and that he should get the police reports on the informant. An order was entered, and, just three hours after the motion was scheduled, Jeremy was on his way to the jail.

Though he arrived during the prisoner feeding time, Michelle made a phone call and got Zeb to the contact room for a visit with Jeremy.

"How's it going, Mr. J.," Zeb said, with a flat smile. It was obviously a fine day in the Wabeno County Jail.

"I'm okay," Jeremy said. "How are you?"

"Good."

"I just wanted to stop by to ask you a couple more questions," Jeremy said.

"Okay," Zeb said. "I wasn't really doing anything, except we were about to eat."

"I'll get you back quick," Jeremy said. "I'm doing some background investigation into the facts of your case. I looked for your website, but I couldn't find it. Is this the right web address?"

Zeb confirmed that Jeremy had been looking at the right site. "The prosecution has not turned over any documents about the site yet," Jeremy said. "So I went there to find out what exactly you wrote, and all I got was a blank page. It just said the site was under construction."

"Oh," Zeb said, "Stevie must have taken the site offline."

"Okay," Jeremy said. "Who's Stevie? You didn't mention him before."

"Stevie Wynn," Zeb said. "He's a hacker. He knows everything about computers. He helped me with my site. Must've gotten scared and taken everything down."

"So does he have any other involvement with this? Is he an anarchist?"

"No, he just does computers," Zeb said.

Jeremy took Wynn's phone number. He tried to reassure Zeb that everything would be okay at the preliminary examination, but in honesty he told the boy again that the exam was not likely to change his situation for the better. On the way out, Jeremy asked Michelle for the visitors' logbook. He flipped through the pages and saw that Steve Wynn had visited Zeb on Saturday. Like most criminal clients Jeremy had come to know, Zeb was having a serious problem with the truth.

5

Charlie skipped up the front steps to the courthouse for another round of Judge Parr's Tuesday morning pretrials and settlement conferences. Charlie's clients would be scattered about the courthouse all morning while Charlie talked with a prosecutor.

He stopped to shake hands with two clients who were seated on the bench outside of Parr's courtroom, zipped back into the secure area to visit a third in the holding cell, and then made for a conference room in search of a prosecutor. The hallway in the courthouse was a carnival of Wabeno County's lower class. Drunks, addicts and small-time thieves lined the hall. Many of them were accompanied by family and friends – a social event, Charlie laughed to himself.

Though his mind was filled with the details of how to best work out three separate felony cases, Charlie's eye was caught by a small boy who sat with his mother and father. The father was obviously the perp, given his face, which bore equal parts guilt, anger and fear. The boy was leaning on his mother's knees, looking at the floor. His face was a youthful replica of his father; a mixture of rage and horror.

Charlie's long fingers fished a quarter out of his pocket, and he stopped in front of the boy. Silently, he held the coin up to the boy's face with his right hand. The boy slowly looked up from his shoes to examine Charlie. Charlie then snapped the fingers of his right hand with a flourish, and the coin seemed to zip sightlessly to his left hand. The boy watched its progress with the beginning of a smile. With the boy fixed on his left hand, Charlie placed the palmed coin behind the boy's ear with his right. He touched the boy and pulled magic from his face. As the boy exclaimed to his mother,

Charlie laughed loud, gave the quarter to the boy, and went on his way up the hall.

Ed Gray was seated in the conference room.

"Why you slumming on the pretrials today? Where's Pamela?" Charlie said.

"She's upstairs trying some juvenile case," Ed said. "I swear, that woman just loves trying cases. It's driving me nuts. Keeping me way too busy."

Charlie laughed.

"Who you got?" Ed said.

Charlie looked at his files. "Gonzales, Wright and Patmore."

Like old dance partners, Gray and Charlie worked through the minutiae of the cases and arrived at acceptable plea bargains.

Before going to discuss the plea bargains with his clients, Charlie said, "So what are we going to do with this new kid we got? The Blue-Mart kid."

"Radamacher," Gray said. "You're handling it, right?"

"I'm giving it to Jeremy."

"Don't do that," Gray said. "The case is too hot for him. Did you see it made the *Free Press* already? He hasn't got enough experience. Still thinking in billable hours and ivory towers, that guy."

"No. He's ready. He's gonna handle it," Charlie said.

"He called me a fascist at the arraignment for crissakes."

"He was a little hot. You shouldn't have even asked for no bond. What was that?" Charlie said. Gray had been elected prosecutor right before Charlie had come to Milton. He was wound a bit tight, but Charlie figured he was better than some prosecutors. Only in the rarest of cases was there not a reasonable plea bargain to be had on files Gray handled himself.

"It was appropriate," Gray snapped. "You got Mark Radamacher's kid there going off the deep end. The kid's a risk."

"Treason? Come on. It's a bit much for some sand in the crankcase and burning a car," Charlie said.

"Well," Gray said heatedly, "you tell Jefferson that if I read any more about what kind of tyrant I am, there aren't going to be *any* deals. Not that the kid is going to get much anyway."

"Don't make it personal. This is a kid we're talking about. He's seventeen. He ain't so bad, really," Charlie said, slightly annoyed at Gray's tone.

"I didn't make it personal," Gray said. "That was your boy who made it personal. But even so, we know this kid wasn't out there alone, and if he doesn't get real serious about giving up his partners, I doubt there is much I'm gonna do for him anyway."

Charlie didn't like the way the case was headed. He thought he might step in and calm things down this morning, but listening to Gray go on,

Charlie started to sympathize with Jeremy's evaluation of the prosecutor as a fascist. He wondered how much of Gray's decision to charge terrorism had to do with fending off any possible contenders in next year's election.

Zeb Radamacher was in for a rough ride if they could not get Gray to cut him a reasonable deal. Charlie knew the kid had done wrong – but it was vandalism, really. Still, if a deal meant giving up accomplices, then that's what had to be done. Jeremy could handle that much, Charlie thought. And he would keep a close eye on the case, just to make sure.

On his way into the courthouse, Jeremy saw Charlie putting his arm around a client and leading him out into the crisp fall air. "Step into my office," Charlie said to his client, nodding to Jeremy in passing.

Jeremy had a 9:00 a.m. plea before Welch on a retained drunk driving case. The public defender contract prohibited Charlie and Jeremy from taking cash cases on felony matters. But they were allowed to take private misdemeanor cases, and representing one or two drunk drivers a month nearly doubled Jeremy's salary. He trotted down the stairs and met his client in the hall.

Out of the corner of his eye, he saw Allie coming out of the clerk's office. She spotted him and walked over casually.

"Go have a seat in the courtroom, and I'll be right in," Jeremy directed his client.

"Hi," Allie said, smiling and extending a hand. She wore black slacks and a short-sleeve black blouse that complemented her sleek frame.

"I'm seeing too much of you," Jeremy said affably. "You must be following me."

"You have the hot case," she laughed. "Really, I was just here reviewing that file."

Jeremy smiled, and a moment passed as they looked at one another. "Well, I have to see Judge Welch," he said.

"Are you going to be holding the exam?" she asked, delaying him.

"We haven't decided yet," Jeremy said. "We might waive it."

"Okay," she said. "Well, we'll see you Friday."

"Okay," Jeremy said. He was not looking forward to having an exam on the case. The evidence was fairly substantial and not much stood to be gained.

He turned to enter Welch's courtroom, but Allie kept on.

"I know this isn't entirely professional," she said quickly, "with me covering your case and all, but I have two tickets for the opening of *Our Town* Saturday night. They're free from work. And – I thought –" Her voice trailed off. She looked up at Jeremy with a face that was at once disarming and lovely.

"I'm not really sure," he said.

"Well," she said, "if you're not doing anything, let me know on Friday. I promise it won't skew my coverage."

As they parted and Jeremy entered the courtroom, he felt like a schoolboy. He had made it awkward for her. He had thought about going to the play anyway. The new playhouse was the height of culture for Milton. But he wasn't prepared to get asked out. Allie was as bold as Hannah in her own way, he thought.

"Nice that you could join us, Mr. Jefferson." Judge Welch had already taken the bench, and his words snapped Jeremy back to reality. "Your client and I have been waiting for you."

6

Mark Radamacher pulled his red Dodge Ram pickup truck into the crowded jail parking lot. "How on the good Lord's earth can the government employ so many people at a jail?" he muttered to himself. He found a spot near the access road that was almost too small for his truck, but he managed to wedge in between cars. He banged his door into a rusted-out Buick and growled.

The glass on the doors to the jail was dark, and, as he approached, it mirrored back his image. Fifty-five and still fitter than most, he thought. Inside, the lobby was warm and stale. A black woman sat bouncing a toddler on her knee. It pained him to think his own son was locked up with black men.

He signed in at the desk and waited uncomfortably, avoiding eye contact with the black woman and her child. Zeb was basically a decent kid, he thought, but his ex-wife had ruined the boy.

"Mr. Radamacher," the guard called his name through the intercom, shaking him from his thoughts of Zeb. He was directed to a visitor's room.

Mark seated himself on the aluminum seat that was fixed to the floor. His hatred of prison came flooding back to him. He looked through the plexiglass, waiting anxiously for his son.

Zeb walked up to a security door and waited for the guard to buzz him through. He wore an orange jumpsuit and was starting to grow a scraggily beard. He entered and took a seat opposite his father. They faced each other through a transparent inch-thick barrier. Mark picked up the phone that hung to his right, and his son did the same after some hesitation.

"Zeb," Mark said.

His son nodded without a word.

"You're lookin' good for the can," Mark said, laughing.

Zeb nodded again.

"I'm sorry I ain't been here sooner," Mark said.

"I didn't expect you at all," Zeb said.

"You have gone and got yourself into a world a shit, boy," Mark said.

"I can't talk about it, Dad," Zeb said. "My lawyer said so."

"I saw your freakin' lawyer in the paper! You got a damn public defender. That Jew bastard is gonna have you in jail for life!"

Zeb didn't respond.

"Your mama asked me for some money," Mark said, "before they took away your bail."

"I didn't ask her to," Zeb said. "I don't need your help."

"What in the hell were you thinking, boy?" Mark said. "They're calling you a freakin' tree hugger and a terrorist. A bunch a commie bullshit. I oughta let you rot."

A moment passed, and Mark sensed Zeb was about to hang up the phone. "I can get you the best lawyer money can buy. My ministry's been doin' real well."

"I don't really need your help, Dad," Zeb said.

"You don't know what you need," Mark said, his voice spiking. "You think that Jew lawyer is gonna save your ass? You got another thing comin'."

"Not that it matters," Zeb said, "but he's not Jewish."

"You don't know shit, boy," Mark growled. "Just because he ain't got a Jewish name don't mean nothin'."

"Well, Pop, I hate to run, but I got lunch," Zeb said.

"I can help you, son." Mark said, regaining his composure. "You'll see what I mean about that damn lawyer. Bad enough we got a crooked prosecutor, but your own lawyer is gonna sell you down the river on this shit."

"Okay, Pop. Gotta run," Zeb said, hanging up the phone.

"Zebediah!" Mark said loudly through the glass, but his son just turned and buzzed for the guard.

Mark sat until his son was gone. He was escorted out by the front desk guard. Maybe he should just let the boy alone to his fate, he thought. Let him think about pulling another faggity, liberal stunt like that while he was doing twenty in the pen. Prison had surely been an eye-opener for Mark. Helped him see the light. Brought him to God and his livelihood.

But Zeb could probably learn the right way without prison. He just needed to get away from his hippie mother. Mark could straighten him out in a year. But, none of that was going to happen unless he got him a real lawyer, he thought.

Jeremy was reading case law in the library when Charlie got back from court. Jeremy's legal method had changed little from his days as a law student. He learned early that preparation was the key to being a competent trial lawyer. Anticipation of legal issues that might pop out in the courtroom was essential.

While his method remained the same, the tools he used to prepare himself changed substantially when he came to practice with Charlie Sage. At Barnes & Honeycutt, he had access to the best databases available, collecting all the law ever written in the United States and bringing it to bear on the most arcane issues in seconds. At his new office, research was much more labor intensive. They had a full set of case books from the state appellate courts and a full set of statutes. The cases and statutes were indexed like encyclopedias. Finding the precise point of law when you needed it sometimes meant spending hours leafing through books.

"Good news on Radamacher," Charlie said, with a wry smile under his ragged moustache.

Jeremy looked up from his reading. "What's that?"

"I think I've found a way to work it out," Charlie said. "Gray wants the kid to give up his accomplices. If we're willing to roll, I bet we can work out a deal."

"The kid hasn't even come off his story yet," Jeremy said. "He was just in the wrong place at the wrong time." Criminal clients, even the smart ones, were always the last people in the world to realize how utterly stupid they sounded in maintaining their innocence against overwhelming evidence.

"Well," Charlie said, "you're gonna have to break him down. And I'd do it before the exam. It'll be easier to get a deal nailed down early in a case like this, before there's some kind of public feeding frenzy."

"I think I know the accomplice," Jeremy said. "Kid named Wynn has been helping him publish his anarchist stuff on the Internet."

"Great. You need to talk to that kid right away. Maybe you can get him to talk and use that to break Radamacher down," Charlie said, aligning pieces on the chessboard. "Now put the books away and let's get down to business. I need some lunch money."

"By, 'right away' you mean right after I get done beating the crap out of you," Jeremy said, with false bravado. The game was on.

As he drove to meet Steve Wynn, Jeremy replayed another crushing loss. He had become a far better criminal defense attorney over the course of his year in Milton. His substantive knowledge of criminal law and procedure increased with daily exposure. It troubled him that his chess skills had not tracked a similar learning curve. He made a pittance as a public defender. It was enough for a rented house in a hick town, a cheap car and a full fridge. But the daily chess tax was becoming a nuisance.

After Charlie had taken him for another two dollars, Jeremy called the Wynn residence. Wynn's mother was a woman so obedient to authority that she did not question Jeremy's motives for wanting to speak with her son. She was nervous when he identified himself as an attorney investigating the Blue-Mart construction fire – she knew Zeb well and had read the story in the *Beacon* – but she agreed to cooperate without hesitation. She invited Jeremy out to talk with Steve when he got home from school.

The Wynns lived north of town. It was a ramshackle, white frame house that Jeremy found within ten minutes of hanging up the phone. He pulled his car into the clay and gravel drive. Mrs. Wynn was at the door to meet him before he made it halfway across a weedy lawn.

She was a short, rotund woman with plastic frame glasses. She wore a Ted Nugent concert shirt that was well past its prime – dating to the '80s, if Jeremy's knowledge of rock history was correct. She took a drag from a cigarette and said, "Hello. Mr. Jefferson?"

"Hello, Mrs. Wynn," he said, fishing a card from his wallet. She took the card, and a phone rang in the background.

"Let me get that," she said, motioning for him to come into the house. The interior was dark, the natural light shut out by blinds. From what Jeremy could make out, it was decorated from the pages of "American Trailer" magazine.

Mrs. Wynn yelled at someone on the telephone. " –and he's a lawyer investigating the Blue-Mart fire. Now I gotta go. Good-bye."

She invited him to sit on a rust-orange couch that was made of cloth but had the feel of wrought-iron. She brought him coffee in a mug bearing the logo of the local radio station. "Stevie should be home any minute," she said, handing him the mug.

He sipped coffee, the taste of which had been slowly boiled away after hours on a warmer, and tried to avoid telling her much about the case. Just as it seemed that Mrs. Wynn was about to cut through the polite chatter to ask why Jeremy needed to talk with Steve, a bus pulled up outside the home. A tall, thin boy with short dark hair tramped off the bus. He wore blue jeans and a brown leather bomber jacket, similar to Jeremy's own.

Jeremy and Mrs. Wynn stood up from the couch as Steve came inside. The boy's face slackened when he noticed Jeremy. His eyes grew large, like a deer preparing to turn-tail and bound through the brush.

"Stevie," Mrs. Wynn said, "this is Mr. Jefferson. He's Zeb's lawyer for the Blue-Mart thing."

Steve's face recovered slightly, and his eyes morphed back to a more human form. Jeremy moved forward and shook his hand. The boy had a powerful grip. Jeremy guessed him for six-feet even, and his slight frame belied a sinewy strength. "Nice to meet you, Steve," Jeremy said pleasantly.

"Uh-huh," Steve said.

"Do you mind if I ask you a few questions about Zeb?"

There was a moment of hesitation. "No," Steve said.

"Great," Jeremy said, sitting again and motioning for Steve to sit down. "You know Zeb's in a lot of trouble?"

"Uh-huh."

"Well, I'm looking for any information I can to help him out," Jeremy said. "And he told me that you were a friend of his."

"Uh-huh," Steve said, "we've been hanging out since he came to Milton. About four years, I think. His parents split up, and he moved here with his mom."

"Great. So he's a good friend?"

"Uh-huh."

"Great. So you'll help him if you can?" Jeremy asked.

Steve nodded. He was definitely involved in the arson. Jeremy could smell the fear oozing from him.

"Zeb said that you helped him maintain a website," Jeremy said.

"Uh-huh," Steve said.

"You didn't tell me you were helping Zeb," Mrs. Wynn said, turning from her son to Jeremy. "He's such a whiz on that computer, Mr. Jefferson. I just love looking at his work."

"Mrs. Wynn," Jeremy said, with sugar in his voice. "There are some things about this case that are extremely confidential. I really need to speak with Steve alone."

"Oh," Mrs. Wynn said knowingly. "It's that client confidentiality thing. Yeah. I seen that on TV." Jeremy smiled and said nothing, not wanting to disabuse her of her made-for-television understanding of the justice system. She excused herself and listened from the kitchen.

"So, you did help Zeb with the anarchy site?" Jeremy said softly, when she was gone.

"Uh-huh," Steve said. "He did all the content. I just handled the tech stuff. I run lots of sites."

"I see," Jeremy said. "So, have you been following Zeb's case at all?"

"Just what I read in the paper," Steve said.

"So you altered the website, right?" Jeremy said, turning his tone from affable to accusing. He wanted to catch Steve in a lie, even a little one, to make him feel guilty. It would increase the pressure on him to talk.

Steve shook his head in an exaggerated motion.

"Oh," Jeremy said. "No kidding. Because Zeb told me you were the only person with access who could have changed the site."

Steve didn't move. Jeremy could almost hear the wheels clicking in the boy's adolescent brain and wanted to turn up the heat. "Zeb told you to take down the bad stuff, didn't he?" Jeremy said. His voice level raised enough so that Mrs. Wynn leaned into the doorway with a watchful look of concern.

"No," Steve said. "I haven't even talked to him since – since he got arrested."

Jeremy smiled at Steve. "Look up here," Jeremy said, pointing to his own forehead. Steve looked closely, his eyebrows pulled together as if he was pondering the Sphinx's riddle. "Do I have the words 'I'm stupid' tattooed here?"

Steve shook his head and looked to the carpet.

"I saw your name in the visitors' log," Jeremy said. "We can stop playing games, okay. I'm on your team. If you were giving these answers to the cops you'd be in jail already."

Seconds passed. Jeremy thought he had broken the boy. He knew Steve was involved with more than just making a website. That fact was palpable. He didn't know the details of the confession that was about to spill forth, but he was sure it was coming.

Jeremy sat firm, fixing the boy with a confident glare. At last, Steve looked up to meet Jeremy's eyes. "It's not a crime to help someone with a website, is it?"

"That depends on what you say on the website, I suppose," Jeremy said. He hadn't expected the sudden resolve he heard in Wynn's voice.

"Yeah," Steve said. "I took the stuff off the website. Zeb told me to. It didn't have nothing to do with this eco-terrorism crap that they're talking about, though. This is a crock."

Jeremy felt Steve wriggling away. "So where were you that night?" he asked.

"What night?" Steve said. "The night of the fire? I was out. With someone."

Jeremy was positive he wasn't getting the whole story. But the kids were proving to have more steel than he thought. He continued to drill Steve, trying to get at something true, but the boy wasn't talking. After a few minutes, Mrs. Wynn finally decided that Jeremy wasn't really on their side and asked him to leave.

Jeremy's face was flushed as he drove back to the office. He hated losing control of a situation, and badgering his client's friend until he was ejected from the house certainly qualified. He stopped for a mocha latte at the Morning Grind and then headed back to his office. He stamped up the creaky stairway, ignoring his phone messages. He closed the door to his small office and plopped down at his desk.

Jeremy had finished near the top of his law school class, he believed, because he had been born with a gift. He didn't know why, but he always had an analytical mind that ground to the bone of any issue and spit out the right answer. If given a set of facts, no matter how complex, and access to the rules of law, Jeremy always came up with the right answer – eventually.

But, the practice of law was far more complicated than a law school hypothetical, because no one gave you a set of facts. Every case had evidence – witnesses, exhibits, analyses and opinions – that were constantly subjected to the winds of change. There was no objective truth about a case any more than there was a tooth fairy. And without a stable truth, how was one to apply a set of laws?

Still, he had done it successfully at Barnes & Honeycutt. He had access to investigators and experts and multi-media equipment. He had the best money could buy. And with these indulgences he had learned to manipulate the truth. The facts became malleable clay to be molded into the law that needed to be argued. Jeremy at least felt in control then – a master of a ship at sea on a wavering surface of reality.

As a public defender, however, he had learned to be afraid of the uncertainty of the available evidence. There was no budget to help tame unruly truths. Investigators and experts were rare and came only with court approval. And even then, they were usually of a far poorer quality than those serving the Barnes & Honeycutts of the world.

The change to criminal practice didn't help matters. Day in and day out, criminal courtrooms were a cesspool of lies. Lying clients. Lying police officers. Disingenuous arguments by lawyers. Academically dishonest opinions by judges who'd vowed to be tough on crime in order to get elected.

There were days when the weight of it made him wish he had stayed in Detroit. He would be looking out a corner window over the city. Hannah would be with him, and they wouldn't have to put in eighty-hour weeks forever. His leaving hadn't brought a halt to the success of the corporations and insurance companies he represented. They were still out there making billions on the misfortunes of the little guy.

His eyes drifted out the window overlooking the Sage Law Office parking lot. At the back of the lot was a chain-link fence surrounding the backyard of a simple home. In the backyard was a boy playing with his dog. The dog pounced on the boy, and the boy retreated. A silent breeze cut through small pines and blew, ruffling the boy's hair. Jeremy remembered the joy of playing with his own dog when he was young and the simplicity of not being responsible for anyone's fate.

He glanced back at the Radamacher file on top of his crowded desk. He had two days to get ready for the preliminary exam on the first life offense of his career. Zeb was in a world of hurt, and Jeremy needed to focus. A client was depending on him. And this client had a face instead of a board of directors.

He checked his appointment book. Tomorrow was Wednesday. He had two client appointments but no court. Thursday was intake interviews at the jail. He supposed Charlie would take those. He buzzed Dena and told her to reschedule the Wednesday appointments. He would see Zeb tomorrow and try to convince him to come clean about his partner in crime so that a deal could be worked out with Gray. And if he couldn't get a deal, he would just have to handle the first phase of the case with whatever version of the truth the prosecutor presented.

Having a plan – any plan – made all the difference in the world for Jeremy Jefferson. He was in control with a plan. Contingencies could be dealt with, as long as there was a path to follow. He cleared five files off his desk, dictated three memos and two motions. He filed and trashed loose papers and returned several volumes of manuals that had been collecting dust on his desk to their permanent home in the library. Charlie said he was happy to cover intake interviews on Thursday, and Jeremy was admiring a clear desk with only the Radamacher file in the in-box when Dena buzzed him just before 5:00 p.m.

"Yes," Jeremy said through the intercom.

"Allie Demming on line one. You got a new girlfriend?" Dena said.

Jeremy thought of blowing Allie off. He thought he would leave the office on time, order a pizza, and get a good night's rest before launching in on the case in the morning. But, Charlie wanted him to get some positive press on the case, and he wasn't going to do that by ignoring Allie Demming. "Thanks Dena," he said.

"Hello Allie," he said, punching up line one. "What's up?"

"Hey. I just wanted to give you a heads up. The governor's office issued a press release on your little case this afternoon," Allie said. Her voice was warm and full, like the smell of baking bread.

"Really," Jeremy said. "What did our good governor have to say?"

"The release said that Michiganders would not give in to threats of terrorism, foreign or domestic, and that people should be on guard for acts by environmental fanatics. He was going to ask the AG to step in to prosecute the case if Gray had dropped the ball."

"I'm sorry to hear the governor has forgotten the constitutional right of his citizens to be presumed innocent of any crime. It doesn't help that the chief executive of our state is out there trying people in the press when he doesn't know anything about the case."

"Can I quote you on that?" Allie asked.

Jeremy thought. "Sure," he said. "And you might quote me on this, too. The people of this state ought to be more afraid of political opportunism by people like Governor Howell and Ed Gray, who are trying to take advantage of the war on terrorism to better themselves politically. I mean, the allegation in this case is that a kid lit a bulldozer on fire and put some sand in a crankcase, and it is only an allegation at this point. Even if it turns out to be true, which my client has fully denied from the outset, I hardly think that this is a case where we are talking about a threat to our national security."

Allie was quiet. Jeremy could hear her scribbling. Speaking off the cuff was a skill lawyers developed, like catchers learn how to block a ball in the dirt. Jeremy could give a five-minute speech at the drop of a dime, and he liked to do it. Many lawyers liked the sound of their own voices, Jeremy thought, and there was some danger he was joining their ranks.

The scribbling sound stopped and Allie said, "Great stuff. You could be a politician some day."

"I'm not so sure that's a compliment," Jeremy said.

"Good point," she said. "I just have one more follow-up question, if you have any time."

"Sure," Jeremy said.

"Have you thought about *Our Town* on Saturday?" she said.

Jeremy paused. "You are one tough reporter, Demming," he said.

"It's a tough racket," she said. "Even in Milton."

"Well," he said, "I've been pretty busy with this case. I'd like to go, but I'm not sure if I've got to work this weekend or not. I'll let you know Friday, okay?"

"All right," she said. "We'll see you then."

He had never been very good at saying no to beautiful women. But, if he decided to go to the play with her, he was going to have to tell her how screwed up he was and nip this thing in the bud.

7

Jeremy was at the Wabeno County Jail when it opened to the public at 8:00 a.m. the next morning. His eyes were gritty and tired. He had washed down a Domino's pizza with a six-pack and watched old movies on cable the night before, and was now prepared to work for forty-eight hours straight, if necessary, to be ready for his case.

He had painfully bounced out of bed when the alarm spiked at 5:00 a.m. He was in the office by 5:45 a.m., where he reviewed every report on the case in detail. He then reviewed the statutes under which Zeb had been charged, and he was ready to take one last crack at breaking Zeb down, when Michelle unlocked the front doors to the jail.

"You're the early bird today, aren't ya?" she said cheerily. Michelle was always the only smile in an unsmiling building. He signed in and had Zeb dragged to the contact meeting room by 8:10 a.m. Jeremy felt like he was going to conquer the world in one day.

"Hey, Mr. J," Zeb said.

Jeremy explained that he had received all the supplemental police reports and materials from the prosecutor. He then went over the basics of Friday's upcoming hearing for a second time.

"A preliminary examination is simply a hearing where the prosecutor has to show the court evidence that a crime has been committed, and that you're the person who committed it," Jeremy said.

"Their burden of proof at this stage is only 'probable cause' – very easy for the prosecutor to show. Judge Welch binds over almost any case, unless the police or prosecutor has really screwed up."

"All right," Zeb said, unfazed.

"There is some good news," Jeremy said. "I've looked at the law in your case – believe it or not we don't get many of these charges, so I had to look it up – and I think there is very strong legal argument that you are not guilty."

"I told you I didn't do it," Zeb said.

"No, no," Jeremy said. "You saying you didn't do it is a factual argument. It's like the prosecutor saying 'he did it because we caught him in the act,' and then you turning around and saying 'I was just walking along and saw the fire, but I didn't set it.' That is a factual difference. They say, 'A.' And you say, 'B.' And someone has to decide if 'A' or 'B' is the truth. The court doesn't get into factual differences at preliminary exams, okay? In fact, we won't be presenting any evidence at the exam. We'll only be challenging their evidence, for just that reason. Our evidence doesn't matter at the exam, because the court has to leave those differences of fact for a jury to decide later. Understand?"

Zeb shrugged with a puzzled look on his face.

"But, what I'm saying is that I think we have a strong legal argument as opposed to a factual argument. A legal argument is kind of like saying, 'So what,' after the prosecutor has put on his evidence. It's basically saying, 'The action you are alleging, Mr. Prosecutor, is not really a crime – or not the crime that you charged anyway,'" Jeremy explained.

"That sounds good," Zeb said. "So what's our argument?"

"Well," Jeremy said. "The prosecutor is going to tell the judge that you burned up a bulldozer in an attempt to further a political cause, basically. That's the factual basis for the crime of terrorism that they have charged you with. But, there are three specific things they have to prove to get you bound over for trial on that charge.

"One, that the act is a violent felony. No problem there. What was done, by whoever, was a violent felony, because the statute defines 'violent' as using a Molotov cocktail, like the one used in this case.

"Two, that the act was done to influence the government or civilians," Jeremy said, holding up fingers as he ticked off the main elements of the crime. "That is not much of a stretch when you add up all the information about your anarchy site and the ELF connection.

"And three, that whoever did it had reason to know they might cause a death or serious injury.

"It seems clear to me that whoever did this, purposely did not intend to cause death or serious injury," Jeremy said. "I think this is a very strong legal issue, and I don't think the charge should hold up in the long run."

"That sounds great," Zeb said, brightening considerably.

"I said, in the long run. In the *short run* things don't look so good," Jeremy said. He liked to explain the details to his clients, where time permitted, but he didn't want to raise any false hopes. "In the last year I've done two dozen felony exams in front of Welch, and he hasn't dismissed any of them. His basic rule is that if the prosecutor says you did it, then you are getting bound over. So, I don't think he's going to rule in our favor on the legal issue. We'll have a better chance with Judge Parr once the case is bound over. He's a little more open to defense arguments. And, if we can't win there, we can appeal. But, this takes time. And none of this is going to get you out of jail today."

"So I'm going to be stuck here?" Zeb said. "For how long?"

"It is up to the court, really," Jeremy said. "It could take three to six months to get your case to trial after the exam. And then, unless the appeals court wants to take it on an emergency application, your appeal could take years. And, while I believe I'm right about this, it isn't a slam dunk. The prosecutor is going to say something like, 'You should have known a fire could seriously injure someone, because everyone knows firemen get called out to fight fires and sometimes get hurt in the process.' So, I can't guarantee you anything, other than we have a good legal issue."

Zeb put his head down. He looked thinner than when Jeremy had seen him last. His hands were bone-white.

"And even if we did get the terrorism charge dismissed, there would still be serious charges of arson and malicious destruction left. The max on each of these is twenty years. You'd probably get a stiff prison sentence even without the terrorism charges," Jeremy said.

"I didn't blow up the bulldozer," Zeb said, looking up, his eyes meeting Jeremy's. If Jeremy hadn't read the police reports and sifted through a forest of evidence against Zeb, he might have believed him. "This ain't right."

"Again," Jeremy said, "that is a factual issue we can take up at trial, but it's not going to do us any good on Friday. But, I've looked at the evidence against you, Zeb. And it looks pretty strong. Would you like to see the reports?"

Zeb did. He perked up and went over all the police and fire reports on the crime.

Jeremy was patient. This was the key moment. He had to get Zeb to come clean about his own involvement in the crime before he could even start talking about giving up accomplices. Zeb read thoroughly and silently.

"So, you can see," Jeremy said, "they have a lot of evidence."

"I didn't burn up that dozer, Mr. J.," Zeb said. "That's all I can really say."

"Do you mind if I ask you some questions about these reports, then?"

43

"No, sir."

"First off, if you didn't do this, what were you doing wearing work gloves and socks on your boots at a construction site on a Saturday night?" Jeremy said tersely.

Zeb said nothing.

"Why were you caught running from the scene? How did the drill from your high school shop class get to the scene that night?" Jeremy asked as Zeb sat in stone-cold defiance.

Zeb had no answers.

"Isn't it coincidental that your website publishes an article complaining about Blue-Mart three weeks before this attack on a Blue-Mart?" Jeremy continued, hoping with each unanswerable question that Zeb would break down.

Jeremy was trying to lose it in a calculated way. His voice rose with each question. But, he felt some anger at Zeb's obstinance as it became clear he was not going to bend. To Jeremy's surprise, Zeb looked more defiant with every question. Jeremy stopped, and the boy stared at him intently, seeming to study his face.

"You don't want an idiot for a lawyer, do you?" Jeremy asked.

"No, sir," Zeb said.

"Well Zeb, it's pretty obvious to me that you were involved in this and that you weren't alone. Whose tennis shoe print was at the scene?"

Zeb looked at him again. His eyes were the clear blue of a cloudless sky. "I can't really say much. I'm already screwed. I don't want to screw over anybody else."

"That's a problem, Zeb," Jeremy said, "because when we are looking at evidence like this, and we are looking at charges like this, we need to make some kind of deal to help you. And the prosecutor has pretty much said there isn't going to be much of a deal unless you give up your friend."

Zeb shook his head immediately. "I'm not gonna to do that, Mr. J. I'll just have to sit in here and take my lumps. I can't say any more about it than that, really."

"Do you know the governor has come out and said you're an enemy of the state? I don't think you're going to like what's going to happen here," Jeremy said.

"I don't care, Mr. J. You just do the best you can. The guys in here say you're the best public defender there is. Just do your best."

Jeremy was starting to hear more and more praise like this through the jailhouse grapevine. He discounted it, because he knew he wasn't half the defender Charlie was, but it still made his chest swell a bit. No insurance adjuster or CEO ever slapped him on the back and said he did a great job when he was at Barnes & Honeycutt.

He knew he wasn't going to get any more from Zeb, and it didn't bother him. The kid's stock was rising all the time in Jeremy's eyes. Now, not only was he idealistic and courageous, but he was loyal to the point of self-sacrifice.

He went over plan "B" with Zeb. They were going to hold the exam and challenge the prosecutor's case as best they could. They would try to get Welch to kick the terrorism charge, and they would try to get him to re-address bond. But, Jeremy knew that there was almost no chance of winning on either score. When they were through, Jeremy packed up his shiny leather briefcase and buzzed Michelle to let him out into the sunlight.

"I don't think you're an idiot, Mr. J.," Zeb said, as Jeremy left. "It'll be okay."

Jeremy knew that absent a miracle, Zeb was going to have the optimistic, charming, boyishness knocked out of him in the state prison system. It was only a matter of time.

Allison Demming's office shared a wall with the press room. When the big offset press churned out an edition of the *Beacon*, it would send a faint quiver through her cluttered desk, which was jammed up against the wall. Her office had no window, but as she spun her chair one hundred and eighty degrees and looked out her door, she could see across the hall and out the window of the advertising manager's office.

The autumn rain that irregularly plinked the window fell from a grey bank of clouds that covered the sky. It fit her mood. She wheeled her chair around again to her computer screen and glanced over the Radamacher story she had been writing for Sunday's paper. She could not finish writing until after tomorrow's hearing, but she thought the initial work she had done on the story was quite good. It was rare to get such a meaty story in Milton. She had worked the local government beat for three years before volunteering for a lateral move to the cops-and-courts beat in the summer, and she had never seen any story with potential like this.

The Radamacher story had some nice elements. Terrorism and environmental angles. Very vogue. Heavy equipment explosions. What story didn't benefit from that? And, a handsome, single attorney battling absurd odds. She liked that part of the story best.

It was what she always wanted. Big, exciting stories. Major headlines. But having a story that was getting picked up regionally, maybe even nationally, only reminded her of lofty aspirations before she had settled for a job at her hometown weekly. Her goal of working for a major daily had almost passed into the category of a pipe dream, she thought, but now with the big story in a little town, she was thinking again of sending out clips and getting out of Milton.

She had even called an old editor she'd known from when she interned at the *Tribune* and casually mentioned the Radamacher story. While they didn't publish much freelance stuff, he offered to take look at a feature if she wanted to write it. But, at twenty-seven, she knew that no major daily was going to take a serious look at her now, unless she went to some medium-sized market and got a bunch of daily experience under her belt first.

She forced her mind back to her copy and, after a few minutes of quick editing, was satisfied that the background for the story was as good it was going to get. Now she just had to wait for tomorrow's hearing.

Allie had called a secretary at the prosecutor's office in the morning and learned that the exam was definitely going forward. After lunch, she'd heard through the rumor mill at the courthouse – information usually slipped from the solitary confines of the judges' offices, through their secretaries and law clerks, to the ministerial clerks in the front offices, and on down to the janitorial and maintenance staffs – that Channel 23 from Mount Pleasant had been granted camera access for the hearing. It was the first time she would have to share her beat with another member of the press corps.

She pulled up other articles for the week to make sure they were in order. Her briefs from the police blotter were all set. A feature about a new bicycle officer on the Milton Police Department was polished and ready for print. She shut down her computer and was ready to leave the office a few minutes early.

Allie looked at the telephone. She had asked Jeremy out directly – had even called him under the guise of letting him know about the governor's press release on Tuesday to prompt him for an answer – and the guy still had not said yes, or even bothered to call her. She was sure from the way he looked at her that there was a spark. She decided she would give him another try.

She dialed his office and got his secretary.

"Law office," a cheery voice said.

"This is Allie Demming from the *Beacon*. Is Mr. Jefferson available?"

"Could you hold, please?" the secretary said. After a minute or so the secretary returned, "I'm sorry, Ms. Demming, he's in a meeting. Can I take a message?"

"I just wanted to know if the Radamacher preliminary exam was going ahead tomorrow?" Allie lied.

"As far as I know," the secretary said. "I can leave a message for Mr. Jefferson to call you about it."

"That's all right," Allie said. "I'm just headed out. I'll catch him tomorrow. Thanks."

In a meeting, she fumed. She had yet to meet a man who had turned her down for a date, and she doubted Jeremy Jefferson would be the first.

"I don't like lying like that for you, Jeremy," Dena said over the intercom, an impish smile embedded in her voice.

"It's your job," Jeremy said. "You got a problem with working? Maybe I should talk to Charlie."

"She sounds very nice," Dena said. "I know her family from my church. Good people. But her poor father. Alzheimer's."

"I'm trying to work," Jeremy said.

"All work and no play makes Jeremy a dull boy," she said.

"Stay out of my life, Poyer," he said. More bonus point for small-town romance; everyone knew everyone else's business, Jeremy thought.

He finished off the last of his cross-examination notes and printed it out. He was ready. As with most cases, the more detailed an examination he gave to the evidence, the more imperfections he saw in the state's case. If he had an open-minded judge on the bench, he thought he might actually be able to get the terrorism charge thrown out. But, with Welch, the exam was really just a discovery hearing to learn about the prosecution case.

He reviewed his notes one last time, stopped by the Milton Diner for a cheeseburger and was snug in bed before 10:00 p.m. Sleep came slowly, and when he dreamed, it was of Hannah. She was on the bench instead of Judge Welch, listening to Jeremy argue about how the whole case was a misunderstanding. She was smiling, just like Allie's smile, and he knew he was winning the case. But, then Hannah stopped listening. She touched up her hundred-dollar manicure with a file. When he finally stopped talking, she ruled against him and ordered Zeb off to jail. Jeremy screamed at her and stomped out of the courtroom. Allie caught him by the courthouse steps. She wanted a quote. But, before he could tell her about Hannah, his dream dissolved into a black sleep.

8

Kurt Bishop loved how his power had grown exponentially with that of the governor. As a law student, he was a nobody. When he started helping with Howell's campaigns for Congress, suddenly people started returning his phone calls. In Congress, as a chief-aide, those who wanted the congressman's ear were eager to be put on hold for a chance to talk to him. And now, as the governor's chief-of-staff, the vast political machine that he had assembled to put Howell in this position was at Bishop's beck and call.

Artie Fisher, the party's best pollster, was in Bishop's waiting room at 9:00 p.m. on Thursday evening and didn't make a peep when Bishop let him sit for fifteen minutes. Bishop was busy vetting a speech the governor was going to deliver to a special assembly of the Detroit Economic Club on Saturday morning, but he would have made Fisher wait, even if he had nothing to do, just because he had that power.

When he finished with the speech, Bishop had to get up to usher Artie into his office personally. Even his power couldn't keep his union secretary beyond normal working hours, much to his displeasure.

"How are you, Kurt?" Artie said, pumping Bishop's hand in greeting. Bishop led him to his office overlooking the lights of Capitol Avenue.

"So how do the numbers look?" Bishop said, taking a seat and kicking his feet up on his desk.

"This is a knockout issue," Artie said, handing a packet of papers to Bishop. "I've got to hand it to you: statistically, it's the best wedge issue I've seen for our guys in a long time. There's still a lot of fear out there across all categories. And this hits the bull's-eye. It takes the fear of terror attacks and turns it against the one area where we are weakest. It neutralizes their arguments on the environment completely."

"These numbers are all plus or minus four?" Bishop said, as he reviewed the raw data.

"Yup," Artie said. "I should be able to get it down to plus or minus three in a day or two, but you wanted an answer so quick."

Bishop continued to review the figures as Artie detailed his findings. This issue had serious play. If he could just get Green Peace to slam a plane into the state capitol, he might be able to get Howell tagged as a vice-presidential candidate immediately, he mused.

So long as they could get out in front on it, the raw numbers told him the issue would likely erode any opposition to Howell by two to ten percent. That would bode well for the party in the mid-term elections and make Howell a player in the next presidential cycle.

Artie was a great pollster, Bishop thought. But you couldn't get him to shut up once he was wound up on an issue. Bishop started roughing out a legislative proposal that would give them a vehicle to drive the issue home as Artie blathered. Bishop then listed notes on how he could best use the governor's bully pulpit to screw over Jefferson's case. Not that Jefferson needed much help there. Bishop had gotten a copy of the police reports from the local prosecutor. Jefferson's client seemed screwed already.

"It plays particularly well among white females, twenty-five to fifty-four. And you know, we could use some help in that demo–"

"That'll be all, Fisher," Bishop cut him off. "Nice work."

He escorted Artie past the night security and headed for home thinking of a new office on Pennsylvania Avenue.

Jeremy packed his briefcase with the essentials. The file, two legal pads and pens, his trial notebook carefully tailored for the hearing, the Michigan Court Rules, and Dubin and Weissenberger on evidence. Normally a file, a pen and paper would have done the trick, but today he packed as if setting out on a large-game safari. He stepped into the bathroom and wrapped a red-striped cream tie snug around his neck. He adjusted the button-down collar on his powder-blue shirt and returned to his office for his navy, Armani dress coat. He pulled the cuffs of his shirt snug, picked up the heavy briefcase, and set out on his short walk to the courthouse.

The morning sun cast his long shadow on the sidewalk before him as he went. The grass was green, and the trees held stubbornly to leaves of yellow and red. It was shaping into a beautiful fall day, but the air chilled his hands as he walked. He passed the Veterans Memorial on the courthouse lawn, centered between the two dominant oaks. It listed the names of Milton's sacrifice in the cause of war. He was reminded of a history professor at Michigan State, who explained the morality of war in historical terms: "Winners write history and are heroes," she said. "Losers, however justified, become villains for all time."

The courthouse was a majestic nineteenth century structure, built with dark red brick. Four marble steps greeted visitors, funneling them through two limestone Doric columns to heavy double doors made of dark-stained oak. The majestic building housed the three courts that governed all legal proceedings in Wabeno County. The east wing of the ground and second floors housed the circuit courtroom of Judge Lawrence Parr, which handled most of the heavy lifting on legal issues that arose in the county. Parr's courtroom could have been home to antebellum trials, with ornate woodwork rising twenty-two feet to a decorative ceiling. It was lighted by tall windows on the north and east walls. Practicing in the room made a trial lawyer feel worthy.

The western half of the top floor belonged to the probate court, which took care of the property and juvenile matters in the county. The east wing of the basement was home to Judge Welch's district court, where Jeremy was headed for the first real action on Zeb's case.

The halls were empty and his footfalls going down the wooden stairs echoed. He rang a security buzzer and was granted access to Judge Welch's office suite. He passed the judge's secretary sitting at her desk and nodded pleasantly to no reply. The law clerk's office was empty, and the door to the judge's chambers was closed. The jury room was dark, and the holding cell at the end of the hall held his client, Zeb Radamacher. Deputy Short, as jovial a law enforcement officer as Jeremy had ever met, had transported Zeb from the jail. He used a large brass key to let Jeremy into the lockup.

Zeb was dressed in a grey pinstripe suit. It was pathetically out of date and ill-fitting. Charlie had used petty cash to purchase it from the Salvation Army. It was only a modest improvement over the jail-issue orange jumpsuit. Normally, preliminary hearings were held in less than an hour with a client dressed in orange, but Charlie had thought Zeb should look as formal as possible, once they were alerted that cameras would be in the courtroom. It was never too early to try and start influencing a prospective jury pool.

Zeb clowned about the suit and was generally in good spirits. Jeremy did his best to be reassuring and then set out to find Ed Gray.

Jeremy found Gray in a conference room across the hall from the courtroom. He was talking in hushed tones with Detective Mary Russell.

"Got a minute?" Jeremy interrupted.

Gray continued to give some instruction to Detective Russell and then motioned Jeremy into the room. Jeremy closed the door as Detective Russell left.

Jeremy plopped his briefcase down and sat at the table. "You know this terrorism charge is baloney, right?" Jeremy said.

Gray chortled out a clip of unamused laughter. "We'll see what Welch has to say about that, won't we?" Gray said.

"Charlie said that we might work something out on this case," Jeremy said. "And I just wanted to get that charge off the table before we get to some reasonable deal."

"I told Charlie that the only way this case is going anywhere but trial is for your guy to give up his partner or partners in crime."

"He tells me there were no partners in crime," Jeremy said.

"Did he tell you he was innocent, too?" Gray's voice rose to highlight his sarcasm. "My God, have I got the wrong kid in jail here?"

"Look," Jeremy said. "You have a fairly strong case on the MDOP and the arson. I am not trying to make light of this. But, this wasn't a terrorist act under the statute, so let's just set that charge aside and negotiate on the other two."

"Is your guy willing to talk?" Gray said.

"I think I could get him to, given the right deal," Jeremy said, fishing for some offer.

"Guilty as charged for a nine-year cap, if he gives up everyone involved and fully cooperates," Gray shot back. Obviously he had given the matter some thought.

Jeremy looked at notes in his file. "The guidelines on the MDOP and arson are something like two to four. He's not doing nine over this. Come on. He's been a decent kid. This is his first ever involvement. Assuming, for the sake of argument, that he did it, it was seriously misguided. But not nine years' worth."

"I have his guidelines at twelve to nineteen on the terrorism," Gray said. "Nine is below guidelines. And you know he's screwed. Did you read the reports? It's a slam dunk."

Jeremy had read everything three times. Factually, Gray was right. The kid was screwed. "This isn't terrorism, Ed," Jeremy said. "You know it. Or you should. The statute says he's got to reasonably believe he could cause serious injury. Again, assuming you're right and he did this, he did all he could to make sure no one would get hurt. It's like the creed of these ELF guys. Damage property only."

"Anybody who blows up anything ought to know that emergency responders are in a lot of danger," Gray said. "That's enough to get him. I don't think Welch or Parr or any other judge is going to throw this out. And I know a jury isn't going to. You take this to trial and you are sending this boy away for a long time."

"He's going away for a long time with what you're offering," Jeremy said. "Dismiss the terrorism and give me three."

"You're dreaming. And if we start taking evidence today, the offer's off the table," Gray said.

"That's crap," Jeremy said. Threats made him want to stand and fight. "This is a life offense, and you're going to threaten the kid that he can't get a deal if he holds an exam? That's close to misconduct."

Gray closed his file and stood up. "File a motion for misconduct, then," he said. "If you start this exam, the offer's off the table." The prosecutor brushed past Jeremy and went into the courtroom.

Jeremy returned to meet with Zeb. It was his obligation to discuss all offers with his client. He laid out the deal and recommended Zeb reject it. Zeb agreed. Nine years wasn't much better than twelve at the low end of the guidelines. And Zeb was nowhere near to giving up anyone. It was an easy call. They might never get another offer, but the kid wasn't going to prison for a decade without a trial.

Jeremy made his way for the courtroom and was surprised at the throng that had gathered inside. He scanned the crowd. A TV-23 cameraman had a tripod erected by the far wall just behind the bar. A television reporter primped her hair in the front row. The rest of the pew-like seats were filled with a smattering of onlookers. Steve Wynn was seated with several teenagers clustered in the back corner. The group was a blur of tattoos, piercings, black clothing, eyeliner and primary-colored hair to Jeremy's passing eye. He hoped they were not rooting for Zeb, but they obviously weren't fans of the prosecution.

Zeb's mother sat in the front row of the gallery near the wall. At the other end of the pew sat a boy that shared so much of Zeb's appearance, it had to be his older brother. Next to the brother was a middle-aged man with a permanent scowl. The infamous Mark Radamacher, Jeremy speculated. An elderly woman dressed in jeans and a sweatshirt sat a few rows behind Zeb's mom. Behind her was a row of three young men and two young women. Twenty-somethings searching for entertainment, Jeremy mused.

Allie had taken up her post next to the television reporter. She smiled and nodded at Jeremy, and he winked a reply without thinking. Two men sat next to Allie behind the prosecution desk. One was a fit man with a young appearance; the other was a man of fifty- something with bronze hair and an expensive coat. Witnesses for the prosecution, Jeremy surmised.

Jeremy settled into his chair at the defense table and unpacked his briefcase. His stomach growled long and low, and he wondered if Gray, seated at the prosecution table to his left, could hear it.

Detective Russell, an attractive woman, in a way only a woman who carried a gun could be attractive, leaned back in her chair and whispered around Gray's back, "Did you skip breakfast, Jeremy?"

Jeremy smiled and shrugged.

Deputy Short led Zeb to his seat next to Jeremy, with the camera panning the perp walk.

The law clerk opened the door at the back of the courtroom. "All rise," he ordered.

Judge Welch and his court recorder entered.

"Be seated," Welch said, settling in behind the bench. "Calling Case Number 03-651-FC, the People of the State of Michigan versus Zebediah Radamacher. Appearances, Counsel."

Jeremy and Gray identified themselves in turn. Gray glanced over and said, "You want the deal?"

Jeremy shook his head.

"Any preliminary matters, gentlemen?" Welch said.

"The People are ready to proceed," Gray said.

"Two small matters, Your Honor," Jeremy began. "First, we'd ask that the witnesses be sequestered. And second, I'd make a motion that Amanda Ratielle be excluded from all proceedings today. She is listed as a witness on the complaint, and, in reviewing the reports, it appears that the prosecutor will be relying on her, at least in part, to identify my client. She was a clerk at the Milton Hardware, Your Honor, who saw someone matching the general description of my client stealing a can of spray paint on the evening in question.

"Allowing Ms. Ratielle to attempt to identify my client for the first time in a court hearing would be improperly suggestive, Your Honor, and a violation of Mr. Radamacher's right to due process. We'd be requesting a line-up or, in the alternative, that Ms. Ratielle be prevented from testifying as to identification."

Welch's eyebrows furrowed as if he had just been presented with a novel theory on relativity. "Mr. Gray?"

"The defense can't dictate a police investigation, Your Honor," Gray said, rising to his feet. "There is no right to a line-up."

"Your Honor, the law in Michigan is clear. The court may order a line-up on request. May I approach?" Jeremy said, extracting a photocopied case out of his trial notebook. He handed a copy to Gray and approached with a copy for Welch. "You see, Your Honor, you have the power to grant a request for a line-up. And, if you fail to do so, any identification she were to make at this hearing could taint her testimony irrevocably if a later court finds it to be an overly-suggestive setting."

Welch glanced at the case without reading. "Well, Mr. Gray, I wouldn't want to allow the testimony today to the State's detriment. Is this evidence necessary to show probable cause?"

"Your Honor," Gray said, rising again, "as Mr. Jefferson knows, the evidence in this case is overwhelming. I could probably find a way to work around Ms. Ratielle's testimony."

"Very well, I'll reserve ruling on this matter unless Mr. Gray should want to call Ms. Ratielle as a witness. And you can raise this in the circuit court," Welch said, pausing. "If I bind the matter over, that is."

"I just want to be sure that she is kept from the courtroom, so there is no chance of viewing of my client. I would also ask for an order preventing Ms. Ratielle from viewing any media coverage of this matter," said Jeremy, motioning toward the television camera. "I wouldn't want her identification tainted due to television coverage."

"So ordered," Welch said. Jeremy had drawn first blood. Gray gave Detective Russell instructions that sent her scurrying from the courtroom. "All other witnesses will be sequestered from the courtroom, with the exception of Detective Russell, and they shall be instructed not to discuss or disclose their testimony with any other person during the pendency of this proceeding. Mr. Gray?"

Gray spoke to the husky man with the bronze mane. The man was animated but eventually complied with Gray's order, and he and his younger companion left the courtroom. From the man's irritation at being excluded from the proceedings, Jeremy surmised it was Ian Cashman, the owner of Cashman Construction, whose equipment was destroyed.

"Your Honor, the People would call Trooper Don Nielsen to the stand," Gray said.

Nielsen entered the courtroom in his starched blue uniform, led by Detective Russell. He was sworn in by the court recorder and led through a rambling narrative of how he had noticed an explosion while patrolling on US-27 and apprehended Zeb Radamacher running from the scene wearing work gloves and socks over his tennis shoes. Zeb seemed disinterested in the testimony, and Jeremy twice saw him looking back, trying to communicate with the teenagers in the gallery.

"Any questions, Mr. Jefferson?" Welch said.

"Thank you, Your Honor," Jeremy said. There wasn't a lot that could be done with Nielsen's testimony. This case was really the epitome of being caught at the scene red-handed.

"Good morning, Trooper Nielsen," Jeremy said.

"Counselor," the trooper said cordially. They had met before in court on minor offenses, and Jeremy thought Nielsen was, by and large, a straight shooter.

"I wanted to start by clearing up some confusion in your report and in the testimony here today," Jeremy said, settling in at the lectern in the center of the courtroom. "You testified today that you were first aware of a problem at the site when you witnessed an explosion. Did I understand you right?"

"Yes, sir."

"It was your testimony that you were traveling southbound on US-27 when you saw an explosion off the highway, correct?"

"That's right."

"About how far away were you when you saw this explosion?"

"I would say I was about a quarter – about an eighth of a mile north of the Milton exit on twenty-seven when I first saw it. And I got there pretty quick after that," Nielsen said.

"I'm sure you did. About how long would you say it took you?"

"I'd say about a minute from the time I saw it, sir," Nielsen said.

"So you went from about a quarter mile away, to the construction site in a minute?"

"I think it was about an eighth of a mile. Yes."

"Now, you eventually made a written report of these events, correct?" Jeremy said.

"Yes, sir."

"May I approach, Your Honor," Jeremy said, handing Nielsen a copy of his police report. "Is this the report you made, Trooper?"

Nielsen studied the report for a minute and said, "Yes, sir. It is a copy of my report."

"When did you write this report, Trooper Nielsen?" Jeremy said.

"I believe it was that night, sir. I actually stayed past my shift – I was supposed to get off at eleven, but I stayed after to finish the report because Mr. Radamacher was lodged, and I needed to get charges authorized."

"Your report doesn't mention any cause of the fire, correct?"

Nielsen reviewed the report again. "No, sir," he said. "That's in the report by the fire department. You should have got a copy. I included it with
–"

"I have a copy," Jeremy interrupted. "My question is simply that your report does not detail a cause of the fire, does it?"

"No, sir, it doesn't."

"But, I take it from your testimony, that you had been made aware of the cause of the fire by the fire investigators, correct?"

"Yes, sir. Chief McGuigan was on the scene that night. He told me it was a Molotov cocktail that burned out the bulldozer."

"And that was before you cleared the scene that night?" Jeremy said.

"Yes, it was. They got the thing under control pretty quickly, and I guess Chief McGuigan did not have a real hard time finding the cause. It was a pretty basic bomb, from what I understand."

"Now, would you say that your exact memory of what you saw that night was better at the time you were writing your report, that night, or is your memory better today, some two weeks after the incident?" Jeremy asked.

"Objection, relevance," Gray said, rising from his chair. "And it's argumentative."

"Sustained," the judge said, before Jeremy could respond.

"You wrote in your report, and I quote, 'a large fire caught responding officer's attention,' didn't you?" Jeremy asked.

Nielsen glanced at the report. "Yes, sir."

"And that description is in the narrative of your report, correct?" Jeremy said.

"Yes, sir."

"You would agree with me, would you not, Mr. Nielsen, that when you are writing a police report it is important to be precise and accurate about what happened?"

"Yes, sir, it is. But, nobody's perfect," Nielsen said.

"Nobody's perfect," Jeremy said. "But, Mr. Nielsen, you do understand that the words 'fire' and 'explosion' have different meanings, correct?"

"Yes, sir."

"And, when you wrote the report about what you saw, you said that your attention was drawn to a large fire, correct?"

"Yes, sir, I did."

"You could have written that your attention was drawn by an explosion, correct?"

"Yes, sir, I could've."

"But that's not how you described it." Jeremy loved cross-examination. Forcing a hostile witness to agree was an art and a pleasure, wrapped together like a vanilla-chocolate twist.

"No," Nielsen said.

"Is it fair for me to say that you did not see an initial explosion, but you saw a fire after an explosion?"

"I think that's right. It seemed like an explosion had just occurred."

"So you didn't see the initial explosion, but you think that it had occurred just prior to you observing the fire?"

"Yes, sir, that's right," Nielsen said.

"And do you have some expertise in explosives or fire investigation?"

"Objection, argumentative," Gray said, springing up again.

"Sustained," Judge Welch said. He turned to Jeremy. "I think we get the picture, Mr. Jefferson."

"It was because of the size of the–" Nielsen started to explain before the judge cut him off.

"I've sustained the objection. You don't have to answer the question," Welch said.

Jeremy looked to his cross-examination notes to regain his train of thought. In addition to being a legal challenge, objections always had the effect of throwing him off his very focused train of logic.

"So I am clear," Jeremy began again, "you did not see the initial explosion, correct?"

"That's correct."

"So when you described seeing an explosion in earlier testimony, that was not correct."

"Yes, I should have said I saw the fire just after the explosion," Nielsen said.

"And you know there was an explosion because of the fire investigation that was done later?" Jeremy said.

"Yes, sir."

"But you don't have any expertise or information to say exactly how long the fire was burning before you saw it, do you?" Jeremy said.

Nielsen thought for a moment before conceding. "No, sir, I don't know exactly how long it burned before I saw it."

Jeremy checked the first point off his list. It was a small point but an important one. If Nielsen didn't actually see the explosion then he didn't know when it had occurred.

Before Nielsen was through, Jeremy led him through several other points in a tug of war. In the end, Nielsen admitted that he hadn't conducted a thorough investigation of the scene, that he hadn't secured the scene in a way that would have prevented tampering after the fact, and that he did not personally witness Zeb Radamacher break any law.

The prosecutor next called Fire Chief James McGuigan, who handled the arson investigation. McGuigan had a grandfatherly kindness and patience that a jury would love, Jeremy thought. Jeremy had not yet had time to seek any independent expert assistance on the cause of the fire, so he didn't have much ammunition to challenge McGuigan's conclusions. The fire appeared to have been set by a Molotov cocktail – a homemade version of napalm made by filling a bottle with gasoline and dish soap and stuffing a rag doused with flammable liquid into the opening. Once lit and thrown, the device shattered and ignited a sticky gelatin across the surface of the target, according to McGuigan's expert testimony.

On cross Jeremy got McGuigan to admit that there was no way to pinpoint the time of the explosion with any scientific accuracy. He then set out to get McGuigan to admit that the fire was not a particular threat to anyone's safety – a fact that, if conceded, might help get the terrorism charge booted.

"Mr. McGuigan, you responded to this fire scene, did you not?" Jeremy said.

"Yes, I did."

"And you had a crew of what? Four or five men?" Jeremy said.

"One truck and my car responded to the fire. There were a total of six from the fire department. I did not have a count on the number of police officers who were there for security."

"This was a fairly standard vehicle fire?" Jeremy said.

"No, I wouldn't say that," McGuigan said. "As I said, the fire was caused by a Molotov cocktail. That's basically the same as a napalm bomb, on a smaller scale. It contains a gasoline jellied with detergent. It's a sticky substance and can be very dangerous."

Jeremy sensed that Gray had prepped McGuigan well for this line of questioning.

"None of your men were injured in any way in responding to this fire?" Jeremy said.

"No, no one was hurt."

"In fact, in your entire tenure as fire chief in Milton, you're not aware of any car fire that resulted in an injury to a fireman, are you?" Jeremy said.

"No, sir, I'm not. But, this is the first time in my memory that we've had a vehicle firebombed."

Jeremy knew more questions on this line were futile. He would need his own expert if he was ever going to get testimony that this fire was not really a danger to any person.

"No further questions, Your Honor," Jeremy said.

Welch adjourned the exam for lunch. Zeb had gotten a two-hundred-and-fifty-dollar-an-hour cross-examination, Jeremy thought, but the evidence of his guilt was still mounting.

Charlie slipped into Welch's courtroom unnoticed in time to watch his friend cross-examine Nielsen. He thought Jeremy was an excellent lawyer technically, and the cross was skillful. But, his protégé had not yet adapted a style that was amenable to the average listener in Wabeno County. Charlie himself, though having an educational pedigree worthy of American royalty, had gradually taken on a Matlock-like rhythm of speaking that was quite effective with the locals. It came natural to him, and he thought of it as more of a discovery of his own true self than a charade he practiced.

He listened to the testimony intently for most of the morning. He stepped out on the lawn for a cigarette as the hour approached noon and enjoyed the autumn sunshine. The day was like a butterfly that could be pinned to corkboard, its beauty preserved in memory for all time, Charlie thought.

He took a last drag from his Marlboro and was about to head in when the courthouse doors opened, and the small crowd that had been watching the exam started to exit. There were two groups of young people talking among themselves. One was a group of kids, probably from the local high school. They looked like a Celtic tribe dyed black. The other group looked like the landed gentry of youth by comparison. They were dressed casually, but there were brand name clothes in the mix. An older woman in jeans and a sweater, with a warm face, walked out with the second group.

Charlie watched as the two groups merged by the Veterans Memorial at the center of the courthouse lawn. The older woman spoke for a moment, very quietly. The merged group numbered eleven, counting the matronly leader. Three boys broke from the group and jogged out of sight behind the courthouse.

They returned a short time later with armfuls of picket signs. Each member picked up a sign, and the group formed a picket line that circled at the bottom of the marble stairs near the courthouse door. The signs were handmade, and, judging from the quality of the work, Charlie guessed that not many of the young people were from the art department. The messages were simple. Charlie could make out the larger block lettered signs. "FREE ZEB." "BLUE-MART = SLAVERY." "FREEDOM FOR ALL, NOT STRIP MALLS."

The cameraman and reporter from TV-23, whom Charlie had seen in the courtroom, were on their way down the steps. The cameraman had his head down and nearly missed the protestors until he was startled by their first chorus.

"What do we want?" the older woman yelled in a rich voice.

"Freedom for Zeb!" went out a strong, ten-person chant.

"When do we want it?" she yelled.

"Now!" the group responded.

The startled cameraman took a misstep on the stairs but recovered without falling. He and the reporter exchanged a look, and he set up for some quick protest footage. The reporter approached the protest leader and asked for a quote on camera.

Charlie moved closer to hear.

The shot was set up, and the reporter asked the woman for her name and position.

"I'm Wilma Quinn," the woman said. "I am a professor of social ecology at Central Michigan."

"What brings you out here today?" the reporter said.

"A student at the local high school alerted my class to the injustice that is being done to Zeb Radamacher," Professor Quinn said. "We decided to come up here and show our support for the young man. Whether he is guilty or not, the crime that was committed here is not so different from the Boston Tea Party. Whoever tried to stop this national corporate behemoth from forcing sprawl on our rural counties deserves a medal, not prison."

"So, are you advocating terrorism, Professor Quinn?" the reporter said.

"This is not terrorism," Professor Quinn said. "This was an act of self-defense. And an act of non-violence. The corporations that are raping our public lands are the real criminals here, and someone should start holding them accountable."

The reporter looked very pleased with her impromptu interview. She and her cameraman set up a closing monologue with the grand, old courthouse as a backdrop, and then headed back to their truck to file their story in time for the six o'clock news.

Charlie introduced himself to Professor Quinn before she could return to her role as cheerleader.

"My office represents Zeb," he said.

"Pleased to meet you," she smiled.

"Are these all your students out here?" Charlie said. "That's not a bad turnout. You must have promised them all an 'A.'"

"No, about half of these kids are from the high school," she said, gesturing to her band of revolutionaries. "There is a lot of cynicism out there among older people, but I'll tell you, these kids today, some of them, are completely idealistic."

"Do you know who at the high school contacted your class?"

"Yeah," Professor Quinn said, pointing. "That girl right there. Melissa Dobbs."

He exchanged cards with Professor Quinn and wished her well before approaching Dobbs. She was a short girl, who could not have been more than seventeen. Her hair was straight and colored an unnatural midnight black with a blue highlight. She had a thin silver ring pierced through her left nostril, and her left ear looked like the lure aisle at the bait shop. She was dressed in a black, button-down shirt, untucked over black pants.

"Miss Dobbs?" Charlie said, walking beside her as the chant to free Zeb started anew. "I'm Charlie Sage. My office represents Zeb. Could I bother you for a moment?"

Charlie guided her to the nearest courthouse step. The protest kept on merrily without her.

"Professor Quinn said that you contacted her class about Zeb. Is that right?" Charlie said.

"Uh-huh," she said.

"How do you know him?" Charlie asked. He figured Zeb's partner in crime might be the protest organizer or at least among the protestors.

"From school."

"You guys friends?"

"Uh-huh."

"I was wondering, you know how Zeb was into anarchy and all that?" Charlie said.

The girl looked at him, her brows closing toward one another, perplexed.

"You didn't know about all that?" Charlie said.

"Not much," she said. "I have him in English. And he's cool. What they're doing to him is wrong."

"You guys going out?" Charlie said.

She thought for a moment before addressing Charlie as if he had a severe brain injury, "No. People don't really go out anymore."

"Do you know if he was alone that night at the Blue-Mart," Charlie said, coming to his point. His circuitous path was getting him nowhere.

"I heard he wasn't even there," Dobbs said. "If you're his lawyer, haven't you talked to him about this?"

"That's confidential," Charlie said. "But it's always good to talk to everyone. Since you got this protest going, I thought maybe you could help me understand things."

"All I know is that trying to put Zeb in jail for life is crazy," she said. "They can't do that."

"I hope not," Charlie said. "Happy protesting."

Allie Demming from the *Beacon* had found the protest and was rounding up quotes from the group. Charlie saw Jeremy exiting the courthouse and decided his associate could use some lunch.

Jeremy had a quick lunch at the Milton Diner. He and Charlie did a brief post-mortem on the morning evidence. He told Jeremy about meeting Professor Quinn and her merry band of protestors. It was Charlie's hunch that Melissa Dobbs may have been involved with Zeb in some way. Jeremy remembered the way Zeb had been incessantly staring back into the gallery at his supporters and thought Charlie was onto something.

Charlie introduced him to Professor Quinn after lunch, and she invited them both to come to an organizational meeting of their *Save Zeb* group at the Milton library that night. She said she had read the coverage of the case so far and was impressed with Jeremy's fire. She wanted him to say a few words at the meeting. Jeremy was flattered and agreed to show.

Jeremy was back in court by 12:50 p.m. for the afternoon session. The afternoon crowd seemed unchanged to Jeremy, except that the television crew had departed. Judge Welch called both he and Gray back into chambers prior to resuming the hearing. Welch made it plain that he wanted them to pick up the pace of the exam because he was intent on finishing it today. Jeremy didn't bother insisting that he'd take as much time as was necessary to defend his client because it would have only inflamed the judge.

Gray took Welch's words to heart. He reeled off three quick witnesses and ran through a tight direct examination of each of them. Evan Ondyer was the foreman of the construction crew at the Blue-Mart site. He described the events of the Monday following the fire. He had been informed of the fire before arriving. The burned bulldozer had already been removed from the site. His crew set about working around the missing dozer, but by mid-morning, a backhoe, a loader and an off-highway truck had all seized up, effectively closing the construction site while replacement equipment was brought in.

On close inspection, Ondyer found that a small hole had been drilled in the oil intake pipe on each piece of equipment that seized. A hand drill, labeled as the property of Milton High School, was recovered in the spot where the off-highway truck had been parked, according to Ondyer.

There was little Jeremy could do with Ondyer's testimony. He had him highlight a seeming contradiction – why was the bulldozer so openly ruined and the other equipment so covertly destroyed? He also confirmed that no workers on the site wore tennis shoes that would account for the one footprint that the state police had collected from the scene. Ondyer also testified that the construction site was closed down in the evenings and that the timing of the fire assured that none of his crew would be present to be injured. Jeremy summed up by making Ondyer confirm that he had no evidence to suggest that Zeb had done anything at the site.

Gray next called Ian Cashman. Jeremy's earlier guess was right; the husky man with coiffed bronze hair took the stand. Cashman explained that he was the owner of Cashman Construction. The damaged equipment was owned by his corporation and damage estimates aggregated to just over one hundred thousand dollars, excluding the costs of time lost on the project.

John Few was next up. He was the mechanic who examined each piece of equipment. The burned-out bulldozer was salvageable, needing only superficial work to restore it to activity. The other three vehicles needed new engines. He found that silicon carbide had been injected into the oil system. This was an extremely hard substance that was fine enough to be suspended in the oil and not filtered yet hard enough to score all the metals inside the engine blocks. It was an ingenious and effective act of sabotage. He testified that in his expert opinion, the drill holes in the oil intake pipes could have been made with the hand drill found at the scene.

Jeremy had virtually nothing to ask either Cashman or Few. There was no proving that the equipment was not ruined. Few confirmed that the silicon carbide was harmless to human beings. Jeremy continued his theme, making each witness acknowledge that they had no evidence that Zeb did any of the acts that were alleged. Cashman fought it, but Jeremy eventually tugged the admission out of him because Cashman had no personal knowledge of Zeb's involvement.

After a mid-afternoon break, Gray called Allen Kryszinski to the stand. Kryszinski was Zeb's shop teacher at Milton High School. He identified the hand drill as one from his class and acknowledged that Zeb would have had access to it. Gray then led Kryszinski off script. Though it wasn't mentioned in the police reports, Kryszinski explained how he had been approached by Zeb at the beginning of the school year about sponsoring a club. The high school had a very permissive policy about extracurricular clubs. Almost any type of club was allowed, so long as it had a faculty sponsor.

Zeb had wanted to start an anarchy club, according to Kryszinski. Zeb had expounded on his ideas at some length and had even shown Kryszinski his Milton Anarchy website. Detective Russell had succeeded in recovering a hard copy of Zeb's website from the Internet provider, and Kryszinski identified the site as the same one Zeb had shown him. The hard copies of the website were admitted over Jeremy's hearsay objection.

The website contained an article criticizing the Blue-Mart development and extolling the harm it would bring Milton. The website also contained Zeb's plan to democratically take over the local government of Wabeno County with an invasion of voting anarchists. To top it off, the site had a link to the Earth Liberation Front website.

"Mr. Kryszinski," Jeremy began his cross-examination, "you did not see Zeb Radamacher take the hand drill from your class, did you?"

"No," Kryszinski said.

"And when Zeb talked to you about sponsoring his club, he gave you no indication that this club was seeking to use violence to forward its agenda, did he?" Jeremy said.

"No, he didn't," Kryszinski said. "He just wanted to change things through the voting process."

"And you have no personal knowledge of any evidence that would suggest that Zeb Radamacher committed the crimes at issue here?" Jeremy said.

Kryszinski paused thoughtfully. "No, I don't," he said.

"Nothing further, Your Honor." Jeremy said.

Jeremy was growing weary. His father, a construction worker, had always encouraged Jeremy to get a job that used his head instead of his body. But, Jeremy had learned that lawyering was demanding in its own way. During hearings and trials, Jeremy spent every second focused on issues that constantly changed and required re-evaluation. After a full day of testimony, he was always completely wiped out.

"May we approach, Your Honor?" Gray said, rising from his seat.

Welch nodded. Jeremy joined Gray at the bench for an off-record confab.

"Judge, I'd originally planned to put on Detective Russell and Amanda Ratielle. But, given Mr. Jefferson's objection to her identification, I don't really see the need. Unless you want to hear more, I think we've met our burden. I'm going to save them for trial," Gray whispered.

"About time," Welch said. His tone told Jeremy he had made up his mind. Jeremy had expected no less. "So you are going to move for bind over?"

"Yes," Gray whispered.

"Mr. Jefferson, there is more than enough here to bind over," Welch said. "You aren't putting on anything, are you?"

"No, Judge," Jeremy said.

"Good," Welch said. "You will be asking me to revisit my decision on bond?"

"Yes, Judge, I would like to address it," Jeremy said.

"I've had my clerk look into the issue," Welch said. "I think you may have a point about the denial of bond based on treason. It's at least a close call."

"My research shows the same, Judge," Jeremy said. "We're going to ask you to reinstate his original twenty-five thousand cash bond."

"Well, go ahead and argue the amount, but I'm inclined to agree with them on this point about treason," Welch told Gray.

"I understand, Judge."

"Okay," Welch said. "Let's wrap this up."

It was cut and dried, like most things with Welch. The judge was going to bind Zeb over on all charges. And he was going to reduce his bond to cash. The only question was the amount of bond. And, if Jeremy understood the subtext of Welch's comments, he knew that the new bond was going to be something that Zeb had no chance of posting.

The lawyers argued. The judge put his decision on the record. Zeb was bound over to the circuit court on charges of terrorism, arson and malicious destruction of property. Welch set a million dollar cash bond, which had the same effect as bond being denied, but eliminated any legal issue that Jeremy might have appealed; Zeb would be sitting in jail until his case was tried.

Jeremy had prepped Zeb well for the outcome, and the boy was not surprised or hurt by the decision. Jeremy packed up his briefcase and wearily made his way toward the exit. He was stopped by Allie at the courthouse doors.

"Tough day," she said.

He didn't talk.

"Off the record?" she said.

"About what I expected," Jeremy said.

"Can I get a quote from you for Sunday's story?" she said.

"I'm wiped out, Allie," Jeremy smiled. "Maybe you should just make something up. But, be kind."

"How about you give me one tomorrow," she smiled, "at the play? It can be a working date."

Jeremy had forgotten. He was supposed to give her an answer. He needed to explain the train wreck his personal life had become, but he was too tired to do it now. "Okay," he said. "When can I pick you up?"

"Seven," she said.

"Okay," Jeremy said, "great."

She gave him her address, phone number and a beautiful smile, which lifted his spirits some.

"You heard about the *Save Zeb* meeting?" Allie said.

"Oh, Christ," Jeremy said. "I almost forgot. I'm the guest speaker."

"Good," she said. "I'll see you there. I'll just take my quote from your speech. You seem to do pretty well when you aren't talking to a reporter."

"Thanks," Jeremy said. He would be glad when the week was finally over.

9

Mark Radamacher clenched his teeth through most of the proceedings. It was a kangaroo court, he thought. When he couldn't stand the bullshit, he muttered low and angry to his oldest son, Zachary, who had come along to watch Zeb get screwed. Radamachers went to prison in every generation since Mark's grandfather had settled in Wabeno County. Zeb's last name never gave him a fighting chance, Mark thought.

In his right hand Mark held a manila envelope. It contained all the information he needed to convince Zeb that his lawyer was a worthless, lying hypocrite. But, the dipshit deputy wouldn't allow Zeb to accept any messages or to speak with his loved ones in court. So through the day, Mark just held the envelope and cursed silently.

As Jefferson left the courtroom, Mark glared at him, but the lawyer paid him no mind. He complained to Zachary as they drove from the courthouse to the jail to visit Zeb. Zachary said nothing, silently listening as always. Zeb was the smarter boy of the two, Mark thought, there was no doubt of that. But, Zeb was ruined because he had chosen to live with his damned mother, whereas Zachary was turning out to be a God-fearing man.

"You wait here," Mark said to Zachary, as he parked his truck at the Wabeno County Jail. "No sense you seeing the inside of a place like this."

Mark jogged to the jail and spoke with the guard at the desk.

"I'm sorry, Mr. Radamacher," the woman said. "He's not back from court yet, but even when he gets here, you're not going to be allowed to see him."

"Why not?" Mark said incredulously.

"He's taken you off his visitors' list, sir," she said simply. "You can't visit unless approved by the inmate."

Mark's face flushed hot. That lawyer had talked some crap into his son's head to be sure. He did not bother to curse or thank the guard. He turned and marched out of the jail, without even thinking to deliver the manila folder. He would make Zeb aware of his lawyer's hypocrisy soon enough. Not two years ago, Jefferson was representing a gigantic mining company as it destroyed the homes of innocent, poor folks. He helped the mining company destroy their homes and made it all legal-like, in the name of the almighty dollar. Jefferson sure as shit didn't give a damn about Zeb and his misguided tree-hugging cause. That lawyer was the devil, Mark thought, a descendant of Cain. And his boy was going to get new counsel, if Mark had any say in it.

Jeremy regretted telling Professor Quinn he would come to the *Save Zeb* meeting. He was weary from battling Gray and Welch for the entire day, and he didn't have the strength to address a bunch of idealists who had no real notion of the amount of trouble Zeb really faced.

But when he had mentioned the meeting to Zeb at the exam, the boy had brightened considerably. Zeb was a cause man, and he delighted at the thought of a band of fellows tilting at windmills with him. Zeb's enthusiasm cinched it. Jeremy would at least make a brief appearance.

He showered, exchanged his suit for jeans, pulled on sneakers and grabbed a beer. He turned on the television. The local news reported on his case, but Jeremy quickly turned the channel. He had been there and didn't need a recap by a second-rate journalist from the north woods.

He vegged out for an hour in front of the tube, world news making a background like wallpaper for Jeremy's thoughts about the case. He lost track of time and when he finally looked up at the clock, he was late. He threw his brown leather bomber jacket around his shoulders on the way out the door and drove downtown to the library.

He parked, walked in and inquired with a librarian, who directed him to a row of meeting rooms lining one side of the building. Professor Quinn was already addressing her brigade of activists when Jeremy entered.

"–dimensions of the problems facing any political prisoner are multifaceted," she said, acknowledging Jeremy with a nod as he grabbed a desk near the back of the room. "They are social, legal and political. As an organization seeking to help this young man, we can support in all of these arenas. I can speak to the social and political activities that we might choose to undertake. That is my area of expertise. I have already spoken about them at length with my students–"

Jeremy surveyed the room. All five of Professor Quinn's college students who protested during the day had stayed for the organizational meeting. The local contingent seemed to have grown since the lunchtime protest. Jeremy recognized the high school students who'd been at court. But their original number of five had doubled. Two adults sat at the back of the room, and next to them was the faithful Milton press corps – Allie Demming. She was a hard-working reporter, Jeremy thought. He had to give her that much.

"As for the legal hurdles faced by Zeb Radamacher, I have invited his lead attorney, Mr. Jeremy Jefferson, to address you this evening," Professor Quinn said. "Mr. Jefferson."

There was a quiet, polite applause from the small group. Jeremy rose to a slouch and trudged to the front of the room where Professor Quinn welcomed him.

"Thank you," he said. "Let me say, first, that I have spoken to Zeb about the support you are giving to him, and he is very pleased. If you do nothing else for his case, you have at least given him some great reassurance.

"Zeb has given me permission to speak about his case publicly, but, as this is an ongoing matter, I do not want to get into factual details about it. But, legally, I believe it is a sham that he has been charged as a terrorist. I do not think the evidence submitted today supports that charge, and we will fight this matter all the way to the Supreme Court, if need be, to prevail.

"I think there is a reason that Zeb Radamacher was charged with terrorism," Jeremy said, glancing at his audience. He saw Steve Wynn, wearing his bomber jacket. Next to Wynn was a girl with dyed black hair and multiple piercings. He guessed the girl was Melissa Dobbs, from the description Charlie had given him. While Jeremy spoke, she whispered to Wynn. For someone who had gotten the ball rolling on this entire movement, it struck Jeremy that she didn't seem very interested in what he was saying. "We have become a nation living in fear. You've all seen Osama bin Laden's face on your TV screens. Popping up, I think, to remind us all to be afraid.

"Now, you can look at your local news. I saw it tonight. And there is Zeb's face, with the word 'terrorism' underneath it. Right here in our own community. So we can still be afraid.

"And why should we be afraid? I think it's helping some of those in power. They want us to forget about things that are important to us. That our environment, that our schools, that our economy, that our civil rights, that the very fabric of our lives are being eroded away. So, I know Zeb's very happy that there is a group of people out here like you, who won't forget these things, just because they have wrongly labeled him as a terrorist."

Jeremy went on to explain how Zeb was facing decades in prison if things didn't go his way. He answered some generally uninformed questions from the group. He would have liked to launch into a passionate argument about how Zeb did not do this or how it was a misunderstanding. But the crowd of environmentalists didn't really want to hear that anyway. They wanted to hear that Zeb did do it, and that he shouldn't be punished like a criminal for doing it. They were blinded by their ideology, no less than the corporations and factory farms they hated. To them, Jeremy could tell, Zeb was much more a cause than a person.

When there were no other questions, Professor Quinn took over. She seemed to be something of a guerilla organizational genius - someone with skills probably forged in the '60s who was now in constant search of a cultural war to fight.

She gave a lecture of fair length about the social and political aspects of Zeb's situation. Jeremy was fascinated. He thought Professor Quinn's own social and political outlook were probably far from the norm, but her grasp of the system of government and society, and the forces that move them, was impressive. She set up a committee to address ways to affect the political pressure on Ed Gray, to raise the stakes for his prosecution of Zeb and hopefully encourage his willingness to come off his hard-line stance on the case. She set up a fundraising committee. And finally, she set up a committee to continue the work that Zeb started. She did not incite the young people to take up Molotov cocktails but instead encouraged them to find legal, and nonviolent ways to bring Zeb's noble goals to fruition. "Whatever the outcome of Zeb's personal battle, let's not let him become a casualty who was lost in vain," she said. "Let's win the war he was trying to fight."

Though he had almost skipped the meeting, he was now enthused by the group's ideals and commitment to a cause. The meeting adjourned for two weeks when they would reconvene and take reports from committees.

While the young people drifted out in groups of two and three, Jeremy stayed behind to speak with Professor Quinn further. Her manner was so warm and upbeat, he was hoping that some of it would rub off. Because, the more he thought about the case analytically, the more he felt Zeb slipping away from him.

As he talked with Professor Quinn and soaked in her positive vibe, Allie nudged her hip against his side in a warm hello. He did not start, and said hello to her as naturally as if he was accustomed to being greeted in such an intimate way, barely pausing from his conversation with the professor.

Jeremy was nearly drunk with a sense of goodness when a sharp thunder echoed from outside the building. Jeremy's head instinctively snapped toward the sound of the blast, looking through the glass doors toward the parking lot. He saw a tall frame – Steve Wynn – slowly toppling to the ground like a felled tree. The blur of motion linked with the sound, and as Jeremy's mind formed the concept of "gunshot," his eyes recognized the unnatural shape of Wynn's head. He tore away from Allie and ran through the doors to the prone body.

Wynn had fallen face down, but the head was obviously not intact. A dark puddle, too visible in the dark, grew steadily beneath it. Some instinctual part of Jeremy knelt to the boy and went through a checklist he had learned in the army, fifteen years past. Breathing first, then heartbeat, then blood loss. He rolled the boy to his back to check his breathing, but the horror that remained of Wynn's face stopped him. Steve Wynn was gone.

Jeremy listened to the relative silence of a crisp autumn night in northern Michigan. He looked around in the darkness, his eyes and ears searching the night. A slight breeze ruffled dead leaves and live pines. He could hear a distant car on Main Street. Melissa Dobbs was in shock, kneeling close to Wynn. As the girl recognized the remains of Wynn's face, she began to rock and wail uncontrollably.

Allie came running out of the library.

"Call nine-one-one," Jeremy yelled. "He's been shot."

Jeremy watched Allie run back to the library, then looked down unwillingly. His own hands were covered in blood. He held Steve Wynn, still warm, in his lap and waited for someone to come and clean up the unspeakable carnage.

A random shot from a hunter; Jeremy's brain tried to bring reason to the chaos. It was only bow season, but everyone in Milton had a hunting rifle. His mind could not wrap itself around any other logical thought. No one would purposefully wreck the boy's beautiful, young mind in such a grotesque way.

He finally gave up on reason and realized he was weeping openly, a silent release. He watched the blood-soaked collar of the boy's coat as it dripped onto his denim-covered thigh. The collar of the boy's coat was identical to his own, except that is was saturated in blood.

Jeremy was suddenly concerned for Dobbs, and for himself. He looked around in the darkness outside the library, for the first time, trying to identify the shooter. A few houses stood in front of a half-wooded lot to the west across Indiana Street. It was the only good cover. The hair raised on the back of Jeremy's neck. Though he doubted any monster could deliberately shoot Wynn, Milton was home to dozens of gun-toting nutcases who might want to take a shot at a lawyer who had the bad judgment to defend a terrorist.

Allie returned and startled him.

"They're on their way," she said, and as she spoke sirens could be heard in the distance.

He laid Wynn softly on the walkway, gathered Dobbs and Allie, and returned to the safety of the library.

10

It was past midnight when Jeremy left the Milton Police Department. After he and Allie had given statements to the police, he had driven her back to the library to pick up her Jeep. There was little conversation. He was too numb. But, even without words, he knew that she wanted to stay with him. He wanted her to stay. He wanted to hold onto to her and erase everything they had seen.

She had been in contact with her editor, though, and she had to get back to the *Beacon*. They had held the deadline for her to file a story about the shooting. It was the first murder in Wabeno County in fifteen years, and her editor wanted to take advantage of his well-placed reporter. Before she left, she hugged him for a moment too long. He almost asked her to come back to his house after her work but held back.

Jeremy's house was dead silent when he returned. Without turning on a light, he grabbed a beer from the fridge and felt his way to the living room. He dropped into the recliner and sat staring at the grey and black and blue shapes around him. He was tired but did not want to sleep. He felt like he was waking from a nightmare but knew that Wynn's death was all too real.

The shooting took place in Milton proper, so the Milton Police had jurisdiction. Detective John Imlach had been called in from his Friday night bowling league to handle the investigation. Everyone in the *Save Zeb* group had been invited to the station to give a written statement about what they had seen. Jeremy had forgotten any distrust in the police and happily met with the detective.

Imlach had spoken with the witnesses individually. Jeremy had told him everything he could recall along with his suspicions even as they were unfolding in his mind. The boy was nearly Jeremy's height, they both had dark, short hair, and their jackets were identical. Jeremy could not help but think that the bullet had been intended for him. Someone upset by Zeb's case – someone who was inflamed at the thought of a terrorist getting representation. Someone who had known about the *Save Zeb* meeting.

Jeremy liked Imlach personally but was not impressed with his skills as a detective. Imlach was the lone detective on a force of seven officers. He was ten years Jeremy's senior and not the sharpest blade in the block. "I appreciate your thoughts," Imlach had said, "but why don't you leave the detective work to us."

Going to the station to give a statement had allowed Jeremy to keep from thinking of the shooting and of the possibility that it could, or even should, be his own body lying on a slab in the medical examiner's office.

Now, sitting in the dark, he could not get the image of the boy's half-destroyed face out of his mind. It must have been a powerful rifle, probably with a scope, given the accuracy. One minute Wynn was merrily walking from the library, and the next minute his thoughts were scattered on the sidewalk along with his brains.

Such traumatic violence probably happened in major urban centers dozens of times a year, Jeremy thought. But it was the fact that it had happened in the middle of nowhere that troubled him. It was a world gone mad. No one could make sense of it because even to try would drive you mad, Jeremy thought.

After three beers full of quiet pity and weeping, Jeremy finally broke through the settling depression. He had to think about it. What if he was right? What if the bullet had been meant for him? He could wallow in the stupidity and injustice of a crazy world. But that wouldn't stop the shooter. He could ignore the whole thing and hope Imlach suddenly morphed into Sherlock Holmes, but that probably wouldn't stop the shooter either. He had to think. And, if his hunch was right, he had to think fast.

Who could hate him enough to try to kill him? Some right-wing nut job who thought terror suspects should be burned without a show trial. It would have to be a seriously disturbed person. A complete wacko. And how could he protect himself against such a person? He would have to give up Zeb's case and move away. And, even then, there were no guarantees the wacko wouldn't hunt him down. So there wasn't much of a plan if a total nut case had fired the gun.

But what if it wasn't a nut case? Maybe it was someone with a real axe to grind. What if Zeb wasn't guilty? What if the real eco-terrorist wanted to off Jeremy because he was afraid a good lawyer was going to find the true culprit? That would explain a motive, but Zeb had tacitly admitted his involvement with the crime when they talked on Wednesday morning. He just wasn't going to give up his accomplice out of loyalty. Even Zeb wouldn't expect Jeremy to believe he was innocent.

A disgruntled client? It was a hazard of working with violent people. But Jeremy had only been at it for a year. Anyone truly capable of a crime of this magnitude would still be serving time. If it was just some petty criminal who flipped out about an imagined grievance with his lawyer, it was really no different than if a total nut case wanted to kill him. What could he do about it, really?

Or maybe he was wrong. Maybe someone had a reason to want Wynn dead. Maybe he was involved in the crime with Zeb, and a third accomplice killed him to shut him up. That could make sense. Another young person, scared by the harsh treatment Zeb was getting, figured it was worth killing Wynn to keep his involvement in the crime a secret. It was a possibility, but it was based on a series of speculations.

Jeremy started to doze off in his chair, his mind rolling over the events of the evening. He dreamt of the wooded lot by the library. Jeremy was huddled over Steve Wynn. He looked to the wooded lot and could see a shooter taking aim at him. He could almost make out a face through the darkness, behind a scope. It was Zeb's face, and the gun exploded in an echoing shot that bolted him out of his sleep.

He stayed still in the living room for a moment, listening. Zeb had his answers, he thought. He rose from his recliner wearily and made for the comfort of his bed but did not sleep again until the early morning hours.

Jeremy woke at 7:30 a.m. without an alarm. He sat up and kicked his feet onto the floor, rubbing the sleep from his eyes with one hand. Life was normal for a few seconds before reality set in like a November gale. Being the possible target of a murder just ten hours before, Jeremy felt scared, and worse, had no plan.

He showered and shaved hurriedly, thinking about what courses of action were available. If the shooting was not some random act, then it was almost surely connected to Zeb's case. It was time Zeb gave him some answers. Jeremy felt he deserved that much. He pulled on jeans and a T-shirt and set out for the jail.

Jeremy arrived early and waited in his car, the heater running to ward off the cold morning air, but it did nothing to ease a coldness that had enveloped him. He turned on the radio for a distraction. Between songs, a disc jockey from WHIP, Wabeno's only FM station, read a news update headlined by Wynn's murder. It said that police had released no information regarding any suspects.

The weekend guard unlocked the doors, and Jeremy bolted from his car to meet him. Jeremy greeted Zeb in the contact visiting room at 8:35 a.m. Zeb had not been told of the murder, and Jeremy broke the news. The boy was paralyzed with disbelief and terror.

"Oh my God, Mr. J.," he said finally. "No way. No way."

"I was there," Jeremy said. "I was with him when he died."

"No," Zeb said, tears welling in his eyes. "That means Melissa's in trouble, too."

"Why is that, Zeb?" Jeremy said crossly. "What have you been hiding from me? I could have been killed last night, and I'm going to know the truth before I leave here."

"Oh no," Zeb said. "That crazy fuck. He's lost it. He's gonna kill Melissa, and he's gonna kill me, too."

"Who, Zeb?" Jeremy said.

"You've gotta protect her, Mr. J.," Zeb said, crying openly. "I'll tell you everything. But, you've gotta protect her. He's insane."

"Okay, Zeb. Okay. I will. I told you I can only help if you tell me everything. I will do whatever I can. But I have to know," Jeremy said.

"It's Jared MacAdam, Mr. J.," Zeb said, bringing his voice under control. "He goes to Milton. He's the one who burned the dozer. I told him not to, but he did it anyway. We were just going to monkey wrench the equipment. We'd have never got caught. And he showed up and torched the damn thing. So stupid."

"Slow down. Slow down," Jeremy said. "You said 'we'd have never got caught.' Who is 'we?' "

"It started out as my idea," Zeb said. "Melissa and Stevie were going to help. I planned it all out. We were going to be really careful. We'd have never gotten caught."

"So there were four of you?"

"No," Zeb said. "At first it was just the three of us. Me, Melissa and Stevie. I can't believe he's dead, Mr. J."

"I know," Jeremy said. "It's okay. But you've got to tell me. How does this – what's his name?"

"Jared MacAdam," Zeb said. "It was just the three of us. We met a couple of times to go over everything. But then, Melissa brought this guy Jared to one of our meetings. The guy followed her around like a puppy, I swear. He's kind of a spazz. Crazy. But, Melissa always felt sorry for him.

"She asked if he could be a part of it. I was against it, but I said okay at first. I love her, Mr. J. She's pregnant," Zeb cried again.

"It's okay, Zeb." Jeremy said. He wanted to hug the boy – give him some comfort – but only patted his forearm. He let Zeb cry for a minute and then urged him to get the story out.

"I'd planned it just like they said to in *The Monkey Wrencher's Handbook*," Zeb continued. "Silicon carbide in the oil system. Wear socks over your boots to cover your tracks. Gloves, so there wouldn't be any fingerprints.

"But then this Jared guy starts talking about how he knows how to make a bomb, and how we should blow something up. Crazy shit. Just trying to impress Melissa, I think. And I kicked him out because I knew he would get us caught.

"I was gonna call the whole thing off. But Melissa said she knew he would never talk. And we decided to go ahead without him."

"So how did the dozer get blown up?" Jeremy said.

"Because, that night, when we were out there, he just showed up," Zeb said. "He started spray-painting the backhoe. Something only an idiot would do. And then when we tried to tell him to stop, he just lit the bomb and chucked it before any of us could stop him. He's insane."

"Why didn't you tell me, Zeb?" Jeremy said. "Why were you protecting him? This could help your case. I'm not sure anyone would believe it, but if it's true, it could help."

"It's not him, Mr. J.," Zeb said. "I could give a shit about him. I'd have told you about him in a minute. It's Melissa, mostly. We're gonna have a baby, Mr. J. And Stevie. I couldn't get them in this."

"So you think it was this – MacAdam – who killed Steve?"

"I would bet on it," Zeb said. "He's not right in the head."

"But, why would he do it?" Jeremy said.

"He thinks we were going to rat him out, I bet," Zeb said. "Everybody loved Stevie at school, Mr. J. Who else would have done this to him?"

Jeremy couldn't answer the question. Zeb's hypothesis was far better than Jeremy's own wild speculation.

"He ain't gonna stop at Stevie, Mr. J.," Zeb said. "I've gotta do something to protect Melissa."

Jeremy had another reason to admire the young man. Not only was he idealistic, but he was in love in that unrestrained way that adults can seldom achieve.

"I've got to think about this," Jeremy said. "I could go to the police with this info, and maybe they'd get MacAdam, but it could really hurt your case. It's like a confession. At least to malicious destruction."

"I don't care about me, Mr. J.," Zeb pleaded. "Just protect Melissa."

"Okay," Jeremy said. "I'll do what I can. But, you understand, I'd be breaking our lawyer-client confidentiality if I tell the police what you've told me."

"I don't care," Zeb said, staring coldly into Jeremy's eyes. "Just keep her safe."

Jeremy thanked Zeb for leveling with him. The story seemed sincere. It may have been improbable, but truth was often stranger than fiction. Jeremy accepted that he finally had the truth from Zeb Radamacher. He had Zeb write down contact information for Dobbs and MacAdam and headed for his office to think through his next move.

The parking lot at the Sage Law Office was behind the building, accessed by a narrow driveway on the east side of the lot. As Jeremy pulled in, he was met grill-to-grill by Allie's old Jeep. Jerked from his thoughts, he slammed on the brakes. His Accord stopped inches from her bumper. He looked up and saw Allie's surprise fade to a smile as her eyes met his. She backed up, and they both parked.

"I stopped by your house first," she said, walking straight to his arms and hugging him. "I wanted to make sure you were okay."

He reluctantly gave in to her embrace and enjoyed holding her for a moment, then let go and established a comfortable distance.

"Yeah," he said. "I'm okay. You?"

"I don't know," she said. "I was on deadline last night, so I didn't have time to think about it until late. And then, it was awful. That poor kid."

"Yeah," he said. "I can't believe it."

He let her in the employees' entrance, gave her a seat at the conference table in the library and started a pot of coffee. Jeremy wanted to tell her about his breakthrough with Zeb but was bound by the rules of confidentiality. No reporter was going to hear the whole story until he figured out what to do.

"Where were you?" Allie said. "I've been waiting here for a half-hour after I checked your house."

"I had to see a client at the jail."

"Zeb?"

"Look, Allie," Jeremy started and then stopped. Explain anything or nothing at all, he thought. He smiled. "I can't really talk about my clients with you. In case you don't remember, you are covering some of them in your paper."

"You can talk to me, Jeremy," she said. "I'm not a reporter twenty-four-seven, ya know."

Jeremy poured two cups of coffee and took a seat across from her.

"I know. I don't mean anything by it. It's just better that I not talk about some things."

"Okay," Allie said.

Allie asked for cream and sugar, and she mixed her coffee just like Hannah, thought Jeremy. The comparisons were driving him crazy. On the one hand, he knew he was attracted to her. And on the other, he knew that his feelings toward Allie were inextricably linked with his remnant feelings for his ex-fiancé. He sipped his coffee, black, enjoying the bitter jolt of caffeine.

Allie's lips were drawn to a pout. She had witnessed last night's carnage with him. She probably deserved better than to be completely frozen out of his thoughts. Jeremy decided he would have to give her some information.

"I had to see Zeb," Jeremy said. "I think what happened last night may have had something to do with his case."

"What?" Allie said, her pout melting away.

"I don't know for sure," Jeremy said, "but I thought Zeb might help me understand."

"Did you tell the police?" Allie said.

"I don't know anything for sure," he said, "but I did tell them some of my suspicions last night, yes."

"So did Zeb help you understand? Do you know what's going on?"

"I think I might know," Jeremy said. He knew he was saying too much, but Allie was a good listener. She was engaged and asked the right questions. The give and take helped him think - the beloved Socratic method of lawyers. But, Jeremy knew that he really needed to talk with Charlie.

"I'm not sure, though," Jeremy continued, "and I don't know what I can do with the information I have. I've got to protect Zeb."

"Do you think Zeb was behind this?" Allie said, alarmed.

"No, no, no," he said. "He's a good kid. He would never do something like last night. But, I think it's related to his case."

"You've got to go to the police," Allie said. "Isn't it obstruction of justice or something if you don't?"

"No," Jeremy said. "What Zeb tells me is privileged. That's why I really can't talk about it with you. But it's not obstruction. I need to think this through, that's all. If the police can help, and I can protect Zeb, I will tell them all I can."

Allie seemed pleased that he had confided in her. She seemed to understand about his conundrum. He could have told Hannah. She was a lawyer, and the two of them were never on opposite sides. But the fact that Allie might publish his inner thoughts to the world was an uncomfortable reality.

"So are we still on for tonight?" she said, her mouth forming another beautiful pout.

"I don't think I can, Allie," Jeremy said. "I'm going to have to take a raincheck."

She frowned but feigned understanding. Jeremy needed to do something to try to protect Melissa Dobbs, and he needed to do it fast.

Allie gave Jeremy a hug. He could sense her fear easing as she held onto him. It had been a frightening night. Jeremy would have liked nothing more than to hold onto Allie and try to make the world right again. She let go at last. Jeremy promised to call her and keep her posted as she left.

As soon as Allie was out the door, Jeremy picked up the phone in the library and called Charlie at home. He let the phone ring repeatedly as he doodled on a legal pad at the conference table. He had narrowed his dilemma to a single issue and wrote it out longhand among his scribbling:

Tell Imlach = risk damaging Zeb's defense

or

Keep secret = risk kids getting killed

Jeremy finally hung up the phone. He doubted that Charlie had strayed from his house. His boss seldom left Milton on the weekends. But, it was not beyond imagination to think that Charlie had been up late drinking on Friday and was sleeping, oblivious to a phone call. Jeremy hopped in his car and set out for Charlie's house.

Jeremy wrestled with his dilemma on the way. First, there was the confidentiality issue. Zeb had given him permission to share the information with anyone. In fact, Zeb had ordered him to use the information to help Melissa. Ideally, a waiver of the attorney-client privilege on such an important matter would be in writing, but a waiver did not need to be in writing to be valid. The waiver need only be given in a knowing and understanding way. Jeremy was comfortable that Zeb had waived the attorney-client privilege.

The second issue that occurred to Jeremy as he drove was more practical. If Jeremy did share Zeb's explanation with Detective Imlach, just how badly would it damage Zeb's own defense? Jeremy would, in essence, be giving his client's partial confession to Imlach. The information would surely go into a report, and the report would surely make its way to Gray.

But the partial confession was not all bad. Jeremy believed the boy was telling him the truth. The look in Zeb's eyes – the honest concern for Melissa – was wholly convincing. And if Zeb's story was true, the information was exculpatory. It helped acquit Zeb of the arson and terrorism charges, but acted as a confession to the lesser charge of malicious destruction. On the whole, as long as a jury believed what Zeb said to be true, it seemed to Jeremy that the statement would do more good than harm.

The final issue that Jeremy pondered, as he rolled up to Charlie's house, was the benefit of sharing the information with the police. Would Imlach even listen to Jeremy? He hadn't seemed interested in Jeremy's own theories last night. How much credence would Imlach pay to the story of a seventeen-year-old prisoner? Would they even consider MacAdam a suspect in Wynn's death? Would they protect Melissa Dobbs? Or Zeb? Jeremy did not know the answers. But he felt helpless holding the information to himself.

Jeremy pounded on Charlie's door to no avail. He peaked in Charlie's garage window. The Pontiac was there. Charlie had to be home. On a hunch, Jeremy looked under the welcome mat and found a key – it was the same place Charlie kept a spare key for the office.

He let himself in. "Charlie," he yelled. "Anybody home?"

Jeremy heard a television coming from Charlie's bedroom. He picked a careful path among the trash in the living room. Charlie was an incurable slob – he was fortunate that the health department did not know where he hid his spare key.

Jeremy found his friend snoring loudly in bed, a tangle of covers obscuring the wretched noise. Jeremy tried to shake Charlie awake. There was an empty fifth of single malt Scotch lying on the floor next to Charlie's bed. With every loud exhale, Jeremy's nostrils were inundated with the sour smell of the whisky on Charlie's breath.

It was no use. The greatest legal mind in Milton was dead to the world. And, even if Jeremy managed to wake him, he doubted Charlie would be in a condition to assist. Jeremy considered waiting for a few hours for Charlie to rejoin the living, but remembered the urgency of Zeb's voice. Melissa Dobbs could be in serious danger. Jeremy did not have the luxury of time.

On the coffee table, he left a note asking Charlie to call him when he woke up. Jeremy resigned himself to the fact that this decision would be his, and his alone.

Getting back into his car, Jeremy decided he was going to act to help Melissa as best he could. He decided to go directly to her parents first, to at least alert them to the danger their daughter faced. Then he would go to Imlach and hope the police would listen to what he had to say.

Jeremy dialed Dobbs on his cell phone as he started toward her home.

11

Allie went to the Beacon building to start planning next week's stories. She felt utterly defeated. She had been working solidly for a week to get Jeremy to take her out, and when things finally fell into place – when she was getting close enough to touch him – her hopes were dashed by the first murder in Wabeno County since the '80s. Though she didn't believe in such nonsense, perhaps fate was trying to tell her something.

"You okay, Al?" Michael Stoops asked, leaning a head in her doorway. Stoops had been the editor at the Beacon for ten years. He was middle-aged, balding, and had been eyeing Allie since he divorced his wife six months ago.

"Oh, you startled me," Allie said, jolting from her thoughts of Jeremy.

"That was great work on the stories last night," Stoops said. "It's the best scoop we've had since I've been here. I can't believe you were there."

"Just lucky, I guess," Allie's attempt at humor fell flat. She would never be free from the memory of Steve Wynn's dead eye staring up from a mangled face.

"Well, that was a helluva story. Good work."

"Thanks," she whispered.

"So you scooped up those tickets to *Our Town* tonight, huh?" Stoops said.

"Oh, yeah. Why, you want 'em?" she said.

"No, no. Who you taking?"

"I don't think I'm going to use them, now," Allie said. "Kind of worn out from yesterday. I think I'm just going to stay in."

"I'll go with you. Come on. Relaxing dinner at The Point. And then *Our Town*, in our town," Stoops said with a corny smile and a ridiculous arch in his uni-brow.

"Thanks," Allie said, "but I'm just not up to it with last night and everything. Let me get them. You should use them."

She fished the tickets out of her handbag and handed them to an openly frowning Stoops. Allie thought she would have to talk with Jeremy about sexual harassment law when he had the Radamacher case under control. She mused over the thought of a large settlement at Stoops' expense financing her move to a bigger market.

"Okay," Stoops fumbled. "Great work, anyway." He ducked out of the doorway and left Allie alone again with her thoughts. Next week would be busy. An in-depth follow-up on the Wynn murder. A police angle on the investigation would be the prime story. A human interest feature on the Wynn boy. A follow-up on the Radamacher case with the defense perspective, if Jeremy would give her something. And the usual police blotter and court notes. All in all, a full schedule.

Her head ached from a lack of sleep. She had desperately wanted Jeremy to invite her to stay with him last night. She felt his body – comfortable against her, just before the shooting. And again when they hugged good-bye, after their trip to the police station. He wanted her; she knew it. But he was holding something back. And she so needed to be comforted.

With her growing feelings for this aloof man, and the fear from being so close to the killing, she half-expected Jeremy to invite her back after she filed her story. When he didn't, what was she to do? She couldn't invite herself to stay the night, could she? There had to be lines, even for a modern woman, Allie thought. He had failed to recognize her needs, and that was one strike against him.

And then cancelling their date this morning. He couldn't work all day and night. He had to go home at some point. Strike two, she thought.

At first she had been understanding. This situation obviously didn't happen every day. But, as she thought it over, she became angry. He had one more chance. She was going to see Mr. Jefferson at his home tonight and, one way or the other, find out if this spark between them was going to ignite.

Jeremy zipped through the small commercial zone that Milton locals passed off as a downtown. Just a few blocks to the north and south of Main Street, Milton became a checkerboard filled with small homes. Milton had never been a prosperous town, so most of the homes were little more than updated shacks that had slowly accumulated on the plotted city blocks in the century or so since Milton was founded.

The Dobbs' home was on the southwest corner of Wisconsin and Sixth Streets. It was a box, sided in weather-aged, green aluminum. Plastic toys littered the lawn, catching beads of rain that fell from the grey sky. Jeremy parked on Wisconsin and walked across a green and yellow lawn to the one-step concrete porch. He banged on the ill-fitting aluminum screen door and heard grumbling and a college football broadcast coming from inside the tiny home.

A short, fat man with a semi-groomed beard answered the door. His face was cast in a half-permanent snarl. His eyes were dull brown, and he turned to look at the television intermittently while Jeremy introduced himself.

"Melissa's asleep," the man told him. "She got in very late."

"That's all right," Jeremy said. "Are you her father?"

The man turned to look at Jeremy. "Why do you need to know?"

"Sir," Jeremy began, trying to break his news gracefully, "I believe your daughter may be in danger."

Two young boys rolled off the couch into Jeremy's view as they chased a small plastic football.

"Whaddya mean? What kinda danger?"

"Did you talk to her last night when she came home?" Jeremy said.

"Listen, mister," the man said. "You'd better state your business, because I don't really feel like answering a bunch of questions."

"Do you know that your daughter witnessed a murder last night?" Jeremy asked.

The man did not respond with word or gesture, but the widening of his eyes told Jeremy that he was completely surprised by the fact.

"I have reason to believe that she may be in danger. That the person who killed one of her friends last night may want to hurt her."

"What friend?" the man said.

"Steve Wynn," Jeremy said.

"Stevie's dead?" the man said, surprised.

"He was shot last night after a protest meeting – to help Zeb Radamacher."

"No shit," the man said. "Stevie's dead? I knew him. Nice kid. That Radamacher fella was up to no good, though, that foul little son of a – pardon my French. What was Melissa doing trying to help him?"

"It's a long story," Jeremy said. "I think a kid named Jared MacAdam may have been involved with Steve's murder. I think he might want to hurt Melissa. I can't go into the details right now, but I suggest that you keep her at home and away from this MacAdam person if you can."

"Jared? No way. Why are you telling me this?"

"I just wanted you to know," Jeremy said. "My client, Zeb Radamacher, was extremely worried about Melissa. He wanted me to do all I could to protect her. That's why I came. Just keep her inside and out of harm's way until the police come to talk to her, okay?"

"What's Melissa got to do with all this?" the man demanded.

"Maybe you should talk to her about that," Jeremy said. "And you might consider getting her an attorney, too, before she talks to anyone, because your daughter might be in a lot of trouble."

"What do you mean?" the man said.

"You should talk to her, sir," Jeremy said. "And then talk to a lawyer. That's all I'm saying."

"I've heard about enough of this," the man said tersely.

"Okay," Jeremy said. "Just keep her safe, okay?"

Melissa's father stopped asking questions. Jeremy had done what he could, but the whole effort seemed futile.

He jumped in his car and tried calling Charlie again. There was no answer. It was time to speak to Imlach, he supposed. He figured the detective would be working, given that most murders were solved in the first twenty-four hours after the crime, so he headed for the station.

On the way, Jeremy saw the Beacon building. He stared in a window and thought he could make out the back of Allie's golden head. He didn't feel good about missing *Our Town*. He hoped she would understand.

She was beautiful and nice. A rare combination. He had spent the better part of a year living in the past, remembering only Hannah. It was good to think of someone new. To think of a future, he thought.

He called Information from his cell phone and was connected to the *Beacon*. He let it ring several times as he parked at the Milton Police Department. An automated voice invited him to enter an extension or listen to the menu. The voice started listing several hundred options for those unlucky enough not to know their party's extension. Even on his best day, Jeremy could not suffer an automated receptionist, and today was far from his best. Maybe he could catch Allie after he saw Imlach, he thought.

12

Kurt Bishop grabbed a seat near the back of the audience of assembled businessmen. He folded his hands behind his head and admired his handiwork. Though his background was in law enforcement, the governor had developed a passable skill at public speaking through his decade-long political career.

Bishop had rewritten parts of the speech on Friday afternoon, following word that the Radamacher case had been bound over, and yet again this morning, when he was informed of the shooting at the environmentalist meeting on Friday night. The local prosecutor, Ed Gray, had proven a valuable asset. He doted on Bishop's requests when he learned that the governor had taken a special interest in the case. Proximity to power was intoxicating, Bishop thought.

Bishop had made the speech largely about security on a state level. He intertwined the economic interests served by security; commerce could only prosper in a secure market. A large section in the middle was dedicated to developments in Milton and the new threat to security from eco-terrorists. And Howell was delivering the prose in bold fashion.

"There are those living in our society, not merely foreign terrorists in sleeper cells, but radical malcontents bent on destroying our very way of life," Howell said with conviction uncommon to a man only introduced to the issue days ago, "who believe that man and nature cannot exist in harmony. They would have us believe that man is the enemy of nature and should be stopped.

"These radical elements have taken an environmentalist agenda out of the mainstream and are, at this moment, at work in our state. They are eco-terrorists plotting and executing plans designed to harm businesses and people to further their warped views.

"These domestic terrorists, opposed to our free markets, are capable of causing millions of dollars in damage to property. They are endangering our first responders – our police, firefighters and emergency workers – with their actions. And as governor, I intend to deal with this domestic terrorist threat with the same unflinching strength this country has shown in combating the foreign terrorist threats to our borders and our people and our critical infrastructure.

"As many of you have probably read, one of these eco-terrorists was apprehended in Milton, Michigan two weeks ago. I have been in communication with the head of the law enforcement community there, Prosecuting Attorney Edward Gray. He has kept me up to date on that case and has given us some of his thoughts on what might be done to strengthen the hand of those on the front lines in this new battle – the police, the firefighters, the prosecutors and the judges.

"In the Milton case, a single young man, a high school senior, has been arrested and charged under our existing terrorism laws for firebombing heavy equipment at a local development site. He caused over a hundred thousand dollars in damage to equipment at the site and closed the construction site for two days, at great additional expense to the local contractor – Mr. Ian Cashman – who is with us here this afternoon," Howell said, motioning to Cashman in the audience to a smattering of applause.

"Just this morning, I have received word from Ed Gray that this act of terrorism has spawned civil unrest in this small town. Apparently a group of supporters of the eco-terrorist movement held a rally at the courthouse Friday and continued their rally into the evening in Milton. I am told that the rally sparked violence – a shooting that killed one of the seventeen-year-old protestors.

"Ladies and gentlemen, firebombings and shootings on the streets of our towns and on the sites of our economic development cannot be tolerated," Howell said with emphasis. The applause line worked as two hundred developers, entrepreneurs and capitalists rose as one to cheer the governor's protection of the American way of life from monstrous tree-hugging hordes.

It was standard political theater. Lay out any opposing viewpoint, however oversimplified, in a way that no one could tolerate. Whip the audience into a frenzy with rhetoric that makes the opposing viewpoint evil personified. And then sprinkle on a list of objectives that, whether meritorious or not, are designed to empower the speaker as the defender of truth, justice and the American way.

The governor polished off the formula nicely, ticking off his new legislative agenda about how we could all pull together to support laws that would help our law enforcement community stamp out eco-terrorism in its infancy. The new statutes, whether constitutional or effective, were designed to combat domestic terrorism specifically with easily-won convictions and harsh sentences. Particularly, the governor bemoaned how Ed Gray could not get bail denied specifically for eco-terrorists – a change that must be made. Gray had to jump through hoops to even charge terrorism as well. It should be easier, the governor insisted. And the pro-business lobby loved it. It was their chance to strike back at a decade of growing support for the environmental movement, and they were seizing the opportunity enthusiastically.

Bishop was pleased with the standing ovation the governor received when he concluded his remarks. This was a red-meat speech that spoke well to their base, no doubt. It wasn't hard to get the business community to cheer when you were handing them tax breaks faster than they could re-invest their windfalls. But, the issue needed to be road tested with ordinary citizens. Bishop was thinking he would like a photo opportunity in Milton at some point, to cement home the fact that Governor Howell was tough on eco-terrorists.

Jeremy arrived at the Milton Police Department at 11:15 a.m. and was told by the desk sergeant that Imlach would be back at the station shortly. He took a seat in the austere lobby and stared at police pamphlets. *Milton Police Department Mission Statement, Your Rights as a Victim* and *Wabeno Area Shelter for Battered and Abused Women.* He leafed through them. From his new perspective as a criminal defense attorney, it all seemed like propaganda.

He tried Charlie's house again but got no answer. Jeremy stared out the lobby window, across a half-empty parking lot, to the back of the courthouse. He considered the case he was about to make to Imlach. Just the bare-bones truth. No defense lawyer posturing. Just spill the truth as he knew it, and Zeb's suspicion on the killer. If nothing else, at least Jeremy knew the truth about what happened, and that made him much more confident about defending the case.

An eternal half-hour ticked off the clock. Jeremy kept rethinking his decision. Charlie's blessing that telling the police was the right thing to do would have been comforting, but with the danger to Melissa, and Zeb's insistence, Jeremy thought he was making the only reasonable decision.

The desk sergeant, locked behind security glass, finally hailed him through the speaker. "Mr. Jefferson," the sergeant said, "I'm going to buzz you through the door on your right."

Jeremy went through the door to the offices of the Milton Police Department and was met halfway down the hall by Detective John Imlach. Imlach, a small, fit man with graying brown hair and a trim moustache, shook Jeremy's hand.

"Mr. Jefferson," he said, "what brings you back here?"

Imlach's eyes were red, and he carried a disposable cup of coffee.

"I need to talk to you, John," Jeremy said. "I've got some new information about last night."

Imlach led Jeremy back to a pit of an office. There was a desk somewhere under a mass of paper, Jeremy was sure of it. Metal filing cabinets walled the sides of the small, square room, and there were three chairs: Imlach had a lima-bean-green imitation leather chair, that was cut and worn, to go with two Spartan office chairs – a pastel orange ensemble, circa 1960, Jeremy thought.

Jeremy sat at Imlach's invitation.

"I think I know who shot Wynn," Jeremy started.

"Is that right?" Imlach said thoughtfully.

"Uh-huh," Jeremy said. He was interrupted by someone knocking and entering the office. It was Ed Gray.

"Mr. Jefferson was just telling me he might know something about the shooting," Imlach said.

"Don't let me interrupt," Gray said.

"Ed," Jeremy said, "what I'm going to say may incriminate Zeb Radamacher. But, he wants it out there, because he thinks he knows who killed Steve Wynn. Just promise me that you'll consider this when it comes time to deal on this case, okay?"

"I consider everything. Cooperation with the police is always helpful," Gray said.

"Radamacher did have partners the night they went up to Blue-Mart. He went there with Melissa Dobbs and Steve Wynn. They were going to put some sand in the crankcases."

Imlach listened patiently, nodding, as Jeremy talked.

"Another kid, Jared MacAdam, who they had previously kicked out of their group, showed up and firebombed the bulldozer. My client and his friends had nothing to do with that. But my guy got popped at the scene."

"Uh-huh," Imlach nodded.

"My client tells me that MacAdam was a real loose cannon. Deadly serious. And violent. That is why they didn't want him in their group. Radamacher was not going to talk about any of this. He wanted to protect his friends. But he's sure that it was MacAdam who shot Wynn. And he thinks he and Dobbs are next."

Imlach gave nothing away as he listened. He took a few notes on a pad of white paper he had fished from the pile on his desk. Gray was all ears, too, listening intently at the growing list of potential terror suspects.

"Anything more specific that makes your guy think –" Imlach paused and looked through his notes, " – MacAdam shot Wynn?"

"He has motive," Jeremy said. "He was afraid Wynn and the others would talk. Who else would do that to the kid?"

Imlach paused, looked to Gray, and then back to Jeremy. "Well," he began, "like you told me last night, maybe it was someone who was after you and just got the kid by accident?"

"Radamacher is scared," Jeremy said. "He wants you to get MacAdam. He's scared for Dobbs. You can get a warrant and maybe get the gun or something from his house."

"We already got a warrant," Gray said proudly. "I just finished drafting it. We are just on our way to see Welch and get it signed. But it ain't for MacAdam's house. We got a witness and a make on the getaway car."

"Not MacAdam?" Jeremy said, surprised. He had been certain that Zeb was right. "Who is it?"

"We'll let you know as soon as the warrant is served," Imlach said. "Can't tell you before for officer's safety reasons, of course. But you'll definitely hear about it."

Jeremy was dazed. He had been so certain that MacAdam was a murderer on the loose that he had betrayed his client's confidence. And now it seemed as if Imlach had solid information leading in another direction. Jeremy had shown all his cards about the case. They had the accomplices now. And, he hadn't secured a plea bargain for the information the prosecutor wanted. Charlie was going to kill him.

13

The phone rang again. It had been ringing incessantly all morning, it seemed. Charlie Sage finally stirred from a deep, but unrestful, sleep. Some people were just stubborn, he thought. How many rings did it take them to realize that there was no one home? He had finished a bottle of single malt scotch while playing online poker until 5:00 a.m., and the world should feel fortunate to see Charlie Sage at all on Saturday, he thought.

He ignored the phone and tried to regain some level of unconsciousness. Even after the phone stopped ringing, sleep would not return. His body twitched every time sleep neared, awakening him again and again until he rolled out of bed and slid into athletic shorts. He started a pot of fresh coffee and retrieved *The New York Times* from his porch. He sat, sipped coffee, lit a Marlboro and read. Eventually, he turned on the television to let college football blare in the background. He had already missed the early games, but he still wanted to get a few bets down online before he ordered food and collapsed on the couch for an afternoon of mindless entertainment.

The phone rang again, and Charlie hoisted the receiver to his ear. It was Jeremy, and he sounded worried. He was on his way over. The house was in its usual condition of disarray, but Charlie was unashamed. The state of the interior would have brought dishonor to any bachelor with the slightest concern for how he might be perceived by others – a sentiment Charlie lacked.

Books, newspapers and sports magazines were stacked on almost every horizontal surface. Full ashtrays were found on two end tables by his couch, near the computer, and on his kitchen table. Empty beer bottles outnumbered empty scotch bottles ten to one. Paper plates, with thin layers of dried food, were strewn about. The garbage can was empty and would only be filled on Wednesday night before garbage day.

Charlie struggled to the bathroom. It smelled of mildew – like an old locker room. He brushed his teeth, trying to erase the taste of the scotch. He threw on a Lions jersey that he retrieved from the bedroom and plopped down at the computer. Michigan was laying one-and-a-half at Purdue. They had looked great early in the year, and he bet a hundred and ten dollars from his Costa Rican gaming account on the Wolverines. It was an easy cover, he thought. As he scanned for another attractive wager, Jeremy entered, his face grave.

"What's up?" Charlie asked, rising to find the remote control. He tuned in to watch the end of the Iowa-Penn State game.

"I've screwed up big," Jeremy confessed, obviously deflated.

Charlie plopped down on the couch and lit another Marlboro. "Grab a couple of beers, would ya?" he said.

Jeremy played barmaid and joined Charlie on the couch. "You did a good job yesterday," Charlie said, pausing for a swig of cold beer that soothed his scratchy throat. "You shouldn't be so down on yourself. There's not much you could've done."

"Steve Wynn is dead," Jeremy said. "Shot in the head coming out of the library last night."

"Shut up!" Charlie said, shocked. He turned his attention away from the game to stare at Jeremy.

"I held him," Jeremy said. "Blood all over me. He walked out of the meeting and got shot like a deer. I saw him go down."

"What the fuck?" Charlie said.

"It's worse," Jeremy said. "I've been trying to get you out of bed all morning. I was here just a couple of hours ago, but you were dead to the world. Didn't you see my note?" Jeremy grabbed the note he had left on the coffee table and flung it at Charlie.

"Sleeping," Charlie said, reading the note. "Tough night last night."

"Happened right in front of me. I was inside talking to Professor Quinn, and – and then he's dead, right outside the doors. It was so messed up. I can't believe it," Jeremy said, his voice unsteady.

"That's an awful thing," Charlie said. He clapped a hand on his friend's shoulder, trying to comfort him. "But, I don't get how you screwed anything up. It's not your fault."

"I went to see Zeb this morning. I had to get the truth out of the kid because Wynn was wearing a jacket just like mine, and he looks a little like me, you know. And I thought maybe I was the target at first. All I could think was that I could've been the one with my brains on that sidewalk. So I wanted Zeb to square with me. So I could figure it out."

"So, what did Zebediah have to say?" Charlie asked.

"He spilled it," Jeremy said. "The whole thing. He was scared shitless. Said there were four of them initially. Dobbs, Wynn and another kid. MacAdam. MacAdam was a freak, though. Real violent. So they booted him out of the 'Save the Earth' club.

"So it was this MacAdam kid who shows up at the scene when Zeb was putting sand in the crankcases and blows up the dozer. And Zeb's scared to death, because he thinks MacAdam is nuts. Thinks he killed Wynn and will kill Dobbs and Zeb, too, to shut them up."

"Did you buy it?" Charlie said.

"Yeah," Jeremy said. "You should've seen him. It's either true or the kid is Marlon friggin' Brando. He's in love with Dobbs. She's having his baby. And he's scared for her. But, I've got no doubt it went down like he told me."

"So," Charlie said, and thought for two seconds. "That sucks for Wynn. Poor kid. But, what's so bad? You got a defense now. You can try to escape the terrorism charge anyhow. You could even get Gray to deal a little."

"I needed to talk to you," Jeremy said, still distressed. "And Zeb was freaking out. He wanted me to help Dobbs. Keep her safe. He told me to go to the police with the info."

"No," Charlie said. "No way. You can't give that info to the police."

"I did," Jeremy said, looking to the floor.

"No way," Charlie said. Defense lawyers were supposed to take secrets to the grave. The less others know, the better. Jeremy had violated that rule. A defense lawyer never shares anything that may tend to incriminate his client. "Did you have him sign a waiver of the attorney-client privilege before you told them?"

"No," Jeremy said to Charlie's scoff. "But he waived the privilege. He insisted I go to the police to protect Dobbs."

Charlie had employed Jeremy for just over a year. He was a friend and an excellent trial lawyer. But he had a lot to learn about criminal practice. Charlie had never had reason to question Jeremy's judgment before. But this was a blunder of epic proportions. Charlie felt like screaming at Jeremy. But his young apprentice *had* come to him for guidance, and Charlie had been passed out from the scotch. There was plenty of blame to go around.

"Well," Charlie said, "it isn't the end of the world. I mean, you did what the client wanted. Maybe if they get – what's the kid's name?"

"MacAdam," Jeremy said.

"Maybe if they get him on the murder, they'll give Zeb some credit," Charlie said.

"I doubt it," Jeremy said. "Gray came in while I was telling Imlach. They have a suspect. And it's not MacAdam. My information was worthless for the murder. They are serving a warrant on someone else today. I gave them Zeb's accomplices for free. And got nothing. I should go back to Barnes & Honeycutt because I'm screwing things up here."

Charlie had a hard time finding words of consolation for his friend. He had screwed up big time. But it was an extraordinary circumstance. Jeremy wouldn't witness a murder every day. Charlie had never even seen a dead body in real life. Jeremy was just going to have to buck up and work this case through because Charlie wasn't ready to pull him just yet.

"We'll work something out with Gray," Charlie said. "Don't be so hard on yourself. I mean, a kid died in your arms."

Charlie drained his beer. The fridge was empty, so he sent Jeremy to the store for a twelve-pack. While Jeremy was out, Charlie showered, his mind wandering over the bizarre case of Zebediah Radamacher. If MacAdam didn't kill Wynn, then who did? He made it back to the television in time to see the Wolverines end the first half, up 14-0 over the Boilermakers. It was an easy cover, but there was still time for a comeback, Charlie thought cautiously.

Jeremy stayed to watch the end of the Michigan game with Charlie. Jeremy was a die-hard State fan, so watching the Wolverines thump Purdue was painful, but taking in the game and a couple of beers with Charlie at least let him forget Zeb and Wynn for a short time.

He finally left Charlie's and rolled into his own driveway as the late afternoon sunlight faded. He realized that in wasting the afternoon, he had forgotten Allie. He was supposed to call her and let her know what was going on. He tried her at the *Beacon*, but even after listening to the instructions from the automaton, he only got her voice mail.

Inside the house, he found her number on a scrap of paper, pinned to his refrigerator with a tiny magnetic sunset by Monet. He dialed, and an older woman answered.

"Hello."

"Hi," Jeremy said brightly. "Is Allie there?"

"No, you just missed her. Can I take a message?"

"No, that's okay," Jeremy said. "Thanks."

It looked like he wouldn't have to explain how he couldn't start something after all. She was the belle of Milton. He was sure she had no problem replacing him for their Saturday date. He was relieved on one hand

and slightly disappointed on the other. A weariness was settling over him. Lack of sleep. Stress. Beer. He took a quick shower and tried to keep Zeb and Wynn from his thoughts. He had earned the rest of the weekend off. Zeb's case would still be waiting for him on Monday morning.

Mark Radamacher sat at a black walnut desk in the study of his small farmhouse. The desk, and the farm itself, had belonged to his grandfather. The desk was Mark's favorite place of refuge. It was early Saturday evening, and he was supposed to be working on a sermon for his Christian Identity congregation that gathered on Sunday mornings in the small-frame church – a church he had built with his own hands on the southeast corner of his one-hundred-and-sixty-acre farm. His flock would turn out in force at 10:00 a.m. tomorrow, looking for his guidance in these troubled times. But, he was having a difficult time concentrating on the sermon.

On the corner of his desk was the manila package which contained a published court decision. It would confirm once and for all the complete hypocrisy of Attorney Jeremy Jefferson. He stared at it, angry at Zeb for forbidding him from jail visits. His anger was interrupted by pounding on the front door.

Mark knew immediately the heavy-handed sound at the door but peeked through the living room drapes to look onto his porch. Six uniformed officers were on the porch. Four police vehicles and a civilian car had pulled up in the turn-around driveway.

The deputy who had been pounding on the door wore yellow sergeant's stripes on the long brown sleeves of his uniform. The deputy glanced at Mark in the living room window. "Mr. Radamacher, we know you're in there," the deputy sergeant yelled. "Come on out."

Mark had several firearms in the farmhouse, and he wished he were holding one now. His rage at the government's encroachment onto his property was so great that the saliva in his mouth tasted metallic.

"You'd better get off my land unless you got a warrant," he screamed from the house.

"I've got a warrant!" the deputy sergeant yelled. "Now, open the door or it's coming down!"

Mark opened the front door a crack and blocked the way. The deputy handed him a warrant, which Mark read over. "It's a warrant to search your home, sir," the deputy sergeant said. "Now step away from the door."

It was indeed a warrant, Mark thought. Signed by the same piece-of-shit judge who was holding Zeb without bail. Radamacher didn't have time to digest the warrant before he was brushed back by a column of officers marching through the doorway.

"Please come with me," the deputy sergeant said, pulling Mark out the doorway and onto the porch. "Is there anyone else in the house?"

"Don't touch me, you fucking pig," Mark said, ripping away from the deputy sergeant's light grasp. "You have no cause to arrest me."

"You're not under arrest," the deputy sergeant explained. "We just need to secure this scene until we are able to fully search the house. Now, is there anyone else in the home?"

Mark said nothing. America had become one giant police state, he thought. A plain-clothes pig got out of an unmarked Olds Eighty-Eight and walked up onto Mark's porch. He handed a card to Mark.

"I'm John Imlach," the detective said. "I'm investigating the murder of Steve Wynn. Does that name ring a bell with you?"

"I wanna call a lawyer," Mark said.

"Okay," Imlach said. "We'll get you to a phone just as soon as this search is completed. For now, why don't you have a seat over here, while these guys do their job. Or would you prefer to wait in the patrol car?" Imlach sat down with Radamacher on weathered porch furniture and sent the deputy sergeant on his way.

"You sure you wouldn't like to talk with me about Steve Wynn?" Imlach asked. "I might be able to help you out here, before they find what they're looking for. But once they find it, there isn't gonna to be much I can do."

"I said I wanna talk to my fucking lawyer," Mark snarled.

"You sure swear a lot for a preacher," Imlach said. "Not very Christian."

Mark sat, watching officers come and go from the home. They carried off clothing he'd thrown down the chute that morning, his dirty laundry now in opaque evidence bags. Then they marched the computer from his study out the front door. The items were taken to a deputy who dutifully scribbled notes on a pad, then secured the items in the trunk of his patrol car.

The deputy sergeant returned from inside the home. "We need a key to unlock your gun cabinet or we're going to have to break it," he said.

Mark led the officers into his bedroom. A fully stocked gun cabinet stood in the corner. He reached up on top of the molding and grabbed a key to unlock the cabinet.

The deputy sergeant ordered his flunkies to bag the long guns from the cabinet. As Imlach led Mark back through the living room toward the porch, a female deputy called out from the study: "Imlach. Check this out."

Imlach took Mark into the study where a female deputy was wading through papers on his desk. The deputy picked up the manila envelope. On the front of the envelope, in black marker, was written, "Zeb Radamacher".

"I thought you might like to see this," she said, handing the envelope to Imlach. Imlach opened it.

"That's United States Mail. It's for my son," Radamacher said. "Get your damn hands off it. You got no right."

Mark reached for the envelope, and Imlach pushed him back. Mark was surprised by the short detective's strength. He lost his balance and fell backwards, his hands instinctively clutching at Imlach's shoulder and sleeve to catch himself. As Mark fell backward, he dragged Imlach on top of him.

"FREEZE!" the female deputy screamed. She was going for her revolver. Mark struggled to get Imlach's weight off him. Mark's right hand had been pinned by Imlach's chest. He tried to force it free to signal the deputy to stop, but it got tangled inside the detective's wool jacket.

Mark physically felt his mind screaming the word "NO" as he saw the mouth of the revolver open toward him just four feet away. The searing pain came first even before Mark heard the explosion or saw the fire from the barrel of the revolver. A bullet tore into Mark's right side and cut through him like a lava flow. The sunset that ebbed into his study, onto his black walnut desk, was exquisite. But it faded fast from his vision as everything washed out to grey, and then black.

14

Allie pulled up in Jeremy's drive next to his car. She walked up the path to his front porch and rang the bell. She waited several moments, hearing nothing inside, and was about to turn and leave when the door cracked. Jeremy peeked around the corner, his short black hair spiked with water. She could see his bare right shoulder covered with droplets.

"Hey," he said, "Just taking a quick shower. Give me a second, and then come in."

He opened the door slightly and scurried back towards his bathroom. She came in and caught a glimpse of his retreating form. Smooth olive skin. A slender, taut torso tapered to narrow hips, covered in a white towel.

"You always answer the door in a towel?" she hollered.

"Only for reporters," he yelled back. "Help yourself to a drink if you want. There's some wine on the counter or beer in the fridge."

She strolled through the living room trying to absorb something about the man who had piqued her interest. A print by Monet from the National Gallery - a small child in a sunlit garden - dominated the room. On the opposite wall was a picture of Jeremy in a green graduation gown. Jeremy smiled from the photograph, his arm around a beaming woman with graying hair. The television was archaic and sat back in an oak entertainment center that looked custom-made.

In the kitchen, Allie pulled a bottle of Zinfandel from a small counter rack and searched his drawers until she found a corkscrew. She hadn't had wine since college. People did not drink wine in Milton. She poured two large glasses and sipped. It was a sweet wine, much to her liking.

"Hey," he said, joining her. He had pulled on jeans and a gray sweater. It was not the towel, but he didn't look half-bad.

"Hey," she said, handing him a wine glass. He raised his glass to hers and they drank.

"I tried calling you just awhile ago, but they said you were out," said Jeremy.

"Oh," she said. "Yeah, I couldn't wait to hear what was going on. So I just thought I'd come over."

"Great," he said. "Do you still want to try and catch the play? I'm sorry about earlier. I've just been scatterbrained about all this. But if you want to – "

"I gave the tickets to my boss."

"I'm sorry," he said.

"It's okay. I didn't really feel up to it, either."

They sat at his kitchen table and drank as darkness filled the room. He told her about his decision to go directly to Imlach. And about Zeb's confession – off the record – but at least he was trusting her more, she thought. And about Charlie's criticism.

"Screw him," she said. "Bosses suck sometimes." She had finished a second glass, and the wine was coursing merrily through her, loosening her tongue.

"No," Jeremy said, "he's right. I should've at least gotten some kind of deal from Gray first. Now Zeb's at their mercy. They got what they wanted, and they don't have any incentive to give Zeb a break. I panicked."

Without thinking, she put a hand to his shoulder and rubbed the soft sweater. The past day had brought them effortlessly closer. Her touching had been unconsciously intimate, and he showed no apparent discomfort, even as he ignored it. She liked touching him, and she liked that he was so nonchalant in his response even more.

"I wanted to come back here last night," she said. "After I got my stories filed."

Jeremy looked at her with his dark brown eyes – as deep as any eyes she'd ever seen. They were kind and intelligent, but in them was some secret. A wall keeping something inside him from getting out, she thought.

"I was so scared. I didn't want to be alone," she said.

"I know," Jeremy said. "I felt the same way. I wanted to ask. But, you needed to work – and –"

"I would've come back," she smiled. She leaned closer to him, drawn to his face. She let her hand slide from his sweater to his soft-shaven cheek. She kissed him gently.

He did not resist. He was not eager or greedy. It was a kiss that held a patient promise, and it was Allie who had to back away, somewhat light-headed. From the wine or Jeremy, she was not sure.

He looked at her again, troubled, and said, "Allie, listen. I've been wanting to talk to you."

She had heard these words before. They were never followed by pleasantries. She thought of kissing him again. Smothering any words he might say to spoil the moment. But she remembered the wall in his eyes and just listened.

"I really like you. I mean, I think I could really like you. I wanted you to stay here with me last night, too. So bad. But, I am just not ready to get into anything serious right now. And I think you ought to know that. And the way I am feeling, I think this thing between us – it would be too serious."

She didn't say anything for a moment. She wasn't sure what he was saying. She did feel the strongest attraction to this man, which was unusual for her. There was nothing casual about the kiss they shared. It had felt like home. "I don't know what you mean. It's not like I'm asking you to marry me or anything, Jefferson," she said, allowing herself to grin. "It was just a kiss."

He laughed out loud. A laugh that was rich and infectious. A laugh that let them move on from confronting serious things, she thought. While their conversation stretched into the night, they emptied the bottle of Zinfandel and opened a bottle of Chardonnay. He told her about his life before Milton. He told her about his ex-fiancé, Hannah, and how much Allie reminded him of her. And, he told her about how much he had been hurt when Hannah chose a career over him. It was Allie's luck in love, she mused, as he rolled out his story, that she would have to catch such a lovely man who had been so recently hurt and who was now gun shy.

In the end, they agreed that the timing was not right. But, that didn't keep them from polishing off the Chardonnay as they watched the end of a movie on cable. They shared a blanket, trying to keep out the cold of the coming winter. He was a perfect gentleman, but Allie was sure she could have made love to him.

She fell asleep on his couch and stirred only when the grey morning light rolled into the room like a tide, making the Monet print look like a monograph. She was alone, and the blanket they had shared was tucked snuggly around her. She rose, put on her shoes and coat and quietly snuck out the front door.

As she drove from his house, she thought of the kiss. It had been magic. Full of promise. There was definitely a spark. She had to be patient.

Driving through town, she passed a paper boy throwing copies of the *Beacon* from bike to porch with a natural cadence. The paperboy looked up at her in a studied way as she passed.

The look made her laugh. She felt just a bit slutty, sneaking home in the early morning after spending the night with a man she had really only just met. She hadn't felt that way since college. She remembered freshman year at Central, her first time away from home, and her sorority sisters at *Alpha Sigma* Tau explaining the walk of shame with equal parts envy and ridicule.

Early Sunday mornings, stray girls could be seen intermittently straggling back to their dorm rooms or sorority houses after drunken encounters. Their hair undone, falling on day-old clothing. Some with a look of bemusement or joy or thought. Some with a distinct look of shame at having prowled past the moonlight right through to the sunrise.

Allie had always hated the double standard. For college boys, such morning walks were victory marches. But, for a large percentage of young women, it was still a walk of public scorn. A walk better made before sunrise. Allie had rejected these old-fashioned ideas, in theory, from first learning about them. But, in practice, when she made her own walks of shame, few in number, she could feel eyes upon her from passing strangers. Sometimes the world placed burdens on your heart, she thought, however unfair. And she knew that if she were going home to her sisters at *Alpha Sigma* Tau this morning, they would never believe that her night with Jeremy had been purely innocent.

Fortunately, she did not have to get past her sorority sisters but only her aging parents. She rolled the car into the drive with near silence, tiptoed through the house, avoiding even the faintest groans from the old floorboards, and snuck toward her upstairs bedroom. Her mother and father had not yet risen. It was like sneaking in after a late date in high school. She stripped completely and crawled under her worn, soft comforter. Curled on her side, she started to drift off, thinking of Jeremy. Alone in the cold bed, she started to wonder if she was investing in damaged goods.

He had been up front about his lingering feelings and anger toward his ex. He was trying to stop her, even though she knew how much he really wanted her. She probably should have walked away when he told her these things, but she did not think she would. She would be patient. He was worth the wait, she thought.

"Mr. Usterman to see you, sir," buzzed his secretary.

"Tell him to have a seat," Bishop said, feet up on his desk, reviewing a copy of the talking points the governor had used at this morning's party caucus meeting. "Get him some coffee if he wants it."

Bishop had no love for the senate majority leader. Fritz Usterman was a big-time farmer who had made a living off conservative values and rural issues that made him beloved in his district. But, he was a politician, and as a rule, Bishop did not trust anyone with enough political skill to have obtained such a high office. They tended to be two-faced, untrustworthy and self-serving – with wonderful smiles.

Usterman had asked the governor to attend the regular Monday morning caucus after he had heard sound bites from Saturday's speech. Because there would be a legislative proposal, Usterman thought the governor should keep the legislators in the loop.

Bishop told the governor that he didn't need to cow-tow to the legislators on this issue, but Howell was an affable man. He actually liked meeting with those old bastards. So talking points were drafted quickly, and the governor was sent down before his noon flight to D.C. Bishop could not imagine what Usterman was doing in his office now.

After letting the Senator cool his heels for a few minutes, Bishop had him sent in.

"How are you, Kurt?" Usterman said with a heavy handshake.

"Very well. And you, Senator?"

"Just dandy," he said, in his down-on-the-farm accent. "I just wanted to congratulate you on this eco-terrorist legislation. Roger was just down with us at the caucus this morning, and he says it was your baby all the way. And it's a humdinger. I can't wait to go over the numbers. Roger said you had Artie working on them."

"Yes, sir, I did," Bishop said. "And they're outstanding. I think this might get us ten points statewide, if we play it right."

"Unbelievable," Usterman said. "Well, Roger had to make a flight, or some business, and he sent me up here to see you. I told him, that while I love the bill – what are you calling it –"

"MEGPAT, sir. The Michigan Economic Growth and Protection Against Terror Act," Bishop said.

"Yes," Usterman said. "While I love the bill, I just want to make sure it isn't going to put a strain on my legislative agenda for the senate. I absolutely have to get this school voucher bill passed this spring. We all need to run on that in the fall. And, I told Roger I'd be happy to expedite this MEGPATH –"

"MEGPAT, sir," Bishop said.

"Yes," Usterman said. "Like I was saying, more than happy to push it along quickly. But I have to have your assurances that you are going to use Roger's political capital to get that voucher bill through this spring."

"We're already committed to it, sir," Bishop said. "The entire party's going to benefit from your bill, Senator. We just need to crack the whip on this MEGPAT bill because of timing. We have to strike while the iron is hot and lock in our gains."

"I completely understand," Usterman said. "I just want to know that we've got a deal." Bishop shook Usterman's meaty hand again. Anything you say, Fritz, he thought. Anything you say. He would own Fritz Usterman in another year or two. And the old farmer would never come into his office and try to harvest Howell's support again.

15

By Wednesday, Jeremy's desk was already recovering from the effort he had focused on Zeb's preliminary exam. The Sage Law Office defended nearly two hundred felonies a year, and whenever a single case required as much attention as Zeb's did, the routine work of countless other cases tended to collect like water behind a dam. Now that Zeb's exam was finished, Jeremy steadily worked on the backlog until all his cases were caught up.

He listened to WHIP – all the hits from the '70s, '80s and '90s – as he worked, tapping his ballpoint pen to "Pour Some Sugar on Me" by *Def Leppard*, and singing in a whispered, off-key voice. Senior year, he thought. The song reminded him of Saturday night and Allie, and the way she had made him feel self-conscious, like a high school boy.

Despite his efforts to concentrate on other cases, Zeb's case kept coming back to him. A suspect was in custody on the Wynn murder, WHIP told Jeremy every hour on the hour since Monday. Mark Radamacher, Zeb's father, had been shot while resisting a search warrant being served on the murder case. He was under protective custody at Mid-Michigan Regional Medical Center. Jeremy was shocked that Zeb had been so wrong about Wynn's killer but was relieved that the shooter was in custody.

It sounded like the elder Radamacher was lucky to be alive. According to the radio account, he had been shot once through the abdomen at close range. He hadn't been charged with Wynn's murder yet, but Charlie was pretty sure that charges were coming soon.

Jeremy was still shaken by Wynn's death, and it was difficult for him to analyze the situation. But during the course of the week, he forced himself to think it through. There were really only two possibilities, as far as Jeremy could see. Either Radamacher had shot Wynn for some reason related to Zeb's case, or the old man was trying to kill Jeremy and had mistakenly shot Wynn. Neither scenario was comforting to Jeremy. But in any case, Jeremy felt better now that the old man was lying in a hospital, under guard.

As Jeremy puzzled through the mystery of the cases of Zeb and Mark Radamacher, his thoughts frequently turned to Allie. She had been a comfort to him on Saturday night. Her presence was calming. He was happy she stayed the night, and was amazed at his own willpower in resisting the urge to take advantage of the moment provided by the wine and her kiss. It would have been easy enough.

Charlie didn't believe that nothing happened. He teased Jeremy relentlessly about being rejected by the hot reporter. Jeremy glanced up from his routine work to look at the clock; it was 11:55 a.m. He dropped his pen and walked over to Charlie's office.

"You ready?" Jeremy said.

"Unfortunately for you, I am," Charlie said.

The game was on. They tramped down the stairs to the library. Charlie opened with white and the King's Gambit. A favorite of the master, Jeremy thought. They both stopped halfway through the opening sequence hearing the words "eco-terror" in a WHIP news update. It was the media's newest favorite adjective for Zeb's case.

A cheerful, disembodied voice read the story with perfect inflection: "Melissa Dobbs has been arraigned in the 89th District Court today on charges of Terrorism, Malicious Destruction of Property and Arson, in connection with an alleged act of eco-terror at the Blue-Mart construction site near the Milton exit off US-27, on October 11, 2003. A preliminary hearing on her case has been scheduled for November 11, 2003.

"Dobbs is the second person charged in the eco-terror case, joining co-defendant Zeb Radamacher, who is currently being held at the Wabeno County Jail, pending trial. Detective Mary Russell of the Michigan State Police said that new information led to the arrest of Dobbs. Russell indicated a warrant has been issued for a third suspect, Jared MacAdam. MacAdam is a seventeen-year-old senior at Milton High School.

"Anyone with information on MacAdam's whereabouts should contact the Michigan State Police. Citizens should not attempt to approach MacAdam on their own, according to Russell, as he is considered armed and potentially dangerous."

"Wow, I wonder what their 'new information' could be?" Charlie said, deadpan.

Jeremy didn't respond.

"I bet they are going to assign Ellis to defend her," Charlie said, finishing his opening in perfect position. "A definite drawback to have her as your co-counsel if you have to try this thing."

The Sage Law Office handled almost all indigent felony work. However, where there were co-defendants in need of an attorney, the court had to assign another local attorney to handle the case. Patty Ellis got many of these assignments. She was a middle-aged divorce lawyer with a penchant for annoying judges and anyone else she had contact with.

"I hope Welch has more sense than to assign her," Jeremy said, returning his attention to the board, where his black pieces were slowly engulfed by Charlie's white onslaught. Jeremy figured his position was worthless, and Charlie confirmed it a move later, his queen leaping forward. "Check," Charlie said. "And mate in five."

WHIP had moved on to more '80s music. Howard Jones crooned that things could only get better, and Jeremy wanted to believe. But after getting stomped two-straight, Jeremy paid the two-dollar chess tax and returned to his office for a quiet afternoon of cleaning up cases. He was there five minutes when Dena buzzed him. It was Allie. He hadn't called her since Saturday night, and he was not looking forward to her reaction.

"You've heard about Dobbs, right?" Allie said, assuming her professional reporter voice.

"Yeah, I just listened to it on the radio," Jeremy said.

"I have to update my story," she said. "How about meeting me at the Morning Grind. On the *Beacon*. Business only."

Jeremy skipped down the stairs and let Dena know he was going out. Indian summer had given way to a cold snap, so he grabbed his coat off the stand and walked over to the coffee shop.

Jeremy couldn't suppress a smile as she walked in, dressed in a tweed cap and matching jacket that played up her schoolgirl charm. She grilled him for his thoughts on the case and his strategy. He played it close to the vest but insisted that his client would be vindicated at trial. And after she finished the professional questions, she got down to the real purpose of the visit, Jeremy thought.

"So, you don't call a girl after she spends the night?" Allie grinned at him, putting her notebook away.

"I've just been swamped. This case has everything else backed up. I wanted to," he said. "I had fun Saturday."

"Me, too," she said. "But, I don't know if we should do that again. People might talk."

If she only knew what Charlie had been saying.

"I appreciate you understanding about Hannah and all that crap," Jeremy said.

"I like you, Jeremy," she said flatly. "Why don't we just get together now and then. Friends? There aren't that many people you can talk to here, ya know."

"That would be great," Jeremy said. He was reminded of a line from the movie they watched on Saturday night – *When Harry Met Sally* – where Billy Crystal tells Meg Ryan that men and women are never really friends.

"How 'bout lunch on Wednesdays, Dutch," she said.

"I don't know," Jeremy said, considering the offer. It was an unwritten condition of employment that he play chess with Charlie on the lunch hour, and he wasn't sure how his old friend would take to Wednesdays alone. "Wednesdays, huh? Okay. I'm in, but only if the *Beacon* keeps picking up the tab."

She laughed, and it reminded Jeremy of the kiss they had shared. He loved being around her, but he knew it was only a matter of time until friendship crossed the line into something that would hurt him, or her, or both of them.

"All right," she said. "Wednesdays it is. I gotta get back."

He watched her go, her steps filled with animal grace, until she turned the corner to the Beacon building.

October turned to November, the autumn colors giving way to the grey morning frost and the first snow, numbered flakes gently guided by a cold wind. For a week or more, Jeremy was able to forget about Zeb and Wynn and old-man Radamacher. He returned to the routines of his work life. Interviews. Motions. Pleas. Sentencings. Every case was dwarfed by the magnitude of Zeb's case, except to the client involved, and to Jeremy, who cared for each of Charlie's charges like a nurse maid.

He scrupulously avoided Zeb at the jail because he did not want to talk to the boy about his father's impending murder charge and the relative lack of activity on Zeb's own case.

The case continued to attract attention on TV-23 and WHIP. And Allie continued to write about it. The defense view got more play in her coverage, and that was good. She also did a feature about the environmental movement and how it had spawned a generation of young people willing to become direct actors to correct a flawed system. The piece probably would have been lauded in New York or California, but Jeremy was pretty certain after reading it that she was in for some nasty letters.

Professor Quinn was quoted in the article, and Jeremy spoke admiringly of her comments when she called him the day after the story ran.

"Thanks," Professor Quinn said. "I haven't had a chance to read the article yet, but I like that reporter. She seems to understand our cause."

"I think you're right," Jeremy said. "So, to what do I owe the pleasure of a telephone call?"

"I wanted to see how you were holding up," Quinn said. "That was an awful thing with that young man. And, I've seen the news about the other shooting. Zeb's father. That's one chaotic situation you have up there."

"Yeah," he said. "Like nothing I've ever seen. I'm okay, though. I'm actually thinking that Zeb's case has gotten better. I think I might have a chance to beat the terrorism nonsense at least."

"Good. Good. Glad to hear that," Quinn said. "I wanted to remind you about the *Save Zeb* meeting on Friday, too. I'm sure our people would be grateful to hear from you again, if you feel up to it."

"God. I thought they'd give it up after the shooting. I can't imagine carrying on with a kid dead. None of this is worth it. There's nothing they can do to help Zeb, really."

"Well, I won't tell the kids you said that," Quinn laughed. "That's a little on the negative side for the public activist crowd. I'd take that bit out of your speech if you want to come, unless you want to get booed off the stage, anyway."

"I'm serious, Professor Quinn," he said with some venom. "If Mark Radamacher wasn't in a hospital right now, I'd be frightened for those kids, and there's no saying if there are other nut cases out there. Radamacher wasn't the only guy opposed to the environmental movement around here."

"I didn't mean to make light of Steve Wynn's murder, Jeremy. I just wouldn't want to see him die in vain. And neither would these kids. They're working their collective asses off for your client. You gotta be the change you seek, you know, and all that."

Jeremy was ashamed at his relative lack of faith in Zeb's cause. He'd never been a cause man. "I wish you the best, Doctor," he said. "I really do. But I just don't think I can be there." He couldn't think of a cause that was worthy of Wynn's life or Zeb's imprisonment.

As the week drew to a close, Jeremy continued his mindless routine – defending the public, those guilty and those poor. But his mind turned back to Professor Quinn's words often. "You have to be the change you seek." She'd paraphrased Mahatma Gandhi, he thought. And by 8:00 p.m. on Friday, he found himself at the Milton library, wanting to be near the idealism of the young activists.

Much to his surprise, the *Save Zeb* movement had grown. He thought the outright murder of a member might suppress turnout. But, the small meeting room at the library was twice as crowded as the initial meeting two weeks earlier.

A group of fifteen students from Milton High School showed up. The college contingent had doubled in size, now ten members strong. A handful of young adults scattered in the seats at the back of the meeting room, locals drawn by Allie's article from the previous Sunday, Jeremy guessed. Allie was also near the back of the room and looked surprised when he arrived. She motioned him to an empty chair on her right.

Professor Quinn smiled and nodded at Jeremy as if she had known he would be there all along. She dragged a lectern to the front of the room, facing the audience. As she was about to begin, Jeremy was jolted by a familiar face entering the meeting room. Steve Wynn's mom entered and silently took a seat in the rear opposite from where Jeremy sat. She was dressed in a black skirt and jacket with padded shoulders, a far more somber figure than when Jeremy had first met her. He was grateful she did not sit near him because he could think of no words to offer comfort.

Professor Quinn opened the meeting in her businesslike style and stuck to a narrow agenda. She made a brief statement about the grief they all shared at the loss of Steve Wynn, and her stirring audience was at once rapt in silence. She welcomed the newcomers and thanked the two-week veterans for their determined presence. And then she called for committee reports.

The committee chairs were all students of Professor Quinn, and it was apparent to Jeremy that they were all quite serious about the *Save Zeb* movement. The first report was given by Lauren Owen, a chunky black student who talked with the ease of a veteran speaker. She was the chair of the fundraising committee and found that money was going to be hard to come by. Young people seemed to be the only demographic interested in Zeb's cause, and other than volunteered time, there was little cash to be raised. Fundraising was going to have to be creative, grass roots in nature, and above all, patient. She suggested that members pay voluntary dues of one to ten dollars per meeting. Professor Quinn called for a voice vote on the motion, and *Save Zeb* had an official, but small, revenue source.

The political committee was headed by Mike Pearson, a politician in waiting, posing as an undergrad. He was a tall, nice-looking young man, whose voice was pleasing. He identified himself as a pre-law senior at Central and laid out the committee findings. His committee had gathered voting rolls for Wabeno County and prepared walking maps for every voting district. He suggested that the group should use volunteers to start a door-to-door campaign to reach the voters of Wabeno with some basic literature about Zeb's, and now Melissa's, plight. Volunteer canvassers would work as continually as possible up until the trial date, collecting signatures on a petition that would inform the prosecutor, in no uncertain language, that he should deal more fairly with Zeb and company, or face a political defeat in the coming election year. His remarks were well-taken, and the small crowd applauded spontaneously. Professor Quinn quickly silenced the outbreak and invited the third committee chair to the podium.

Katie Reader was a slight bohemian girl with wide eyes set large under straight, brown hair. She chaired the social action committee. She explained that the committee had examined state election law. Zeb's plan to have a democratic revolution in Wabeno County was at least legal, and at best achievable if the group was well-funded. Unfortunately, since funding was not likely to reach those levels, the plan's prospects were of questionable efficacy.

It didn't stop her enthusiasm as she outlined a detailed plan of how election law would permit the group to start a revolution. Voters and candidates could become registered in Wabeno with only thirty days' residence in the county. Ballot access could be gained by sending in an advance team to claim the Green Party nomination, since the Greens were recognized statewide but had no established committee in Wabeno County. Once Green Party control was established, *Save Zeb* would be able to put their own candidates on the county commission ballot, carefully targeting four out of the seven districts in the county in order to gain a bare majority and control of the county government.

Going after only four seats instead of all seven would limit the number of voters the group would need to win control. Her committee projected that control could be won if they could register seven hundred and fifty voters in each targeted district. The committee outlined what it thought was the most realistic plan to reach this level of registration: rent a farm in each district and create a kind of rotating commune. The farms would nominally be designed for college students to work raising organic agricultural products. If the rented farms could be operational by May, and they could each rotate one hundred and fifty workers per month, the numbers could be reached. It would work like a migrant worker operation, which was common in Michigan agriculture. She indicated that the committee would begin to scout out one farm to act as the advance operation, so a small group of volunteers could get to work on hijacking the Green Party nominations for next year's November ballot.

The plan sounded extraordinarily far-fetched to Jeremy. Ingenious, but far-fetched. But the girl was obviously pleased, and her committee cheered wildly when she concluded her remarks.

Professor Quinn thanked the committees for their hard work She also suggested that a new membership committee be created to encourage participation in the organization. Finally, she invited Jeremy to say a few words about Zeb's ongoing case.

Jeremy had no prepared comments but was happy to speak to the supportive group. He spoke very briefly about the addition of Dobbs as a co-defendant and about the prosecution's continued unwillingness to offer any reasonable terms for a plea bargain. He would know more after a pretrial hearing in mid-December. He thanked them for their encouragement and assured them that he would pass their support on to Zeb. He finished to polite applause from all but one member of the audience. He had avoided looking at Mrs. Wynn during his remarks. He couldn't bear it, really. But now as he looked out, he caught her eye. She had risen at the back of the room and started to talk over the scattered clapping.

"You killed my Stevie!" she said, strongly at first, pointing directly at Jeremy. Then her voice cracked and faltered between sobs. "You dragged him into – all of you – he is DEAD! – for this – my poor, sweet Stevie –"

A stunned silence followed. The young people looked around, their own enthusiasm for the cause muted. Jeremy felt as if ice water had been poured into his heart. He had felt guilty, holding Steve Wynn's bloody remains, and Mrs. Wynn's accusation found its mark. He looked to Allie, who stared at him with hurt eyes. Without thinking, Jeremy approached Mrs. Wynn. She was slumped now, broken and sobbing uncontrollably. Jeremy put his arms around her and held her. He could feel warm tears on his neck as he bent to her short frame. "I'm sorry," he whispered in her ear. "I am sorry." Be the change you seek, he thought, holding on as his eyes burned and his head swam. Be the change you seek.

16

"Welcome back to *In Focus*. I'm Don LaBelle, and we're pleased to be joined today by Kurt Bishop, chief-of-staff to Governor Howell. And, as always, our panel," LaBelle said, motioning to three other journalists who sat with Bishop around a prop-like conference table. It was warm under the lights, and Bishop was already sweating profusely. He hated makeup for television appearances and did not enjoy the spotlight. But, the governor wanted him out there, so he had accepted LaBelle's invitation to do the show.

"Mr. Bishop," LaBelle said, turning to look right past Bishop and into camera number two. "Let's talk about the legislation that the Governor introduced this week. The Michigan Economic Growth Protection and Anti-Terrorism Act. MEGPAT. That is a mouthful. First off, why don't you tell our viewers a bit about it. And second, isn't this act just political posturing? Don't the current terrorism laws on the state books deal with the domestic terror threat adequately?"

Even before Bishop met LaBelle, he had not liked the man. LaBelle had been the face and voice of state political journalism since Bishop could remember. His face was rat-like, his voice was grating, and it was an amazement to Bishop that he reached this level. Success in journalism must be even less based on merit than success in politics, he thought.

"This is anything but politics, Don," said Bishop directly. "Governor Howell does not play politics when it comes to protecting the people of our state. Domestic terrorism – eco-terrorism – is on the rise in our state. These liberal extremists have resorted to force and violence where their ideas could not compete in the free market, and Governor Howell has responded

111

strongly to them. Environmental extremism is not going to be tolerated on the governor's watch."

LaBelle shifted in his chair to face camera one, in the general direction of a liberal reporter from the *Free Press*. "Luke, what do you think about MEGPAT? Is this necessary protection or politics as usual?"

"Well, it's clearly politics," said the reporter, a borderline socialist, from the columns Bishop had read. "Governor Howell has taken one of the best issues for his opponents, support for the environment, and turned it against them," the reporter said. He reminded Bishop of one of his professors from college. Smart, but clueless. "It's brilliant politics. But, the Act is frightening in scope. It is broader than the USA Patriot Act. And what I'd like to know from Mr. Bishop is, with a state budget that is already nine hundred million dollars in the red, where is the governor going to get the money to fund additional policing and an additional department, headed by a MEGPAT czar that is called for in the Act, should they succeed in enacting it into law?"

"Governor Howell would never place a price tag on the safety of our people," Bishop said. Getting his own message out on the air waves was child's play, really. Answer what you want. Stay on message. Propaganda 101, he thought. "Take this case up in Wabeno County. Your paper covered this story back in October. It's a good example.

"There, we had four young people, from what we know, armed with gasoline bombs and common tools. They sabotaged a construction site up there. Four teenagers. Avowed eco-terrorists. And they shut down a site for two days and caused millions of dollars in damage. If it wasn't for some heroic work by our police and firefighters, it could have been worse, and people could have been hurt or killed."

"But how are you going –" the reporter tried to redirect his question, but Bishop just rolled over the top of the intellectual geek.

"If I might finish," Bishop said. "Now, there are these radical environmental causes shooting up everywhere. The WTO protestor types. Disaffected. Not able to win on their ideas. Because they would rather save an owl at the cost of taking jobs away from people and taking food off people's plates. But when they're not able to win on their ideas, they take to blowing things up, to intimidate us.

"And it's not just the initial act of terror, which is bad enough. But, if you've followed the story, now there have been radical protests connected to the terrorism, and a shooting at one of these protests. The first murder in that county in almost two decades.

"Now, the prosecutor up there has told us repeatedly that the tools he needs to fight cases like this are not there under current law. And Governor

Howell is not going to sit by and do nothing. His administration is going to act decisively, and I think the House and Senate are going to act quickly on this thing. Senator Usterman tells me that this is going to be fast-tracked in the Senate. And I know the House will follow. It's good legislation. Important legislation. To protect our people from a real threat."

"We're running short on time," LaBelle shot in, turning back to camera two. "But, I'm glad you brought up Senator Usterman. Because I've been hearing everywhere in Lansing that his school voucher proposal –" LaBelle went on.

Plenty of good sound bites about those nasty eco-terrorists, Bishop thought. He loved this issue. It was impossible for them to rebut. Americans were ready to be frightened and protected. It was a beautiful formula. The 9/11 attacks had been a political godsend.

His own agenda having been addressed, he answered a few questions from the panel on other issues. When the interview was over, he headed for his own office to map out the passage and promotion of MEGPAT.

Mark Radamacher spent three weeks in the hospital, drugged into a mind-numbing oblivion. He was happy to be discharged, but his first steps outside the hospital took him from a wheelchair into the back of a patrol car. Detective Imlach was the last person Radamacher remembered seeing before being shot, and was now the first person Radamacher saw upon his release. Detective Imlach and a uniformed officer escorted him from the hospital to the courthouse in Milton.

It had been touch and go for Mark early on. He had lost a lot of blood from the gunshot wound. When he woke up three days after the shooting, the doctor told him that he had lost a kidney and a portion of his large intestine. That bitch who shot him point-blank had almost buried him, he thought.

As if being shot in his own home wasn't enough, Radamacher had been informed that the government was going to charge him with the murder of a boy he didn't even know. The prosecutor was rabid, he thought. First Zeb; then a trumped-up murder charge. But he was confident that his lawyer was going to sue the crap out of everyone involved.

Mark had hired Harold Karljevic. Some of his old prison contacts told him Karljevic was tough as nails and gaining a name for himself as a top-notch defense lawyer. Having spent time in the pen on weapons charges because of an incompetent public defender, Mark was willing to pay a high premium to ensure he was never going back. Karljevic was supposed to be a prosecutor's worst nightmare.

Mark hoped that Zachary had gotten Karljevic the money yesterday, because he sure as hell did not want to show up at court without a lawyer.

When they arrived at the courthouse, Detective Imlach led Radamacher in the back door, down a service elevator to the basement. He was placed in a tiny holding cell and released from his handcuffs.

Mark sat in the cell for an eternity. There was no clock to keep time. The walls were block and painted a numbing cream color. Iron bars and a security door cut him off from any sound or sight outside the cell. He was alone with two benches, a stainless steel toilet and a small sink. Infinite minutes later, the security door was unlocked and a barrel-chested man in his fifties stepped through.

"I'm Harold Karljevic," his attorney said. "You must be Mr. Radamacher."

Karljevic explained everything with clarity in about five minutes. His only advice was for Mark to remain silent during the hearing. Beyond that, Karljevic said he would take additional information from Mark about the crime after the arraignment. The guy was a pro.

A deputy interrupted their conversation to cuff Mark and lead him into the courtroom. Mark rejoined his attorney at the lectern in the center of the courtroom, and together they listened as the judge read two counts: Open Murder and Resisting a Police Officer. From what Mark could understand, the charge of resisting must have had something to do with falling down and getting shot in his own home. He chuckled to himself.

Bond was denied, as Karljevic told him it would be. The judge was going to give Mark a preliminary examination date in just two weeks, but Karljevic asked for more time, and Mark reluctantly waived his right to a prompt hearing. The judge set the exam for December 19, a full month away. A month in jail for falling down and getting shot, Mark thought. America really was going to hell. It was outrageous. But he knew he would be released soon.

Karljevic looked at his watch. He had another court appearance downstate, he explained. He said he would be back to talk to Mark in full about the case as soon as his schedule allowed it, and he beat a hasty retreat.

Mark didn't get much time with his learned counsel. Fifteen thousand dollars down was a lot of money to talk to a guy for less than five minutes, he thought. But you get what you pay for – and this guy was good.

17

"Up next, we've got a pair of gentlemen closely involved with the war on environmental terror," said Studs Nolan. Bishop had the radio in his office switched off and heard the voice over the phone line. It sounded more muted than when he had heard Studs talk on his daily broadcast. "Joining us by phone in Lansing is Kurt Bishop, the chief-of-staff to Governor Howell. And also by phone, from Milton, Michigan, is Jeremy Jefferson. He is an attorney for one of the eco-terrorists charged in the now infamous Milton Blue-Mart firebombing. And we will debate this issue and take your calls after we pay the bills with these commercial messages."

Bishop was astounded to learn that Jefferson accepted an offer to appear live on *The Studs Nolan Show*. Nolan was a hot commodity in talk radio. His show was broadcast from Grand Rapids and syndicated throughout the Midwest. He was a cross between Rush Limbaugh and G. Gordon Liddy. Bishop had contacted Studs to try to promote MEGPAT on a friendly media forum. He had initially laughed off Nolan's suggestion that they get Jefferson on to talk about the issue, figuring Jefferson would have enough sense not to appear on such a hostile battleground.

An engineer came on to let Bishop know that the show would start in thirty seconds; just turn the radio down and talk to Studs directly, the engineer said for the twentieth time.

"And we're back," said Studs. His voice was deep and rich. Slightly southern. Bishop had never met the man, but he understood he was short and frail, in contrast to the bold voice. "This should be a treat for you Nolanites out there. As you know, we have been talking for the past few weeks about environmental terrorists.

"We were among the first news outlets to bring this story to the public's attention. A group of teenage environmentalists, here in Michigan, upset with the building of a Blue-Mart in their community. Rather than going out and getting a job at what was undoubtedly a gem in the rural economy of Milton, Michigan – I mean if these kids were not malcontents they could be working at the Blue-Mart today – but instead, these young people decided to turn to terrorism.

"That's right. They blew up a bulldozer on the construction site. And they damaged several other pieces of heavy equipment. Millions of dollars in damage to a local construction company – another source of jobs – and they shut down the site. Millions of dollars in damage to the local economy. And to Blue-Mart. And any of us Nolanites who own shares in Blue-Mart – we ultimately pay for this act.

"I could go on setting this up for you. Because it is fascinating what is happening up there in Milton now. I understand that it is a community divided. There is a small group of radicals that have taken up the cause of the jailed eco-terrorists. There has been violence. A murder at one of the eco-terror rallies. But, let me introduce – we have two of the principals on opposite sides of this issue. I am pleased to welcome Kurt Bishop, chief-of-staff to Governor Howell of Michigan. And Jeremy Jefferson. He is a public defender in Milton, Michigan. Defending one of the eco-terrorists. Or should I say alleged eco-terrorists. Welcome gentlemen, to *The Studs Nolan Show.*"

"Thanks," Jeremy Jefferson said, a voice Bishop had not heard since law school.

"Thank you, Studs," Bishop said. "Long-time listener, first time caller."

"Great," Studs said. "Well, let's get to this issue. Environmental terrorism. What is it? And what can we do about it? Mr. Bishop, what's been the governor's response to this crisis in our state?"

"First, Studs, you've hit the issue right on the head in your opening comments," Bishop said, stepping in to crush the first of many softballs he anticipated would be floated his way during the radio debate. "This is about a group of frustrated environmentalists, who, when they can't get their way through the democratic process, have essentially taken up arms to try to force their cause down the throats of ordinary people.

"The governor has set out an agenda from the beginning of his term that seeks to balance legitimate environmental concerns against economic stability. His policies seek growth, jobs and a better environment. But when it comes to dealing with these eco-terrorists, Governor Howell has been quick to act.

116

"He has supported the local prosecutor, Ed Gray, up there in Wabeno County, who has charged these young people with the harshest crimes available under the law. Governor Howell has committed whatever resources are needed to ensure these individuals are brought to justice.

"In addition to that, the governor immediately set out to toughen our state's laws, which will specifically target eco-terrorism. He has proposed a law called MEGPAT. That's the Michigan Economic Growth Protection and Anti-Terrorism Act. MEGPAT gives our law enforcement officers the tools they need to battle these eco-terrorists. It also sets up a new department to monitor our response to domestic terrorism aimed at hurting our state's economic growth. It is a good law. We can be one of the first states in the Union to pass something this focused on a growing problem. And Governor Howell is proud of his efforts to lead the fight in this area."

"That sounds like a logical response," Studs said. "You've got a bunch of environmental radicals who can basically cause millions of dollars in damage with a bottle, a rag and some gasoline. Sounds like maybe we should be beefing up law enforcement's ability to deal with these acts of violence. Who would be against stopping this type of terrorism? Mr. Jefferson?"

There was a pause before Bishop heard Jefferson start to respond. His old nemesis was shell-shocked, he thought. Very good.

"I thought you wanted me to talk about the merits of my client's case," Jeremy said. "I'm not really here to defend terrorism, Mr. Nolan. My client is not a terrorist, despite how he's been charged, and I don't think that story has been getting out in the media."

"Now, you represent Zebediah Radamacher, right?" Studs said.

"Yes. Zeb is my client –"

"And if I understand it right, he is the one who was caught on the scene, red-handed, so to speak," Studs said.

"Yes," Jeremy said. "He was at the scene. But he did not participate in any act of terrorism. They are trying to lock my client up for what really amounts to a high school prank –"

"High school prank?" Studs said with his characteristic astonishment when he heard things he found incredulous. "Millions of dollars in damage. A high school prank. I know a few hundred thousand people who listen to my radio show who would probably disagree with you about that."

Jeremy tried to explain, but there were few in the vast audience of AM talk radio who believed him, Bishop thought. After fumbling around for a few minutes, Studs cut in again over the music that signaled a commercial break.

"We're going to pick this up in a moment," Studs said. "I'd like to have our guests talk more about this new radical movement that has been spawned in Milton. And the violence that has been associated with that movement. And we'll take your calls. After we pay the bills with these commercial messages."

It could only get better with the Nolanites calling, thought Bishop. Jefferson would think Studs was fair and balanced after listening to the questions the audience was likely to pose. The interview was only a third over, and Bishop was already basking in triumph over his law school rival. He couldn't wait to get up to Milton to see Jefferson in person.

Every public defense client of the Sage Law Office was instructed not to call collect from the jail. The instruction was written and distributed universally. Still, at least a quarter of the clients made collect calls from the jail. They were refused without exception. The county did not reimburse the expense, and to accept a single call would have only encouraged an onslaught of more.

When Jeremy picked up his messages after lunch, he found three refused calls from Zeb. Jeremy had only seen Zeb twice since the preliminary examination: once after Wynn was killed and a second time after Zeb's father was charged with Wynn's murder. And that was two more visits than any other client got between the exam and pretrial. Little happened in the case between these court appearances, and, on most cases, Jeremy's public defense clients simply did not see him during this lapse in the case.

Jeremy pocketed the messages and took Zeb's file to court with him in the afternoon. After finishing up his usual business late in the afternoon, he headed to the jail.

They met in the contact room. Zeb stared at the floor when he first entered, but as he raised his head, Jeremy saw that the boy's eye was swelled and blackened.

"Are you okay?" Jeremy asked, sincerely concerned for the boy.

"Oh," Zeb said. "Yeah. This? It's nothing. Got it a couple of days ago."

"What happened?" Jeremy said. "Is there something I can do?"

"No," Zeb said. "It's fine. Really. Looks worse than it is."

"How'd it happen?" Jeremy asked, pointing to his own eye.

"I was just watching the *X-Files*," Zeb said. "Re-runs. In the common room. And this guy comes up and wants to change it to Springer. I told him I was in the middle of a show. Big mistake."

"Who was it?" Jeremy said. "You know the guy?"

"Nuccio, I think his name was," Zeb said. "Somebody told me he was in for armed robbery."

Jeremy knew Doug Nuccio; he was Charlie's client. Perhaps the angriest young man on the face of the planet, according to Charlie. At just twenty-two, he had already done three and a half years in the Indiana state prison system. Nuccio was going to go down hard on his new robbery case, and telling him he could not watch *Springer* would definitely be the last thing Jeremy would consider.

Zeb was not smiling, and his usual buoyancy had evaporated.

"So I see that you called," Jeremy said, taking the messages out of his pocket and laying them in front of the boy. "Don't tell anyone that just because you call three times, your public defender shows up. I'm not a genie in a bottle."

Zeb did not smile. "I gotta talk to you about a couple of things."

"Okay," Jeremy said. "What's up?"

"One of the guys in here said he heard you on a radio show the other day," Zeb said.

"Oh," Jeremy said. "Studs Nolan. Yeah. You're making me quite a celebrity."

"I didn't hear it," Zeb said. "I would've liked to. But, this guy said that you were just getting killed on this show. Said they made you look pretty bad."

"Yeah," Jeremy said. He had looked, or at least sounded, pretty bad. "Well, like I've told you before, Charlie thinks that we should not be shy about media attention in your case. So I haven't declined any interviews. We want to get your side out there in the media, you know."

"But that guy," Zeb said. "He is a right-wing nut job. Nobody with my political views is going to get good coverage on a show like that. I don't even like people who listen to that guy's bullshit."

"Well," Jeremy said, smiling wide, trying to get Zeb to cheer up, "I didn't know that. I never heard of the guy before. I promise I won't go on his show anymore, okay?"

Zeb did not smile. He stared at his hands. The swollen eye looked painful.

"Did you ever hear of Huey Long?" Jeremy said, trying again to cheer the boy.

Zeb shook his head.

"He was a politician in Louisiana," Jeremy said. "And he once said that the only way he could lose an election was if he was caught in bed with a dead girl or a live boy."

Zeb said nothing.

"His point, I think, was that any publicity is good publicity. So I'm not too worried about *The Studs Nolan Show*," Jeremy said.

"My dad wants me to get a real lawyer," Zeb said.

Jeremy hated the term "real lawyer." His initial impulse was to reach over and slide his fingers around the throat of those ignorant clients who muttered those words. But, he had learned the more appropriate response.

"I think it's important for people to feel comfortable with their attorney," he countered. "And if you're not comfortable, and you can afford to hire someone else, I would encourage you to do just that."

"I'm comfortable with you," Zeb said. "I think you're doing great. I mean, my case isn't the greatest, is it?"

It was Jeremy's turn to remain silent.

"It's just my dad," Zeb said. "He had another guy pass me copies of some stuff in his police reports. Some papers they took from his house."

"Really," Jeremy said. He had heard few details about Mark Radamacher's case.

"Uh-huh," Zeb said.

"So," said Jeremy. "What are they?"

Zeb paused and then looked up at Jeremy with his one clearly visible eye. "They're from a case you took to the Supreme Court," Zeb said. "It's got your name on 'em as lawyer for some mining company. The case is really fucked up. These people got screwed."

Jeremy's conscious mind stopped listening when Zeb said Supreme Court. There was only one case he had ever argued before the Michigan Supreme Court. *Northwest Michigan Mining Company v. Della Passman, et al.* He was an associate with Barnes & Honeycutt at the time. It was his great contribution to the common law. He had practiced the argument so often that he could still quote large passages of it on the spot. As his mind refocused on Zeb, he heard him say someone had gotten screwed. Zeb was right about that. Della Passman and her neighbors had gotten screwed. Jeremy had done that with his own legal hand.

"So, after reading about that, and then hearing about how crappy you did on the Nolan show, I started wondering," Zeb said. "Maybe I should go with another lawyer."

He had heard expressions of doubt from many an indigent client, and generally, such ruminations had lost their sting. But, hearing these words from Zeb, Jeremy felt defeated. Here was a boy willing to risk life imprisonment for his cause. And, here was his attorney, who had once been willing to argue any side of any cause, without regard to social good or his own personal beliefs, in order to pull down a six-figure salary and a trophy wife. Jeremy thought for a moment that he should advise Zeb to get another attorney, because the boy deserved someone who stood for something.

"I think I believe in you, Mr. J.," Zeb said. "I think you're gonna fight for me. But this has me wondering."

"That's my case, all right," Jeremy said. "I remember it like yesterday."

"So you screwed these people over, knowing that the mining company was ruining their houses?" Zeb asked.

"Yes, I did," Jeremy said. "I took every fact I knew in that case. And I molded them. I took the law, some of it a hundred years old, and I twisted it. And I put it all together, and I argued for that mining company, Zeb. Because they were my client. And I was getting paid to argue for them. I saved them millions on that case. I did my job as good as I've ever done it, right there in that case you read."

"So you don't believe in anything about my case," Zeb said. "I mean, you think I'm a terrorist and that I was basically doing wrong to Blue-Mart?"

Jeremy thought for a second. "It doesn't matter what I think, Zeb," he said. "What I think is completely irrelevant. The only thing that matters in this case is what kind of plea bargain we are going to get. Or, if, God forbid, there is no deal, then what a jury is going to think. Those are the only things that matter. And, I'll tell you something. I'm the best lawyer in this county. If anyone is able to make a jury believe that you're not guilty, I think I'm that person. So, I think you'd be wasting your money on someone else. But you do what you want."

Jeremy's eyes had drifted to the left, as they often did when he was thinking out loud, and he had to shift his gaze to see Zeb. Zeb stared intently at him, his one good eye boring right through Jeremy's head.

"It matters to me," Zeb said. "I care what you think, Mr. J. I don't want no lawyer who doesn't give a damn about my case. I think that's what makes you a good lawyer. I think you care more about us than some of the lawyers guys in here got. But, I don't want a lawyer on my case unless he believes in what I'm all about."

Jeremy felt his eyes burn. Somewhere inside, in his heart or mind or self, he felt something for this boy. Zeb was right. Jeremy did care about his clients in the Wabeno County Jail. He cared about all of them. He worried about the treatment they would receive as they were being ground through the system. Whether they were right or wrong, guilty or innocent, he cared about them. And, he cared about what side of an argument he was on, too.

He had left Barnes & Honeycutt not long after the *Northwestern* case, because he could not stand plying his considerable trial skills in order to screw people over. He remembered Della Passman. An old woman whose only real asset was her tiny house in the upper peninsula. He had crafted a beautiful argument to deprive her of the value of that home. He had done exactly what needed to be done for the mining company, for his boss, for his firm and for Hannah. But in the end, Jeremy cared about Della, and people like her. Jeremy had been a witness to the pained expression that

Della Passman had worn for three years as the case slowly wound through its course. It had been that face that finally drove him out from being a cog in the machine, out to seek some meaning in his daily labor.

Zeb had helped Jeremy remember something about himself that had been dormant. Deep inside Jeremy knew right from wrong without a law book to explain it. Helping the Northwest Mining Company legally rob Della Passman and dozens like her was wrong. And that wrong had driven him here to Milton.

"For what it's worth, Zeb," he said finally, "I believe in everything you've done. I hate Blue-Mart. I hate sprawl. And I hate authority about as much as you do.

"I hate what I did to those people in that case. But whatever I think doesn't really matter. It's not going to help win your case. What you need is a great lawyer. And I don't think you're gonna find anyone better than me."

A hint of Zeb's usual grin returned. Jeremy was unsure if he really was the best lawyer to handle Zeb's case. But, for the moment, his belief in his client had made Zeb smile again. And that was worth something.

That night Jeremy picked up his ragged copy of *To Kill a Mockingbird* from his nightstand. He opened the yellowing pages and read for five minutes until his eyes grew weary. He marked his page with a dog ear, turned out the light and drifted easily to sleep.

He dreamed of a green sky. From the putrid clouds, a funnel leapt to the ground and spun grotesquely toward him. Trees and debris were ripped through the air as a cold wind struck his face. He ran to the basement, into his downstairs office. He was surprised to see Zeb and Doug Nuccio there, arguing over a television remote. Nuccio had leapt on Zeb and was beating him. Jeremy ran and struggled to pull Nuccio off. When he finally pried them apart, it was Hannah, not Nuccio, in his arms. "What are you doing to Zeb?" he screamed.

She didn't talk. She only smiled and looked at him with those longing blue eyes. It was warm now. They were not in his cellar. It was a bed in a bungalow. There was gauze screening around the bed, and he could smell the ocean. The Caribbean.

She pressed herself to him on the bed. They were both wonderfully naked, Hannah's skin smooth to his touch. He stopped kissing her and told her he needed to tell her something about Zeb, about how the boy had made him remember what it was like to believe in something. But, Hannah would not let him talk. She kissed him greedily.

When the alarm went off at seven, he hit the snooze with his left hand and reached out with his right, feeling for her before remembering she had been gone for more than a year. As sleep cleared, he remembered his conversation with Zeb. It had shone a light on a sense of justice that had been buried inside him by the cynical practice of law. It was good to feel it again, and he lay in bed savoring the feeling until the alarm sounded again.

18

Jeremy plowed through regular business in the morning and met Allie for their Wednesday lunch. Charlie had taken the lunch meetings with Allie well, hardly complaining about giving up a chess game once a week. Though Charlie was frequently hostile to newcomers, Jeremy was fairly certain his friend liked Allie a great deal.

At lunch Jeremy was still consumed with the conversation he had with Zeb the day before. He tried to explain to Allie. She listened like no one had ever listened to him, he thought. Rapt. Smiling. Wanting to know what was going on inside him.

He felt more deeply for her with each passing moment they spent together. He thought of her often during the week and found himself constantly looking forward to their weekly luncheons. He still did not believe they could ever be just friends, but he tried to enjoy whatever their relationship was becoming.

"That's great," Allie said, when he had finished. "I'm so happy for you. You could do with a little less cynicism."

They sipped coffee and shared a piece of blueberry pie for dessert. Jeremy did not feel like going back to the office. He would have been content to talk all day.

"You haven't talked much about your case," she said through a mouthful of blue, "for someone with such a renewed zeal."

"Too consumed with myself," he said. "You heard about MacAdam?" Jeremy had got the news from WHIP. Zeb's co-defendant, Jared MacAdam, had been arrested in New York City on Monday.

"Yeah," Allie said. "I'm doing a story for this week. Gray says he's waived extradition. Should be back here in a couple of weeks. How's that gonna effect Zeb's case?"

"I don't know," Jeremy said. "Could be motions to join, I suppose. We might end up getting delayed. Too early to say."

"So what are you doing for Thanksgiving?" Allie said.

Jeremy hadn't really celebrated any holidays since his mom passed eight years before. He and Hannah had traveled. New York for one Thanksgiving. Vegas for one Christmas. It was hollow.

"Nothing probably," he said, laughing slightly. "Swanson turkey roll and Stove Top. Tradition."

"No way," she said. "You're coming to our house. You can't have a turkey roll. What would you do if the press got a hold of that? You think they paint you un-American now? If this leaked, you'd have no credibility with the jury."

He agreed without a fight, and the next day, he arrived at Allie's house at 2:00 p.m., as scheduled. He wore his best grey wool coat, black pants and a pheasant tie. He brought a bottle of Chardonnay from the rack. It was the first time Allie had invited him to meet her family, and he wanted to make the right gestures.

She lived with her parents in Milton, in an old house that showed its age gracefully. The house was white with a green roof and grey porch. The grey matched the sky and the frosted grass. The porch swing swayed in the blustery November wind. The house needed a coat of paint, but looked otherwise sound.

"You must be Jeremy," Allie's mom greeted him at the door. She led him into the house and hugged him warmly. "We've been hearing so much about you."

"Nice to meet you," Jeremy said, handing her the wine.

"Oh, isn't that sweet," she said. "You can come on in and have a seat in the living room. Dinner will be ready in just a minute. Allie should be right down."

She yelled for Allie and returned to the kitchen. The scents from the kitchen danced past Jeremy and struck him with memories of his own mom and the Thanksgiving meals she had made for him.

He walked past a linen-clad dining table, set for four, and into the little living room at the front of the house. The Lions were on, and a large man was watching them from his recliner. He stood.

"Who are you?" Allie's father said.

"Hello, sir," Jeremy said, moving to shake his hand. "I'm Jeremy Jefferson. A friend of your daughter's."

125

"A friend of my daughter's?" he said, confused.

"Yes, sir," Jeremy said. "Nice to meet you."

"We haven't met before?" Allie's father said.

"No, sir," Jeremy said. "It's a pleasure."

"You watch football?" he said, motioning to the television.

"Sure," Jeremy said. "Love the Lions. Nothing like the Thanksgiving Day game."

"Want a beer?" Mr. Demming said.

"Sure," Jeremy said. "That'd be great."

Mr. Demming disappeared into the kitchen. He was gone only a moment.

"Who are you?" he said, upon his return.

"Uh, hi. I'm Jeremy, sir."

"Do I know you?" Allie's father said. He had no beer to offer Jeremy, only a befuddled look.

Allie came down the stairs. She looked like casual elegance, wearing a black sweater with matching slacks. She helped with the introduction, but Jeremy was sure that Mr. Demming would never know him.

Allie led Jeremy to the kitchen where they helped with the last-minute preparations. "I hate to have a guest working so hard on Thanksgiving," Mrs. Demming said, but her protest lacked conviction.

The dinner was a match for Jeremy's memories. The turkey was moist, the potatoes creamy and the stuffing homemade. He eagerly accepted a second helping of everything when it was offered. The wine complemented the meal to perfection.

Allie kept the conversation light and lively, including her father at every chance. It was no small task, given Mr. Demming's dementia.

"So, Allie tells me you two have been having lunch together every week?" Mrs. Demming said, serving generous slices of pumpkin pie under dollops of whipped cream. Allie shot her mother an annoyed look, but Mrs. Demming was oblivious.

"Yes," Jeremy said. "We have been. Your daughter is keeping me well-informed about the case I'm working on. She knows things I don't even think the police know yet."

"That's my Allie," Mrs. Demming laughed. "She's been writing for so long. Did you know she was the editor of the high school paper?"

"No," Jeremy said. "She's been holding out on –"

"Mom," Allie interrupted. "He doesn't need a history lesson."

As forks fell silent on the dessert plates, Mrs. Demming rose and cleared some of the scattered dishes. Allie helped her father back to his recliner. She pulled Jeremy to the couch, close to her, and they watched the Lions coast to an unlikely victory over the Packers.

Mrs. Demming offered coffee, but Jeremy was much too stuffed. The turkey was already making his eyes feel droopy.

"This place is great," he said to Allie. "It must have been fun to grow up here."

"What do you mean?" Allie asked.

"I don't know," Jeremy said. "The porch swing. The small-town atmosphere. It must have been –"

"I love that swing, too," Allie's mom said, coming in and sitting on the couch, close to her husband's recliner. "It's beautiful out there on summer nights."

"I grew up in a duplex. No porch at all. We always wanted a swing like that," Jeremy said.

"It's not too cold out there," Mrs. Demming said. "You should try it. This is a lovely neighborhood. John and I have been here, what honey –"

She paused, but John Demming was lost watching the television, oblivious to them. She continued, "It must be, what Allie, you're twenty-seven –"

"Mom," Allie said, a hint of annoyance creeping into her voice.

"What? You're twenty-seven. That means we've been here thirty years. A beautiful home."

"It really is," Jeremy said sincerely. They sat for a while, talking little. Allie's parents dozed off, John Demming snoring freely.

"I think I'm going to take off," Jeremy said.

The corners of Allie's mouth frowned, almost imperceptibly. "Okay," she said.

"Thanks for having me," Jeremy said. "That was great. I haven't had a home-cooked Thanksgiving in forever."

She slid on a coat to walk him out. On the porch, he paused to thank her again.

"Do you want to try out the swing?" Allie said, smiling that beguiling smile.

"It's a little nippy," he said. The sun had set and the cold of November was setting in. The first snow had come and gone last week. But Jeremy could not stand Allie's pout.

"Okay," he said. "But just for a second."

They swung together slowly. The gusty wind had subsided, but it was still cold. The chilled air made Jeremy more alert, counterbalancing the turkey.

127

"I'm really glad you came," Allie said. "Dad's not going to have many more of these at home. It was nice to have someone else here."

Jeremy put an arm around her and pulled her close to him.

"Jeremy," she said, looking at him directly, too close. "These lunches. Being friends –"

Jeremy ended her search for words with a kiss. Her lips were wonderfully warm, contrasted with the arctic air. He pulled her close. He was completely taken with Allie Demming.

Charlie was impressed by the small crowd that had gathered outside the Wabeno County Jail. He looked around the gathering and guessed that there were about fifty people in attendance. They had parked mostly in the sheriff's parking lot and congregated on the small grassy area to the south of the jail building.

A stiff wind and driven snow had kicked up in the morning and some of it had stuck on the ground. Charlie had almost decided not to go to the vigil, figuring that the snow would dampen, if not cancel, the event. But Jeremy had insisted that Charlie come out to see *Save Zeb's* candlelight vigil. So, Charlie ignored his Saturday night online poker game and made it to the jail by 7:00 p.m.

He spotted Jeremy and Allie through the dusk, huddled together against the wind, standing at the back of the gathering. He meandered around the crowd and came up behind them.

"I want to light my candle now," Charlie said. "It's cold."

Jeremy gave him a candle that had been stuck through a small paper plate. "Just wait," Jeremy said. "This is very organized. They'll tell you when to light it."

Charlie looked around the gathering. It was dominated by young people. Children really. Some probably in high school. Some probably undergrads. But, there was a smattering of townsfolk among them. Charlie recognized the faces, if not the names. Four students stood facing the group alongside Professor Quinn. They stood above the gathering on a small rise that nestled up to the south wall of the jail.

The crowd made little noise, save for individual conversations, muted by the wind. Then someone in the crowd started chanting, "Free Zeb Now." Like a wave, the chant was picked up by two, then ten, and soon the crowd was yelling out the phrase. The rhythm broke down and clapping broke out. The young crowd cheered its own enthusiasm, and Charlie's skin crawled. These people really believe Zeb Radamacher ought to have a license to burn down Blue-Marts, he thought.

Professor Quinn stepped forward on the small hill and raised her arms to quiet the gathering. "Thank you for coming," she said. "Thanks. We know Zeb Radamacher and Melissa Dobbs and now Jared MacAdam would thank you, too, if they were given a voice."

The crowd cheered Professor Quinn fervently.

"Thank you," she said again. "And we know that Steven Wynn would thank you if his voice had not been taken from him."

The crowd cheered louder.

"I just want to take care of a few housekeeping matters," she said. "And I'll do it quickly, because I know you're all cold."

Laughter. These people loved this woman, Charlie thought. And he understood why. She had a natural magnetism that he hadn't felt since he had heard Bill Clinton give a stump speech during the 1992 presidential election.

"We're treating this as a regular meeting. So, your contributions are welcome. We've set a goal of one to ten dollars, per person, per meeting, so give as you can best afford. Please see Lauren Owen, our finance committee chair after the meeting," Professor Quinn said.

"Also, for those of you who are new, and I see quite a few new faces out there, we are moving our regular meeting times. Starting in January, we will meet on the first and third Friday of each month. That's at 8:00 p.m. at the Milton library," Professor Quinn said and laughed. "But, if our crowds continue to get this large, we might have to rent a hall."

The crowd cheered itself again.

"We've got two speakers tonight, who I know are going to be as brief as I am," she said, turning and giving a mockingly stern stare to the students by her side. Charlie hoped she was right, as his toes were starting to numb. "Let me turn it over to Katie Reader, chairperson of our social action committee."

The crowd hooted as Katie stepped forward. She tugged a scarf off her mouth and addressed the gathering in a slight voice. "We're here tonight, on this Thanksgiving weekend, to show our support for Zeb Radamacher, Melissa Dobbs, Jared MacAdam and Steve Wynn."

The crowd was silent as Wynn's name faded into the cold night. Again, Charlie felt gooseflesh crawl up his spine, partly from the cold, but also from the momentum of the gathering.

"These people have given of themselves for a cause that we hold dear. They set out to protect our mother earth. To defend her. Some of them have given up life itself so that others might live.

"And in return, the government – a government set up to promote and preserve unsustainable growth – has thrown these defenders of the earth in jail. And it's threatening to throw away the key.

"We come together to say thanks to these brave people who have given so much for our cause. While they have been forced to spend Thanksgiving away from their families, we gather here tonight to say that we are one family. We support you. And we honor you. And if you will please light your candles now," Reader said, lighting her own candle, pausing, and then raising her candle up over her bowed head. "We light these candles to show our support for Zeb. And Melissa. And Jared. And Steve. And for our mother earth. Please join me in a moment of reflection and thanks."

The wind subsided and the hush was complete as the group collectively bowed, save for Charlie. He looked around, amused by their reverence. From the young girl's tone, you would have thought she was addressing a Russian mob in 1917, he chuckled to himself. But, even as he laughed internally, he wondered how many contented souls had stood laughing as the Bolsheviks began to rally their cause.

"Thank you," Reader said to polite applause. "Now, let me introduce the chair of the political committee to those who haven't met him. Mike Pearson."

Polite applause continued until the young man stepped forward.

"Thank you. Professor Quinn, I won't talk long. I can hardly feel my mouth," he said. He was tall, and his voice resonated even in the open field. Charlie was immediately struck that he was seeing a future political leader. "I want to thank so many of you for giving up a part of your Thanksgiving break to come out here tonight.

"There's a song from the '60s by Buffalo Springfield. I won't make you listen to me sing. But, he says, 'there's something happening here.' And friends, there *is* something happening here. I can feel –" he was drowned out by a heartfelt cheer and muted applause. Charlie was unaware of his own clapping, candle askew as he brought one gloved hand down repeatedly on his forearm.

"I've been out walking through Milton. And Watson. And Perkins. I've walked with some of you, door to door. To the houses in the towns. To the farms. To the businesses. And I haven't been welcomed by all. But I have been welcomed by some. They want to know about our cause. They want to know why our government is persecuting young people, who are doing no more than defending their communities."

The crowd again roared approval. Charlie could smell schnapps, but the crowd's warmth was more from the heart than from the bottle, he thought. Pearson continued to speak, but Charlie's attention shifted to the jail parking lot. He saw, under the yellow light of the street lamps, a group of sheriff's patrol cars come from the side of the building up through the lot. There were four cars, and they turned their overhead lights on as they parked in a line on the side of the lot. The small crowd had turned with Charlie to look at the cars. And, though Pearson continued, his voice became distracted as he, too, turned to look at the police presence.

Eight deputies exited the vehicles and marched in a line toward the crowd. Charlie recognized Deputy Short's skinny, angular frame as the wall of officers approached the hill where the speakers were. Mike Pearson had drained away to silence, and the crowd stood together in quiet apprehension. Charlie found himself frozen, certain that things were going to get out of hand.

"All right, folks," Deputy Short said in a loud, pleasant tone. "We've checked with the county, and you all do not have a permit to have a demonstration. So we're going to have to wrap things up and move along."

Short was a bumbling deputy, but kind, and Charlie thought his affable appeal might salvage a tense moment.

"This is public property," Professor Quinn said, stepping up to meet Deputy Short. "We are here exercising our rights under the First Amendment of the United States Constitution to peaceably gather and petition our government for redress."

Charlie was no civil rights scholar, but he was impressed by Professor Quinn's ability to quote the Constitution. Still, in this day and age of free speech zones, he doubted that she had much of a legal argument.

The crowd let loose some guttural support for their leader, and this time Charlie thought it was the schnapps talking.

"I'm sorry, ma'am," Deputy Short said, "but you need a permit for a protest of this size, and I'm going to have to ask you all, again, to leave."

Shouts of "Hell No!" and "Fucking pigs!" answered Deputy Short from the crowd. Professor Quinn turned to her gathering and raised her hands. As she was about to speak, Charlie saw a bulky deputy dart into the crowd and grab one of the protestors.

"This is the one who said it!" the bulky deputy screamed, now fully immersed in the crowd. Then Charlie saw a bottle fling out from the crowd toward Deputy Short. And the melee was on.

Charlie, Jeremy and Allie made their way out of the back of the crowd, which was pushing forward toward the deputies. They circled to the side of the conflict. Charlie saw bodies going down and punches flying. He smelled the sting of pepper spray and heard the thump of batons.

The skirmish lasted only seconds, until deputies had wrestled Mike Pearson and Professor Quinn into custody. Two deputies minded the detainees, while six others moved the crowd back with batons.

Charlie pushed his way past the crowd, a mob that was scared but still angry, judging by its sound.

"I am her attorney," Charlie said to the bulky deputy who was now guarding Professor Quinn. "There's no reason to manhandle her."

"She'll get an attorney later," the deputy said. "Now back off. Unless you want to go to jail, too."

"Is she in custody? Or free to leave?" Charlie shot back.

"She's under arrest. Now back off," the deputy said, through gritted teeth.

Charlie knew if he said more, he would have to bail himself out of jail in addition to posting bond for Professor Quinn.

The candlelight vigil was over, and it looked to Charlie like the *Save Zeb* protestors had lost the battle, if not the war.

19

Ten days later, Jeremy went with Charlie to Professor Quinn's pretrial hearing. The prosecutor had charged Professor Quinn and Mike Pearson with disorderly conduct and permit violations, both misdemeanors, after the confrontation at the jail. Charlie was representing both defendants *pro bono*.

Jeremy was entertaining Pearson as Charlie met with Professor Quinn in a conference room. While talking with Pearson, Jeremy glanced to his left and saw the back of an attorney entering Judge Welch's courtroom. The attorney had short, sandy hair streaked with grey, and wore a blue suit. He had only seen a glimpse of the man, but it looked like Michael Fuller.

Fuller was something of a legend in the metropolitan Detroit area. He was the criminal concierge at Barnes & Honeycutt. He had been the prosecuting attorney in Oakland County until he was forced out by one of his ambitious protégés. But Fuller had the softest of all landings. Jeremy's old law firm had brought him on as a partner to run a small criminal section which defended the relatives of rich clientele. It was a fluff job for the most part, helping the children of the elite avoid convictions on simple possession and drunk driving. Young lawyers at the firm were encouraged to offer *pro bono* time to Fuller's division, and the only criminal experience Jeremy had before coming to the Sage Law Office were the few pleas and sentencings he had done under Fuller's tutelage.

Jeremy continued to banter with Pearson, keeping an eye on the door to Welch's courtroom, hoping to get a better look at the attorney when he exited. When Charlie came out to exchange Professor Quinn for Pearson, Jeremy excused himself and slipped into Welch's courtroom.

Watching him in the courtroom, Jeremy had no doubt. It was Michael Fuller standing at the prosecution table, talking with Ed Gray. A young prisoner with wild, red hair was being escorted out of the courtroom. Jeremy slowly recognized the prisoner as Jared MacAdam from pictures he had seen in the paper.

"Michael," Jeremy said, approaching the bar separating the courtroom and the gallery, and extending a hand over to his old colleague.

Fuller turned from Gray and took Jeremy's hand in a vice grip. "Jeremy Jefferson of the North," he said. "How are you?"

"Not bad," Jeremy said. "What brings you all the way up here?"

"Oh, nothing much," Fuller said casually. "One of our client's kids, as usual. Guy runs a natural gas supply network. He's worth eight digits. And he's got his bastard kid up here trying to bring the capitalist world to its knees."

"Jeremy represents Zeb Radamacher," Gray interjected.

"Oh," Fuller smiled. "So we're going to be working together, huh?"

"You represent MacAdam?" Jeremy said.

"Yeah," Fuller said. "Just got him arraigned. Tough old judge." Fuller flicked his head toward Welch's chambers.

"Careful," Gray whispered, glancing to the microphones on the counsel table. "We're miked up."

"The guy just set a million dollar bond," Fuller laughed. "I don't give a damn if he does hear it. He's a tough, old judge."

Jeremy smiled at Fuller. The old rogue was so drunk with the power he had once wielded in the metropolitan southeastern part of the state that he did not understand, or care to understand, the sensibilities of the more rural out-state region.

"I gotta get running," Fuller said. "Tennis with old Barnes at Oakland Hills at two-thirty. I hope you can fix a speeding ticket for me if I need it, Ed."

Fuller told Jeremy to call him about the case and blew out of the courtroom like a storm. Gray trotted after him like a puppy, star-struck in the presence of the former Oakland County legend. Jeremy wandered slowly out of the courtroom. He hadn't talked to anyone at Barnes & Honeycutt for over a year. He hated the idea of working with someone from his old firm. Just seeing Fuller had reminded him of Hannah. Some things never change, he thought.

November gave way to December, and Zeb's pretrial date finally arrived. It had been months since Jeremy felt anything like nerves on his way to the courthouse. His first exam and his first sentencing day had made him slightly anxious, but he could never remember any nervousness, as he felt now, before a pretrial.

Judge Parr took no interest in pretrials. Consequently, the hearings usually consisted of informal chats in a conference room with the prosecutor handling the file. If a plea agreement was reached, the judge would slide the case onto his docket so the plea could be placed on the record. If no plea agreement was reached, papers would be filed to set the matter down for a trial date.

More than ninety-five percent of the cases were pled out at the pretrial, meaning only about ten criminal cases a year were set down for trial in Wabeno County. Of those set for trial, about half were either dismissed by the prosecutor or the judge because of defects in the case. The other half, generally about five cases a year, were tried to a jury. The numbers were from Charlie's experience, but Jeremy knew them to be true in his own short time in Milton.

The percentages made him hopeful that something could be worked out on Zeb's case. But the stakes were high for Zeb, and this made Jeremy's stomach knot as he walked into the courthouse and buzzed for access to Judge Parr's suite. He passed Carolyn, Judge Parr's secretary, with a polite hello and found Zeb in the lockup. They talked nervously. Jeremy knew that the outcome today would likely control Zeb's fate. A reasonable plea bargain would be nearly impossible to turn down in the face of such strong evidence; and the lack of a plea bargain would likely doom Zeb to a fruitless trial and convictions on at least some of the charges against him, with a hefty prison term to follow.

After a brief conversation, Jeremy left Zeb and found Gray sitting alone in a conference room, making notes in the top file on a large stack.

"What do you say, Ed?" Jeremy said, congenially. For Zeb's sake, it was time to swallow any pride and start kissing serious butt, Jeremy thought.

"Hey," Gray said. "Who do you got?"

Jeremy took easy deals on two other files he was handling and then broached Zeb's case. "All I got left is Radamacher," Jeremy said.

"Saving the best for last," Gray laughed.

"Yeah," Jeremy said. "We gotta do something with this kid, Ed."

Gray closed his file and sat listening.

"I don't want to overdo it," Jeremy continued, "but he is really a good kid. He's smart. He could go places. I know he screwed up here in a big way. But you don't want to send this kid away forever."

"Why not?" Gray said matter-of-factly. "I told you, if you had an exam, my offer was off the table."

"C'mon, Ed," Jeremy said. "Think about this. This kid's father is a nut case. This case has to be worked out. Give the kid a break."

"I did give him a break," Ed said. "I offered you nine before, and you rejected it. Your client is a fool. And a dangerous one. He was the ringleader here. I should've never offered nine."

"He wasn't the ringleader. He didn't blow anything up. He never would have. I told you that. My guy was the one talking about nonviolence. MacAdam is the one who went off the deep end," Jeremy said, noticing the TV-23 cameraman walking past, toward Parr's courtroom. He could not believe they sent a crew to cover a pretrial, and then thought Gray was going to give him some sort of plea deal and wanted the cameras to record the case resolution. "Don't forget. My kid gave up MacAdam and Dobbs. Without his statement, you'd have never gotten them. You gotta factor that in."

"I am factoring that in," Gray said. "That's why I'm going to give your guy one last chance. Guilty as charged. Nine-year cap. And he'd better take it, because MacAdam has rolled. He nails your guy right down the line. You've got no prayer."

"What? You cut MacAdam a deal?"

"Someone from Fuller's office is going to be up this morning to put it on the record," Gray said. "He's agreed to cooperate fully. Your guy is toast. So go get him ready to plead with the nine-year cap, and we'll get him on right after MacAdam. I'm not going to make this offer again."

Jeremy felt heat flush through him. MacAdam, the guy who actually torched the bulldozer and then fled the state, was getting a deal, and Zeb was going to spend his formative years in a state prison. "What's the deal?" Jeremy said, trying to compose himself. "What's MacAdam getting?"

"He's pleading to MDOP and arson, and we're recommending HYTA," Gray said. "In exchange for his full cooperation."

"You've got to be kidding," Jeremy said. Gray must have been licking Fuller's boots. HYTA, or the Holmes Youthful Trainee Act, was a way for young felons to get probation. If they kept their noses clean, the case would be dismissed outright after the probationary period expired.

"He's the guy who showed up and torched the dozer. It was his idea. He's your terrorist, you –" Jeremy stopped himself.

"That's not the way I hear it," Gray said. "But whether your guy is telling the truth or MacAdam's telling the truth, I don't really give a good goddamn. This case is starting to be a pain in my ass. And I'm done. Take the nine or we're setting it for trial. It doesn't matter. I shouldn't be giving your guy anything. We've got him dead to rights."

"Look, Ed," Jeremy said, calming his voice with great effort. "If this is about me calling you a fascist, I'm sorry. But, don't let it hurt my guy.

He's a good kid. I'm not blowing smoke up your ass. You can talk to him if you want. I won't even sit in. You're making a deal with the wrong guy. Zeb's not going to grow up to kill people, which is more than I can say for MacAdam."

"I don't want to talk to him," Gray said. "You talk to him. And I'd lean on him hard. Because if he takes this to trial, I'm going to be asking for basketball scores. Forty to sixty maybe."

"Okay, thanks," Jeremy said. He wanted to grab Gray by the lapels and knock some sense into the dense prosecutor, but he refrained. He swiped his files from the table and spun out the door before he lost it completely. He could feel sweat breaking on his forehead and back. He'd never been so close to screaming at another attorney. Had Gray really just said he didn't care who was telling the truth? He was the prosecutor. How could he not care about the truth? Jeremy walked straight out the front doors of the courthouse into the freezing December air. He watched his breath as he paced on the steps, feeling the biting cold in his lungs.

Freaking out was not going to help Zeb, he thought. Focus on what can be done, he told himself. Taking one last breath of cool air to calm himself, he returned to the courthouse. He met with his two bonded clients, who would be taking plea bargains. The routine of it set him back on form. He filled out the plea forms and advice of rights paperwork for each. He explained the deals, which they were both happy to take. He got their files to the clerk and had plenty of time to get back to the holding cell for Zeb.

"Mr. J. How'd it go?" Zeb said, coming to the front of the cell. Three other inmates talked trash to one another in the back.

"Not so good," Jeremy said. "He made the same offer he made at exam. Plead as charged with a nine-year cap."

"Nine years. That'd be on the minimum, right?" Zeb said.

"Yeah. You'd serve at least nine before being eligible for parole," Jeremy said. "No one can promise you what the parole board would do in the future, but my best bet is that you'd serve nine."

"We should reject that, right?" Zeb said. "You told me that was an awful deal before."

"Yes," Jeremy said. "It was an awful deal. Because we had a decent chance to beat the terrorism charge. But, the prosecutor tells me that Jared MacAdam has agreed to testify against you. So that might make their case on the terrorism charge stronger."

"What?" Zeb said. "He's going to testify against me? But he's the moron that got us into this mess. He blew up the bulldozer. Did you tell them?"

"Yes," Jeremy said. "But, the prosecutor isn't really interested. He's siding with MacAdam. He said we can take it or leave it, but it's his final offer."

"What do you think?" Zeb said, his face wrinkled with worry.

"I don't know, Zeb. I don't know exactly what MacAdam is going to say or how effective he's gonna be as a witness. And Gray is going to push for a steep sentence if we take it to trial and lose. You could be looking at nineteen instead of nine."

Jeremy looked at the boy. Zeb said nothing. What could he say? His lawyer was giving him no helpful advice and asking him to choose between Scylla and Charybdis.

"Zeb. I've got to know, now. No bullshit, okay?" Jeremy said finally. "You've told me the truth about everything? You didn't have anything to do with firebombing that bulldozer? That was all MacAdam."

"Yeah, Mr. J.," Zeb said. "That's what happened. I'm not that stupid. It says right in *The Handbook* – don't blow things up. It's not that effective, and it gets the police all wound up. I can't believe the prosecutor is taking his side in this. That blows my mind."

"Well," Jeremy said, picking the lesser of two evils, "I guess I'd advise you to reject this deal, then. I'm not gonna sit here and tell you to plead guilty, because if you had nothing to do with the incendiary device, the Molotov cocktail, then you're not guilty. We're just going to have to take our chances with a jury. Okay?"

Zeb agreed and slunk back to the other inmates, who glibly talked about who would serve more time at what institution. Zeb didn't belong with them. And the only way he was going to avoid an extreme prison sentence was to take the matter to trial, Jeremy thought.

He left the security door to Parr's corridor and turned to head toward the conference room to talk to Gray. As he looked for Gray, he saw her. Her face seemed out of time and place. She was talking with Gray at the door to the conference room. He could see her clearly over Gray's shoulder. Her eyes were stark blue and clear. They were striking, even from an angle. Her lips were painted on as if by a master's hand. Jeremy's legs carried him forward toward her as his mind swam. When he was halfway down the hall, she glanced at him, then back at Gray. Jeremy saw recognition wash over her face, and she turned back to look at him again.

Hannah beamed at him, her smile a white perfection. "Jeremy?" she said, stepping past Gray.

She met him with an embrace. Fifteen months were washed away. Jeremy's body was on auto-pilot as he struggled with his emotions. He hugged her from muscle memory, their bodies fitting together like a child's puzzle.

"How are you?" she said. "I've missed you."

"What are you –" he started, and realized the answer as she spoke.

"Fuller needed some help with one of his wayward youth," she said. "I told him I'd come up. It's good to get away from that place sometimes."

Jeremy saw a deputy leading MacAdam up the stairs.

"We're ready, Ms. Yale," Gray said.

"Oh, all right," Hannah said, her eyes still locked on Jeremy. "Could you do a city girl a favor and take me to lunch?"

"Okay," Jeremy said, still stunned to see her before him.

"I can't imagine where you eat around here," she said.

Jeremy watched Gray and Hannah as they disappeared into Parr's courtroom. Together, they were driving another spike into the coffin that Zeb's case had become. Jeremy drew himself back into the conference room and closed the door. He let himself sink into the generic office chair.

His eyes burned at the fresh memory of Hannah's face. He did not cry when she left him, when she sat at their apartment the year before, with that cold stare, telling him he was weak for running out on Barnes & Honeycutt. But he remembered his eyes burning then, as they did now. A rush of emotion wanted to escape him into the wide world. But, he did not give in. He sat and concentrated on holding back that part of him that had once loved Hannah Yale.

The door opened, and Tommy Hughes stuck his smiling face into the room.

"Oh, Jeremy," Hughes said warmly. "You using this room? I've got a client I need to go over a settlement with."

Jeremy tried to smile.

"No problem," he said, leaving. He brushed past Hughes and a heavyset woman wearing a neck brace.

"You okay?" Hughes called after him. "You need to stop doing all that criminal baloney and come work for me."

Jeremy laughed without conviction and turned into the men's restroom. He locked himself in a stall and sat, trying to control his eyes. He had two pleas to put on the record, and Zeb's pretrial, all with Hannah Yale hanging out in the courtroom, and he wouldn't give her the satisfaction of seeing him undone.

He concentrated on each breath without feeling. He did not love Hannah Yale, any more than he had ever loved practicing law at Barnes & Honeycutt. He had once loved the idea of those things. He had believed they were steps toward the American dream. Some concrete manifestations of wealth that he'd desired as a boy growing up in a blue-collar world.

But, when those things were literally in his grasp, he rejected them. They were false. They did not satisfy him as he had always dreamed they would. Hannah, and the money, and the condo, and the car, were all empty shells. Mythical symbols he'd been told to desire since childhood by an army of mass-marketers. But, once these products were consumed, they were not filling. And this nostalgia he felt for Hannah was nothing more than a dream. He knew that.

Hannah was window dressing compared to Allie. Seeing Allie made him feel like hot chocolate on the first day of winter. Touching her was like pulling on worn jeans. His feelings were growing so deep for Allie that he had been afraid even to examine them himself, until seeing Hannah. He took out his wallet and removed the picture of Hannah.

He stopped to check his eyes in the mirror. He concentrated on pulling himself together. When a collected lawyer finally looked back at him from the mirror, he turned for the door. He dropped Hannah's picture in the trash can as he left.

20

Bishop sat quietly with the governor and took in the rural squalor of Ed Gray's office. The prosecutor had given them the dime tour before excusing himself for court. The entire suite consisted of three small offices and a reception area, all tucked in the rear of the second floor of the Wabeno County courthouse. The walkways of the suite were crowded with file boxes. There was no security. All in all, thought Bishop, it was substandard by any measure.

Gray's private office was just a continuation of the mess throughout the suite. Boxes and files were scattered without order around a desk and chair. There were two chairs that sat facing Gray's desk. The walls were adorned with photos of Gray fishing and hunting in the north woods.

Gray had left his staff prosecutor, a young woman with a shrew-like face, to entertain them.

"So you were in the FBI," the shrew said to Howell, who was engaged by her attentions. "I always wanted to move over to the federal side of things."

"With experience like this," Howell said, "it shouldn't be a problem. I know the U.S. Attorney in Grand Rapids very well. Perhaps –"

"Governor," Bishop interrupted, "if I might excuse myself for a moment. I think I'll go check on how things are progressing. It was nice meeting you, Ms. –"

"Pamela Fitchett," the shrew said, shaking his hand. "Good to meet you, too."

Bishop closed the office door behind him, leaving the governor to his devices. As he headed out of the reception area, he let the security detail know that the governor was engaged in an intimate discussion. The governor was

141

prepped and ready to go. They had reviewed his speech for this morning's press conference as the King Air turbo-prop ferried them from Lansing to Milton. But Bishop was still annoyed by Howell's easy willingness to be distracted by anyone wearing a skirt. That the man had ever been elected to any office was a testament to modern marketing, Bishop thought.

He exited the office to the left, crossed a large hallway and took a seat in the balcony, which overlooked the stately circuit courtroom of Judge Lawrence Parr. The courtroom, in sharp contrast to Gray's office, was a jewel of interior design. He looked down on Gray, who was reading a plea bargain into the record. Bishop's eyes moved right. He recognized MacAdam from the news coverage. MacAdam's defense attorney was a striking blonde, her long legs shown off by a dress that was too short to be professional, Bishop thought. MacAdam and the defense attorney walked to the lectern to offer their plea.

Bishop had been kept advised of plea negotiations by the ever-eager Gray. When the prosecutor advised him that a deal with MacAdam had been struck – a deal that would assure convictions against Zeb Radamacher and Melissa Dobbs – Bishop had been quick to seize the opportunity. Radamacher and Dobbs had become the Bonnie and Clyde of the eco-terror movement, according to some press accounts. So Bishop arranged for the governor to come up and capitalize on this significant victory in the war against domestic terrorism.

Bishop had been anxious to get to Milton since the beginning of his political gambit. He wanted to eye his old nemesis again, to see the great Jeremy Jefferson struggling as a public defender on the edge of total defeat. As Bishop watched, he saw Jefferson enter the courtroom directly beneath the balcony. Jefferson sauntered in casually and took a seat behind the press corps that had jammed the courtroom. He looked far older and wearier than Bishop had remembered him. Bishop stared at his one-time rival until Jefferson turned to look up to the balcony. Bishop hazarded a slight wave, but Jefferson looked away, as if he had not seen Bishop or did not recognize him. This angered Bishop. Jefferson would damn well recognize him when this sad affair was over, he thought.

The governor's press secretary interrupted his viewing. It was almost time. Bishop directed her to get the press corps set up just inside the courthouse entrance. The governor would be down five minutes after Gray finished his court proceedings. Bishop then returned his attention to the courtroom.

MacAdam flashed a large smile at his attractive lawyer. The young man was to be freed on bond pending sentencing. The boy had no clue how lucky he was not to be caught up in the avalanche that was about to bury his partners in crime.

Zeb Radamacher's pretrial followed. It was short and uneventful. Jefferson formally rejected the offer of nine years in prison, as had been anticipated. The matter was set for a January 19 trial date, just five weeks off. Bishop punched the date into his electronic organizer. Parr then took a recess, and Bishop returned to get the governor.

The assistant prosecutor, Fitchett, flinched when Bishop entered Gray's office. She had taken the seat next to the governor, and their chairs were slightly closer than when he had left, Bishop thought. Surprise, surprise. Howell was going to be a headache to deal with as a national candidate.

"Sorry to interrupt," Bishop said, smiling, "but we're almost ready, Governor."

"I'd better get down to court," Fitchett said nervously.

"Well," Howell said, pulling a card from his breast pocket. "It was nice meeting you. Here's my personal secretary. Send me that résumé, and we'll see if we can't get someone over there at the U.S. Attorney's office to take a look at it."

Bishop smiled again as the shrew left. They went over the main points of the speech again. Howell had it cold. As long as the man could deliver a speech, Bishop thought, his personal qualities would not keep him from the White House. Bishop straightened Howell's jacket and tie, and when the press secretary knocked on the office door, they were ready for the press conference.

The security detail led the small group down the stairs to the main floor hallway, where a cluster of reporters, cameras and microphones were waiting. The governor stopped on the last stair, flanked on the right by Bishop and on the left by Gray. Bishop saw that the network affiliates had all responded with cameras. The *News*, the *Free Press*, the local paper and the local radio station had also sent reporters.

"The governor will have a brief statement," Bishop said, "and will be available for questions after."

"I've traveled here to Milton," Howell began, as lights flooded the hall, "because today we have won a small battle in the war against those who would harm our way of life.

"Milton is a small town. Until recently, you might have called it a sleepy town. It is not unlike other small towns in American history. Lexington. Gettysburg. They were sleepy towns, too. Until they became focal points in our country's struggle for liberty and justice.

"Two months ago, the calm and decency of Milton, and of our state, was shattered. Shattered by a cell of eco-terrorists who do not respect the simple rules of American democracy. The right to have an economy that creates jobs. The right to have a neighborhood free from violence. The right to have all voices heard, but heard in peace and respect. They broke that peace, here in Milton.

"But, I'm proud to be here today with Ed Gray, the prosecuting attorney for Wabeno County," Howell said, putting his left hand on Gray's shoulder. "Mr. Gray, and the police and firefighters of Milton have been on duty in this war to stop these domestic terrorists. To root out and destroy this eco-terrorist cell.

"And today, Ed Gray has won a small battle in a much larger war. Today, the first member of this terrorist cell has pled guilty. Admittedly, today's plea is from a low-level member of this eco-terrorist cell. But, he has pled guilty to his crimes and will now cooperate in bringing down the entire cell that he was a part of. It's a small battle, on a small battlefield. But, it is a great victory. And it is with these victories that we will win the war against these groups that would try to sabotage our very way of life."

Howell took a moment to pad his forehead with a handkerchief, and Bishop made a note to break him of this habit immediately, as it made the governor look like the buffoon he actually was. At least he was nailing the speech. Bishop was certain that anyone watching the six-o'clock news would get a great sound bite from the governor.

Howell continued, drumming up support for MEGPAT, before yielding to questions.

"Paul," the governor said, pointing to the reporter from the *News*.

"Governor," the reporter said, "analysis from around the state has consistently compared your MEGPAT initiative to the USA Patriot Act. Are you concerned at all that MEGPAT will be tarred with some of the same criticisms as the Patriot Act?"

"No, Paul," Howell laughed. "I think the people of Michigan have risen to the call of duty since 9/11, and I think that they believe the USA Patriot Act is a pretty darn good thing. It's a positive. So I'm happy that MEGPAT is being compared with the Patriot Act. I think there are a lot of similarities. And I think that's a good thing. Next question. Let's get someone local?"

"Sam Oster. WHIP. Milton," a local reporter said with a microphone. "Governor, I wondered if you could comment on Ed Gray's role in this process? And a follow-up. I understand there will be an eco-terror czar created under MEGPAT. I wondered if Ed Gray would be someone who you might consider to fill that post?"

"Thank you for the question," Howell said. "Like I said, Ed Gray has been on the front lines of this battle. And I think he's proven himself to be a soldier who you'd want to go to battle with. As for your second question, we'd just like to make sure the State House gets this law passed. Because Michigan needs it. But, when it comes time to pick an eco-terror czar, Ed Gray would be a fine candidate for that post."

"I'm very happy here, Sam," Gray stepped forward to respond. "He's just trying to get rid of me, Governor." The press pool laughed politely.

"Allie Demming. *The Milton Beacon*," Bishop turned to see a young, blonde reporter who'd edged her way near the front of the small press junket. "Governor, what would you say to the growing minority here in Milton who see the prosecution of Zeb Radamacher as a political ploy designed to distract attention from real issues, like the loss of manufacturing jobs in our state, and the loss of farm land to sprawl caused by developments like the Blue-Mart shopping center right here in Milton?"

Bishop saw Howell's eyes widen when he got a look at the drop-dead gorgeous reporter who had thrown him the hardball. "I'm sorry," Bishop interjected. "The governor is out of time. He's due back in Lansing." Bishop led the governor back up the stairs and away from the press gathering, who were already breaking camp to file their stories.

"Did you get a load of her," Howell whispered to him.

"Obviously not in our demographic with a question like that," Bishop said.

"Who cares about the question, Bish?" Howell chuckled. "She was a knock-out."

Bishop was far more concerned with the question. He wanted to know more about Allie Demming from *The Milton Beacon*, and whether she should be neutralized.

The courtroom had nearly emptied after Zeb's pretrial. The entire media contingent had followed Gray out of the courtroom, as did several onlookers. Jeremy had even seen an onlooker in the balcony during the hearing. Now, the gallery was empty except for Hannah, who had taken a seat behind the prosecution table. Jeremy could see her watching him out of the corner of his eye. He glanced at her a couple of times, and she smiled warmly.

Zeb had been whisked away by Deputy Short, and Jeremy was left with two other indigent clients. Pamela Fitchett from the prosecutor's office had come to take Gray's place. The pleas were routine. The paperwork was completed. Jeremy's clients played their roles to simplistic perfection. Yes, sir. No, sir. Guilty, sir. They responded to Parr's interrogation. And they were sent to the probation department to handle more paperwork. It took all of fifteen minutes to complete.

Parr recessed for the morning, Fitchett left, and Jeremy was alone in the courtroom with his audience of one.

"Kind of quiet around here," Hannah said, standing up.

"This is about as exciting as it gets," Jeremy said, packing his briefcase. "This case you're on has gotten more media attention than anything that has ever happened around here."

"Yeah," she said, "I know. It's a cause celeb all over the place. Major coverage. Even in Detroit."

Jeremy brushed through the swinging doors that separated the courtroom from the gallery, and Hannah met him in the aisle. He started for the door, but she stepped in front of him, moving with aerobic quickness.

"I thought you were gonna buy me lunch," she whispered with a seductive smile. "I didn't come all the way up here for nothing."

Jeremy was irritated. He could not believe he had wasted more than two years of his life with someone so shallow, and then another year missing her. Yet, if she had been here two months ago with some coy line, he knew he would have taken her in his arms.

"I'm seeing someone, Hannah," Jeremy said, looking up to meet her pale blue eyes.

"All's I'm asking for is lunch," she laughed blithely. "For an old friend. I've missed you, Jeremy. That place isn't the same without you."

"It's kind of a shock to see you," he said. "I really don't think I'd be good company."

"You were always good company," she said. She stepped close to him like a spirit, wrapped her arms around his neck as she had done a thousand times, and kissed him. She smelled like lavender and tasted like a familiar mint, but Jeremy was repulsed.

Before he could push Hannah away, he saw Allie enter the courtroom from the hallway. She stood in the doorway, at first a look of childlike bemusement on her face, followed by a storm cloud that darkened her brow and weighted the corners of her mouth. Even in complete anger, Allie was beautiful, he thought. Then she was gone, the door closing again.

"Enough!" Jeremy said, finally pushing Hannah back, too hard. She stumbled and looked genuinely hurt. "It was over a long time ago," he yelled.

Tears welled in Hannah's eyes, but Jeremy felt nothing. "Good-bye, Hannah," he said and brushed past her to the door. He did not see Allie in the hall, only a horde of cameramen filming reporters. Jeremy felt an immediate emptiness in her absence.

146

21

Allie ran from the courthouse, her coat over her arm, and drew a sharp winter breath. She was uncertain why she was running or why her eyes stung. She knew Jeremy had meant more to her than a silly conquest. But she had not realized the depth of her own feelings. She slipped on a patch of bare ice that covered the walkway to the parking lot and threw out her arms for balance. She stumbled on toward her Jeep, seeking some cover for how exposed she felt.

He had never lied to her, she thought. He had told her he still had feelings for Hannah. But his honesty did not comfort her. He was still a dog.

Allie got her first look at his ex-fiancée while covering MacAdam's plea deal. She was beautiful in a sophisticated sense, Allie thought. But Allie had felt no petty jealousy for her on first sight. Jeremy could not control who Barnes & Honeycutt sent to handle a plea hearing.

But the tramp was only in town an hour before Jeremy was back in her arms. In the middle of the courthouse, no less, Allie steamed. She didn't know whether to scream or cry or laugh.

The Jeep slowly cranked to life when she turned the key, and cold air from the heater met her burning face. She sped out of the lot, down a side street, and onto Main in front of the courthouse. She saw Jeremy running down the stairs toward her car, and, without thought, her right foot jammed on the accelerator.

Since she was a child, she'd always dreamed of Prince Charming. She'd internalized the stories she was told. Some day, she thought as a young girl, the right guy really would ride in and sweep her off her feet. Slowly, through awkward high-school romances and superficial college relationships, she had shed herself of this child's fantasy. Jeremy had re-awakened those silly feelings. But he was no prince, she thought now. There were no princes.

Back at the *Beacon*, she threw her notes down on her desk. She told the receptionist she was out for the day and drove to the supermarket. Chocolate for heartbreak was such a cliché, she thought, but she bought a pint of Haagen-Dazs and headed for home.

Jeremy's stomach ached as Allie refused his phone calls for the rest of the day. After work he went to her house. Her Jeep was in the drive, and the conflicted look on Mrs. Demming's face assured him that Allie was barricaded inside. But Mrs. Demming insisted she wasn't home, despite Jeremy's protestations.

He was tortured through a fitful night of sleep. He needed to speak with her. She had to understand how he felt about her, and that what she had seen with Hannah was not of his doing.

Jeremy arrived at the office early the next morning. It was vacant and silent. He had beaten Charlie in, which was a rare feat. He went to the downstairs waiting room and took a seat near the corner window overlooking Main Street.

He waited patiently until he saw her burgundy Jeep crawling up Main Street, cold exhaust trailing away into a sunny December morning. He bolted out of the waiting room through the front door. He ran haphazardly across Main Street and toward the *Beacon* parking lot, timing his jog so he could intercept Allie.

Her brow furrowed as he approached her Jeep, in anger or pain, he could not tell.

"Allie, I called you all day yesterday," he said, as she got out of the Jeep. "We've got to talk." Her eyes were puffy. It looked like she hadn't slept.

"What's there to talk about?" she said, jerking her arm away to avoid his grasp. She was pouting like a child.

He caught her wrist and she stopped, her eyes fixated on the freshly plowed parking lot.

"I can explain about yesterday, Allie," he said, not liking the sound of the words as they left his mouth. In his blind need to see her he had not considered what he would actually say, and he struggled for words. He could not tell her he loved her. It would explain nothing, and she would think him insane. They had only known each other for two months, and the relationship had only recently turned romantic. She would surely think him a freak if he told her how he felt, he thought.

"There's nothing to explain," Allie said, still avoiding his eyes. "We're adults. You warned me you still had feelings for her. You don't need to say anything."

"But, I do," he said, releasing his gentle grip on her wrist.

"She's beautiful –" Allie said, her voice cracking. She started toward the building. "I've got to get to work."

"Allie," he said, urging her to stop.

"I think you were right," she said, looking up. It was the first time he had seen her face directly since yesterday. Looking in her eyes, he ached to tell her how he felt. "I just don't think the timing is right for us, Jeremy."

"You don't?" he said, trying to hide his pain. "What happened yesterday was noth–"

"It might have been nothing to you," she said, her voice breaking again, "but you hurt me, Jeremy. I can't believe you were with her like that, in the courthouse."

He stepped toward her, and she let him put his arms around her. He wanted to tell her it was nothing. But she was rigid in his arms. He sensed that this might be the last time he ever held her, and it was bitter.

"I want to see you, Allie," he said. "I don't want us to end like this. I think there may be someth–"

She stepped back and dried her eyes with the inside of her wrist. "I – just – don't," she struggled with her breath, "think – the timing is right, Jeremy."

She turned and walked toward the Beacon building, leaving Jeremy alone in the parking lot. He grew colder with each step she took away from him, and he cursed under his breath. How could he have let himself get here, he thought, shaking his head. He walked slowly back to the office to bury himself in the day's work and savored the biting breeze on his cheeks.

Underneath a stoic face, Mark Radamacher was seething. The Friday morning preliminary exam was a welcome distraction from the mind-numbing boredom of the jail. He would rather serve time in state prison than a county jail, he thought. It was more violent there but certainly a lot less chickenshit than the local site of confinement.

The prosecutor was completing the redirect examination of Detective Imlach, but Mark's thoughts were elsewhere. He had plenty to be angry about. First, he was shot for no reason, costing him a kidney and a large chunk of his intestine. Then, a month in the hospital and another month in the damn jail. But, the thing that pissed Mark off the most was his attorney.

He'd plunked down fifteen grand in cash for Karljevic. And the shyster had basically disappeared. He didn't see him for a month. Mark's phone calls and letters went unanswered. The guy didn't know the first thing about his case. And then, the bastard shows up at the jail on the night before his murder exam smelling like gin, Mark thought. Mark was going to sue the shit out of this clown as soon as he got out of jail.

Mark had no doubt that he would be free shortly. He knew exactly where he'd been at the time of the murder, and if Karljevic didn't have his head so far up his ass, Mark figured he would have been free already. Guys in his cell block were telling Mark that the public defender would have had him out already, and that just pissed him off more.

He had listened to the testimony off and on throughout the morning, through periods of rage. He was damned happy to have an alibi, because the prosecutor's evidence was not half-bad.

The prosecutor's case started with a librarian who had seen Steve Wynn exit the library and then seen him fall to the ground after a gunshot.

The prosecutor then called the pansy-assed bike cop who had seen Radamacher's truck parked on Wisconsin Street, two blocks from the library on the night the boy was killed. The cop recognized the truck because local law enforcement kept special tabs on Mark's activity due to his involvement with the Christian Identity church.

Another patrolman was called to say that he searched the woods between Wisconsin Street and the library. The officer had found what he believed to be the shooter's location. There was a fresh beer can on the ground and a .30-06 casing. The patrolman later went to Radamacher's to serve a search warrant, where they confiscated his guns. The patrolman's testimony took a detour, as he described how he had seen Radamacher trying to grab Imlach's gun as the two struggled on the ground, just prior to Radamacher being shot. At this blatant lie, Radamacher had to physically cover his mouth to keep from screaming, "Liar!"

Milton's crime scene officer testified that he had collected evidence at the scene and from Radamacher's home. All the evidence was sent to the state police crime lab. Three reports were admitted into evidence: one was from the autopsy performed on Steve Wynn which, big surprise, showed he had been shot with a hunting rifle; the second said that Mark's fingerprints were on the beer can; and the third said the bullet fragments recovered from Wynn's head, and the casing found in the woods near the beer can, were both from Mark's .30-06.

Mark was shocked from his self-consuming anger as the physical evidence poured in. He had been baffled as to the identity of the real killer, but the evidence made it clear; either he was being framed, or someone had used his truck, his beer and his rifle that night.

Imlach was placed on the stand to tie the evidence together. He explained the prosecution's theory of the case. Radamacher parked his car on Wisconsin Street, took his rifle and can of beer, and walked to the wooded lot across the street from the library. He waited for the *Save Zeb* rally to break up, and then shot Steve Wynn in the head. The police were unsure if he had been gunning for Wynn, who was Zeb's accomplice or for Jeremy Jefferson, who Radamacher had reason to believe was mishandling his son's case. The two were of similar build and wore identical jackets to the rally, so Wynn may not have been the intended victim.

Karljevic had failed to lay a glove on any of the prosecution's evidence. Mark had watched Zeb's exam only two months before, and Jeremy Jefferson had made some headway with his cross-examinations. Radamacher was convinced he had hired a clown.

Just before the lunch hour, the private investigator that Karljevic had hired the night before, after he had finally taken the time to listen to Radamacher's alibi, returned from the Mid-Michigan Regional Medical Center in Perkins. The investigator quietly handed a bulky manila envelope to Karljevic and whispered something Radamacher could not make out. Karljevic held up the envelope and smiled at Radamacher, as if he had just discovered the polio vaccine.

Before Karljevic could explain, Gray finished the redirect of Imlach. The witness was excused, and Gray moved to bind Radamacher over on charges of murder and resisting an officer.

"Anything, Mr. Karljevic?" Welch asked.

"Your Honor," the buffoon said. "I've just been handed new evidence in this case, discovered by our private investigator. I would like to request a brief recess to review this evidence, if I might?"

"New evidence?" Welch said, like a man who was looking forward to the lunch hour. "What new evidence? What is it?"

"It's a videotape, Your Honor," Karljevic said. "We have been investigating a possible alibi defense in this case, and this videotape clears my client, I am told."

"I'd object," Gray interjected. "An alibi defense is not cognizable in the district court, Your Honor. It has no relevance as to whether you bind this matter over."

"Mr. Karljevic?" Welch said, raising an eyebrow toward the bumbling defense lawyer.

"Cognizable or no, Judge," he stammered, "I believe it shows my client's innocence, and I'd ask for a few minutes just to review the tape, if I might."

"I'll give you five minutes," Welch said. "Then I'll hear arguments on bind over. We stand adjourned."

The gangly deputy recuffed Radamacher's hands, and he was led back to the holding cell. The cell was like a tomb, Radamacher thought. He couldn't stand the tiny space for too long. Radamacher counted out the seconds before the deputy brought him back to the courtroom.

Karljevic had time enough to whisper, "The tape clears you. It backs up exactly what you told me."

Welch resumed the hearing. "All right. Mr. Gray, you've already moved for bind over in this matter, as I recall. Mr. Karljevic, you wish to oppose the motion?"

"Yes, Your Honor," the mesomorphic attorney said, rising to his feet. "Judge, this tape, which I would be happy to play for the court, absolutely exonerates my client on the murder charge. He was at the Mid-Michigan Regional Medical Center comforting a family that belongs to his church at the time of the killing. The tape is only one piece of evidence that establishes a clear alibi. I understand from my investigator that there are several very credible witnesses who will back up this claim. We'd have no opposition to your binding Mr. Radamacher over on the resisting count."

Welch looked down from the bench at Karljevic. His eyes sparkling with bemusement, incredulous. He paused for several seconds. "Anything further, Mr. Karljevic," Welch said.

"No, Your Honor," the defense lawyer said. "Unless you want to view the tape."

"I find that the evidence is sufficient to show probable cause that Mark Radamacher did knowingly and intentionally take the life of another human being, one Steve Wynn, and that said killing was willful, deliberate and pre-meditated. I further find that Mark Radamacher did assault, obstruct, oppose, disrupt or resist a peace officer, to wit, Detective John Imlach, while said officer was dressed in a recognizable uniform and while said officer was engaged in the lawful performance of his duties, to wit, executing a search warrant.

"I further find that the defense made some half-hearted effort to introduce evidence of an alibi at this preliminary examination. The defense attorney did not offer the evidence formally, choosing instead to make an offer of proof in argument only. In any event, an alibi defense is not cognizable by this court and would have no bearing on my decision.

The defendant is bound over to the circuit court on both counts. Bond is continued. We are adjourned."

Radamacher found his own mouth slightly ajar as Welch quickly disappeared from behind the bench. He looked angrily from the departing judge to his own attorney. "What the–" he started.

"Don't say anything," Karljevic interrupted. "I'll take care of this. It's an outrage."

"It's an outrage that I paid you fifteen grand and you didn't find this stuff out before last night, you fucking moron!" Mark screamed. "You're fired!"

Mark boiled as the deputy cuffed him and led him away.

22

Charlie took care that his Jerry Garcia tie fit nicely. As a rule, he hated ties and formal attire of all kind. He wore a coat and a tie to court – from J.C. Penney, circa 1990 – only because etiquette required it. But, he wanted to look cordial for tonight's *Save Zeb* meeting.

Jeremy was avoiding Allie at all costs, so he had asked Charlie to make an appearance at the meeting on behalf of the firm. Charlie accepted readily. He had thought of going anyway, and now he had an excuse. He slipped on a tweed jacket that had been with him since Cambridge and headed for the Milton library.

He got there ten minutes early, but the library lot was full. Cars overflowed out of the lot and lined the side streets. He found a parking spot a block away and jogged through the slush and cold, trying to spare his shoes.

Outside the library entrance he saw a young man lecturing three counterparts. "This is it," Charlie heard as he passed. "This is where Steve Wynn died."

The *Save Zeb* movement had slowly grown on Charlie. He had initially thought the group silly. A bunch of bloated youth charged up by a cause they could not possibly understand at their tender age. But, as he soaked in the atmospherics of the group, and especially the energy of their leader, Professor Quinn, he became more and more enamored. It reminded him of the groups that had come together at Harvard Yard to protest U.S. state-terror in Latin America in the '80s. He had been among them, with some deranged notion that their collective voice would change something. While

154

this group was far from the intelligentsia he had mingled with at Harvard, they had the same naive charm.

He spotted Professor Quinn in the library hall, speaking with her core cadre, directing their young energies like a general. "Charlie," she said, after she had dealt with her troops. "How are you?"

"Doing fine," he said. "I've got the easy part, though. Just showing up and enjoying these events. You look like these youngsters might wear you ragged."

"Keeps me young," her weathered look evaporated with an easy smile. "But I could use a hand, if you're not doing anything."

Charlie lived by the motto of Groucho Marx; he didn't want to belong to any group that would include him as a member. But his affinity for the professor outweighed his apathy. "Sure," he said. "But only if you'll let me buy you a cup of coffee or a beer after this is over."

"You got it," she smiled, and then promptly ordered him to check with the library staff about using some of the other meeting rooms. *Save Zeb* was becoming a hot ticket, apparently, and the small meeting room they had started in was not going to handle tonight's crowd.

Milton had a far nicer library than any little town was entitled to, thanks entirely to an endowment from a long-deceased lumber baron. The library was happy to accommodate the overflow crowd. In ten minutes, Charlie had arranged three extra rooms. Professor Quinn split her student leaders into four groups, each responsible for a different part of the agenda and sent them into four rooms. They evenly dispersed the guests, both *Save Zeb* veterans and newcomers alike. There were just over a hundred people. Charlie thought that half were certainly college kids up from Mount Pleasant. But the other half looked like locals to Charlie.

He followed Professor Quinn into a room and took a seat near the rear.

"Good evening," Professor Quinn said, as soon as she reached the front of the room. "I'm Wilma Quinn. For those of you who don't know me already, I teach social ecology at Central Michigan University. I want to thank you all for coming tonight. This is a larger turnout than we expected. So we're a little cramped.

"What we're going to do tonight is kind of like a buffet. We've spread out into four different rooms. In each room, you'll get an update on one of the various projects we are working on. This room will give you information on our social action program, which I think is one of the most exciting. When we're done here, we will all move as a group to the next room.

"So, without further ado, I'm going to turn you over to Katie Reader, our social action committee chair. Katie."

Professor Quinn scurried out, off to brief the other rooms. Charlie scanned the room, impressed by the diversity of the audience. About half were young people, mostly from Central Michigan, probably recruited by Professor Quinn, he surmised. But the other half was a hodge-podge of townsfolk. Men and women, old and young – faces he recognized from around town. Milton was responding to *Save Zeb*, and this surprised him a great deal.

Katie Reader introduced herself and was educating the newcomers on her committee's role.

"The social action committee, or SAC, as we've started calling it, is basically trying to accomplish Zeb's larger goals. It was something Professor Quinn said at our very first meeting that I remember. She said, 'Whatever happens in Zeb's legal battle, at least we can carry on and try to win the war Zeb was fighting.' And that is really what SAC is all about.

"So to get you all up to speed, we're setting out to try to reform Milton's government. To make it less hierarchical. And to make it more responsive to people. And we're doing that by establishing a Green Party here in Wabeno County, and then trying to get enough like-minded people registered to vote here, so that we can effectively control the local government. The plan is really pretty simple.

"So far, we're off to a good start. Since the last meeting, we have rented a house in Milton. We initially wanted to find a farm, but this house was the best we could do.

"It's going to serve as our headquarters. It's over on Maryland Street, if you want to drive by tonight. Maryland and Sixth. 522 Maryland. The committee chairs have all moved in, so that we can establish residence in Wabeno County and then get our Green Party affiliation started.

"Let me see. What else?" the young woman was a decent speaker, Charlie thought. Not spellbinding, but efficient. "Oh. I almost forgot. The Blue-Mart is set for its grand opening on January 9, I think. That's our next meeting date, so we're going to protest at the Blue-Mart that night instead of coming to a meeting. We're trying to organize a picket line. And we'd like to do some other cool stuff to basically disrupt things there. We haven't finalized the details yet. But, if you give your contact information to the membership committee tonight, we'll be sure to let you know. And we would really love to see you all out there with us.

"I don't think I have anything else as far as SAC business to report. So, if we just wait another five minutes or so, then we can change rooms. "Unless there are any questions?" Katie said.

Charlie saw a man wearing a John Deere hat raise his hand.

""I was just wondering what you guys, *Save Zeb* or SAC or whatever you call yourselves," said the man, who was seated near the front of the room, "plan on doing about helping organic farming?"

"I'm not sure what we call ourselves, either," Katie laughed and some snickering broke out in the room. "But, that's a really good question. You know, I can't speak for everyone. Because, if anything, our group is really about giving regular people a voice. You know, like a true democracy. So, I'm not up here to, kind of like, give you a policy directive or something. But I can say that it is a core principle that we want to protect our environment. Because it belongs to all of us. So, organic farming is a great thing. In my view, anyway."

Charlie liked the youngster's ability to handle the question. The answer had the man engaged, and the locals in the crowd seemed intrigued by her response.

"Well, I was just wondering. Because I've been reading about your group in the paper," said the man. "And it sounded pretty good. Like maybe someone would listen to us. Because I can tell you that no one is listening to small farmers right now. Politicians just talk and talk. But, none of 'em are doing anything. And you know, it's hard to compete with these factory farms. And you've got these builders out there buying up our farmland. You can't practically afford to farm anymore."

"Yeah," Katie broke in. "I know. It's called sprawl. And over-development. Building all those McMansions for people trying to run away from our cities. Professor Quinn can tell you a lot more about it. But, just from what I've learned from her, yeah, our group definitely would support organic family farms. And we're definitely opposed to sprawl. That's why we want you guys to come out and help us protest against the Blue-Mart. Because they are a part of that same problem."

A second farmer, seated next to John Deere, raised his hand.

"How much are you guys paying for rent in the city? Because, I've got a couple of farmhouses just sitting empty on land I work. And let me tell you, if you guys are going to stand up for the small farmer, then I'd like to help out. This is something that we've needed for a long time."

Charlie first thought that he was witnessing a spark of history. If these children were inspiring local farmers, then *Save Zeb* might actually catch fire. Maybe they were going to change the world. But then he thought he was being overly dramatic. Hanging around with Jeremy too much, he thought.

But, hearing Professor Quinn's ideas pour out of Katie and into the farmers of Milton made Charlie admire his academic lady friend even more.

157

*

The Christmas weekend started early for Jeremy. The courts were closed starting on Wednesday, and with five days off, Jeremy had agreed to go with Charlie on his annual Christmas pilgrimage to Toronto.

Charlie talked up his own secular holiday ritual like a travel agent. A snow-frozen city. The New York City of the north. A suite at the Royal York Hotel. Bourbon in the Library Bar. Dinner at Alice Fazoli's. It all sounded a lot better than a Christmas alone in Milton to Jeremy.

They were packed and ready to take off right after work on Tuesday night. On the way to the highway, Jeremy made Charlie stop at the Wabeno County Jail.

"Just five minutes," Jeremy said.

Inside, the evening guard set Jeremy up in a contact room with Zeb.

"Mr. J.," Zeb said, with his indefatigable smile. "How are you?"

"Great, Zeb. Merry Christmas," he handed Zeb his beat-up copy of *To Kill a Mockingbird*.

"Thanks," Zeb said, embarrassed.

"I've got to get out of here. Me and Charlie are taking a road trip. Few days of R and R. Thought you'd like this book, though. It's all about true justice. You ever read it?"

"No," Zeb said. "We were going to in English class this year. But, I've kind of missed some classes, ya know."

Jeremy laughed. "Merry Christmas."

"You, too, Mr. J."

A white Christmas, Allie thought, as she watched the snow fall like tickertape outside. She was seated at the dining table in her parents' home. It was Christmas Eve, and alone, she stared out the double windows watching the snow. She hadn't stopped thinking of Jeremy since she left him in the *Beacon* parking lot one week ago. He'd looked confused and saddened, his eyes those of a puppy dog.

She'd wrapped all her presents, save one. *Chess for Dummies* sat on the table, waiting for colorful wrapping paper. She had grown tired of Jeremy's constant complaining about his lunchtime chess losses and thought the book might help. Now, she wasn't sure what to do with it.

She'd been serious when she walked away from him. She did not want him to call. She did not want to see him again, except in court – and then only because it was her job. Her feelings were deep, and she wanted a clean break. There was no sense in involving herself in some strange triangle where she could only be hurt.

But a week later, thoughts of him were a constant annoyance. She could not physically avoid him in a small town where their jobs intersected. And everything she saw or did reminded her of him. Being alone made her question her resolve. Maybe it would be better to try, she thought. To risk being stung even harder. Last week it was clear. But now her feelings were like the directionless snow that swirled outside.

He was alone, too, she thought. His parents gone. Spending a Christmas Eve with his case files. Impulsively she picked up the phone and dialed his number. After several rings, she heard his tape recorded voice. She listened to the entire message, missing the cadence of his speech, and hung up without leaving a message.

She wrapped his book, carefully folding the edges. She would try him again tomorrow, she thought. Alone was no way to spend Christmas.

23

Bishop was less than pleased to be disturbed at home by Artie Fisher. He led Fisher to his basement office. Once seated, Bishop took great care to ensure that his stare communicated his displeasure.

"I'm sorry to bother you on New Year's Eve," Fisher said. "But you said you wanted to hear about any changes in the MEGPAT data immediately. I just got done working up the new numbers today."

Bishop had donned his tuxedo for the New Year's celebration at the governor's mansion. His hands knotted the bow-tie as he continued to glare at Fisher. "Why couldn't you give it to me over the phone?" he asked.

"I thought you'd want to look at these numbers in person," Fisher said, sliding a stack of paper across Bishop's desk. Bishop's cell phone blared out a techno tone, and he pulled it from his pocket.

It was Colonel Scott Thibodeau, the Director of the Michigan State Police, returning his call. Bishop motioned for Fisher to stop talking as he spoke with Thibodeau.

"Thanks for getting back with me so quickly, Scott," Bishop said.

"No problem. What can I do for you?" Colonel Thibodeau said.

"Well, we've been having some problems with a group of protestors up in Milton. They call themselves "*Save Zeb*" or something. You know, that Blue-Mart eco-terror case up there."

"Oh yeah," Colonel Thibodeau said, "Sure. The governor's been in the headlines a lot with that one. Sure."

"I've been following the activities of this group. There's a local reporter up there who's been covering them," Bishop said. In two weeks, Bishop had learned a great deal about Allie Demming. He had read everything she had written about the Radamacher case, and there was a definite pro-defense slant to her work. The quality of her writing was top notch; Bishop could have used those skills for his own propaganda initiatives. The local prosecutor had confirmed that Demming and Jefferson were becoming something of an item, and that they had both been at the *Save Zeb* rally in November that had turned violent. After his initial research, Bishop viewed Demming as a formidable weapon of the enemy. Both she and the movement she was reporting on deserved additional scrutiny.

"They've held a number of meetings and a couple of protests," Bishop continued. "You probably saw some of it in the papers. At one of the meetings a kid got shot. And, another protest turned into a riot, basically."

"Yeah," Colonel Thibodeau said. "I did see about the shooting. A crying shame. Kid was seventeen, right?"

"Yes," Bishop said. "Well, I'd like to keep an eye on this group. They seem pretty radical, and I'd like to have an eye on the inside. Keep them in line, if I could."

"Uh-huh," Colonel Thibodeau said. "I can understand that. Maybe we could bring in the FBI. A Joint Terrorism Task Force operation?"

"No," Bishop said. "No way, Scott. This is a state issue. The governor is all over it, and we don't want it going to the feds. We want to keep it at the state level. You think you could put a guy on the inside of the group? Keep an eye on them? Get info directly to the governor about their activities?"

"Sure we can. That's not a problem. You tell the governor we'll have someone inside in a week," Colonel Thibodeau said. "But, I've heard the Bureau of Investigations is backed up. I may have to steal someone off the security section."

"Sounds good," Bishop said.

"Okay," Colonel Thibodeau said. "I'm on it. I'll get you set up with reporting as soon as we have someone in."

"Great," Bishop said.

"See you tonight," Colonel Thibodeau said.

Bishop pushed the button on the cell and returned himself to Fisher's impatient face. "Okay, Artie," he said. "What we got?"

"See for yourself," Artie said, pointing to the thick report.

"I haven't got time for all the details tonight, Artie," Bishop said. "Just give me the headlines."

"I wanted to get a much more robust look at the numbers after that initial set I ran for you. So this latest data goes a lot deeper than the first numbers we looked at. It looks to me like your support on this issue is a lot softer than I thought at first. Especially among middle-of-the-roaders.

Libertarians. Conservatives. This thing might even give you problems with your base."

"I can't see the base deserting us on this one," Bishop said.

"Well, look at the numbers. MEGPAT has kind of got lumped together with the USA Patriot Act. And the numbers on that cut both ways. There's lots of strong support among our constituents. But, the other side gets a boost any time the Patriot Act is mentioned. And even some of our own folks are a little leery. It is kind of like 'Big Brother' to some of these arch-conservatives."

Fisher was a political hypochondriac. He was all theory and no practice. His numbers were always the best, but he had the political instincts of Czar Nicholas II. "Okay, Artie." Bishop patronized his numbers guru, "I'll take a look at the numbers. I promise. But not tonight. Got to go press some flesh at the governor's mansion."

Bishop led Fisher to the door and then returned to his basement office. He fastened his gold cufflinks and then laid Bishop's report in his crowded in-box. There would be time for political theory later, he thought. Now was the time for crowded rooms and false smiles; the real world of politics.

The days between his return from Toronto and New Year's Eve dragged for Jeremy. And now the nights dragged, too, he thought, as he sat in a booth at the Roadhouse Bar, staring at Charlie's grin and listening to Professor Quinn's intermittent laughter. The booth where the trio sat was cramped, and the high-backed wooden seat felt very much like the church pews that his mother had insisted he sit in on the Sundays of his youth.

Desperado, an *Eagles* tribute band, belted out their namesake song at a decibel level strong enough to make Jeremy's efforts at conversation pointless. Charlie and the professor were enjoying each other's company anyway, he thought. Three really did seem like a crowd tonight.

"I'm headed to the bar," Jeremy roared over the music. "Need anything?"

Charlie held up two fingers pointing at the bottles he and Professor Quinn had nearly drained. Jeremy headed for the men's room through the crowded bar. The bathroom door muted the music behind him. While he stood in a small line for the urinal, his hand brushed against the carving he had stuffed in his pocket.

He bought the small, Inuit soapstone at a shop in Toronto. The tiny figure, a bear dancing with a contorted human mask, reminded him of Allie and her love of native crafts. He paid a small fortune for the trinket, knowing somewhere in the back of his mind that he wanted to give it to Allie as a belated Christmas present.

He hadn't seen her car in the lot at the Beacon during the shortened holiday work week, and he really did not want to call her house, so he had let the dancing bear sit on his dresser for almost a full week. He had brought it to the Roadhouse tonight on the off chance that he might run into her. When he finished with the bathroom, Jeremy headed out of the noisy bar, into the cold, black New Year's night. He dialed Allie on the cell.

"Hello," Mrs. Demming answered the phone.

"Hello, Mrs. Demming," he said. "This is Jeremy. Is Allie home?"

There was a pause, and Jeremy thought he had lost his signal.

"No, Jeremy," Mrs. Demming said. "She's in Chicago for the weekend."

"Oh," Jeremy said, disappointment leaking from his voice.

"She has a job interview there on Monday," Mrs. Demming said, both proud and sad at once. "With the *Tribune*."

"Oh," he said. "Well, if you could let her know that I called."

"I sure will," Mrs. Demming said. "She gets back Monday night."

"Happy New Year," Jeremy said unenthusiastically.

"You, too, Jeremy. Happy New Year."

Jeremy rubbed his hands against the cold as he walked back into the bar. He got three beers and shimmied his way back toward the uncomfortable booth, through the undulating mass of New Year's revelers.

"Here's to a Happy New Year," Charlie yelled a toast. Three beer bottles clinked together. Jeremy let the beer roll down his throat and thought of Allie, celebrating somewhere on Lake Drive in Chicago. It would be hard to start the new year any worse, he thought.

Jeremy rose late on New Year's Day. His house was silent, except for occasional knocking from the hot water pipes. His head ached slightly from too many New Year's Eve toasts. But his heart ached more. He had an empty pain in the pit of his stomach. He thought of Allie, wondering where in Chicago she had slept, and whether she was alone.

He brewed a small pot of coffee and sipped the first cup, looking out his kitchen window. An ice storm had already begun to lay a coat over Wabeno County. He decided to spend the rest of the holiday weekend working on Zeb's case. He had piled several trial manuals and the case file in his car when he left work on Tuesday, and he walked barefoot on his frozen driveway to retrieve the materials. He spread them out across his kitchen table, poured a second cup of coffee and turned on the radio.

Sitting in his T-shirt and sweatpants, he plowed through the case again and again, pausing to think, scribbling notes, reading and rereading points of law. As the hours passed, he was able to release thoughts of Allie, turning himself fully to the task of defending Zebediah Radamacher.

Around noon his stomach ached again. But this time the craving was satisfied with a sandwich piled high with roast beef and turkey, and mustard slopped along the sides of white bread. He cracked a beer – the first of a case he had laid away for the weekend. He stopped his work to watch a bowl game of no particular importance.

Outside he saw the ice storm rage on, covering bare tree limbs and clinging to power lines. After lunch and a second beer, he stared at the game, but his thoughts drifted idly back to Allie. She'd always been ambitious, Jeremy knew. She was too big a personality for such a small town. It was amazing he had ever met her here in the first place. He had to admit to himself, that a part of the motivation for moving somewhere so small was to avoid people just like her. The beautiful, the ambitious, the self-important people of the world.

He thought of the meaninglessness of existing in a house alone, as he had existed for more than a year. And how he had found comfort in sharing the boredom of such moments with Allie. He thought another beer would suit his melancholy disposition well but then thought better of it. A third beer would lead to a fourth, and before he had given it much thought, he would be drunk and lonely, probably on the phone trying to call hotels in Chicago. An altogether pathetic vision.

He turned off the television and turned his attention again to the complexities of Zeb's case. Parr was hearing motions on the case on Monday, just four days off, and it was time for Jeremy to buckle down. Zeb's case kept looking worse as time wore on, but it was no excuse to be unprepared.

The storm blew itself out by late afternoon, leaving a crystallized world in its wake, all exposed surfaces casting shards of sunlight in through the windows toward Jeremy. WHIP was reporting downed power lines in the north of the county. Watson and Whitfield would likely be without power for two days. Poor bastards, Jeremy thought.

His narrow focus on Zeb's case held thoughts of Allie at bay, and Jeremy kept the same pattern of work on Thursday and Friday. A great holiday, he reminded himself sarcastically, over and over. The routine was broken when Charlie called on Saturday afternoon.

"You sound like crap," was Charlie's first meaningful comment.

"Thanks," Jeremy said, feeling worse to know that his pain was leaking out for the world to hear.

"What have you been up to?"

"Not much," Jeremy said. "Just getting ready for Zeb's motions on Monday."

"There's not that much to do, is there?" Charlie said.

Jeremy paused. "No. I guess I am about as ready as I'll get."

"Good," Charlie said. "We gotta go out tonight. You can't shut yourself up like this, man. She'll be back. You don't know anything about what's going on, so it's no time to start another round of depression. God, you were just starting to snap out of it."

"Thanks," Jeremy said. "You really know how to pick a guy up."

"The Roadhouse. Tonight. I'll swing by and get you at eight," Charlie said. "And take a shower, for God's sake."

Jeremy packed up Zeb's case file. He was as ready as he was going to be. It was going to take another distraction to keep his mind off Allie, and hanging with Charlie at The Roadhouse would have to do the trick. He napped until nightfall, showered and was just ready when Charlie got there to pick him up.

The Roadhouse was the best drinking establishment Wabeno County had to offer. It was situated on the bank of the South Branch River, about midway between Milton, Watson and Baudeau, and it drew a cross-section of Charlie's clientele from all over the county.

Saturday nights featured live bands, usually covering both country and rock tunes that were appreciated by Wabeno County's less desirables. When Charlie pulled into the packed parking lot, Jeremy saw that *Daddy's Still* would provide the evening's entertainment. No doubt they would fill the house, he thought.

They found a seat at the crowded bar, and Charlie ordered the first of an endless round of drinks. The beer was cold, and Jeremy drained one after another, trying to keep pace with his ivy-league associate. Charlie had a seemingly endless tolerance to beer. It was only when Charlie turned to harder drink that Jeremy had ever seen him inebriated.

The crowd was typical for a Saturday night, Jeremy thought. The bar was filled with bikers, hunters and aging women who escaped desperate trailer parks for an evening of possibility. As Jeremy became more and more intoxicated, his view of the bar became more narrow. He focused hard on what was before him, the periphery becoming an impressionist blur.

Charlie was explaining how he had shacked up with Professor Quinn on Thursday and Friday. She did not want to leave on account of the storm, and Charlie made room in his reclusive lifestyle to accommodate the fascinating scholar. The normal smile that spread under his thick moustache was noticeably wider as he talked of his liaison.

"She's your client," Jeremy said, his tongue thick and dragging at his words. "Have you no shame, man."

"Full disclosure. Full disclosure," Charlie said. "I advised her of the potential conflict, and she fully consented."

Time became disjointed as Jeremy poured down beer after beer. He looked at his watch frequently, with the evening being eaten away in large chunks. *Daddy's Still* covered pop-country tunes to the delight of the locals. Bodies brushed past Charlie and Jeremy on their way to the dance floor. At one point, someone stumbled into Jeremy and poured a cold drink down the back of his pant leg.

He turned and saw a woman, swaying with intoxication, who smiled and shrugged. She was attractive, relative to the crowd at The Roadhouse. She was Allie's age, Jeremy thought. She wore a tight pink shirt that exposed her midriff and hip-hugger jeans.

"I'm sorry," she hollered over the music, her voice rasped by years of smoke, Jeremy thought.

"It's okay," Jeremy said, staring at her and swaying slightly.

The girl stepped closer to him, standing on her toes to whisper in his ear. "Let me make it up to you," she said. "Wanna dance?"

Jeremy leaned back to look at her. "No thanks," he said, fumbling for words to avoid offense. "I – I'm not really interested –" Seeing a flash of hurt in her eyes, he realized he had failed miserably.

"Screw you!" she yelled and walked away, jostling others as she went.

"Well done," Charlie said.

"How about another," Jeremy said, but before he could hail the bartender, a large man stepped to the bar between Jeremy and his friend.

"Charlie Sage!" the man bellowed. Jeremy could only see a mane of greasy black hair and a broad back covered in a leather coat. "How the hell are you?"

"Adam Kann," Jeremy heard Charlie say. "Good to see you."

Kann grabbed another large man in biker garb and introduced Charlie. "Hey man," he said. "This is that lawyer I was telling you about. He's the best thing going. Got me probation last year after that beef with the old lady. Pretty slick."

"You're not drinking tonight," Charlie said with a laugh. "Wouldn't want to be violating your probation, now."

Kann laughed loudly. "Don't you worry yourself about that," he said. "Let me buy you a drink." Kann bought a round for Charlie and Jeremy. Conversation was stilted, but Charlie kept it going, and then Kann bade his lawyer farewell.

"He'll be in jail again soon," Charlie said, as Kann cleared earshot.

"Looks like it," Jeremy said. "You must be proud to have freed such an upstanding young man."

Charlie drank from his beer and bristled. "You don't believe in what we do, do you, Jeremy?"

"I dunno," Jeremy said. "I mean, when we do our job right, if we do a really great job, then what. A guilty guy gets off. What's not to believe in there?"

"We don't get any guilty guys off, my young apprentice. If the state hasn't got the evidence necessary to convict, then our guys are not guilty in the first place. There's no objective truth out there. A guy is guilty if he's convicted, or if they have the goods and make him plead. Our job is to make sure they have the evidence. That's all I do. In every case. I've never got a guilty guy off."

"If you can live with that bullshit," Jeremy said, "you go ahead." Charlie went on, defending his life's work with nuances, but Jeremy was distracted. He looked out across the dance floor and thought for a moment that he saw Zeb's face through the crowd. He scanned back to where he had looked but the face was gone. Too many beers. He checked his watch. It was after 1:00 a.m.

"I've had it," Jeremy said. "Let's hit the road."

"All right, pilgrim," Charlie said. "But, only one problem. I can't drive anywhere. I'm drunk." It was a rare admission from a man who drank daily and knew almost every cop in the jurisdiction.

Jeremy got the bartender to call them a taxi. They ordered one for the road, and by the time they'd finished their drink, the taxi had arrived.

"You hold the cab, brother." Charlie said. "I've got to piss."

Jeremy made his way through the crowded bar. He needed fresh air to clear his head, but the bodies jammed together, gyrating to the final honky-tonk set of *Daddy's Still*, slowed him. He finally reached the door and saw the taxi idling exhaust into the freezing night air. He approached, waved at the driver and opened the front passenger door.

"It'll just be a second," Jeremy slurred. "Someone right behind me."

"No prob," the driver said.

Jeremy left the passenger door open and walked back toward the bar to check on Charlie's progress when he heard a car door open to his left. He turned and saw Zeb again, standing under the yellow streetlights of the parking lot. Slowly, Jeremy realized it was not Zeb's face. It was his brother, Zachary, whom Jeremy had seen in court. Zachary reached into the back of a truck and pulled out a long-barreled gun. A shotgun, Jeremy's drunken mind noted. Zachary pivoted with the grace of a tiger, racked a shell and raised the barrel toward Jeremy. His motion was fluid.

Jeremy froze, his mind a blank, no time to think of terror or horror or reason. He waited an instant for the blast, knowing it was coming as surely as the sun would rise. The barrel was only feet away. A free throw, Jeremy thought.

Simultaneous with the roar of the shotgun came a jarring impact. Jeremy's body was thrown toward the open door of the taxi-cab, rather than being blown backwards by the blast, as he had feebly anticipated. As he landed, half in the cab, he thought himself lucky to be drunk. The shotgun blast did not hurt in the way he imagined it would.

He felt for blood and realized that another body was lying on top of him. He recognized Charlie's hair, the grey streaks a strange shade of yellow under the lamps. Charlie leaned his head back, and his mouth opened, releasing a strange combination of a moan and a grunt that sobered Jeremy. Jeremy pushed up against Charlie, his hand trying to feel for the blood he knew must be flowing from his friend.

As he struggled to get Charlie's weight off him, the driver started to move the cab forward slowly. "He's coming! He's coming!" the driver started to scream. Jeremy and Charlie slid from the cab as it moved, Jeremy's butt falling to the ground. Jeremy worried that his arm, or worse, his head, would be crushed by the moving taxi. But, that worry was washed away as he looked over Charlie's shoulder and saw Zachary Radamacher walking up, re-racking the shotgun.

I'm going to die in The Roadhouse parking lot with a soundtrack provided by *Daddy's Still*, Jeremy thought. He was more calm and sober now than he had ever been in his life, concentrating on a last, long breath. As Zachary inched forward, a blur of black came out of the bar, leapt through the air, and bowled the boy to the ground.

The blur and Zachary fell out of Jeremy's vision, and Jeremy rolled Charlie off him. Charlie's moan became a scream. His friend was alive, but blood was pouring out from Charlie's lower extremities. Jeremy did not want to look at his mentor.

The taxi had come to a stop, and Jeremy quickly peeped up over the open passenger side door. He saw the black blur, Adam Kann, and Zachary struggle briefly. Zachary freed himself from the burly biker and ran for his truck. No one gave chase. As Zachary peeled from the lot, Jeremy turned to Charlie and tried to stop the bleeding with his jacket. Jeremy did not vomit until the ambulance arrived; and then he threw up until his stomach was empty.

24

Jeremy had knocked his head against the door of the taxi, causing a small gash on the left side of his skull. With the blood and the vomiting, the paramedics insisted that Jeremy go along to the hospital with Charlie. He and Charlie were each laid out on separate gurneys on opposite sides of the ambulance. Jeremy watched one paramedic work feverishly over Charlie as they rolled away.

They were taken to Mid-Michigan Regional in Perkins. Charlie was rushed into surgery while Jeremy was parked in the hallways of the emergency room. Jeremy sat in stunned silence until a deputy came up to take his statement. He told the deputy who the shooter was, and was left alone again. The emergency room was cold, and Jeremy curled as best he could on the gurney and closed his eyes.

Charlie had saved his life, Jeremy thought. He had been ready to die one moment and inexplicably spared the next. In the aftermath, he could see that Charlie had been hit badly. And, as he lay shocked in the ambulance, he had heard the paramedics talking vaguely about the amount of blood Charlie had lost. Charlie was about the only person Jeremy had left in the world, and the thought of losing him was overwhelming.

Jeremy knew his own head was fine. He'd never lost consciousness. After a nurse put three stitches in the side of his head, he was discharged. But Jeremy stayed at the hospital for word on his friend.

He waited until dawn and learned that Charlie had been choppered to Ann Arbor. He needed more extensive surgery than the regional medical center could competently provide, according to a nurse who had been kind enough to bend the rules and let Jeremy in on Charlie's condition. Charlie was stabilized before he was flown out, and it sounded like he was going to make it.

Alone at the hospital, Jeremy realized he had no one to call for a ride. Allie was out of town. Charlie was fighting for his life. Jeremy's only real human connections in Milton were out of the picture. He called a taxi. When he got home, he slept until Sunday afternoon.

The University of Michigan Hospital wouldn't give Jeremy any information over the phone, other than confirmation that Charlie was admitted. Jeremy jumped in his car and drove three hours southeast to Ann Arbor. He found the hospital and found Charlie there, recovering from surgery.

Charlie was groggy from anesthesia, but the doctors said he would be fine. It was going to take some time to recover, but Jeremy's old friend was going to be around for a long time.

Jeremy finally left Ann Arbor at 3:00 a.m. and was home by 6:00 a.m. He caught one hour's sleep before the alarm sounded, signaling the beginning of a strange new work week.

He made it to court on time, ready for his motions, only to be told that Judge Parr was running late. Court would start at 9:30 a.m., Parr's apologetic secretary said.

Jeremy found Gray in the hallway. "Where have you been?" Gray asked. "Imlach's been looking for you everywhere."

"I went down to Ann Arbor."

"How is he?" Gray said, a look of genuine concern on his face.

"He's gonna be okay," Jeremy said. "He's a tough old bird. Lost about a quart of blood, but they said he's gonna be fine. Just needs a little rest. So have they caught that psychotic –"

"Not yet," Gray said. "He's on the run. But they'll get him."

"So does this tell you you've got the wrong brother in jail?" Jeremy asked.

Gray laughed. "I think the whole family ought to be sent to the penitentiary. If Mom would just step out of line, I'd nail her, too. The old man is here today on a motion. They're keeping him in the basement, away from your guy. I sure as hell would like to know what's going on with these lunatics."

"Me, too," Jeremy said. "So'd you get a chance to look at our motions? Anything you'll stipulate to?"

"Yeah," Gray said. "Let me grab the file." Jeremy followed Gray to the conference room. Gray paged through his files and said, "I'd stipulate to the expert fee. Your own forensic fire expert ain't gonna help much in this case, but I won't oppose it. No sense in injecting any error in this thing on my part. Our case is solid."

"What about the identification by Ratielle at the hardware store," Jeremy said. "Why not stipulate to a line-up?"

"Because I don't think you've got an issue there," Gray said. "I don't really want to concede it. Let Parr decide."

"You're not going to stipulate to a dismissal on the motion to quash, then?" said Jeremy, a crooked smile crossing his face.

"Yeah, right," Gray said, pausing. "You know, Jeremy, with all that's gone on in this thing, the shootings and everything. Charlie, for crissakes. I'm feeling kind of forgiving. I tell you what. It's against my better judgment, but I'll give your guy one last shot to plead. And I'll make it an eight-year cap. I'm cutting him a break, here. Otherwise, he's going down hard. You know it."

Eight instead of a possible twenty, Jeremy thought. Gray was probably right. Zeb was going down. Eight might be a life preserver. Grab on, and come out the other side a hardened activist at twenty-five. Zeb would still be young. But prison would break him. Jeremy knew it in his heart.

"I don't think we can take that," Jeremy said. "I'll discuss it with him. But, this kid is going to die in the joint if you send him for that long. Why don't you just give us what you gave MacAdam without the HYTA. We'll take our chances on the arson and MDOP in front of Parr, if you really want to cut the kid a break."

Gray shook his head. "Man," he said. "You don't know a gift when it's being handed to you. Take the eight, Jeremy. Talk to him. Let's do it today, or we're trying this thing."

Jeremy left to talk with Zeb. He found the boy in his oversized, pin-striped suit, in Parr's holding cell.

"Mr. J.," Zeb said quietly.

"You heard about your brother?" Jeremy asked.

"Uh-huh," Zeb said. "I can't believe it. I don't know why he'd try something like that. He's stupid, but I've never known him to hurt anyone before. I'm sorry Mr. J."

"You don't have to be sorry," Jeremy said. "It's not your fault. But, I have to tell you, you could probably get the county to give you another attorney on this case if you wanted it. I'm pretty certain that your brother trying to shoot me and almost killing my partner qualifies as a conflict of interest. You might not want me as your lawyer anymore. Who knows what I might do at this point?"

Zeb, missing any sarcasm, looked shocked. "No way," Zeb said. "I don't want another lawyer. You can't be my lawyer because of this?"

"I was kidding," Jeremy said. "But seriously, if you were uncomfortable. You know, if you thought I might sell you down the river because I'm pissed at your brother, then you probably could get a new lawyer."

"No way," Zeb said. "You're my lawyer. I don't want a new one."

"The prosecutor made a new offer on your case this morning," Jeremy said, shifting the conversation. "Plead as charged to an eight-year cap."

"Why does he keep coming at us with offers, Mr. J.?" Zeb asked. "He knows he has a crappy case, doesn't he?"

"I don't think so, Zeb," Jeremy said. "His case has gotten better, if anything. Having MacAdam to explain the inner workings of your little group really solidifies things for him. He made this offer out of charity. Because Charlie got shot, I think."

"Well, it ain't much better than his last offer. We're rejecting it, aren't we?" Zeb asked.

"That's not up to me," Jeremy said. He didn't like to lean on clients. He wanted them to come to their own decisions, even when the deals were a lot sweeter than what was being proposed to Zeb Radamacher. "It's up to you. He's saying you'll only serve eight on the minimum. And you could definitely do worse than that at trial. If you lose at trial, guidelines on the terrorism charge will be twelve to nineteen years. So this deal gets you four less than the guideline minimums. That's nothing to sneeze at. It is a significant deal. You should consider it."

"So you don't think we can win at trial?" Zeb said.

"I didn't say that," Jeremy said. "But, like I've told you a hundred times, they have some pretty strong evidence. And it's stronger with MacAdam. We could lose at trial."

"So you think I should take the deal, then?" Zeb said. His eyes looked pained.

"I'm not saying that either," Jeremy said. "I am just saying, you should consider it. Taking an assured eight years, versus taking a big gamble, where if we lose you're looking at twelve to nineteen. Maybe more, if Gray gets his way."

"We're not going to lose, Mr. J.," Zeb said, smiling again. "I've got faith in you."

"So you want to reject the eight-year deal, then?" Jeremy said.

"Yeah," Zeb said. "Eight or twelve or nineteen. Who cares? What's the difference?"

"You won't be saying that if we lose, Zeb," Jeremy said. "When you're inside, and eight years have passed, you're still going to be serving time. And that's going to be hard time, if we reject this."

"You're going to win, Mr. J.," Zeb said. "I can feel it. I'm not gonna take eight years."

Jeremy was touched by the boy's faith in him, but he questioned his own judgment. Charlie would probably be jumping up and down, leaning on Zeb to plead at this point. But Charlie wasn't here, and forcing a plea on a client wasn't Jeremy's style. Zeb had more than enough brain power to make his own choices. He just hoped the boy showed the same courage if they lost at trial.

Jeremy went back to the conference room, but Gray was already gone. Jeremy slipped silently into Parr's courtroom and grabbed a seat behind the prosecutor. Parr had taken the bench. The judge's natural demeanor was that of a stern grandparent. His presence was at once friendly and intimidating.

"Let's take the Mark Radamacher case first," Parr said. "I've sent Gaylord to bring him up."

There was a short span of dead time in the courtroom until Deputy Short led Mark Radamacher into the courtroom. To Jeremy's surprise, Tommy Hughes stepped up to represent Zeb's father.

Tommy explained to Parr that he was substituting into the case to replace Harold Karljevic. Once Radamacher consented to the change in lawyers, Tommy launched into his motion to release Radamacher on bond. It was a pretty persuasive argument. Apparently, Radamacher had an iron-clad alibi for the night of Steve Wynn's murder. There were affidavits from multiple witnesses and a videotape that showed Radamacher at the hospital at the time of the killing. When Tommy had finished his presentation, Jeremy had a hard time believing the murder charge was likely to move very far forward.

Ed Gray rose and tried to defend the murder accusation. He sputtered on about how the police had not had the opportunity to investigate the alibi evidence, and about how he fully intended to proceed with the case. But he was getting nowhere. Jeremy looked up at Parr's face and could see growing impatience. Finally, the judge stopped the prosecutor.

"Mr. Gray, this man is being held without bond, and there appears to be a very significant question as to his factual innocence," Parr said. "And we've all known about this since – when did this come to light, Mr. Hughes?"

"The videotape was disclosed to Mr. Gray at the exam," Tommy said, paging through his file. "December 19, Your Honor."

"So, you've known about this tape for over two weeks, Mr. Gray," Parr continued. "And you're telling me the police haven't had time to look into this alibi? I find that hard to believe." Parr paused, waiting for some answer from Gray, but the prosecutor said nothing.

"Well," Parr said finally, "it's within the sound discretion of this court whether to modify bond. There is significant evidence, which has been brought to the court's attention, that makes the likelihood of a conviction questionable, at best. I'm going to reduce bond in this case to ten thousand dollars cash or surety, which I think is more appropriate, given the state of the evidence. If you don't like that, Mr. Gray, you can file another motion to have me reconsider bond once your officers have a chance to review the evidence of alibi in this case."

Tommy Hughes beamed with his criminal court victory. Radamacher would be free for only a thousand dollars with a bondsman. Not bad for a civil lawyer, Jeremy thought. Mark Radamacher was also pleased, slapping Tommy on the back and crowing about the best lawyer in town. Gray's face was slightly reddened from Judge Parr's rebuke in open court. He'd been taking a lot of heat in the local media for his mishandling of the Wynn murder case, and this was not helping him.

"The only other motions we have this morning are on the Zeb Radamacher file, Your Honor," Gray said, ready to turn the page to a more solid case.

"All right," Parr said. "I see we have Mr. Jefferson here on that matter. Mr. Jefferson."

"Good morning, Your Honor," Jeremy said, taking his file to the defense table. Jeremy leaned over to Gray and rejected the prosecutor's offer. Gray rolled his eyes.

"Good morning," Parr said. "You have a number of motions on this case, Mr. Jefferson. Five?"

"Four motions, Your Honor," Jeremy said.

"All right," Parr said. "Could counsel please approach on this matter."

When Jeremy and Gray reached the bench, Parr leaned forward and smiled. "My law clerk didn't get a chance to brief me on these this morning," he said. "I was running a little late. Maybe we could talk them over in chambers for a while, and let me get a handle on the issues? Might be more productive than hashing it out on the record?"

Jeremy and Gray answered with the only acceptable response to the judge's confession of unpreparedness; they agreed and followed the judge to his chambers.

"Carolyn," the judge called, taking off his robe and placing it on a hanger at the back of his office. When his secretary peered around the door, he said, "Could you get the three of us some coffee, dear?" Carolyn disappeared.

Jeremy and Gray took seats in front of the judge's desk once Parr had settled into his chair. Parr's chambers were comfortable. Floor-to-ceiling bookshelves lined the north wall with an entire library of Michigan cases and statutes. His desk was natural oak, and the desktop was uncluttered. A leather couch nestled against the east wall, mostly for show. The south wall was dominated by a row of windows that looked over the courthouse lawn.

"So how are you, Jeremy?" Parr said, a look of honest concern on his face.

"I'm fine, Judge," Jeremy said. "A little rattled, I guess, but I'm okay."

"And Charlie?" Parr said. "I heard he was in critical condition for a while there?"

"Yes," Jeremy said. "It was touch and go for a while, but they tell us he's going to make a full recovery."

Parr leaned back in his chair, the fingers on his hands touching together in front of him. "This is a crazy world," Parr said after a moment's reflection. "I've been on the bench sixteen years and it just keeps getting crazier every year. But, I've never seen any case like this. So, from what I understand, it was your client's brother that tried to shoot you?"

"Yes, sir," Jeremy said. "Zachary." Jeremy remembered the barrel of the shotgun, its wide mouth yawning at him in what he thought was his last moment on earth.

"Maybe I shouldn't be getting into this," Parr said. "I mean, if you have any objection, Ed. Because you might end up trying to kick me off Mark Radamacher's case. But what in the hell is going on with that case? I mean the guy was somewhere else at the time Wynn was killed?"

"You're right, Judge," Gray said. "We probably shouldn't get into that case, at least not without Tommy here. He'll be crying about an *ex parte* communication if we talk about it."

"Well, I don't think he's too worried about that, Ed. He's got you beat. Why haven't you looked into the alibi? You've got the wrong guy. It looks like it was this other son. What's his name –" Parr turned to Jeremy.

"Zachary, sir," Jeremy assisted.

"– Zachary who went off the deep end. Killed Wynn trying to get Jeremy here. And then took another crack at him," Parr concluded.

"Well, that's a theory the police are looking at, Judge," Gray said. "But, it's too early to tell."

"I don't know, Ed," Parr said. "It looks pretty cut and dried to me. You ought to start looking out for your re-election campaign, because I'm telling you, mistakes like this on a murder case are not good news for an incumbent prosecutor."

"We'll get to the bottom of it, Your Honor," Gray said, reddening again.

Carolyn came in with coffee. "Did you want cream or sugar, Mr. Jefferson?" she said. Gray apparently always got the first class service, Jeremy thought, because Carolyn had already tanned his coffee with cream.

"Black's fine, thanks," Jeremy smiled. He was happy to be part of the club for a change. It was too bad he had to get shot at to get preferential treatment, he mused.

"So how long is Charlie going to be laid up?" Parr asked.

"He's going to stay down in Ann Arbor for about a month, they said," Jeremy said. "They've got really great rehab facilities down there, and they said he'd need that. Then another month or so off work is what they're saying."

"It's a shame," Parr said, Gray nodding in agreement. "Well, I'm just glad he's okay. Tragic thing."

Jeremy and Gray both nodded, waiting for the judge to end the Hallmark moment and get to the case at hand.

"Well," Parr said finally, "let's get down to business, then. First things first. Don't you guys think you ought to disqualify yourself, Jeremy, what with Charlie being shot by the defendant's brother? I mean you can't be much more conflicted than that, can you?"

"No, sir," Jeremy said. "I talked about it with my client, Judge. He understands the potential conflict, but he wouldn't consent to a substitution. He's happy with his representation."

Parr knitted his brow and shook his head. "Boy, I don't know. I don't want him to come back later and cry ineffective assistance. What do you think, Ed?"

"I don't care who his lawyer is, Judge. Just as long as we put the potential conflict on the record. I don't think there is any worry about reversible error there," Gray said.

"All right," Parr said. "Well, are we having any meaningful discussions about settling this thing?"

Gray looked at Jeremy and then back at Parr. "We've made a good offer, Judge. An eight-year cap. Four years under minimum guidelines. I don't even know if you'd go along with that. But, the defendant has rejected it."

"Four years under guidelines?" Parr raised his voice to emphasize the magnanimity of the offer, Jeremy thought. "Why isn't your client beating down the door to my courtroom to plead to that? I don't even know if I could go along with it, but what is wrong with that offer?"

Parr had a reputation as a friendly and competent judge. But he was notoriously lazy. He had honed arm-twisting to a science in order to resolve cases and keep his docket relatively trial-free.

"The problem is my client is not guilty of terrorism or arson, Judge," Jeremy said. "He can't plead as charged, because he can't even put a factual basis on for the crime. I told Ed that we'd be happy to plead straight-up to the MDOP with no recommendation. Leave sentencing to the court. That way, you can look at what happened and give him what you think he deserves for his role in this."

"So that's where we're at, Judge," Gray jumped in. "I've got him dead to rights on a life offense. Jeremy knows it. A trial is just going to be a slow plea. But that's where we're at."

"Is there anything I could do?" Parr said, still obliviously optimistic about settling the case. "I could give him a *Killebrew* or a PDI. Fix some sentence that he could live with."

"Judge, the guidelines on the terrorism are twelve to nineteen years," Gray said. "I don't think you're going to want to *Killebrew* a terrorist at less than the eight-year cap I've offered. I'm not the only one in the county who has to run for re-election."

Parr's enthusiasm dampened. "I suppose you're right there," he sighed. "Well, I guess if we have to try it, then we ought to get through these motions today. What do you have, Jeremy?"

"I've got four motions up, Judge," Jeremy said. "I think we may have resolved some things. First, I was asking for a thousand dollars for an arson expert. It's necessary for the defense case, and I don't think Ed's going to have any objection."

"I don't know about necessary, Judge," Gray said. "But, it's a life offense. I don't really care one way or the other."

"I'll give you seven hundred, and we'll be done with it," Parr said. "You can ask for more later if you still need it."

Jeremy considered it a victory. He had inflated his request by thirty percent on Charlie's standing order, borne out of years of experience with Parr. Jeremy had the seven hundred dollars he needed for his expert.

"I've also got a motion to suppress identification," Jeremy said, looking to Gray. "I think we might have something worked out on that, too."

"Judge, we'd obviously disagree that you should suppress anything on this one," Gray said. "But, a part of what he is asking for is a line-up. It's completely discretionary with the court whether to grant one, and frankly, I don't even care at this point. This case is so solid, you might just as well go ahead and give him his line-up. So we can stop arguing about this baloney."

"All right," Parr said, scribbling on a notepad. "That was easy enough. Grant line-up."

Jeremy sipped the coffee. "Good stuff, isn't it?" Parr said. "We have it ground fresh at The Morning Grind. Right there by your office."

"Great, thanks. I love that place. Go there all the time," Jeremy smiled. This informal confab on cases was what Charlie had called the practice of chambers law. It was a vestige of the good-old-boy network, and Jeremy had always felt uncomfortable with it. But today, he found himself a member of the club, and he had a momentary longing to be a good old boy himself.

"What's left?" Parr asked.

"I've brought a motion to quash, Judge." Jeremy said. Parr's eyes looked vacantly at him. The judge's attention span was waning. "The gist of it is that there was no evidence at exam to show that my client knew his acts were dangerous to human life. My client, if you believe the prosecution, basically burned a bulldozer. They're saying that it could have been harmful –"

"Did you brief this issue, Jeremy?" Parr interrupted.

"Yes, sir," Jeremy said. "A brief is attached to the motion."

"Well," Parr said, "I'll take argument on the record on that one. And I'll probably take it under advisement. Give my clerk a chance to go over the issue. But I doubt seriously, unless it's just cut and dried, that I will reverse Judge Welch on a case like this. Anything else?"

"Just bond, sir," Jeremy said. He was discouraged that Parr gave him short shrift on the motion to quash, especially after Jeremy had played his best game of good old boy, too. "Welch initially denied bond. Illegally in our view. At exam, he realized he was wrong to deny bond, so he did my client a great favor by lowering it to one million cash. We'd really like to get the kid a reasonable bond, Judge."

"One million is reasonable," Gray interjected. "This kid is the leader of a domestic terrorist cell, Judge. He is about to be convicted on a life offense."

"I'll listen to you out there on bond, then," Parr said. "Anything else?"

"No, that's it, Judge," Jeremy said.

"Great. Well, let's get out there and put all this on the record."

They rose. The judge put on his robe. "Oh," he said. "I almost forgot. I meant to tell you two. I've been contacted by Court TV about this trial. They want to broadcast it."

Jeremy rolled his eyes. He was about to defend a terrorism case against overwhelming evidence, without much of a defense, and now his performance would be broadcast to hundreds of thousands of courtroom junkies. He could imagine the hate mail already.

Zeb was led out to join Jeremy in the courtroom, and the judge put the discussions about the defense motions on the record. Parr then decided the contested motions in just a few words. After Jeremy and Gray argued the motion to quash, Parr said, "I'll take this matter under advisement and issue an opinion before trial." After Jeremy's impassioned plea for Zeb's freedom, Parr said, "I find no abuse of discretion by Judge Welch. Bond is continued." And with those few words, Parr ended the motion day. The trial was set to start in two weeks.

Jeremy spent the rest of Monday and all day Tuesday trying to get things organized at the Sage Law Office. Though he was a master in the courtroom, Charlie was a horrible manager. That much could be seen just looking at his desk. It was stacked high with open files, closed files, bills, both paid and unpaid, gifts, cards, overflowing ashtrays, scribbled notes, and enough books to open a secondhand shop. Some of the items appeared to pre-date the existence of the Sage Law Office itself, and when Dena ever dared to move any item, Charlie could always be heard howling later in the day about how he couldn't find some prime memorabilia.

With Charlie gone, Jeremy sorted through his boss' desk as best he could. Not only was he going to have to assume Charlie's caseload, but he'd have to take on the administrative headache of running a small office. Into Wednesday morning, Jeremy worked, and just as he felt things were starting to get organized, Dena buzzed him in Charlie's office.

"Allie Demming's on one," Dena said.

"Take a message, Dena," Jeremy said. "I'm swamped."

"She says it's important. Sounds like she's crying."

Jeremy took the call. Though his heart was leaping, he really did not have time for a distraction. But Dena was right. Allie was crying. Sobbing really.

"It's my dad. He's miss–" Allie sobbed. "He's missing."

"What?" Jeremy said.

"My mom called me at work," Allie said. "He's just gone. He's not in the house. She's looked all over the neighborhood. We're afraid he's gonna get hit by a car or something."

"It's going to be okay," Jeremy said. "Have you called the police yet?"

"N-n-no," Allie sobbed again. "You're the first person I called."

"I'll call Imlach and see if they can help," Jeremy said. "Then I'll be by to pick you up. You shouldn't be driving."

"Okay," she said. "Thank you, Jeremy. I'm so sorry to call. But my mom is so scared."

"It's okay," Jeremy said. "It's going to be okay."

Jeremy got Imlach on the phone. The official department policy was that missing persons had to be gone twenty-four hours before a complaint could be made, but Imlach said he'd send a couple of officers out just the same.

Allie was waiting at the *Beacon* entrance when Jeremy rolled up. She hopped in the car, drying her eyes, and they sped off.

"Thank you, again, Jeremy," she sighed.

"It's okay," Jeremy said. "Really."

A squad car had already arrived at the Demming house when Jeremy pulled up. A young patrolman was trying to calm Mrs. Demming on the porch.

"Any idea where he might have wandered off to, Mrs. Demming?" the patrolman asked in a soothing voice.

"I don't know. I've looked everywhere," Mrs. Demming bawled. "I've called all the neighbors. I only left him for a second. I don't know."

"Did you check down by the park, Mom?" Allie said. She had calmed herself on the ride over.

"No, I didn't go that far. I looked around the neighborhood and came back, because I thought he might have come home," Mrs. Demming said.

"Does he go to the park a lot?" the patrolman asked Allie.

"He used to," Allie said. "Before the Alzheimer's. Let's get down there and check."

"Okay," the patrolman said. "I'll send my partner to look around the general vicinity again, and I'll head down to the park to help you look."

But Jeremy and Allie were already on their way. It was only three blocks to the park entrance. The park was just across a small bridge on Ohio Street. A group of swingsets, a wooden playground and several snow-covered picnic tables were nestled on the bank of the South Branch River. A wooden walkway with a simple banister ran along the river's edge to the southeast into second growth forest.

Jeremy parked the car, and Allie sprinted toward the walkway.

"There are footprints," Allie said, running in front of him. Jeremy ran to catch up, and the two jogged along the wooden walkway, following the trudging footprints. The wind whipped along the frozen river and into their faces. The sting of January's breath made him feel alive.

Their jog slowed to a fast walk as they followed the path for some way.

"He used to take me fishing here," Allie panted, short of breath. "When I was little. There's a dock up ahead."

They ran again, and in a moment, they could see the dock through a thicket of leafless trees. On a bench at the end of the dock sat Allie's father. He was dressed in sweatpants and a T-shirt, and he sat staring out at the snow-covered ice on the river, paying no attention to the cold or to his own shivering body.

"Daddy!" Allie yelled as she ran down the dock toward him. "Daddy!" But Mr. Demming's stare did not move. Jeremy had to run hard to keep up with Allie. He was taking off his jacket as he ran, to cover Mr. Demming.

Allie got to him first and hugged him, as she sobbed. "Daddy! Daddy!" she said, over and over. Jeremy saw Mr. Demming's eyes. Perhaps it was shock, Jeremy thought, or perhaps he was remembering a perfect day from long ago, but there was a certain peace in his eyes that trumped the old man's rattling teeth. Jeremy put his jacket around Mr. Demming's thick shoulders and helped him to his feet. "Let's get him home," Jeremy said.

Mrs. Demming shrieked with relief when they brought her husband home. She warmed him with blankets and hot chocolate. He had not talked on the way home, but when he was with Mrs. Demming, he said, "Honey, where did you go?"

Jeremy thanked the patrolmen and called Imlach to thank him as well. When Jeremy finished his call, he said good-bye to a grateful Mrs. Demming, and Allie walked him to his car.

"Thank you," she said, hugging him.

"No problem," Jeremy said. "Glad he's okay."

He started to leave and stopped. "I missed you," he said.

"Me, too," a smile squeezed onto her face. "How's Charlie? I heard about what happened. I'm so scared for you."

"Charlie's going to be fine. I'm fine," Jeremy paused. "How'd the interview go?"

"Not bad," she said. "Let's talk about it over lunch tomorrow."

"Tomorrow," Jeremy said. Allie smiled at him, and he looked long into the depths of brown in her eyes. Looking at her, Jeremy remembered the calm in Mr. Demming's eyes as he had stared over the frozen river, and Jeremy was almost certain that the old man had been remembering the beauty of his daughter.

25

Though he didn't really have the time, Jeremy went to the Milton Diner and had lunch with Allie on Thursday. They hadn't talked for three weeks prior to her father's disappearance, and their conversation was stilted in the early going.

Allie was finally calm enough to let him explain what had happened at the courthouse with Hannah. He wasn't sure if Allie actually believed that Hannah had instigated the kiss in the courtroom. But she said she did, at least, and their conversation moved forward.

Allie seemed equally relieved to be able to explain her trip to Chicago over New Year's. She'd gotten a call from an old contact she'd made when she interned at the *Tribune*. They liked the stories she had written about the Radamacher case, and they wanted her to interview for an entry level reporting job. She said she was only interviewing for the position out of curiosity, to see if they would take her, but Jeremy saw the excitement that lit up her face as she talked about the big city newsroom at the Tribune Tower. The interview went well. They said they'd call her, but she hadn't heard anything yet.

Allie was full of questions. She was a reporter who was off the beat for a week, and she wanted to know all the details of Zachary Radamacher. Jeremy had already told the story ten times to the police, and clerks, and judges and Dena. But he told it again. He was still amazed to be alive and thankful to his old friend and to Charlie's old client.

They exchanged Christmas presents. She looked genuinely happy with the dancing bear. She bought him *Chess for Dummies*, and he feigned insult but was secretly glad to have a thorough review of the basics. With any luck, he would be ready for Charlie when his boss made it back into the office.

Near the end, just before leaving, there was a moment where everything seemed okay. They genuinely cared for one another, Jeremy thought. At that moment, he almost told her how he was falling in love with her, but his emotion was overcome by practicality. He knew she would be gone for Chicago if anyone at the *Tribune* had the sense to give her a job. If he confessed his love, it would only hurt them both when she had to leave, he thought.

After lunch he returned to the office to catch up on his trial preparation for Zeb's case. He needed days of solitude to get ready on the case, but Charlie's absence made that impossible.

"Ed Gray's on line one," Dena said as Jeremy walked in the back door.

"I'll take it, thanks," Jeremy said, and marched up the stairs to his office.

He settled into his chair and picked up the phone.

"You have to be careful what you ask for," Gray said.

"Why's that?" Jeremy said.

"Ratielle nailed your guy at the line-up," Gray gloated. Jeremy had forgotten that Zeb's line-up was set for earlier in the morning. Though Jeremy could not have attended anyway – independent lawyers were assigned for line-ups so that trial lawyers would not become potential witnesses in the case – Ratielle fingering Zeb was one more nail in Zeb's coffin, he thought.

"Did you get our motion to join?" Gray said.

"Yeah," Jeremy said. "Got it Monday, I think."

"Are you going to beef about it?" Gray asked.

Jeremy found little reason to complain about Zeb's case being joined with that of Melissa Dobbs except for the fact that he would have to work alongside Patty Ellis, a divorce attorney who had no business practicing criminal law. Zeb and Melissa had the same defense, and the case law supported joinder of defendants in these situations.

"I don't know," Jeremy said. "We'll see."

Once he got Gray off the phone, he threw himself into trial preparation with everything he had. He worked until late in the evening on Thursday and was back at the office before dawn on Friday for another marathon day. He left his office only for coffee, snack food and the restroom.

Dena disturbed him at quitting time Friday. "Don't forget," she said, knocking lightly on his open door. "You've got that *Save Zeb* thing on the book for tonight."

"Thanks. I would have forgotten about it," he said.

"You should go home," Dena said, worry in her voice. "You've been working too hard this week. You're getting those dark circles under your eyes."

He could feel the circles as she spoke of them. Dena was no older than Jeremy, but she had the quality of all good mothers – honest concern.

"Things will get back to normal soon," he said. "Now, go. Have a good weekend."

Hunger abated somewhat for Jeremy when he was under stress, so he skipped dinner to continue working up Zeb's file. At 7:45 p.m., he closed the file, left his desk in a state of organized confusion and headed to the grand opening of the Milton Blue-Mart.

Traffic, a fact of life that Jeremy left behind when he fled Detroit, was a snarled mess at the Milton exit off US-27. Minivans were backed up along the exit ramps in either direction, and there were lines of light trucks and cars in both directions along Milton Road. Wabeno County was turning out *en masse* to celebrate its own conduit to globalization. Low prices, low wages and low quality, coming to a rural paradise near you, Jeremy thought.

Jeremy was heartened when he saw dozens of protestors gathering at the entrance to the Blue-Mart parking lot. While looking for a parking spot, he saw Professor Quinn with a bull horn, directing a herd of protestors. Once parked he searched her out. She gave him a hug.

"I got down to see Charlie yesterday," Professor Quinn said. "He looks good. Said to tell you to hang in there. He'll be back in no time."

"I almost wish he hadn't saved me," Jeremy said. "Doing his job is probably worse than getting shot. What can I do?"

"We've got a sign-in table over there. Could you be a doll and go help them man that? We're getting a really heavy turnout. I think we could top two hundred tonight."

Jeremy did as he was told, and left Professor Quinn to her generalship of the protest. He found Katie Reader at the registration table, and she set him up with a clipboard to take people's names and contact numbers as they arrived. Jeremy was immediately surprised by the number of people who signed up at the table, grabbed picket signs and started marching. College students no longer led the way; well over half of those who showed up were regular working men and women from Milton. Some farmers. Some seniors. All enthusiastic in their support.

After a half-hour, Katie had passed out all one hundred and fifty protest signs. Jeremy saw there were more than two hundred people on the sign-in sheet. Professor Quinn seemed to have the ungainly group organized, and they began their picket of Blue-Mart, in Zeb's name. Songs of protest echoed from their frosty breath.

A large man, with crew-cut, blond hair, came to the table a little late for the protest. "Do I need to sign up?" he said to Jeremy.

"Only if you'd like to get on the *Save Zeb* membership list," Jeremy said.

"What's that?" the man said.

"We use it to contact members for fundraising and protests and stuff," Jeremy said. "All you need is an address or phone number. Or e-mail."

"All right," the man said. "Sounds good. I've got e-mail." He wrote, "Colin Green, cgreen74@email.com" in the space for contact information.

"Nice to meet you, Colin," Jeremy said, shaking the man's hand. The guy had a grip like channel locks, Jeremy thought. "I'm Jeremy Jefferson."

"Hey," the man said. "You're that kid's lawyer. You're Zeb's lawyer, aren't you, man?"

"Yes, I am," Jeremy said, smiling and looking at the ground.

"You're awesome," Green said. "You're doing a great job, from what I read, anyway."

"Thanks," Jeremy said. He could adapt to fame, he thought.

"Got any more signs?" Green asked Katie.

"Nope. Sorry," she said. "But you can join in. You look like you've got a great set a lungs."

Colin Green grinned at Katie and set off to join the picket line. Jeremy took off his gloves to blow on his fingers. He was ready to march and yell, too, if only to get warm. Out of the corner of his eye, he saw two men approaching in the shadows across the Blue-Mart parking lot. As they came under the parking lot lamp, he saw they were dressed in cheap slacks. The lead man's tie blew in the blustery wind. They headed straight for Professor Quinn.

Jeremy left his post to see what was up. As he approached he could hear the lead man. "This is private property, ma'am. If you don't leave now, we're going to have to call the police."

"We're picketing on a public sidewalk," Professor Quinn said. "Go ahead and call the police."

The Blue-Mart men walked slowly back to their store, the lead man pulling a radio from his coat pocket and talking.

"I don't suppose we bothered to get a permit for this protest?" Jeremy said to Professor Quinn.

"You're our lawyer now that Charlie's in the hospital," she smiled. "You were supposed to be in charge of that."

"Charlie's not going to be happy if you get arrested again," Jeremy shot back.

"Civil disobedience," she said emphatically. "It's our duty in the face of oppression." She put the bullhorn to her mouth. "All right, ladies and gentlemen. I've just been told that the police are on their way. Remember what I said about nonviolence. If the police come, just sit down and lock arms. I will lead the chant, if that happens."

It did happen. Ten minutes later, three sheriff's cars, one state trooper and an officer from the Milton Police Department all converged on the entrance to Blue-Mart. Jeremy walked back into the dark of the parking lot, away from the action. Someone needed to be around to bail them out, he thought to himself. A figure walked gracefully away from the protestors, and even in the dark, Jeremy could see it was Allie. She joined him, and together they stood and watched the drama unfold.

The protestors went to the ground, and, loud and clear through the January night, Jeremy could hear Professor Quinn's raised voice. "We Are!" she yelled, and the echo came from her ever-growing band. "Nonviolent!" "We Want!" "Justice!" The police response was better than the night at the jail, Jeremy thought. They had obviously received some training in dealing with the protests. The officers separated the human chain, intermittently handcuffing and carting off some, while others were taken to an impromptu holding area the police rigged with crime scene tape. The protest was effectively broken up in an hour. Only a handful of protestors were arrested; the rest were issued citations. Professor Quinn, her rank marked by the loud speaker, was taken to the Wabeno County Jail.

All the while, the good consumers of Wabeno ignored the protest as best they could. They parked and headed to the Blue-Mart entrances, where Jeremy imagined them doing their patriotic duty, shopping for cheese puffs, towels, tennis shoes, video games, snow blowers and thousands of other products made by peasants half a world a way.

Jeremy had Professor Quinn out on bail by 11:00 p.m. Charlie would have been proud.

26

Mark Radamacher rose early with the sun. It had been six days since his release from the Wabeno County Jail, and on each morning he woke with the sun. He'd spent over a month in jail, on account of the shyster lawyer, and his time there had brought back his nightmares of his time in prison. The finality of the metal doors, closing each man off, compartment by compartment, stealing every moment of freedom. There was no privacy in confinement. And over days, weeks, months and years, it was this inability to find even a moment's worth of time to oneself that was unfathomable when it came to doing hard time.

He grabbed a cigarette from his night table, lit it and headed for the kitchen. It was 6:30 a.m. His flock would be rising now, readying themselves for church on Sunday morning. It was his first chance to address them since he had been shot and taken away. He was driven with the anticipation of seeing them again. The energy they gave him was immense.

He had thought often of his son Zachary during the past two months, and what the boy had wrought out of his own naive goodness. As the evidence fell into place, what had happened became obvious to Mark. Zachary was an obedient son. He had the heart and courage of a Phineas Priest – a solider enforcing God's will. And God had spared the boy from an intellect that would cause him a moment's indecision. When Zachary was told what to do, he always did it. And if left to his own device, he always did what he thought was right, without hesitation.

Zachary had known that Zeb was in great danger from the liberal, Jew lawyer from Detroit. That message had permeated Zachary like stain on weathered wood. And though he wasn't told to erase this danger, he had

187

tried to do what needed to be done. Mark had pieced Zachary's actions together from what he knew and from what he could surmise, so that they ran like a motion picture in his mind.

Zachary had found himself alone on that Friday night after Zeb's exam when Mark went with a family from his congregation to administer last rites at the hospital. He had heard Mark repeatedly preach about the evil incarnate that Jeremy Jefferson represented. He drank a few beers, probably to calm himself before the act he was about to commit. He'd taken Mark's .30-06 out of the cabinet, grabbed Mark's keys and set off to the Milton library, where he knew Jefferson was meeting with the other commie environmentalists. He'd taken a final beer along for the drive.

He parked on Wisconsin Street, where the police officer saw Mark's truck, and snuck into the lot across from the library. He probably used the tree-blind from the back of the truck to get a good angle on his prey. He waited for the meeting to let out, and he sighted Jefferson through the scope. It was dark, Mark had imagined, but Zachary saw the tall figure with the brown bomber jacket walk out of the library. It was an easy shot from less than one hundred yards.

Then, like a boy who first shoots a buck, Zachary panicked. He left his sniper's nest without policing the casing from the rifle. Worse, he was drunk enough to leave a beer can at the scene. And his son sped home, thinking he had taken care of a great evil, believing he had done God's will.

It was really only luck that Mark's alibi was as tight as it was, because the evidence Zachary left behind surely would have sent Mark to prison for the rest of his life. As it was, Mark was out a kidney, some intestine and two months of freedom – a heavy price. God had made Zachary righteous, with the faith of a child. But, the boy's simplicity had almost cost Mark his life.

Undeterred, and knowing his mission had not been completed, Zachary was even more rash in his second attempt on the lawyer. He just walked up with a shotgun, in front of at least three witnesses, and tried to blow Jeremy Jefferson away. Bad luck that he missed him; but, now Zachary had thrown his own life away. He was looking at attempted murder at a minimum, and they would surely understand his role in Wynn's murder in good time. The boy could not hide forever, and Mark shuddered to think of the horrors that would await his simple son in the modern day dungeons of Sodom and Gomorrah.

He cooked some bacon on the stove top while a pot of fresh coffee brewed. He looked out of his kitchen window at the sunlight rising up and making the icy crust of snow sparkle like fool's gold. He buttered toast, sopped grease from the bacon and took his breakfast into the study. He sat down at the black walnut desk and studied the notes he had written for today's sermon.

Today's sermon would be impassioned. He could feel the energy held by the words on paper. And when the words passed up through him and out to his flock, mirrored back by their eyes, and by their shouts of praise to God, it would be powerful.

He eyed the passage from Genesis. Today he would tell his flock again the story of Abraham, that great patriarch of all Aryan men, whom God made show his loyalty by commanding him to sacrifice his only son. Today, the story would have renewed life in Mark's voice.

Mark was not surprised by the knock on his front door. Al Devine had come to give Mark the news himself, and that was an honor.

"Good morning, Pastor Radamacher," Devine said.

Mark showed Devine to the kitchen and got him a cup of coffee. It was the least he could do for the Grand Dragon of the Michigan Klan.

"Your parcel is safe, Pastor Radamacher," Devine said. Mark knew that Zachary had made it to the safety of Al Devine's compound. That would keep him away from the police and the animals in prison, at least until the matter could be handled respectfully.

"Thank you," Mark said. "I will retrieve it as soon as I am able."

They did not speak of Zachary again, instead turning their morning conversation to their love of God, and his righteous hatred of the sons of Cain.

Jeremy's weekend consisted of Zeb's case and little sleep. When Monday rolled around, he was exhausted. He hit snooze three times but still managed to make it into the office on time. He had court on his two most difficult cases. There was the prosecutor's motion for joinder on Zeb's case, and there was a pre-disposition investigation on Doug Nuccio's case, a very delicate matter.

Judge Parr cleared off his civil docket through the early part of the morning, and Jeremy used the time to study up on Doug Nuccio's case. Charlie had been the lead attorney on the file, but with him out of action, the case fell to Jeremy.

Nuccio was a vicious thug. The predisposition report that Jeremy reviewed confirmed this conclusion with each paragraph. Nuccio's father had abused him, according to the report, before the father was sent to prison on criminal sexual assault charges. It was an inauspicious start for the young Nuccio.

He spent the better part of his adolescence in state homes in Indiana, due to convictions for cruelty to animals, auto theft and felony battery. At seventeen, he stabbed a neighbor boy in a fight over a girl. Somehow he managed to get only three and a half years in prison for battery with a dangerous weapon.

By the time he was twenty-two, the prison system had, quite literally, raped any inkling of human decency out of the young man. When he emerged from prison in the spring, he moved to Michigan to live with family friends. He wore his prison anger as openly as the tattoos that marked his torso and arms. He was resentful of almost everyone and everything. He played every bit the role of rabid dog that society had come to expect from him.

The charges he now faced, which were sure to earn him a formidable prison sentence, were an act of criminal genius, Jeremy thought. Nuccio and his girlfriend were angry at her parents, who lived in Perkins, because the parents would not offer money to help the young couple start a new life. Nuccio hatched a simple plan to get even. When nightfall came, he broke into the parents' home while armed with a nine millimeter pistol, outfitted with a laser-sight. He wore a mask, but it did little good, because the parents recognized his voice. He used the pistol barrel to strike both parents in the head when they did not respond quickly to his orders. He even racked a round in the chamber, while pointing the laser-sight on his girlfriend's mother, causing the poor woman to piss herself. Scaring the piss out of his future mother-in-law was going to get him bonus years with Parr, Jeremy thought.

The robbery was less than a success financially. He got away with a bottle of change worth $24.53, several PlayStation 2 games, and the parents' 1991 Ford Ranger. He panicked when he saw a police officer sitting behind him at a red light and hit the gas, even though the officer had no idea Nuccio was just leaving the scene of a robbery. He led a high-speed pursuit back to the trailer park where he and his girlfriend lived. He abandoned the truck when he realized several police cars made his escape impossible. He ran on foot into his trailer. The police found him hiding, breathless, in his closet. The pistol and the stolen items were on his nearby bed.

And, as if the evidence against him were not strong enough, Nuccio proved he had learned nothing about his chosen profession when he gave two full confessions to the police; one at the scene and a second at the station, with videotape rolling. Nuccio thought it was best to talk immediately, and spent a large part of his confession trying to get the cops to bring in a prosecutor so they could work out a good deal. He ended up being charged with armed robbery, home invasion, unlawful driving away of an auto and fleeing and eluding the police.

When Jeremy finished reading the predisposition report, he turned to the notes Charlie had made in the file. Pamela Fitchett, the assistant prosecutor, was handling the case. She had made no offer at the pretrial because she didn't have to. Her case was too good, and Nuccio was too bad. So Charlie had turned to Judge Parr's disdain for trials in an effort to get Nuccio some deal. Parr offered to do a PDI – a pre-disposition investigation. PDIs were the creation of Judge Parr himself, as far as Jeremy knew. The procedure couldn't be found in any law book that Jeremy had read.

A PDI wasn't much of a deal, but it was the best Nuccio was going to get. Nuccio pled no contest to the charge, and the case proceeded as if Nuccio would be sentenced. The probation department made a report and recommended a specific sentence. The judge, after reviewing the recommendation, then gave his opinion on what he thought an appropriate sentence would be. Nuccio got a chance to accept the prison sentence or withdraw his plea and go to trial. A PDI was the deal of last resort before Parr, and it was a difficult deal to finesse. Defendants getting PDIs were almost always going to serve lengthy sentences, and their cases were almost always hopeless.

The probation department had recommended fifteen to thirty years in prison for Nuccio. It was at the low end of his guidelines, and Judge Parr would probably go along with that, Jeremy thought.

As he finished reading through Nuccio's file, Parr called the Radamacher case and the Dobbs case, together. The motion to join the cases for trial was granted with little objection from either Jeremy or Patty Ellis. The trial date was moved back from January 19 to February 9, and Jeremy was thankful that he would have a few extra weeks to cram for Zeb's trial.

Parr took a mid-morning recess so that Jeremy could talk to Nuccio about the PDI. Jeremy buzzed through to Parr's office suite, and, as he waited for Deputy Short to open the holding cell, he was approached by Parr's law clerk.

"Mr. Jefferson," the clerk said, shuffling down the hall toward him, his head bowed like a servant. "I just wanted to get you a copy of this opinion. The judge just signed it."

"Thanks," Jeremy said, as the clerk shuffled away.

Jeremy scanned the decision as he waited. It was a two-page opinion denying his motion to quash on Zeb's case. The judge found that there was sufficient evidence that Zeb knew or should have known that the firebomb would have been a threat to human life so that the case could proceed to a jury. It was not unexpected but only another step toward Zeb's inevitable trial.

Jeremy shifted his focus to a less desirable client once Deputy Short opened the lockup. Nuccio was a short, broad young man with an openly surly disposition. When he learned that the PDI called for fifteen years in jail, he started yelling loud enough so that Jeremy was sure that Nuccio's voice could be heard outside the holding cell. Nuccio screamed about Jeremy, Charlie, the prosecutor and the judge. He could not get over how unfairly the entire process worked, and he was damned certain that he was not going to go to prison for fifteen to thirty years without having a trial. When Jeremy broached the fact that there was really no basis on which they could hope for an acquittal, Nuccio yelled some more, until Jeremy just left him to calm down.

Apparently Parr had heard Nuccio yelling, because when Jeremy and Fitchett were invited back into chambers to discuss the matter, Parr needed no prompting to say, "You better tell your guy he should take that sentence, because if he doesn't –" Parr reached into his desk drawer and took out a tiny noose fashioned from twine. It was definitely bush league and could have drawn a grievance against the judge anywhere but Milton, Jeremy thought. But practicing chambers law here meant getting used to such crude anomalies.

By the end of the morning, Nuccio had rejected the deal, much to Parr's displeasure. Parr ordered the trial to begin Tuesday, over Jeremy's protestations. Jeremy was about to start trial on his first life offense; it was just on the wrong case, he thought.

The only good thing about Doug Nuccio's trial was that it was mercifully short. The case was not circumstantial or scientific. Both parents testified that they recognized Nuccio's voice as he robbed them, and a string of police witnesses ran through their pursuit and capture of a suspect who had been driving a stolen vehicle shortly after the armed robbery occurred.

The trial was a pointless exercise that could only result in Nuccio getting many more years in prison. Jeremy had done his best to explain this to the angry young man, but his efforts were in vain. Doug Nuccio had made up his stubborn mind; he was not going to prison without a trial. So a trial was had.

They had picked a jury on Tuesday morning, and the prosecution's stream of evidence was complete by the end of the day. Nuccio took the stand on his own behalf Wednesday morning, contrary to Jeremy's advice. Nuccio told the same lie he had been telling Charlie in the jail. He'd met a guy named Mike on the night of the robbery. The two of them got high on crack cocaine, and Nuccio started to tell Mike about his problems with his girlfriend's parents. Nuccio then went home to sleep, and was awakened by Mike running through his room late at night, throwing something on his bed. That's when the cops came and arrested him. He was hiding because he was scared, and he told the police of his involvement because he was high. And, of course, as with all such stories, Nuccio did not know Mike's last name.

It was a variation on a theme about how someone else had done it that Jeremy had heard at least a hundred times in the past year. It was natural for human beings to deny responsibility, Jeremy thought. Even the best people did not like to admit their most heinous wrongs.

It took the jury less than twenty minutes to consider Nuccio's lie. They then brought back a verdict of guilty. Nuccio had probably cost himself an extra ten to fifteen years in prison, Jeremy surmised, for his pointless need to maintain his innocence to the world. Now he could serve decades of his life telling other inmates that he was just another guy, wrongly trapped by the system.

Allie was waiting for Jeremy when he left the courtroom. "Lunch?" she said. "I'm buying."

"Can't turn down a free lunch," Jeremy said. "Not after a trial like that. I don't think I'm going to get a lot of retained cases if my name keeps getting into the paper with these convicted clients."

A small yellow sun, at its apex in the southern sky, did its best to warm them as they walked across Main Street and a half a block down Ohio to the Milton Diner. The diner was one of Milton's oldest establishments. It had opened as a boarding house in the 1890s, when the South Branch River was filled with freshly cut Jack Pine headed down river to the mills in Saginaw. Until prohibition it was a saloon serving lumbermen, fishermen and hunters, but in 1919, Ada Hudson turned the old saloon into the Milton Diner, and the establishment had been serving lunch to the locals ever since.

Hudson's story was memorialized on the walls of the establishment and on the menus. She cooked pies and breads and short order for every hungry soul in town until her death in 1993, at the ripe age of 90. Now her granddaughters carried on for her using her original recipes. The diner was, in many ways, the glue that held Milton together.

Jeremy and Allie grabbed a seat in the back, far from the drafty windows that looked out on Ohio Street. They stripped off layers of scarves and gloves and coats, and ordered potato soup and egg salad on homemade bread.

"Nuccio didn't really expect the jury would believe that BS, did he?" Allie asked.

"Is this on the record?" Jeremy smiled, and sipped water from an amber glass.

"Everything's on the record, Jefferson," she said.

"I don't know what he thought," Jeremy said. "I told him to just take the fifteen years they were offering. But, sometimes guys just need a trial."

"That was horrible," she said. "I can't believe he pistol-whipped those poor people. And the woman. God, that must have been awful for her with that laser thingy pointed right at her."

"Yeah," Jeremy said. "Parr's going to appreciate hearing all of that. He's going to launch that guy. But you know what the worst part is, really?"

Allie shook her head.

"Sitting next to him for two days. You can feel the jury's eyes on you. I look at them, and I know they're looking at me like, 'How can you defend that guy.' It makes you feel guilty just sitting at the table with him. I mean, you can't imagine the shame and loathing that guy must feel. It's right there with you when you're at the table."

"I don't know," Allie said. "You may feel it. But, that guy looked like an animal. I don't think he was feeling any of that. The only thing he looked like he cared about was trying to get free. I swear I thought he might make a break for it sometimes."

A waitress came with two steaming earthen bowls of soup. Jeremy admired the creamy soup, swirls of oil and seasonings mixing as he watched. Ada had done some good in her life. Her potato soup recipe alone was a contribution to mankind, Jeremy thought.

"Well," Allie said, dabbing soup from her lip. "My folks are headed for Florida."

"Vacation?" Jeremy said.

"Nope," she said. "They're moving. My mom's been looking at a residential home down there for him for a while. Sunny Willows. It's very structured. It supposedly helps. And then there's a retirement community right next door where she'll be."

"Wow," Jeremy said. "That was out of the blue, huh?"

"No," Allie said. "They always planned on retiring there. Just got sidetracked when Dad got sick. I was talking to her about it, and then with Dad getting out last week. He could have frozen to death, really. So she just thinks it's time."

"Are you okay with it?"

"I don't know," she said. "I cried at first. I haven't really been away from them that much, you know. Just college. And that was only at Central, so it was kind of like being close."

"Yeah," Jeremy said. "You don't really miss them until they're gone. My mom – not so much my dad, because he and I were always kind of distant – but my mom, you know. I mean, I always loved her. But, we weren't really close. It's just life. Kind of takes you away. But, then when she got the, you know – cancer – I mean she was just gone so fast. And then it hits you."

"I know," she said, reaching out a hand across the table to touch his. "I know. I'm going to miss my mom a lot. But with my dad, it's like he's gone most of the time now anyway. I don't even think he recognizes me."

Jeremy thought of telling her what he had thought last week, about her dad staring off down the frozen river. No sense making her cry, though. He used the crust of his egg salad to sop the last of the soup from his bowl.

"I got a call back from the *Trib*," Allie said. "Second interview on Monday."

Jeremy knew they would call, but the inevitability of her going away hurt him. "Great," he said, through a mouthful of sandwich. He inhaled a piece of the bread and coughed violently.

"Wrong pipe?" Allie said. He drank a sip of water and rubbed tears from his eyes.

"Great news," he said again. "I knew they'd love you."

"Yeah," Allie said. "I guess. I'm really nervous, though. It's such a big jump up."

"Don't be, Allie," Jeremy said, looking directly into her eyes. He was searching for some indecision there. Something that said, "I don't really want to go, Jeremy." But her eyes were just deep and beautiful, with no secret message.

"You're going to do great," he said. "You're bigger than this place, really."

She smiled, reassured. They split a piece of Ada's Dutch apple pie, Jeremy savoring every sweet, shared bite. And then the small-town reporter, true to her word, picked up the check. Jeremy was warmed by the restaurant, the soup, the pie, and mostly by Allie's company. He did not want to walk back through the cold to his car, but Zeb's case, and the rest of Charlie's files, needed work.

27

"It passed," Bishop said, bursting into the governor's office. Howell was looking out at Capitol Avenue. "A hundred and seven to three. Only Ashby, that pansy, and a couple of his Communist cronies from Washtenaw voted against it."

Howell said nothing. He turned slowly and offered a wan smile, "What's that, Bish?"

"MEGPAT. It passed. It should be on your desk within the hour. I can get a signing ceremony set up so we can make the six o'clock news."

"Do we have to do it today? I was thinking of knocking off after lunch," Howell yawned.

"It has to be today, Roger, or we'll miss the news cycle for the entire weekend."

"All right, but can we get it done early?" Howell yawned again.

"I'll do my best, sir." Bishop turned and left to make the necessary arrangements. He had growing concerns about Howell's lethargy. He was going to have to snap the boss out of his funk if they were going to even think about a run in 2008.

As Bishop walked through his own waiting room, he saw Trooper Richard Alarie waiting to see him. "Good morning, Richard," he said, and escorted the trooper back to his office personally.

"Give me just a minute," Bishop said, picking up the phone and setting the MEGPAT signing press conference in motion.

"Get it done by two o'clock," Bishop barked, before he hung up the phone. "Good to see you, Richard. How's our little assignment going?" Bishop loved the guy Colonel Thibodeau picked from the governor's security detail. He had the crew-cut, ram-rod straight back and no-nonsense attitude of a marine. The only thing Bishop doubted was the guy's ability to infiltrate a group of tree-hugging environmentalists.

"Good, sir. I'm officially a member of *Save Zeb*," Trooper Alarie said. "Started getting my e-mail updates this week."

"That was fast," Bishop said. "How'd you get in?"

"They're not a particularly secure organization, sir," Trooper Alarie said. "Anyone can join. I just showed up at a protest they organized last week. It's no secret. It said in the local paper that they'd be picketing the Blue-Mart Grand Opening up there, and I just showed up. Gave them a fake name. I'm Colin Green, sir. I thought they might like my last name."

"Colin Green, huh?" Bishop chuckled. "Well, that's good work. So what have you been able to find? Anything?"

"Well, sir," Alarie said, "I made contact with the attorney you spoke of the very first –"

Bishop's secretary interrupted on the intercom. "Senator Usterman on the line, Mr. Bishop."

"Tell him I'm in a meeting," Bishop snapped. "So Jefferson's involved with this group – what's it called?"

"*Save Zeb*, they call themselves," Alarie said. "Yeah. I made contact with him the very first day. He was taking names down for mailing lists and donations."

"He was taking donations?" Bishop said, excitedly.

"Well," Trooper Alarie said, "I didn't see any actual donations, but they do some fundraising, apparently."

Like a dog uncovering a bone, Bishop dug a copy of the newly-enacted MEGPAT statute from his cluttered desk. He flipped through the hundred pages of small print before settling on Section Three of the law, dealing with financial assistance and support to groups designated as domestic terrorist organizations. If the governor proclaimed *Save Zeb* to be a terrorist organization, as was his right under the sweeping new law, raising funds for the group would be a felony. Jeremy Jefferson, a felon. Bishop liked the ring of it.

"I think you may be on to something, there," Bishop said, handing the bulky statute to the officer. "This is the new MEGPAT law. It will be signed by the governor this afternoon. In about three hours, actually."

"No kidding," Alarie said, flipping through the document aimlessly.

"Check out Section Three. It makes it a felony to provide financial support to groups designated as a terrorist organization. Also, Section One. All kinds of new ways to get any information you need when doing an investigation like this. It's actually broader than the Patriot Act."

Alarie was obviously pleased with the new legislation, "No kidding."

"Have Marta make you a copy on the way out. You're going to be the first troop to take down an entire terrorist cell. Keep me posted."

"Yes, sir," Alarie said. He whirled for the door and marched out.

Bishop was gleeful. Everything was falling into place, as if by design. He didn't care for church too much come Sunday, but maybe someone up there was looking out for him, he thought. Maybe he was destined for the Oval Office. So long as he could keep Howell focused for another five years.

Another January week passed, with Jeremy doing his best to run the entire show at the Sage Law Office. He thought he was definitely Charlie's better when it came to management. Jeremy was everything Charlie was not: organized, punctual, and detail-oriented. And yet, with Jeremy in charge for the past three weeks, the office looked much the same as when Charlie had left. Old files were strewn everywhere, new clients needed to be seen at the jail, the clerk's office called daily about paperwork that was not filed, or was somehow misfiled. If he could get a contract lawyer, Jeremy would certainly give up a part of his meager salary for the help. But what lawyer in his right mind would want to come to Milton, even temporarily, Jeremy thought?

The real cold of the northern winter was setting in. A high pressure cell had dropped down from Canada and was literally freezing the entire county into a block of ice. Snowfall had been lighter than usual according to the locals, but there was still too much for Jeremy's liking.

Charlie had kept the budget for the Sage Law Office tight, and that meant Charlie took care of all the office maintenance himself. So Jeremy spent the first fifteen minutes of every workday shoveling the drive and lot, and applying liberal amounts of salt to the walkways to avoid one of Tommy Hughes' slip-and-fall lawsuits. Even when it didn't snow, the wind always blew enough of the powder around to make Jeremy work at keeping the premises reasonably free from snow and ice.

He had taken to coming into the office early to accomplish all the chores Charlie had done silently and unnoticed. The lot was always dark, and Dena, who had a habit of being late, was never there to bother him. Such was the case on Thursday morning, when a car pulled into the parking lot of the Sage Law Office, just as Jeremy had broomed a dusting of snow off the back porch to the employees' entrance. Jeremy saw the lights coming up the drive first and thought that Dena had miraculously made it in early, but the car did not belong to her.

The car parked and out hopped a man, putting on a blue winter parka and pulling a fur-lined hood over his head. He was a large man who Jeremy failed to recognize on first glance.

"Good morning," the man yelled through the cold. As he approached, Jeremy recognized him. It was the man with the crew-cut and vice-like grip who he had signed up at the *Save Zeb* rally two weeks before.

"How are you?" Jeremy said, struggling to remember the man's name.

"Good. Good," the man said. "Too damn cold, though."

"Yeah," Jeremy said. "You're Mr. – I'm sorry. I forgot."

"Green," the man said, reaching out a gloved hand to shake. "Colin Green. That's okay, Mr. Jefferson."

Jeremy tried his best to meet the man's overbearing handshake and managed not to grimace. "What can I do for you, Colin?"

"Well, I'm just headed down south. Sales trip. And I'm not going to be able to make tomorrow's meeting."

"That's no problem," Jeremy said. "You left contact information, right? They'll send you a report about what's happening. Professor Quinn runs a really tight ship. Very good on distributing information."

"Well, I'm going to be gone a week. Maybe two. And I haven't got anything about fundraising just yet. And I really want to contribute. I was wondering if I could give this to you, and maybe you could pass it on for me?" Green said, fishing a thick envelope from his front pocket.

"I really don't handle the fundraising," Jeremy said, but Green handed him the envelope anyway. It felt like quite a bankroll.

"Well, just pass it on for me. To whoever does do the fundraising. Could you? I think this group is really doing something important here, and I want my money to help out, you know."

"All right," Jeremy said. "How much is in here?"

"Two thousand. Cash," Green said, nonplussed.

Jeremy gasped. It was larger than any retainer he had received in the year. "That's mighty generous, Mr. Green."

"Yeah. Hey, I'm single. And I do some cash jobs on the side. So, when I see a good cause, I can do something about it."

"Well, I'm sure Professor Quinn will be grateful. I'll make sure it gets to the fundraising committee with proper credit to you."

"Thanks," Green said. "I better get on the road. I heard a storm was rolling in. I gotta make the Ohio border before noon."

"Drive safe," Jeremy said. He was relieved when the man did not offer a departing handshake. Jeremy went inside and started a pot of coffee. He took the cash out of the envelope. Twenty crisp one hundred dollar bills. Green was lucky he'd brought it to an honest man, Jeremy thought. He tucked the envelope in his coat pocket and delivered it to the chair of the finance committee the following day at the *Save Zeb* meeting. News of

Colin Green's generosity buzzed around the meeting; the man couldn't have bought better publicity within the small organization, Jeremy thought.

28

It took two weeks for the *Tribune* to call her back after the second interview. Allie had started to let go of her revived dream as if she were waking and coming to her senses that reality was Milton and the *Beacon*. The editor from the *Trib's* metro desk had called on Monday. He offered her the position starting March 1, and he wanted her to keep up with her freelance coverage of the Zeb Radamacher case until then.

She had accepted with little thought. When the offer was made, it was like opening the papers to see the winning lottery numbers matched her ticket. She never thought it would happen, but here was the seventh largest paper in the country offering her a job. There was just no turning down a winning lottery ticket.

She told Jeremy at their Wednesday lunch. She thought she saw a touch of sadness in his eyes, despite his congratulatory words. She wanted to hear him say something, anything really, about wanting her to stay. But he did not. Though she still had three weeks in Milton to ready herself, she was already beginning to feel regret in her heart about Jeremy. This love that never was, was going to ache, she thought.

She went with him to the *Save Zeb* meeting on Friday night. They drove in his old Honda Accord, east on Adams Road, until it turned from asphalt to icy dirt. The meetings had been moved to a barn donated to the cause by one of the local farmers. There was a whole contingent of them, *Farmers to Save Zeb*, she had dubbed them in a recent article. They were small farmers trying to compete with the factory farms but losing badly. They had been driven to niches, most trying to grow organic crops and scrape out a living off their lands.

The farmers had donated four small farms in total, all in different county precincts, and the social action committee was busy staffing the farms with a rotating regiment of college students. The students signed up to live and work on the farms, just long enough to establish voter registration in Wabeno County – thirty days. By a quirk in state election law, registered students could maintain their voting status once established, even if they moved on. The plan was to rotate a new batch of motivated students in once a month on every farm. Interest in the program was small, but growing, but, from what Allie could see, there was no way that they could get enough student volunteers to sway the Wabeno elections. Still, Professor Quinn and the *Save Zeb* army marched on.

Jeremy was quiet on the drive to the meeting. Allie glanced at him, his dark eyes fixed on the icy road, catching the moonlight reflected off the snow. "So, how's Zeb's case going?" Allie said, wanting to hear his voice.

"Slow," he said, not lifting his gaze. She knew that the case was up on Monday and could see the stress it caused Jeremy.

"When's Charlie getting back?" she asked, after another moment.

"He's supposed to be released on Monday," Jeremy said. "But, he's not coming back to work until the beginning of March. At least that's what the doctors have told him. Rest and rehab at home."

Allie didn't feel like trying to coax Jeremy to speak. She turned and watched the pastoral beauty of Milton pass by. Under the full moon of February, the ice-crusted snow that covered the fields glistened like a gem. Houses, sheds and barns lay like silent mausoleums on the landscape, broken by patches of woods and wire fences.

"So, are you all ready to go?" Jeremy said. His voice was softer, matching the hard-frozen landscape.

"I've still got three weeks," she said. "But I don't know if I'll ever be ready."

"Wh–" he started.

"Leaving this place behind. I've spent a lot of years here. I'm going to miss it."

"Oh," Jeremy said. "Yeah. It's beautiful." He bobbed his head up from the road and admired the landscape for a moment.

Cars lined the side of the road as they approached the farm. They parked at the end of the line and trudged along the road to the drive. The driveway was double-parked, and a lot that had been plowed near the barn was full, too.

The meeting was inside a weathered barn. Light bulbs cast a harsh yellow glow from string lighting. With the farm equipment removed, the barn could have served as a small warehouse. Professor Quinn and a few of the student leaders were assembled on a makeshift platform at the end of the barn opposite the main doors. Allie checked in with Jeremy at the sign-in table, and the pair mingled about the large crowd. It appeared to Allie that locals now outnumbered students by a fair margin.

"Mr. Jefferson," a large man with a loud voice had snuck up on Jeremy's side.

They shook hands, and Jeremy introduced Colin Green. "Nice to meet you, Allie," Green said, enveloping her hand in a firm shake.

"You, too," Allie said.

"So, did you get that donation turned in last week?" Green asked Jeremy.

"Sure did. I turned it in to Lauren Owen, on the finance committee." Jeremy said, pointing Lauren out on the makeshift stage. "She said to be sure and thank you. It was the largest single donation they've gotten so far. Although, I understand that there are some big contributors in the works now. Philanthropists and the like."

"No problem," Green said. "Thanks. Say, do you know Professor Quinn at all?"

"Sure," Jeremy said, pointing her out on stage. "She's right there. I know her well."

"Do you think I could get a chance to meet her?" Green asked. "I mean, this is really amazing. This organization you two are building."

"Well," Jeremy said. "Thanks for the credit. But, it's really all her. She's incredible. She's really accessible, too. We'll talk to her after the meeting. I'm sure she'd like to meet her biggest donor."

"Thanks," Green said, before moving on through the crowd, close to the stage.

When he was out of earshot, Allie asked, "Who's that guy?"

"I dunno," Jeremy said. "Just met him last month at the Blue-Mart picket. Another soldier for Zeb, I guess."

"Looks like a soldier, all right," Allie said. "But, doesn't really look like a *Save Zeb* type, does he?"

"Takes all kinds," Jeremy said. "Check out half these farmers. To look at them, I'd bet that they would vote against teaching evolution in schools. But they're the biggest supporters Zeb's got, now. Strange business."

"I guess so," Allie said.

Professor Quinn got the meeting started. She gave a quick update on Zeb and Melissa Dobbs. It was followed by reports from the major committees. Membership was up and going great. *Save Zeb* was set to establish the Wabeno County Green Party this month, and with it, gain access to their own slate of candidates on the November ballot. The college farm-worker program was a storming success – great thanks to the gracious farmers, who were establishing their own committee to work on agricultural issues and sprawl. The petition drive to influence the local prosecutor to ease up on Zeb and Melissa even seemed to be turning the tide. Early canvassers had dealt with much venom from the locals as they tried to get signatures, but now, more and more locals were signing the petition. And fundraising was starting to pick up, with a special thanks to Colin Green. It was an efficient and informative meeting, and Professor Quinn brought it to a close in under an hour and fifteen minutes.

Jeremy found Colin and took him to meet Professor Quinn when the meeting formally ended. Allie decided to mingle about and get a few quotes. She was running out of angles on the *Save Zeb* story, but there was still at least three weeks' worth, she thought.

She happened upon a group of farmers' wives who were talking animatedly among themselves, excited by the political fervor that Professor Quinn had whipped up. As Allie approached to get their comments, she overheard a redhead in a snowmobile suit say: "Isn't that Marge Alarie's boy up there on stage?" The woman was pointing up toward Professor Quinn, who was talking with Jeremy and Colin Green.

"You mean the big guy? With the crew cut?" Allie jumped in.

The farm wives looked at her warily.

"I'm Allie Demming," she said. "*The Milton Beacon.*"

"Oh," the redhead said. "I just love your stories. We would have never heard about these guys if it wasn't for you. Your stories are great. We all loved that farm piece you did last week."

There was a cackling agreement, and Allie was accepted into the circle.

"Thanks," Allie said. "Did you mean the man with the crew-cut, up there? You said he was Marge Alarie's son?"

"Yeah, I'm pretty sure," the redhead said. "He's grown a lot. But that's Marge's boy. Rich, I think his name is. She said he was going into the police academy awhile back. But, I've lost touch with her. That was so long ago. But, I'm pretty sure that's Richie. I should go say hello."

The redhead set off through the milling crowd, and Allie was after her. They were jostled by bodies, mostly headed for the barn door and the cold February night. A group of students walked in front of Allie and the stage, obstructing her view, and when they passed, Allie no longer saw Colin Green on the stage. Jeremy was alone talking with Professor Quinn.

It was straight-up 6:00 a.m. on a Saturday morning, but Alarie was waiting for Bishop at the security entrance, as Bishop had instructed. They might have to bring this kid along for the ride when Howell was ready to make his run at the White House, Bishop thought.

"Good morning, sir," Alarie said as Bishop approached. Bishop swiped his security card, and they entered the stale warmth of the George W. Romney Building. Bishop swiped his security card again to access the employee elevator to his office suite.

"So you think you've got him," Bishop said in the elevator.

"Undoubtedly, sir," Alarie said. "The way this law is written, it would be hard not to. You helped write it?"

"Helped?" Bishop said, a crooked smile breaking over his grey teeth. "I wrote it myself, practically."

"I thought so, sir," Alarie said admiringly.

"It's nothing really," Bishop said, enjoying the company of his subordinate. "Just start with the Patriot Act and make it a little tougher. Something you troops can really use out there in the field, I hope."

"Yes, sir," Alarie said. "If this case goes well, I can't wait to share it with the troops. It would make for a good training seminar, don't you think?"

"I suppose so," Bishop said.

The elevator opened to the governor's suite. The governor had flown to Florida on a golf outing, so Bishop decided to use his office as a base of operations. It was more spacious and entirely underused, Bishop thought.

Bishop reclined in the governor's leather chair and stretched his folded hands in the air, resting them on the top of his head. "What have you got for me?" he said, kicking his feet up on Howell's desk.

"All right," Alarie said, laying his file on the edge of the desk and shuffling through his reports. "The Act makes it a ten-year felony to solicit funds or contribute funds to a group designated by the governor as a Domestic Terrorist Organization, or DTO.

"The governor's first act after MEGPAT passed, was to designate *Save Zeb* as a DTO, right?"

"Them and ELF," Bishop said; he had deliberately squelched any publicity about the executive orders to give Alarie some time to work. Ignorance was no excuse in the law, but Jefferson, who was a good attorney, was likely to hear about the DTO designation soon. "Right. It was the first executive order he took under the act. Right after the signing."

"Good," Alarie said. "I dropped a marked donation off with Jefferson on Thursday, January 22. Six days after *Save Zeb* was designated. He accepted it and said he would get it into the right hands.

"I then pulled a warrant with that first administrative law judge the governor appointed for domestic terror oversight. I got a warrant for the deposits of *Save Zeb*. They have registered as a not-for-profit corporation, and they have an account up in Mount Pleasant at Michigan National.

"The marked money was deposited on Monday, January 26, by the group's financial officer, one Lauren Owen.

"Next, I conducted an authorized sneak-and-peek of the suspect's home. Not much there. Just some literature that Jefferson had taken from the DTO.

"Finally, I pulled a warrant for a wire and recorded the suspect and the DTO's leader, one Wilma Quinn, at a meeting of the DTO last night. I had the tapes transcribed for my report. It's amazing," Alarie said, beaming. "Jefferson says on tape that he passed the money on to Owen. And, get this: Quinn basically admits that the group's purpose is to overthrow the elected government in Wabeno County. I think we've got enough to take them both down, sir."

Bishop sat back and tried to objectively view his victory. He was about to have Jefferson's job – to humiliate his old rival in a most public scandal. It would catapult this wedge issue onto a national stage, he thought. He could see the headlines – "Lead Attorney Charged with Aiding Terror Group." He could almost taste the victory.

"Let's get more on Quinn before we take her down," Bishop said. He did not want anyone else clouding the cruel spotlight Jefferson was about to face.

"But, sir. She's unquestionably the leader of the DTO," Alarie started, then caught himself. "But, I, eh, understand that Jefferson is the priority. Yes, sir. My reports are ready to seek an arrest warrant on him now."

"Very good work, Alarie," Bishop said. "Let me get Gray on the line. We'll get this show on the road."

Bishop called Ed Gray on his home line. "Gray," he said. "Bishop here. How are you?"

"Good," came the tired voice of the Wabeno County Prosecutor. "A little tired. I was up late working on the Radamacher case last night. Trial starts – what time is it?"

"Six-twenty-two," Bishop said. "I told you I might have something hopping this weekend. I'm just sitting with my undercover officer, who has been investigating that *Save Zeb* group up your way."

"Really," Gray said, sounding more interested. "What's going on?"

"Well, he's been working the group for a couple of weeks now, and he's ready to seek an arrest warrant."

"Couldn't it wait until after the trial?" Gray said. "I mean I got a two-man office, you know, and this trial is just killing me."

"I don't think so, Gray," Bishop said, his voice smiling. "The defendant is Jeremy Jefferson."

"What?" Gary's voice was almost a yell. "What in the – why Jefferson? What did he do?"

"You've been keeping up on MEGPAT?"

"Yeah," Gray said. "It passed couple of weeks ago, right?"

"Yes, it did," Bishop said. "Have you got a chance to read it yet?"

"I'm just swamped," Gray said apologetically.

"That's okay," Bishop said. "I don't think three-quarters of the lawmakers read it either. It is kind of tedious. But at any rate, when it passed, it gave the governor the power to declare certain groups as Domestic Terrorist Organizations. DTOs, we've been calling them. The language is all new. Long story short, that group up your way is a DTO, and Jefferson is guilty of procuring funds for them. It's a ten-year felony."

"You're kidding," Ed Gray said, shocked.

"Scout's honor," Bishop said. "Now, I've got the undercover officer down here with me. I'm going to send him up to you ASAP to get an arrest warrant. You ought to be able to pick up Jefferson by tonight at the latest."

"That might take care of my trial on Monday," Gray said, amused.

"It might," Bishop said. "Maybe Radamacher's next lawyer will have a little more sense and take the deal you've been offering."

Bishop made arrangements for Gray to meet Alarie and hung up the phone. "He said he'd meet you at the courthouse at ten. You better get up there," he said, turning to Alarie.

"Sir, this is going to blow my cover with the group," Alarie said respectfully. "If we waited, I might be able to get evidence where they wouldn't need me as a witness, so I could keep working the DTO."

"That's not important now, Alarie," Bishop said. "We've got the guy we want. We'll get someone else inside if this doesn't break the group."

Bishop escorted Alarie out of the Romney Building and went back to the governor's desk. He soaked in the power of the office for ten minutes before he set to work on the governor's Monday statement on the success of the new MEGPAT law.

Jeremy broke the late Saturday silence at the Sage Law Office by snapping his three-ringed trial folder shut for a final time. Zeb's case was all there, distilled down to a two-inch thick folder of notes and documents and reports. Jeremy had worked on the case enough to try it without reference to anything, but he would cling to his trial folder just the same, as he had done in every trial he'd had since law school.

Jeremy saw the remnants of the winter sun, low in the sky, turning the frost on the windows gold and yellow. He would get a good night's sleep and review the file once more on Sunday. Then, after taking Zeb through his testimony one last time, he'd get another good night's sleep on Sunday, and he would try the case of Zebediah Radamacher on Monday morning. His plans were laid, and Jeremy was content.

He closed the trial folder and left it on his desk. He ran a hand down the railing of the creaky staircase on his way out of the office. He was almost asleep already. He turned off the lights and locked the employee door behind him, glad that the preparatory work was done.

On the way home, Jeremy was startled by a state police cruiser in his rearview mirror. He had not seen it in passing, and it seemed to descend on him from out of the sky. He checked his speed instinctively. Only five over. No problem, he thought. He could not make out the trooper because of the glare from the setting sun.

Jeremy was conscious of his driving for half a mile, checking his speed and his steering while glancing at the patrol car in the mirror. As he neared the turn to his street, the cruiser activated its overheads, and Jeremy pulled to the side of the road. Jeremy put his hands at ten and two and waited for the trooper to approach.

A minute passed, and the trooper had still not exited the patrol car. Jeremy thought he might get out and see what was happening when a second cruiser, with overhead lights blazing, came up from Jeremy's street and circled in behind the first.

Jeremy saw officers approaching his car from both sides. He still couldn't see their faces in the light, but Jeremy was bewildered to see the officer approaching on the passenger side set a hand on his firearm. Jeremy sat very still.

A young trooper, who Jeremy recognized from appearances at the courthouse, approached the driver's window slowly. His face was wooden. Jeremy rolled down the window.

"Jeremy Jefferson?" the trooper said in a loud voice.

"Yes, Officer," Jeremy said.

"Could you please step out of the vehicle," the trooper said.

"What's this about–"

"Please step out of the vehicle," the trooper said in a commanding voice.

Jeremy's blood was starting to boil. He thought for a moment that they were playing some game with him. Intimidation before the trial? The absurdity. But, after thinking for a moment, he calmly stepped from the car.

The trooper grabbed him roughly and moved him against the car.

"Do you have any weapons or contraband on your person, sir?" the trooper said.

"What's this about–"

"Do you have any weapons or contraband, sir?" the young trooper commanded again.

"No," Jeremy said, his own voice rising. "What's this all about?"

"Spread your hands on the car," the trooper commanded, physically directing Jeremy's body. "Feet apart." He did a rough pat-down.

Jeremy started to look back, his body resisting the trooper's pat-down, "What is this all about, Officer?"

The young trooper then cuffed Jeremy's hands behind his back. "I have a warrant for your arrest, Mr. Jefferson."

Jeremy was stunned to silence. He said nothing as the young trooper led him to the second cruiser, where he was placed in the back seat with care. Seated next to him was Detective Mary Russell. She looked uncomfortable and did not smile.

Jeremy, seeing a more familiar face, regained some composure. "What's going on here?" he said, controlling the rage inside himself. "What's this about, Detective Russell?"

"You are under arrest, Jeremy," she said, patting her folder. "You have the right to remain silent. If you give up that right, anything you say can and will be used against you in a court of law. You have the right to an attorney, and if you can –"

"Spare me!" Jeremy shouted. "What's the charge?"

Detective Russell opened her folder and read, "Soliciting or Providing Material Support to a Domestic Terrorist Organization, it says."

The cruiser sped off, and Detective Russell continued reading Jeremy his rights as Jeremy's own thoughts spiraled out of control. Someone had gone completely off the deep end, he kept thinking. This was either a particularly foolish prank or someone had completely lost their mind. But, as they neared the jail, Jeremy realized that Detective Russell was not joking. She was trying to get him to answer questions.

"I've got nothing to say," Jeremy said, regaining some legal acumen. "I want an attorney."

29

Charlie was dreaming, as he often did in the days after he was shot, of the moments just before the pain. The music blasted inside The Roadhouse of his dreams, and he walked from the restroom to the front door to meet Jeremy for the taxi ride home. The faces and the bodies about him in his dream were distorted, dancing figures in dark light. He could only see the door as his steps led him forward in slow motion.

His head swam with a drunken buzz, just as it had that night, until he reached the door and was sobered by the sight of the shotgun. The dream sped up then, through microseconds of terror. The Radamacher boy was wheeling with the gun he'd pulled out of the back of the pickup. Jeremy was flat-footed, a deer in the headlights, staring at the Radamacher boy. Charlie's body leapt forward, not as the result of some logical calculation, but propelled by some instinct or grace or stupidity. And, with an awful blast, came a crushing pain in his right leg.

As he landed on top of Jeremy, it felt as if his leg had been severed, or nearly so. Consciousness waned as blood pumped out of him in the rhythm of his own pulse, and with his reason, the pain receded. He could hear a hum in his head turning to a ring. And Charlie was suddenly bolt upright in his hospital bed, sweating. His room phone rang again.

"Hello," Charlie said, trying to shake the sleep away.

"Charlie, it's Allie Demming. I hope I didn't wake you."

Her voice sounded sweet on the phone, Charlie thought. "What time is it?"

"It's coming up on ten," Allie said.

"No problem. That's all I do is sleep in this place."

"I wouldn't have bothered you," she said. "But, Jeremy insisted I talk to you first."

"Problems with his trial?" Charlie said, finally starting to shake off the remnants of his nightmare.

"No," she started. "Well, yes. Sort of. He's been arrested, Charlie."

"What?" Charlie said. "What, was he drinking or something?"

"No, no. They've just arrested him on some terror charge. They're holding him at the jail. And he used his phone call to contact me. He wanted me to talk to you first and then get him a lawyer."

Charlie looked around the room. The clock said 9:57 p.m., and it was dark out. He knew it was Saturday night, and that he was being released to go home on Monday. This wasn't part of his dream, he thought.

"A terror charge?" Charlie said. "That's insane. What is the charge exactly?"

"I forgot what he said when he called," Allie said. "But it was giving support to a terrorist group or something. I was just so upset when he called, I didn't write it down."

"Oh Christ," Charlie said. "I can't believe that. Must be something under that new law. This whole world is going insane, I swear."

"He needs a lawyer," Allie said. "At least for his arraignment tomorrow. He wanted to know who you'd suggest."

Charlie could not think of any lawyer in Milton who should be handling this, except himself. "I don't know," Charlie said. "I guess I'd call Tommy Hughes on short notice. His home number's probably not listed, but I got it in my Rolodex at the office. What time is the arraignment?"

"They said it would be sometime around two o'clock tomorrow. I'm going to be there to post bail. How can I get the number in your office? It's locked, right?"

"Usually, yes," Charlie said. "But, I keep a key under the mat. By the employee entrance. Get Hughes' home number from my Rolodex and call me back once you've checked to see if Tommy can cover this thing."

Charlie hung up the phone. He had followed the development of the new state law as much as he could from a hospital bed. It sounded gigantic in scope, and ill-conceived to Charlie, a staunch defender of civil rights. But that hadn't stopped the State House from jamming the measure through in a hurry. Constitution be damned, Charlie thought.

Allie called a half-hour later, as Charlie puzzled over Jeremy's supposed infraction. Tommy Hughes was so offended at the notion that Jeremy was in jail, he said he would do the arraignment for free. Charlie told Allie to give Jeremy a thumbs up from him, and said good night.

He tossed in his hospital bed until midnight. He knew there would be no sleep. He picked up his phone and dialed Professor Quinn. She was a great comfort to him over the past four weeks. She visited often, called even more, and snuck him the necessities of life that were forbidden by hospital policy. A chili dog one day. A pack of smokes the next.

Though they both possessed Ivy League degrees, their communication was simple and direct. There was no wasted use of language. It took him seconds to tell her he needed a ride from the hospital to Milton, so that he could appear at the arraignment personally. Letting himself out a day early wasn't going to hamper his recovery, he thought. He just had to be there to take care of his partner.

Quinn arrived by 4:00 a.m. and helped Charlie sneak from the hospital on crutches, unnoticed. She drove the rest of the night in her Toyota Prius, as he ranted to her about the end of the rule of law.

Milton, thirty days older, looked unchanged, Charlie thought. It was still frozen. He wished the same could be said for his upper leg. His surgeon said he was lucky to have a leg at all. It was badly mangled, but the artery was repaired, and the bone was healing, so his prognosis was good.

Professor Quinn was nearly asleep at the wheel when they rolled into his driveway at 9:00 a.m. He set his alarm for 11:30 a.m., and he and the professor settled in under the covers.

He did not dream, and when the alarm went off, he sat up straight away. He took as quick a shower as was possible for a man who was only semi-ambulatory, and had Professor Quinn drive him to the office. He called Tommy Hughes first, to thank him and to call him off. He then made call after call to the network of defense and appellate lawyers he had built up over the years, trying to catch one at the office on a Sunday, so he could get a copy of the MEGPAT statute. He finally found an old friend in the State Appellate Defender's Office who faxed him a copy of the new law. It wasn't computer-assisted legal research, but it was enough for Charlie.

He studied the statute over as thoroughly as time would permit and thought he had pinpointed the applicable section:

MCL 750.54313 (Sec. 3)
* * *

(4) Prohibition on Material Support for Domestic Terrorist Organizations. No person shall knowingly provide, solicit, collect, or otherwise assist in the procurement of any remuneration, or in the procurement of any other aid or assistance, to an organization designated by the governor as a Domestic Terrorist Organization,

> pursuant to Section 1 of this act. A violation of this subsection is a felony punishable for not more than 10 years or a fine of not more than $50,000, or both.

Charlie turned the corner of the page down, so he could find the language again. He breezed through the entire statute once more, for familiarity's sake. The law was astonishingly broad, Charlie thought, as his eyes danced over the words. Words could hold so much power. The governor had almost blanket discretion to name entire groups of people enemies of the state, or Domestic Terrorist Organizations, as the statute referred to them, and then the statute gave vicious teeth to prosecute designated groups. And if that wasn't enough to make Thomas Jefferson roll in his grave, the statute set out extraordinarily minimal standards for a wide variety of searches and seizures that were not previously authorized under Michigan law. They could eavesdrop on lawyer-client meetings, they could make secret entries to homes authorized only by an administrative warrant, and they could tape and tap almost any form of communication known to man. The law was almost laughable, making criminal any act at the whim of the governor. As words on paper, it was amusing. But seeing it in practice against his friend, Charlie was in no laughing mood.

He complained about the abuses to Wilma.

"I told you," she said, laughing where Charlie could not. "Big Brother really is watching."

At 1:45 p.m. they left for the courthouse. Arraignments on weekend warrants were something Charlie rarely attended. Minor crimes were never arraigned on the weekends, as it required disturbing a prosecutor and Judge Welch, along with the hassle of rushing to put police reports together. But for serious felonies that required immediate action, the necessary parties came together. The police phoned in the on-duty prosecutor, and the prosecutor phoned in the judge, and they would all meet as early as the paperwork could be generated. Defense attorneys were rarely a part of the initial arraignment process, and almost never for a public defender like Charlie. Only a very large retainer would secure Charlie's attendance at such a hearing, or a very close friend.

Professor Quinn parked in the lot behind the courthouse. There were a handful of cars and a state cruiser. Charlie gimped his crutches over the ice in a sprint toward the front of the building, but the doors were locked. He was about to leave and try the side door, when he saw Ed Gray through a window. He tapped an upraised crutch on the window, and Gray came over to let him in.

"What in the hell is going on, Gray?" Charlie said, as he eased himself into the courthouse. Charlie was hot and itching for a fight.

"Charlie," Gray said, breaking into a smile at first. "Good to see you."

"What in the hell is going on?" Charlie said. "You've arrested my associate, you idiot! You know he's not a terrorist!"

"Hey. Look," Gray said, raising his voice to meet Charlie. "I'm dealing with shit here that you could not imagine. I'm getting calls from the governor's office every other day. And, I've got this trial with this moron who should just be pleading guilty. And I don't really need to hear any more-"

"You know he's not a terrorist, for God's sake!" Charlie's scream echoed in the empty hallway. "This is Jeremy, Ed. You *know* him! How could you let this bullshit go through?"

"Have you seen the law on this?" Gray said. "Clear violation. Cut and dried. I didn't write the damn thing. But it's a clear violation. And I can't sit by and not charge something like this when I've got the governor's office breathing down my goddamned neck."

"You know this statute is unconstitutional!" Charlie yelled louder. "Did you read it? Fuck! It makes you a terrorist tomorrow if the governor decides the Prosecuting Attorneys' Association is a threat to domestic order. This is fucking crazy!"

Charlie saw Detective Russell coming up the stairwell. "Judge Welch is ready for us," she said.

Charlie swung himself past Gray, Professor Quinn in pursuit. "You tell them, you old radical," she said, her voice a constant positive, Charlie thought. "I love it when you get riled."

He crutched to the elevator and descended to the basement, trying to bring his temper back under control. But, he thought, his outburst was not unwarranted. And, if anything, Gray had seemed defensive about his own action.

Professor Quinn held the door, and Charlie crutched into the courtroom. There, at the lectern, dressed in an orange jumpsuit, was Jeremy. When his eyes turned to Charlie, the slack look on Jeremy's face changed to a look of genuine relief.

Gray and Detective Russell had taken their places at counsel table as Charlie awkwardly managed to get through the swinging doors of the bar that separated the gallery from the courtroom.

As Charlie made his way to the lectern, Jeremy embraced him, almost causing him to lose his balance. Charlie saw Deputy Short start forward, as if to break the prohibited contact, and then Short looked away.

"Charlie," Jeremy whispered. "What are you doing here? You're not supposed to be out–"

"Well, someone had to run the office with you going and getting yourself arrested," Charlie said, mock sternness fading to a chuckle. "You okay?"

"I'm all right," Jeremy said, his voice hushed against the prosecutor just five feet away. "I can't believe this, though. I kept waiting for someone to walk in my cell last night and say, 'April Fools',' and for it to just be over."

"It's the craziest thing I've ever seen," Charlie said.

The door from Welch's chambers opened, and everyone in the courtroom rose to their feet, but it was only Welch's court recorder.

"The judge would like to see the lawyers in chambers," she said. She led Gray and Charlie back to Welch's office.

The office was small and windowless. The furniture was wood frame, from the '60s, probably about the time that Welch took the bench, Charlie guessed. A bookshelf on the side of the office had several pictures – a tour of Welch's own path through life. There were a couple of pictures of a young soldier. Pictures of family. Pictures of Welch and his brother judges in Wabeno County, and several of Welch with politicians from various decades.

Welch sat behind his desk, peering down through square reading glasses, while he read the file in front of him. He said nothing as Gray and Charlie entered. The court recorder closed the door as she left.

Charlie hesitantly seated himself, as did Gray, when Welch did not look up from his reading. His steady breathing was loud and filled the silent space.

"O'Brien signed off on the warrant," Welch mumbled to himself, still reading.

"Yes, Judge," Gray said. "We couldn't reach you on the pager yesterday, so we got the magistrate to take care of the swear to."

Welch took a last deep breath and looked up at Gray with a fury Charlie had never seen on the judge's face. His voice did not raise, but something about its tone made the hair stand up on the back of Charlie's neck. "What in the Sam Hill is this all about, Ed?"

Gray started to mumble something, but Welch cut him off. "You charged a member of our bar with aiding and abetting terrorism, Ed. He practices in my court. He practices with you. He is a member of the Wabeno County Bar Association. How, do you suppose, is Jeremy Jefferson a terrorist?"

Welch paused, but Gray did not dare to speak. Welch's face had risen past a flush pink and was turning deep crimson. Charlie saw spittle flying from his mouth as the bitter words spilled out.

"I've read the statute you charged him under," Welch said, rising to his full height and maintaining an even, but angry, tone. "And I don't think I have ever seen anything quite like it. I've been following it in the paper, but reading the actual language – You're going to try to turn my courtroom into a kangaroo court, are you?

"You see this picture here, Ed," Welch said, pointing to the closest picture on the bookshelf. It was a black and white photograph of a young soldier. "This was my older brother, Ed. Lieutenant Alan Welch. The Big Red One, if that means anything to you. He died about two months after this photograph was taken. Battle of the Bulge. You know who he was fighting?"

Gray said nothing. Charlie was about to chime in with the right answer but remembered an old adage he had learned – from Welch, coincidentally – "Keep quiet when opposing counsel is in trouble."

"He was fighting the Nazis, Ed. He was fighting fascism. He was fighting to stop a system where people could be taken in the middle of the night and shot in the head because their political opponents arbitrarily decided they were criminals. My brother died fighting that battle, Ed. Did you know that?"

"I didn't," Gray managed to speak.

"I know you didn't," Welch went on. "You don't know anything. You certainly haven't learned anything about history. You kids today. Never served in the army, most of you. Never had any idea about sacrifice or duty to country.

"Well, Ed. I want to teach you something, now. This is a great country. It is a country of laws. A country that follows a constitution. A country that doesn't arrest people – arrest their own co-workers for God's sake – just because a governor decides it should be so.

"I'm going to follow this law, Ed. Because I am sworn to follow the law. But I want you to think real hard about using your prosecutorial discretion in a case like this. Because you and I have a lot of business together. And I make a lot of discretionary calls in your cases. And my brother," Welch said, pointing at the photograph again, "he wasn't the only man in my family willing to stand up for what is right."

Welch grabbed his robe from a coat rack. "All right," he said. "Let's go put this case on the record."

Gray and Charlie got up to leave. "Good to see you back, Charlie," Welch said. "We've missed you."

"Thanks, Judge" Charlie said.

Welch arraigned Jeremy with kid gloves. Absent were the tough words reserved for the average defendant. Charlie waived the reading of the charge, Welch advised Jeremy of his rights, and a plea of not guilty was entered.

"All right," Welch said. "I'll set a preliminary examination date of February 20th. And I'll set bond in the amount of five hundred dollars, personal recognizance."

"Judge," Gray jumped to his feet, objecting to Jeremy being released, in essence, on his signature alone. "Can I address bond?"

"I suppose you can," Welch said. "If you want to waste more of the court's time."

"Judge, the statute in question–" Gray went on, "–I know the court is familiar with it. But, it does allow the court to deny bond to persons charged with providing material support to a DTO."

"I'm aware of what the statute says," Welch said. "And you can feel free to appeal my decision if it distresses you. But I personally know Jeremy Jefferson. And he is not a danger to the public or a risk of flight. We're adjourned."

Charlie turned to Jeremy, whose face registered appropriate shock at Judge Welch's sudden shift in allegiance from the prosecutor. "Thank you, Your Honor," Jeremy said.

"You're welcome, Mr. Jefferson," Welch said.

30

It was an hour before Jeremy was transported and processed out of the Wabeno County Jail. The last hour in custody was the hardest, he thought. His arrest and incarceration coagulated into one ugly feeling that permeated his mind and body. It was a feeling of unreality – disassociation, a psychiatric expert might have called it – where his mind would literally not accept that he had been arrested on terrorism charges. He had laughably labeled the war on terror "fascist" often in the past two years, but he had never thought he would experience this ugly war in such a palpable way. They had stripped him of freedom and dignity with just one night in jail.

Welch's ruling on bond had been a boost, but Jeremy found himself almost unable to wait as his bond paperwork was processed. He wanted to see Allie and Charlie, and process this Kafka-esque ordeal.

Deputy Short finally got the necessary paperwork straight. "I don't really know what to make of all this," the old deputy said as he returned Jeremy's valuables. "But I'm glad you're getting out of here, Jeremy."

Allie, Charlie and Professor Quinn were waiting in the lobby when Deputy Short released him.

"Thank you," Jeremy told Charlie. "Thanks so much. I just couldn't believe–"

"C'mon," Charlie said. "Let's get out of here."

They agreed to get a late lunch at the Milton Diner. Jeremy rode with Allie. She touched his hand and smiled at him often, but they spoke hardly at all. The foursome grabbed a booth at the busy diner. Jeremy felt grungy. He could see greasy strands of his own hair hovering in his line of sight. They were silent until the waitress left with their order.

"So what did you say to Welch back in chambers, Charlie?" Jeremy fired off the question that had been hopping in his brain since the hearing.

"I didn't say two words," Charlie said, a grin breaking under his moustache. "The old bastard just snapped. I thought he was going to wring Gray's neck. You should have seen him. He was seething. 'How could you think Mr. Jefferson was a terrorist? My brother died fighting the Nazis!' He was off his nut. I could see spittle flying out of his mouth."

"Really," Professor Quinn said. "I didn't think that guy had it in him. Some common sense finally."

"Thank you for coming, Charlie." Jeremy said. "I couldn't believe it when you walked in. Allie told me Tommy was going to cover it. Thanks, Allie, for everything."

"Not going to let my associate rot in jail," Charlie said. Allie rubbed Jeremy's shoulders.

"So Welch is that pissed, huh?" Jeremy said. "I can't believe it."

"I think I might finally win a preliminary examination in that court," Charlie said.

"God," Jeremy said, a chill making him shudder. "I don't like the sound of that. I'm going to have to go through an exam. I just kept telling myself over and over all night, this must be a joke. What is Gray thinking?"

"You haven't had a chance to read the new law?" Charlie said. "MEGPAT."

"No," Jeremy said. "I've been kind of busy, you know."

"It's the broadest damn thing I've ever seen," Charlie said. "The governor has the power to designate groups as Domestic Terrorist Organizations. And if he does that, then anyone assisting the designated group is considered a felon. I'd like to meet the dumb bastard that wrote this."

"So *Save Zeb*, they're a designated group?" Professor Quinn said.

"Apparently so," Charlie said.

"How can they do that?" Professor Quinn asked.

"The law is just that broad," Charlie said, shaking his head. "Ridiculous. But it'll never stand. If it's got Welch up in arms, then I can't think of many judges who are right-wing enough to let them get away with it."

"I swear I just want to move to Canada sometimes. Or New Zealand. Anywhere they speak English," Allie said. "I mean what is going on in this country that they can pass a law like that? How can people just sit around and let them do this?"

"You can't run away from things like this, dear," Professor Quinn said. "You have to stand up and fight. You have to make it so people will stand up with you and stop them in their tracks. Speak truth to power. You, of all people, are in a pretty good position to do that."

Professor Quinn was interrupted by the waitress, who was saddled with a tray full of Ada's steaming homemade fare. The professor was right, Jeremy thought. He couldn't run from this fight. It sickened him that his license was on the line if he was convicted of a felony. But Charlie knew the law was wrong, and Jeremy would just have to sit back and let his lawyer do the work - advice he was fond of giving Zeb. Charlie would fight for him. And Jeremy would concentrate on Zeb's fight. One battle at a time. Jeremy devoured a plate of chicken and dumplings and still had room for Ada's Dutch apple pie.

After lunch Jeremy retrieved Zeb's file from the office and had Allie drop him at home. He would have liked nothing more than to lounge away the last hours of Sunday with her, but he needed to review Zeb's file one last time. He gave Allie a kiss good night, and since his car had been impounded, she agreed to take him to court in the morning.

His last review of the file was more of a gesture toward preparation than an actual exercise. He was as ready as he would ever be. There was no other lawyer on the planet that was more ready to defend Zeb Radamacher. But even this thought did not let Jeremy sleep easy.

His sleep was tormented with one unending dream. It was Zeb's trial. As Jeremy rose to give his opening statement, he realized he had left his trial notebook on the kitchen table. Still he managed the trial, piece by piece, witness by witness, from a tortured exercise of memory. Jeremy had all the right answers, but they were slow to come, and at every turn it seemed as if the jury was lost. As the trial neared its conclusion, Melissa Dobbs took the stand in her own defense. Her pregnant abdomen was modest when she started to testify.

As she went on, two curious things started to happen. She started condemning Zeb in her testimony, and as she testified she became more and more pregnant until her water finally broke.

"Your witness," Welch told Jeremy from the bench. Jeremy rose and moved to the lectern, but, without his notes, he could not think of anything to ask the young woman. Minutes passed, and just as Jeremy had formulated a question, Dobbs began to scream with labor pains. Jeremy was awakened by his piercing alarm clock.

Slowly he donned the equipment for court. His best black Armani suit. A red pattern tie. Black socks made from silk and black leather loafers. He skipped breakfast in favor of coffee. Allie rang the bell at 7:45 a.m., sharp. Jeremy was ready for Zeb's trial.

He first knew that there would be no trial when they turned off Main Street on their way to the courthouse parking lot. The lot was almost empty, when it should have been filled with the cars of prospective jurors. A large television satellite truck with a Court TV logo was being loaded with cables and monitors.

"No jury," he pointed out to Allie.

"Hmm?" she said. "What's going on, do you think?"

"I dunno," Jeremy said. "Maybe Parr is going to bring them in later?"

When he walked in the courthouse, Jeremy saw Gray in the hallway. He did not wish to talk with the prosecutor, but he had no choice.

"What's up?" Jeremy asked. "Where's the jury?"

"Parr called them off," Gray said, not looking at Jeremy. "His secretary said he wants to see us in chambers as soon as Ellis gets here."

Jeremy walked away from Gray. The level of discomfort was too great. This was going to be a difficult trial. But he had to work with the man. Jeremy knew he needed to put his own personal traumas out of his mind so that he could focus on Zeb.

Ellis did not arrive until 8:15 a.m. "Hello Ed," she said, her heels echoing in the main hall of the courthouse. "Where is everybody?"

"Parr wants to see us in chambers. He called off the jury. I'm not sure what's going on," Gray said. Gray buzzed Parr's secretary from the hallway. Jeremy heard her tell Gray to have the attorneys wait in the lawyers' lounge. The judge had not yet arrived at the courthouse.

The lawyers' lounge was a small room with three couches, a phone, a coffee table, a Mr. Coffee, and a small sink. It was paid for by the Wabeno County Bar Association. It served as a place to relax while cooling one's heels, waiting for Parr, mostly, Jeremy thought. Jeremy did not wait with Gray and Ellis. He paced the hallway outside the lawyers' lounge. The start of a trial was an extraordinarily stressful event, Jeremy knew. But he liked the stress. It was as close as he was ever going to get to being a jet pilot, he often thought. The only way to relieve the stress, really, was to just get the damn thing started, and he was irritated with Parr for this glitch.

Parr's law clerk retrieved them just after 9:00 a.m. The three attorneys made their way back to the judge's office suite. They cooled their heels for another five minutes in Parr's lobby before they were invited back into chambers.

Jeremy took a seat on the sofa, leaving the chairs for Gray and Ellis.

"I called off the jury this morning," Parr said, after an informal greeting. "I heard about the, um – when I heard you'd been arrested, Jeremy I thought the case would have to be adjourned. So I have put off the trial until next week."

"I'm ready to go," Jeremy said. His tone was more bitter than he would have liked, and the comment was physically directed toward Gray. Control, he thought, taking a deep and silent breath.

"Really," Parr said. "Remarkable. But I can't imagine you'd be on top of your game after – I don't want to get this trial off on the wrong footing. Another week isn't going to kill anyone. And I thought we might take one more chance to try and settle it in the meantime. So where are we at? Have there been any offers?"

"Judge," Gray said. "I've done about all I can. I offered Jeremy's kid an eight-year cap. That's four years under guidelines. He rejected it. And I offered Patty's client a six-year cap. Six years under guidelines. She's rejected it, too. I can't really do much else."

"Oh, yes," Parr said. "I remember now. And neither was interested in a *Killebrew* or a PDI?"

"No, Judge," Gray said. "Because, you're not going to be able to give them more than I've already offered. There's just no way."

"That's right. I recall now," Parr said, a look of slight confusion on his face. "So, Jeremy, what about that offer? Or maybe, first we should talk about whether or not you should really continue on this case?"

"I'm ready to try it, Judge," Jeremy said, sitting up toward the edge of the soft couch. "And my client wants me to continue."

"Have you talked to him since the, uh, arrest this weekend?"

"No, Judge. But I'm quite sure that the charge against me," Jeremy shot another look at Gray, "will not change his mind. I'll double check with him on it. But I know Zeb wants my representation. And I'm happy to be representing him. Somebody's got to stand up to this fascist crap–" Jeremy turned to stare at Gray again.

"You're charged with aiding a terrorist organization, Counselor!" Gray finally yelled at Jeremy. "I think you should take him off the–"

"We'll see how long that's the case!" Jeremy yelled back. "I think Welch is going to show you a thing or two about charging people, and then I'm going–"

"Hold on! Hold on!" Parr boomed over the top of the yelling attorneys. "I'm not going to have this kind of talk. We're going to be civil, boys. Now, this is a prime example of why I think it might be prudent to have you step down from the case, Jeremy."

"I'm not going to, Judge," Jeremy said, "unless you order me off. And even then, I'll be appealing. Somebody's got to stand up to this, Your Honor. You can talk to Zeb about it, on the record."

"Okay. Okay," Parr said. "That's a good idea. I mean, if the boy wants you as his attorney, then I doubt I would remove you."

"All right," Parr continued, talking louder, as if he had restored order in his chambers – despite the heavy air that still rested between Jeremy and Gray. "I want the three of you to keep talking about a resolution for the rest

222

of the morning. I'm going to get caught up on a couple of opinions. We'll keep your clients here in case we can get a plea. I'll be available if you need to talk to me as a group or individually - if you think that will help. But it doesn't seem to me that you're that far apart. We should probably get some kind of deal in this case."

The three lawyers left Judge Parr's chambers. Jeremy milled about the court's main hallway. He had no intention of talking with Gray about anything. Gray and Patty Ellis sat in a conference room and laughed about something that Jeremy could not hear.

Jeremy found Deputy Short. Short took Jeremy to the lockup so he could talk with Zeb. The young man was in the holding cell alone, his face distressed.

"Mr. J," he said. "What are they doing? They told me we aren't starting my trial today."

"Nope," Jeremy said. "I just got done talking with the judge. He has put it off for one more week."

"Why?"

"You didn't hear?" Jeremy said, not surprised. Because he had bonded after his arrest, Jeremy had not made it past the intake section of the jail to the general population. "I got arrested this weekend. On charges of supporting a terrorist group. Your little friends at *Save Zeb*. I'm with you now."

Zeb's jaw dropped, and he almost laughed. "Shut up, Mr. J." the boy said. "Really? What's going on? I can't wait to get this thing over with."

"I'm dead serious," Jeremy said. "I got arrested on charges of aiding a terrorist group. There's a new law. They've declared *Save Zeb* to be a terrorist group. And I supposedly helped them procure funds. So I'm being charged. I spent a good part of this weekend in jail. I thought maybe you would've heard about it on the radio."

"Serious?" Zeb said. "So we can't go to trial because of that?"

"Well, Parr thought it would be better to give me another week. He didn't check with me. Because I was ready. He just adjourned it. Judges can do that kind of thing. They wear the black dress. It's their show, you know."

"God," Zeb said. "I haven't been able to sleep all weekend. I just couldn't wait. I've got to get out of here. And then this morning, when I asked about my court clothes, they just said not to worry about it, the trial wasn't going to happen today. I was pissed."

"Now Parr wants us to hang around here all morning to try to resolve your case," Jeremy said. "He wants us to plead guilty."

"I'm not pleading guilty," Zeb said. "I've been talking with Melissa, through this guy I know who's an orderly. She's ready for the trial. We're gonna win this thing no problem."

"I'm glad you're so confident," Jeremy said. "You know what I've told you about trial, though?"

"I know, I know, Mr. J.," Zeb said. "Anything can happen. But we're going to win. I just know it. But, I don't think I can take another week of this."

"Well, Zeb," Jeremy, smiled. "Just take as much of it as you can."

"All right, Mr. J.," Zeb said. The boy's smile was infectious. He had lifted Jeremy's spirits.

"So the judge wants to get rid of me as your attorney now," Jeremy said, broaching a more difficult topic.

"What?" Zeb said, alarmed.

"Because I've been arrested on terror charges," Jeremy said. "He asked me to step down basically."

"What did you tell him?" Zeb said.

"I told him that you really wanted to stick with me, and that you wouldn't let me go as your attorney."

"You got that right," the boy beamed.

"All right," Jeremy said. "The judge will probably want to confirm that the next time we're in court. You just tell him what you think of me being your attorney when we talk to him then, okay?"

"Got it," Zeb said.

"I'll let you know if there are any more offers from Gray, okay?"

"All right," Zeb said.

Jeremy returned to the hallway, but Gray and Ellis were gone. He was about to go ask the judge for permission to leave when Gray came walking down the main hall. They ignored each other, and Jeremy continued to pace the hallway.

Jeremy spotted Ellis coming up the stairway from the basement. She wore a wide smile as she flicked her hair back. Jeremy walked toward her. In her hands was a file, and plea paperwork.

"Wha-" Jeremy started.

"Ed," she said, walking toward Gray in the conference room. "She said she'd take it."

"Great," Gray said. "You've got the paperwork?"

"Uh-huh," Ellis said. "I'll just get it filled out, and let's get this thing on the record."

"Okay," Gray said. "I'll just have a few questions of her to make sure we know what she's going to say at trial."

"What? Who's pleading?" Jeremy said, stunned.

Patty Ellis walked toward him and put a hand on his forearm. "He just gave her a deal she couldn't refuse," she smiled. "You should really try to work something out for your guy, too."

"What?" Jeremy said, his voice louder. "Dobbs is gonna plead? You told me she was supporting Zeb's story right down the line."

"Well," Ellis said, "that was before Ed offered her four this morning. To attempted terrorism."

"She didn't commit attempted terrorism," Jeremy said. "Did you read the statute? If MacAdam brought the Molotov cocktail without our guys knowing about it, then they're not guilty. Just on the MDOP."

"Well, she's taking this deal," Ellis said bristling. "We're not going to risk fifteen or twenty years when she can take four and be done with it."

Jeremy started toward the conference room to talk to Gray but then did an about-face. There were no sane lawyers to talk to in Milton, save Charlie. He stormed out of the courthouse and let the cold air suck the heat from his face. He thought of Allie's suggestion about moving to Canada. It didn't sound half-bad.

When he regained his composure, Jeremy returned to Parr's courtroom. He watched Dobbs' plea in disbelief. He did not have the heart to tell Zeb what had happened through the iron bars of the holding cell, so he left the courthouse for the Sage Law Office.

Jeremy took advantage of the adjournment by catching up on Charlie's office work. Things were starting to shape up. He had managed to stay on top of all the cases, to take care of bills, and the day-to-day running of the office. Still, he couldn't wait for Charlie to get back to work full time. He missed playing chess with his old friend.

Jeremy stopped by the jail after work.

Seated across from Zeb in the contact room, Jeremy was still hesitant to tell his client what had happened. But it was better he learned from Jeremy than through the jailhouse grapevine, he supposed.

"I've got some bad news," Jeremy said.

"I'll take the good news first," Zeb smiled.

"Sorry, Zeb," Jeremy said. "There's only bad this time."

"When has it been good, Mr. J.?" Zeb joked. "Every time you're here, it's bad news."

"Melissa took a deal today, Zeb," Jeremy said, finding no better way to state it.

"Huh?" Zeb said.

"She pled guilty today, at the courthouse," Jeremy said.

Zeb's smile faded. Jeremy could see hurt and anger welling up in his eyes.

"No, she didn't. We rode back together from the jail. She didn't take a deal."

"Yes," Jeremy said. "I was there. I watched it. She pled guilty to arson, MDOP and attempted terrorism for a four-year cap."

"Guilty as charged," Zeb said. "She would have never done that."

"Not as charged," Jeremy corrected Zeb. "Attempted terrorism instead of terrorism. That takes her guidelines way down."

"I don't believe it," Zeb said. "We're going to trial. She's been telling me that through Ronnie, in here, every day."

"Well," Jeremy said, "I don't know Ronnie, but I know he's got it wrong as of today. I just know what I saw."

"That's crazy, Mr. J.," Zeb said. "She wouldn't do that to me."

"As part of the deal, Zeb, she's gonna have to cooperate with the prosecutor, so she's going to be one of their witnesses now. Against you."

"The fuck she is!" Zeb screamed, rising up and rattling the stainless steel table like a backboard after a slam dunk. "That's bullshit, Mr. J.! I don't believe it."

Jeremy remained calm. He had no fear of Zebediah Radamacher. Zeb was just a skinny kid, and, rage or no, Zeb would need a weapon if he wanted to hurt Jeremy.

"I watched the plea hearing, Zeb," Jeremy said, with an even voice. "She told the judge, under oath, that you planned this all. That it was your idea to blow up the bulldozer."

Zeb sat back down. "But I didn't," he said. "Why would she say that? We're going to have a baby together."

"People say a lot of strange things when threatened with twenty years in jail," Jeremy said.

"You don't believe her?" Zeb said.

"No," Jeremy said honestly. "I don't. The whole plea sounded like bullshit to me. But we've got no one left now, Zeb. We're all alone. It's just your word against everything else now. And I don't know if we can win like that. I'd have to tell you, in my professional judgment, that a conviction is likely now. It might be time to go back and try to beg for the eight-year cap again."

"I'm not pleading to anything," Zeb said. "I didn't do it. I don't know what they told Melissa to get her to say that, but I'm not pleading. That's just bullshit, Mr. J."

Jeremy expected Zeb to say no less, and he was pleased with the boy's answer. It was time to take a stand against Gray, and the governor, and public opinion at large. Zeb was going to have to go first, but Jeremy was going to have to make his own stand in the not-too-distant future.

"You know that book you gave me, Mr. J.?" Zeb said, regaining some calm.

"Yeah."

"Did you ever read it?" Zeb said.

"*To Kill a Mockingbird,*" Jeremy smiled. "I've probably read it half a dozen times."

"You know all the innocent people get screwed in that book, Mr. J.?" Zeb said. "The black guy gets convicted and dies. The crazy guy gets shut up by his parents. The lawyer gets spit on. It's not very positive for someone like me, you know."

Jeremy thought for a moment. "That's true, I guess," Jeremy said finally. "But the point of it is, how did it make you feel? Did it hurt you inside to know that the really good guys were getting screwed?"

"Yeah," Zeb said. "It sucked."

"So as long as you can see that," Jeremy said, "you know what's right and wrong. And the world isn't always fair, but the more of us who can see right from wrong, the better off it is."

Zeb was quiet, seeming to ponder Jeremy's dime-store analysis.

"I can't believe she did this to me," he said somberly.

"It was wrong, Zeb." Jeremy said. "But, we've just gotta get through it."

31

Mark Radamacher was annoyed that he was forced to visit the courthouse on consecutive days. Yesterday he had driven all the way from Watson to watch the beginning of Zeb's trial, only to be told it was cancelled. And today, he was here again, defending himself against baseless charges.

"Next case, Ms. Fitchett," Parr said from the bench.

"Could you please call the Radamacher case, Your Honor?" Fitchett said.

Mark was annoyed by the female prosecutor's whining voice. He stood with his attorney and approached the lectern.

"Do we have a deal worked out in this matter?" Judge Parr asked.

"No, Your Honor," Fitchett said. "However, the People would be moving to dismiss count one of the information, on the charge of open murder. We've had an opportunity to review the alibi evidence that was submitted by the defense in this matter, and at this time, it is our conclusion that we could not meet our burden beyond a reasonable doubt."

"Any objection?" Parr said to Tommy Hughes.

"None, Your Honor," Tommy said. Mark leaned back and gave a sneering smile to the prosecutor before Tommy had a chance to stop him. The government was being run by incompetents, Mark thought.

"All right," Parr said. "Count one will be dismissed on the motion of the prosecutor. Your office will provide a *nolle prosequi*, Ms. Fitchett?"

"Yes, Your Honor."

"Okay," Parr said, "what about count two, resisting and obstructing a police officer? Has an offer been made on that charge?"

"Your Honor," Fitchett said, "We have offered to cap the defendant at one year in the county jail, but that offer has been rejected."

"Is that right, Mr. Hughes?" Parr said.

"Yes, sir, Your Honor," Tommy said. "We would ask that the court set this matter for trial."

"All right," Parr said. "I'm going to set a trial date of April the fifth, at eight o'clock. Please have all motions scheduled and heard not later than two weeks before the trial date. Anything further on the pretrial?"

"Nothing, Your Honor," Fitchett and Tommy confirmed.

"Bond is continued," the judge said.

Mark walked out of the courtroom with his lawyer. Hughes had accomplished in short order what Karljevic could not do in two months, and Mark was pleased to be one step closer to total freedom. But the weekend ahead weighed on his mind, and he could scarcely enjoy the clear February sunshine as he walked from the courthouse.

Though he had only been back for four days, Charlie was slowly losing his mind in the confines of his small home. He had been doing his exercises three times daily, as ordered. But the pain of rehabilitation, even the home variety, had been biting. He consumed Vicodin at an alarming rate. He would need a refill well ahead of schedule. But the Vicodin buzz was the only thing keeping him in the neighborhood of sanity, he thought.

When he wasn't in a drug-induced nap, he played online poker or watched Oprah. He was just in the middle of a rush of good cards at Omaha Hi/Lo, when the phone rang.

"Charlie," Professor Quinn said, "I just heard about a new case in the Federal District Court, in the Eastern District. One of my colleagues says it basically castrates MEGPAT. Could you possibly take a look at it for me?"

Charlie pulled up a computer database that was available to him through the state bar. He found the case within two minutes. *ELF v. Howell*, the case was entitled.

Charlie scanned through the case silently, with Professor Quinn on the phone. "Great case," Charlie said, when he understood the basics. "The ACLU has weighed in against MEGPAT. It says that the statute is vague, overbroad and unconstitutional on its face. The judge down there struck the whole thing. Now, that's what I'm talking about."

"That's kind of how it was described to me, but I wanted to hear it from my lawyer," Professor Quinn said. "We've got that Green Party organizational meeting coming up in a couple of days and I was thinking about cancelling after Jeremy's arrest. I mean, if they can get him, they can certainly get any of us with that statute."

"I know the thing is unconstitutional," Charlie said. "But the problem is getting an appellate court to say it. The way courts are stacked with right-wingers these days, I think they might stand the constitution on its head, just so they don't interfere in this great war on terror."

"This decision is good for us, though, right?" Quinn said.

"Oh yeah," Charlie said. "It is definitely a step in the right direction. I mean, unless that decision gets reversed, you're okay. But, as an attorney, I'd always be cautious about advising a client to flaunt a law. Even such a bullshit law as this."

"So I'm just a client, now?" Quinn said, a girlishness in her voice. "Funny how men forget so quickly."

"Hey," Charlie said, "you called me as your attorney, so don't go pulling that."

"So you would advise against going ahead with the meeting on Friday night, then?" Quinn said.

"Yeah, I think that would be the prudent thing to do, until the law is more settled."

"Good," Professor Quinn said. "I like going against your advice. It makes me feel naughty."

"I'd have expected no less," Charlie laughed. "Well, I'll be there afterward to bail you out, if it comes to that."

Charlie hung up the phone. He had never made time in his life for another person. He had never even understood the concept. But Wilma was slowly making him see the point.

He reread the case from the Eastern District. It was a blueprint for Jeremy's defense on the MEGPAT charges. And if Welch held on to the hostility he had shown Gray on Sunday, all the old judge would need was some solid law to hang his hat on. Charlie printed three copies of the case and stashed them in Jeremy's file.

Allie had expected the Friday night crowd to be much smaller, but the *Save Zeb* organization was continually defying her expectations. The barn was full for the Green Party organizational meeting. One table had been erected on the freshly-built stage at the end of the barn. On stage, the Green Party functionaries were busy shaking hands with Professor Quinn and her cadre of student leaders.

Long tables filled the floor of the converted barn. They were made with sawhorses and plywood, covered by stapled-on paper tablecloths. Folding chairs faced the stage on one side of the table only, so the *Save Zeb* membership could watch as their leaders formally organized the Wabeno County Green Party.

Allie grabbed two seats at a table near the middle of the convention hall, while Jeremy went to scope out the refreshments. The seats were filling fast, and it seemed as if the barn would be at capacity by the time the meeting started.

Allie was tired from the week's work. Since learning that *Save Zeb* had been infiltrated by an undercover officer at last week's meeting, she had been working hard to learn the agent's identity. And, with Jeremy's arrest over the weekend, she had redoubled her efforts. The intellectual idea that citizens were losing their civil rights was compelling; but the reality of the arrest drove her forward. She knew firsthand that the people at *Save Zeb* were no more subversive than any freedom-loving American. And the idea that the group was being targeted in this way made her think of the Gestapo that she knew only from *Hogan's Heroes* reruns.

So far, she had only been able to peg Richard Alarie, a.k.a. Colin Green, as an officer with the Michigan State Police. But he wasn't attached to the state police post in Wabeno County, and her contacts at the state hadn't turned up his actual assignment. A friend in the FBI office in Grand Rapids checked out the Joint-Terrorism Task Force, a group she believed would have jurisdiction over operations like the one being run against *Save Zeb*, but they denied any knowledge of Richard Alarie. The mystery was beginning to bother her, and she recognized the irritation as a feeling she often had at the root of a good story.

"Man, the quality of the refreshments has sure gone up since they've gotten the farmers' wives on board," Jeremy smiled. He set a small plate of cookies and a glass of cider down next to Allie.

Allie tried a soft chocolate-chip cookie. "Um-hmmm," she said as the homemade cookie melted in her mouth.

"That's the state chairperson up there," Jeremy said, pointing to a tall, balding man who was engaged in a smiling conversation with Professor Quinn on the stage, "Joel Hamady."

"Can you believe all this?" Allie said, through a second mouthful of cookie, as she swept her hand in a gesture at the growing crowd. "When I went to that first *Save Zeb* meeting I was thinking, like, a couple of college kids who don't have jobs. But, look at this place."

"I know," Jeremy said. "I never thought it would get anywhere near off the ground, like this, I mean."

"I forgot to tell you," Allie said. "I had an old friend, a source, down at the treasury department in Lansing pull up payroll records on Richard Alarie for me. She couldn't tell me which post he was at, but she confirmed he is with the state police."

"Yeah," Jeremy said. "I know. Charlie got the police reports today. His name is disclosed in the reports. He's a sergeant in the Michigan State Police."

"Don't you think that it would rub the public the wrong way if they found out that our state police are being used to infiltrate groups like this? You know, against peaceful political protestors, I mean?"

"I dunno," Jeremy said. "I'd like to think that, but I think they're so scared out of their wits right now by all the anti-terror crap that they probably wouldn't care much. You know, 'what's the threat level today' kind of stuff has them paralyzed, I think."

Allie thought the public would be offended by the undercover nature of the surveillance used against *Save Zeb*. She certainly was.

"I think you're wrong, Mr. Negative," she said. "I really think people will be pissed about this kind of crap."

"Well," Jeremy said, "when you gonna tell them about it then, Ms. High Falootin' *Tribune* reporter?"

"As soon as I can get the story nailed down," she giggled. "I'm thinking I might win the Pulitzer before I leave for the *Tribune*. What do you think?"

"Didn't Bob Woodward start out at the *Beacon*? That's where he broke that whole Watergate thing, wasn't it?"

Allie slapped him playfully. "Seriously," she said. "I think there might be something to this. Don't you think a story like this would have any impact on your jury? I mean, folks around here may be more pro-police than most places, but I think they're kind of anti-government at the same time, if you know what I mean. I don't think they'd like something like this. It stinks."

"Well," Jeremy said. "I don't see how it could possibly hurt, so you just get cracking on your story. I'll give you all the glory if I can get Zeb off."

The meeting was called to order. Professor Quinn talked for a short twenty minutes about how Green Party values were going to take the group to an election win in the fall. She was followed by the state chairman, who gave his warmest welcome to the newly-established local of the Wabeno County Green Party. Allie felt an energy in the barn that made her think that she might have a bigger story here in Milton if she stayed through the November elections than she was ever going to get as a beginning reporter working the metro beat at the *Tribune*.

32

Radamacher looked out the dark tinted windows of the extended cab pickup truck. The southern Michigan landscape that rolled past outside was lifeless. Farm fields lay regenerating under two feet of icy snow. Occasional stands of trees stood leafless against a grey sky.

The Aryan brotherhood had taken great pains to ensure his visit to Al Devine's compound would not be observed by law enforcement. Radamacher met with a group of brothers at a cabin in Gaylord. He gave a rousing lecture about the coming race war, riling the crowd into a frenzy. He was then taken to another remote cabin near Petoskey, before he was shuffled into the tinted confines of the extended cab. Radamacher had visited Devine on several less solemn occasions, but he never felt the overwhelming dread that crept over him now.

"You're really a credit to your race, Reverend Radamacher," the young driver said, breaking a three-hour silence. The young man was about Zachary's age, with greasy, dark hair covered by a baseball cap. "That speech you gave back there. I know I wouldn't mind sharing a foxhole with you when the battle comes."

Radamacher stirred from his own thoughts and nodded at the boy with a faint smile.

"It must be an honor getting called to Mr. Devine's compound, huh?" the driver said.

"Yes," Radamacher croaked, his voice weighed down by silence. "An honor."

The young man spared him further conversation as they covered the miles to Devine's compound. An hour and some south, past Lansing, the driver exited US-27. He took a series of turns going from the super-highway to pavement, to asphalt, to a rough gravel road. He turned into a dirt drive, muddied with snow and tire tracks. Up the drive a quarter mile was a guard shack. Two men armed with AR-15s approached the vehicle.

The driver lowered his window.

"Billy," one of the men said in greeting.

"How's it goin' fellas?" the driver said. "I got Reverend Mark Radamacher with me."

The man with the rifle looked in the cab, nodding at Radamacher. His partner searched the pickup bed.

"Okay," the man with the rifle said, waving the truck through the checkpoint.

The driver followed the dirt road to a large house with a turnaround drive. He parked near the front of the house and rushed to open Radamacher's door like a world-class chauffeur.

"It was an honor to meet you, Reverend Radamacher," the boy said.

"The honor was mine," Radamacher said in a half-whisper.

As the extended cab pulled off, Skeeter Connely greeted Radamacher from the front door. Skeeter was Devine's sergeant-at-arms.

"Too long, brother," Skeeter said, extending a hand to Radamacher.

"Too long," Radamacher said, at a loss for words. Thoughts of Zachary whirred in his head at a dizzying pace.

"The Grand Dragon is ready to see you," Skeeter said with a sweeping gesture, beckoning Radamacher to enter. Skeeter, dressed in battle fatigues, led Radamacher through the austere mansion to a den. Hunting trophies covered the walls, and a giant fireplace blazed under a confederate flag.

"Mark," Al Devine said, rising from a stuffed chair near the fireplace, a glass of bourbon in one hand and a cigar in the other. "I'm sorry about all the extra driving. Security's become something of an issue, you know."

Radamacher nodded in silence. Skeeter left, drawing the den door closed behind him.

"You look pale," Devine said. "Can I get you something to drink, brother?"

"Thanks," Radamacher said. Devine poured a large tumbler of bourbon for his guest, and Radamacher drank. The bourbon was old, its scent jumping straight to his brain. He let the rich caramel liquid wash back in his mouth, warming him all the way to the gut.

"Everything's ready, according to plan," Devine said. "You should go and see him. Square up accounts."

Radamacher nodded half-heartedly and finished his drink. His eye caught a broadsword hanging as an ornament on the far wall. He could seize the weapon and end Devine's life on the spot. But nothing would be solved. Devine's order was clear. Moreover, his order was right, requiring no less obedience than the order of God to Abraham. Radamacher could only hope for some last-minute reprieve for his son.

"Could we get him out of the country?" Radamacher said weakly.

"It has to be this way," Devine said patiently. "You know the kind of heat the police are putting on to find him. And he can't be trusted. He is too simple, Mark. If they bring him in, there's no telling what kind of damage he could do to the organization. You know that."

Radamacher did know that. And, he wanted to handle the matter personally, with some dignity. But his faith was flagging. How could Abraham have raised the knife against his own blood? Was it amazing faith or fiction? Radamacher thought.

"I just thought, if we could get him down to Brazil," Radamacher said, helping himself to a second tumbler of bourbon. "You know, the movement is growing strong there."

"It can't be done," Devine said, with tender finality.

Radamacher drained his second glass and nodded, his eyes searching the worn brown carpet for some pattern he could recognize, finding nothing.

"He's in the safe house," Devine said. "You should go and see him. Daylight is wasting." Devine called for Skeeter.

Skeeter led Radamacher out the back of the mansion, weaving through several outbuildings to an old barn. In the back corner of the barn, the sergeant-at-arms swept away a loose covering of hay and opened a trap door. It was lighted below.

Radamacher went down the steps and hugged his oldest son.

"Dad," Zachary said. His face was marked with dirt. "Good to see you. Are things blowing over?"

"Yes," Radamacher said. "You shouldn't have to be here much longer at all now."

"Good," Zachary said. "This place is awful. I'm alone, and there's nothing to do."

"Not much longer," Radamacher said, wiping his stinging eyes.

"I'm so glad to see you," Zachary said. "I thought you'd be mad at me. I let that fucking Jew lawyer get away. I was weak, Dad."

"You did good, son," Radamacher said. "Don't worry about that."

"So your court trouble is gone now, they told me."

"Yup, everything worked out okay. No worries," Radamacher said, the bourbon coursing through his veins, giving him some small courage. "Al's got a job for us today."

"Really," Zachary said. "I've hardly seen him at all. He's busy, I guess. But that sounds great. I'll do anything to get out of this hole for a while."

"It's not easy work, son." Radamacher said. "One of the brothers has been talking to the police. We have to take care of him."

"Which one," Zachary said. "Is it someone I know?"

"I don't know who he is. Al just wants us to go dig a hole for him. The guy who brought me here, he's going to lead the traitor out to us. And that'll be that."

"Good," Zachary said. "It'll be great to work. Acts, not words, right?"

"Yeah. Let's go get it over with," Radamacher said, turning his back.

They climbed up out of the safe room. A shovel, a pick and an AR-15 were leaned against the barn wall. Radamacher grabbed the rifle, letting Zachary take the tools to dig his own grave.

They marched out behind the barn, through a thick tangle of brush for a half mile, until they found a clearing. Radamacher showed Zachary the spot to dig the grave. The ground was frozen solid, but Zachary's strong hands churned up the earthen bed like a blender. It was a shallow grave that would have to be moved in the spring, Mark knew.

Radamacher seated himself on a felled tree trunk and watched Zachary work, his son's muscled body cutting through two layers of clothing, sweat forming on his brow, the grey sun back-lighting his form. Zachary was God's creation, Radamacher thought, seeing him churn the frozen earth. What God created, God could destroy. But how could Abraham have held a knife aloft over his infant son? Was it a creative work of fiction? Because Radamacher doubted any mortal could obey this command.

Radamacher called Zachary over when he was done digging. His son sat next to him. "You are my good son," Radamacher said, putting a cold arm around the young man's steaming shoulders. "I just want to know why you did it. What was going through your mind?"

"You mean trying to kill that lawyer?"

Radamacher nodded and searched Zachary's innocent eyes.

"Well, for Zeb, I guess," Zachary said slowly. "You was saying how the Jew lawyer was gonna sell him down the river. I could see it in his eyes, too. He's up to no good for Zeb."

"Didn't you know I was going to take care of that?" Radamacher said, rubbing his burning eyes again, looking away from his son.

"Well, I guess it was the commandments, then, Dad," Zachary said.

"The commandments?"

"Yeah, honor your father. You know. I knew you wanted to take care of him. And Zeb needed something to happen fast. I'm sorry I messed it up. But we can still get rid of him, right?"

Radamacher nodded and heard boots trampling across frozen underbrush. Skeeter approached, with a rifle trained on the back of a husky stranger.

"We got ourselves a traitor here, boys," Skeeter said, marching his mock quarry toward the shallow grave.

Zachary rose and stepped toward the pair, as was intended. It was all part of God's plan. Radamacher fought to keep his stinging eyes from exploding in grief. He stood and raised the AR-15, training it on the back of his son's head.

He looked through the sight, at the blond flowing hair. He remembered that hair, reflecting the sunlight of a golden autumn day long past, as Zachary had drawn a bow on his first deer. Tears flowed silently down Mark's cheeks at the memory. His finger rested on the trigger, unmoving. God could not ask this of any mortal. The story of Abraham was as much a lie as was the Jewish distortion of Nazi atrocities.

Skeeter stood, staring at Radamacher. Silence surrounded the four men in the clearing. Zachary, following the sergeant-at-arms' stare, turned to face his father. Radamacher saw a last divine sparkle in Zachary's blue eyes, before a monstrous explosion roared from the rifle in Skeeter's hands. Zachary tumbled half into the shallow grave. Watching his son fall, through a bloody mist, Radamacher felt the heavens fall about his own head. The world had cracked open; hell was no longer a future destination, he thought.

Jeremy arrived at the courthouse at 8:00 a.m. sharp on Monday morning. The parking lot was full; the jury had arrived. A handful of media trucks arrayed themselves on the east side of the courthouse. The trial of Zebediah Radamacher was set to begin.

The mood of the little courthouse could be fickle, Jeremy knew. It was quiet on slow summer days, somber for sentencings, and mournful when Tommy Hughes was arguing a wrongful death case to jury. But this morning the courthouse was a macabre carnival. The main hall was a mass of humanity. Participants, jurors, gawkers and reporters to cover it all. If there was a freak show set up somewhere in the main hallway, Jeremy thought, the illusion would be complete. He drew in a deep breath, taking in the atmosphere, comforted only by the weight of his briefcase.

He checked in with the judge's secretary first, then went to see Zeb in the lockup. Zeb was dressed in defendant casual. Jeremy had taken enough money out of petty cash in Charlie's absence to outfit the young radical for trial. Two pair of slacks; one tan, the other black. A black belt. Casual brown shoes. Three button-down shirts. Enough to get him through the week if he mixed and matched well. The casual dress was perfection, Jeremy thought. But, the untamed blond hair that held stubbornly to the boy's head betrayed Zeb's unwillingness to conform.

"Hey, Mr. J.," Zeb said, his easy smile too exuberant for the trial he was about to endure, Jeremy thought.

"Good morning, Zeb," Jeremy said. "You ready to get this show on the road?"

"Can't wait," Zeb said. "You?"

"There's no lawyer on the planet more ready to handle your case this morning than me," Jeremy said – and he meant it.

Parr's law clerk popped his head into the lockup and gave Jeremy the five-minute warning. Contrary to his usual lack of punctuality, Judge Lawrence Parr was always on time with a jury present. It was his one chance to appear before the electorate, Jeremy thought, and it changed him from a lazy, aloof judge to a prompt administrator of justice.

Jeremy left Zeb, exited Parr's office suite, and walked through the crowded hallway to the main courtroom entrance. Jurors were busy making their way to seats in the gallery, like bees coming to a hive. Jeremy waded through them, smiling, and casually parked himself at the defense table. He unpacked his briefcase as prospective jurors continued to roll in. His stomach let out a low grumble, which Jeremy did his best to control.

Gray came into the courtroom, a false smile plastered across his plain face, looking this way and that through the gallery of jurors. He was flanked by Detective Russell, a study in blue, her freshly-starched uniform broadcasting authority.

"Good morning, Counselor," Gray said, his voice rising to a theatrical level.

"Good morning," Jeremy said, hoping a forced smile covered his gritted teeth. Once a jury pool was in the room everything was for show. Jeremy remembered hearing stories from old trial lawyers in Detroit about juries that would decide cases based on the most innocuous details; a lawyer's shoe shine, an untimely objection. He did his best to project professional civility, though inside he wanted to throttle Gray.

Deputy Short brought Zeb through the public courtroom entrance rather than the rear doors that were normally used for prisoner transport. The staged entrance was designed to avoid showing the assembled panel that the defendant was in custody, but it was a ruse that could have only fooled the most dense jurors. Deputy Short preceded Zeb into the courtroom, and they were followed by a junior deputy. Zeb was herded to the defense table without restraints or touching, but when he sat next to Jeremy, there could have been little doubt in an attentive juror's mind that Zeb was the bad guy.

Parr and his court recorder were the last to enter. The courtroom rose to the call from Deputy Short: "All rise. The 79th Circuit Court is now in session, the Honorable Lawrence Parr presiding."

"Please be seated," Parr said magnanimously with a sweep of his hand. "Good morning. I'd like to welcome you to the 79th Circuit Court. I am Circuit Judge Lawrence Parr. And this is my court recorder, Emily Forbes.

"I want to thank you all for being here today," Parr said. "Jury service is one of the few duties we have as citizens these days." Parr went on with a good-natured civics lesson that he had learned over the course of a dozen years on the bench. It was informative and charming. It prepared the jurors for an experience most had never had. But, to Jeremy, who had heard Parr's lecture four times in the past year, and dozens of variations from more qualified judges, it was a mind-numbing anesthesia he needed to overcome to stay sharp. Jeremy found staying awake challenging, and feigning interest was almost more than he could pull off with any credibility.

He did his best. He smiled, nodded and laughed on cue, as did Gray, trying to bond with the prospective jurors at every opportunity. After ten minutes, the judge wrapped up his introduction and invited the attorneys to introduce themselves.

Gray rose abruptly and turned toward the jury pool.

"Good morning ladies and gentlemen, I'm Edward Gray, the Prosecuting Attorney for Wabeno County. This is Detective Mary Russell with the Michigan State Police," Gray said, motioning to Detective Russell, who rose and acknowledged the jury.

"As the Prosecuting Attorney, I represent the People of the State of Michigan, and the People have charged Zebediah Radamacher," Gray paused and pointed a long index finger toward Zeb, "with three different crimes – counts we call them. The defendant is charged with the crimes of malicious destruction of property worth more than twenty thousand dollars, arson of property worth more than twenty thousand dollars, and terrorism.

"We are going to call a number of witnesses to prove these charges," Gray continued, finally lowering the accusing finger he had pointed at Zeb. "I'd like to read you a list of these witnesses, and if you could remember these names as best you can, and let me know if you recognize any of them when you get a chance to talk, I'd appreciate it."

Gray listed the names. Jeremy ticked them off in his mind as they were read by the prosecutor, envisioning his cross-examination of each. When Gray was finished with his introduction, Judge Parr turned the floor over to Jeremy.

Jeremy rose fluidly. Zeb joined him, just as Jeremy had instructed him during preparation, and together they turned to face those souls who would sit in judgment of the boy. Jeremy buttoned the middle button of his jacket, and when he reached his full height, he addressed them.

"Good morning. My name is Jeremy Jefferson," he began, smiling pleasantly. He imagined himself an airline steward, instructing a group of passengers about flight safety with a practiced message and a plastic smile.

"I represent Zeb Radamacher." Jeremy laid a hand firmly on Zeb's shoulder. "As the prosecutor just told you, Zeb stands *charged* with three crimes. But, as the judge warned you in his instructions, these are only charges. Zeb has pled not guilty to all of them, and this trial has been called for the State to prove its charges beyond a reasonable doubt.

"This process – the *voir dire* – is the only chance I get to talk to you directly, and for you to talk to me. The purpose is to pick a fair jury. One that can sit and judge this case without any preconceived ideas about what the outcome should be. A jury that will sit and listen to the evidence, and follow the judge's instructions before deciding on a verdict.

"Some of the questions you might face during *voir dire* may seem probing. I just want to be sure that you understand that no one here is trying to embarrass you. I am here representing Zeb," Jeremy said, again laying his hand on the boy's shoulder, "and I'm going to do my best to do that. And that involves asking some tough, perhaps uncomfortable, questions. So let me thank you in advance for your candor."

After Jeremy introduced the defense witnesses by name, the court recorder called fourteen jurors to the jury box by number. The battle was on. Jeremy had not lied when he said the nominal purpose of *voir dire* was to select a fair jury. But the truth was, each lawyer would ideally select an entire jury that was completely predisposed to his position, fairness be damned.

Jeremy surveyed the first prospects called from the gallery. As a trial lawyer, Jeremy had come to classify jurors into two broad categories. Most abundantly, there were sheep. They were people who would likely say little during deliberations and vote with the herd. Far fewer in number were the wolves. This second category of jurors were people bold enough to speak up, whatever their opinions. They were likely to be leaders on the jury panel. The foreperson of a jury was almost always the most dominant wolf. And, in Jeremy's experience, selecting the right wolves and excluding the wrong ones went a long way toward winning a trial.

Both Jeremy and the prosecutor could exclude twelve jurors for any reason by using their peremptory challenges, so the first fourteen people called to the box were almost inconsequential.

Parr started the questioning of the panel. He asked questions designed to identify only the most blatant bias. Several members of the panel started the trial with the firm belief that someone charged was almost certainly guilty. And a few admitted to distrusting the police in most circumstances. But Parr, whether through ineptitude or design, led each of these jurors back to the claim of neutrality by asking them a series of leading questions. He always finished with the same question: "You can be fair to both the prosecution and the defense, can't you?" And the answer was always "yes."

Gray followed with his own onslaught of inquiries. Jeremy recognized the lines of questioning straight from the prosecutor's manual. It was Gray's standard *voir dire*. Rarely probative of the truth, but encouraging cohesion among the jurors; instilling the virtue that they could do their duty and convict the criminal that faced them in the courtroom.

Jeremy felt somewhat detached as he approached the lectern for his turn to address the jurors, his analytical mind focused on two tasks: Foreshadow the main points of the defense case; and ferret out the hostile wolves. He scanned the panel for a moment, trying to let his face show pleasant confidence. He found a young mother, and set out defending Zeb.

"Juror number nineteen," Jeremy said. "Good morning."

"Good morning," the young sheep said, a genial smile looking back at him.

"Do you have any children at home?" Jeremy asked politely.

"Uh-huh," she said.

"Yes or no, for the record," Jeremy smiled. "We've got to have an accurate record of this, and sometimes uh-huh doesn't get the job done."

"Yes," she said, smiling back at Jeremy. "I have two daughters."

"How old?" Jeremy said.

"Seven and four," the woman said.

"Let me ask you something about them," Jeremy said. "Do they ever tell you a fib, trying to cover up a mistake they've made?"

The woman thought for a moment. "N-n-," she started, but quickly changed her mind when eyes of the other jurors turned upon her. "Yes. I suppose they do. Not about anything important. But, you know, they're kids. Of course they tell fibs from time to time."

"Of course," Jeremy nodded in agreement. "Let me ask you this. Are they more likely to tell a little fib like that when they know they might get into big trouble, or would they just lie any old time, about anything, even if they knew they weren't going to get in trouble?"

The juror paused again, eyes searching her neighboring jurors, obviously uncomfortable in the spotlight. "'Course that's right," the young sheep said. "All young kids might tell a fib if they're in trouble. Right?"

Jeremy nodded in agreement again. "I was just asking you, from your experience."

"Oh yeah," the woman said. "Sure. They might tell a fib if they thought they were in big trouble."

"Of course they would," Jeremy said. "Would anyone disagree with juror nineteen's experience, that kids might be more apt to lie if they were in a lot of trouble?"

None of the jurors responded. "Good. We all agree. Now, juror one-thirty-two," Jeremy smiled at a retired policeman. "You will be taking an oath, if you are a juror in this case, where you will swear to follow the law as it is given to you by the judge. Do you understand that?"

Juror one-thirty-two was a retired policeman according to the jury questionnaire he had filled out, and he had obviously taken his dislike for defendants with him when he left the force. He regarded Jeremy's question with an open, silent hostility, his arms crossed on his chest.

"Yes, sir," the ex-policeman said warily. "I understand, and I'll follow the law."

"Excellent," Jeremy smiled. "So you won't have any problem going through the elements of every crime charged in this case. Weighing them separately. Deciding based only on the evidence produced in this courtroom?"

"No, sir," the ex-policeman said. "None whatsoever."

"And for every crime – each separate count – where the evidence fails to show beyond a reasonable doubt that Zeb Radamacher is guilty, you will vote not guilty, correct?"

"Yes, sir," the juror said with faint hostility. "*If* I doubt the evidence, I'll vote not guilty."

"And, if there's a reason, based on the evidence, for you to doubt Zeb Radamacher is guilty, you'll vote not guilty."

"Yes, sir," the ex-policeman said.

"Does everyone on the panel agree," Jeremy said, "that if the evidence doesn't show Mr. Radamacher's guilt beyond a reasonable doubt, you will all vote not guilty?"

The panel shook its head obediently. Jeremy sensed the ex-policeman's hostility as if it were heat radiating out of his eyes. He stepped warily with his next questions, knowing that the ex-policeman might try to poison the jury pool at any opportunity.

"Sir, it says here that you retired from the Detroit Police Department," Jeremy continued.

"Yup."

"Do you still see any of your friends from your days on the police force?" Jeremy said.

"Yeah. Some of the guys will come up and stay once in a while. Hunting and fishing, mostly."

"Let me ask you this," Jeremy said. "If you brought back a verdict of not guilty in this case, how would your friends react?"

The officer thought for a moment. "I dunno," he finally said.

"Do you think it's possible that they might give you a hard time about a finding someone not guilty?"

"Yeah, that's possible," the ex-policeman said. "Considering that most def–"

"Do you think it's something that you might not even tell them about," Jeremy cut off the juror's venom, "if you brought back a verdict of not guilty?"

"I might not," the ex-policeman said. "It depends on which friend, I guess."

"Okay," Jeremy said. "So it might be difficult for you, socially, to bring back a verdict of not guilty, because many of your friends are police officers? Is that fair?"

"Yeah," the ex-policeman said. "It might be, but it wouldn't stop me from doing the right thing."

Jeremy made a note and then continued: "You were on the force how many years?"

"Twenty-five," the ex-cop said.

"Twenty-five years," Jeremy said. "That's a long time. Did you find police work to be very consuming?"

"Yes, sir," the ex-policeman said. "The job just takes everything you got. World's full of a lot of–"

"Would you say," Jeremy redirected the juror again, "after all those years in such a demanding position, the job had an effect on your world view?"

"What do you mean?"

"I mean when you're a policeman for that long, doesn't it affect the way you view the world?"

"Oh," the ex-policeman said. "Definitely. Definitely. You know, you start to see the world like a cop, and–"

"And would it be fair for me to assume that most cops take a pretty poor view toward defendants in criminal cases?"

"Yeah," the juror said. "I guess that would be true."

"So it would be fair for me to say that, having been a police officer for so many years, you would start out this case with a pretty poor view of Zeb Radamacher?"

"I think I can be fair," the ex-policeman said. "But, yeah. I mean, I would feel that way, too."

"Your Honor," Jeremy said, turning his gaze toward Parr, who was scribbling something at the bench. "Juror one-thirty-two has just expressed a preconceived bias against Mr. Radamacher. We'd ask that you remove him for cause."

Parr sat up straight in his chair, and craned his neck toward the juror. "I'm going to instruct you in this case, that you are only to decide the matter based on the evidence or lack of evidence. You haven't even heard any evidence yet. So, you do not have some preconceived idea about the defendant's guilt or innocence in this case, do you?"

"No," the ex-policeman said carefully.

"And you will listen to the evidence and base your verdict solely upon that evidence in a fair, unbiased manner?" Parr said.

"Yes, sir," the ex-policeman said.

"You'll set aside any preconceived notions you have, so that you can reach a fair verdict?"

"Yes, sir," the ex-policeman said.

"I'm not going to strike him for cause, Mr. Jefferson," Parr said. "You'll have to use a peremptory."

"Thank you, Your Honor," Jeremy smiled.

Jeremy asked a few more careful questions of the police officer. Parr was rarely willing to exclude a juror for cause. Jeremy just hoped to lay enough of a basis so that the other jurors – those lambs who might be listening – would understand completely when Jeremy rose later and sent the ex-policeman on his way.

He turned his attention to an elderly woman, juror number eighty-five.

"Ma'am," Jeremy said, "you understand there are three separate crimes charged in this case?"

"Yes," the old woman said in a steady voice.

"You understand that you must consider each of these crimes separately?"

"Yes," she said. "If that's what the judge says."

"So, if the evidence showed Zeb Radamacher was not guilty on one of the charges, but guilty on the other, you would bring back a verdict of guilty only on the charge the evidence supported, correct?"

"Yes," she said pleasantly.

"Does everyone on the panel agree with juror number eighty-five?"

The jurors nodded, understanding.

The morning became repetitive. Jeremy laying a basis for cause with all potentially hostile wolves, only for Parr to deny removing the juror for cause. But, after four hours, Jeremy had worked his way through ten peremptory challenges, and a good jury was starting to take shape. There were seven men and five women, along with two alternates; ten lambs and two wolves as far as Jeremy could determine.

Rose Galbraith was a twenty-five-year-old woman, juror number eighty-six, who was vibrant and outspoken. Jeremy liked her because her hair was as wild as Zeb's. She started her own landscaping company and specialized in earth-friendly designs. She sat, clear-eyed, in the back center, and Jeremy figured Gray would probably kick her off the jury panel because she had admitted earth-friendly tendencies.

The other wolf had larger teeth, Jeremy thought. Kevin Vontom, juror number one-forty, in the bottom right, just next to the alternates. He was a heavyset blond man of thirty-five. Jeremy liked the fact that he was a blue collar guy. But he was loud and certainly capable of moving a jury with the force of his voice alone. He had also worked on heavy equipment for a couple of summers and so had some familiarity with the machines that were sabotaged, and with monkey wrenching in general. Jeremy was not sure how one-forty would cut.

It was Gray's turn to exercise a peremptory challenge, and Jeremy was surprised when the prosecutor, who had several challenges in reserve, rose and said, "Your Honor, the People are satisfied with this jury."

Jeremy looked out at the remaining jurors who had yet to be called to the box. The remaining pool was largely older and male. It looked like an army of conservative, grumpy men to Jeremy. If he dismissed one-forty now, he could easily end up with an old man who would like nothing better than to convict Zeb out of envy for the boy's youth. And, if Jeremy accepted this panel, then the jury would be locked in, with earth-friendly Rose Galbraith helping to decide Zeb's fate.

"I like this panel," Jeremy whispered to Zeb. "I think we should keep them. I don't think we can do better."

Zeb nodded his agreement.

"Your Honor, the defense is satisfied," Jeremy said, making eye contact with a smiling eighty-six. Zeb's jury had been selected.

33

Charlie's doctors had told him that the leg would heal much faster if he rested at home and did his painful rehabilitation exercises religiously. After just eight days of this routine, he was already losing his mind. He couldn't bear the thought of missing Zeb's trial completely, so he had Professor Quinn pick him up on her way to the courthouse for the lunchtime *Save Zeb* rally.

As she helped him get into her car, Charlie was chilled by the northern Michigan winter. It was hitting its peak in mid-February. In another three or four weeks things might begin warming to the inevitable spring. But today's sunny cold was bitter to Charlie, icing him to the healing bone in his leg. The small heater in Professor Quinn's Prius did little to warm him on the way to the courthouse.

Professor Quinn was jubilant. Her wide smile spread across her coppery, weathered face and gave no indication that the boy she had fought for over the past four months was on trial for his life. She told Charlie that as many as a thousand protestors might show up to support Zeb today. Charlie thought she must be suffering from delusional optimism but kept silent.

As they neared his office and the town center, he was glad he had not spoken. Professor Quinn was right. A very large crowd assembled at the Milton courthouse. Cars lined the street, parking three or four blocks in every direction from the courthouse. A number of chartered busses were parked in the *Beacon* parking lot.

People who had poured out of the cars and busses headed for the courthouse mall. Protestors dressed in parkas and snowmobile suits, mittens and gloves, scarves and mufflers, prepared for arctic weather. Professor

Quinn dropped him off by the mall in front of the courthouse and zipped off to find a place to park.

It was not yet noon, and Charlie imagined Jeremy was still picking a jury. He wished that Zeb could have a chance to see his supporters gathering like a storm.

Many in the crowd were carrying homemade signs, demanding Zeb's freedom. Charlie could not find a friendly face, as most of the protestors wore masks to keep the frigid air from burning their skin. But, even in the faceless mob, Charlie felt its youth and vitality.

Professor Quinn jogged up toward the courthouse steps in her green snowmobile suit. She was surrounded by young people; her student leaders, Charlie thought. A megaphone was placed in her hands. Charlie crutched his way carefully over the ice and snow, around body after body, and made it to her side.

"What do you think?" she hollered, gesturing out toward the crowd.

"I think they're going to arrest you again," Charlie smiled. "But, don't worry. I've got plenty of money for bond."

"No way, Sage," Professor Quinn said, pulling a piece of paper from her pocket. "I've finally started following my lawyer's advice. We got a permit for this one."

Professor Quinn started warming up the crowd. Behind her, a steady stream of people poured out of the front doors of the courthouse. Jury selection was over, Charlie thought. Jurors who had not been selected ran like freed wild animals toward the parking lot, looks of astonishment on their faces as they saw the *Save Zeb* crowd. Media types came out next, in search of lunch, and stumbled upon the larger story.

As Professor Quinn whipped the crowd into its signature chant, Jeremy pushed his way out of the courthouse. Charlie saw Jeremy smile at the sea of support.

"What do we want?" Professor Quinn yelled into the megaphone.

"Freedom for Zeb!" the crowd roared back as one.

"When do we want it?" she said.

"Now!" the crowd screamed. Jeremy looked over the crowd, seemingly awestruck. Charlie walked over to his friend and waited for a lull in the crowd's enthusiasm.

"This is getting totally out of control," Jeremy spoke loudly, close to Charlie's ear.

"Off the chain," Charlie said, "as our young friend might say. How about some lunch?"

"Sounds great," Jeremy said. "Let's go back to the office. I think we could squeeze in a quick game of chess before I have to be back."

The pair made their way slowly through the frothing *Save Zeb* crowd and back to the Sage Law Office. In the library, Charlie found himself in a changeless world. He ordered a greasy pizza from Fatty's. And the chessboard came to life for the first time in over a month.

Jeremy put up a game fight. His best effort since he'd signed on at the Sage Law Office, Charlie thought. But, he was still no match for the master, Charlie smiled to himself. After a solitary win, Charlie accompanied his friend back to the courthouse, sure that his young associate was ready for the trial of his life.

Radamacher hung his head as he meandered through the throng that had gathered in support of Zebediah. He had not slept since Zachary was silenced, and knew he would not sleep again. His head throbbed with every numbered beat of his heart. His eyes lost focus repeatedly, and light danced before him. It took an act of will to draw the world back into a clear, if incoherent, picture.

The crowd reminded him of the Jews that had gathered before Pilate and screamed for the release of the murderous Barabbas. Like the crowd that had condemned the Lamb of God, this crowd, too, shouted for the wrong son. Zachary was gone from the world, while Mark's less innocent son, Zeb, received these shouts of reprieve.

Radamacher would have joined their chanting but lacked sufficient will. He knew that his own life had leaked away on the same ground where Zachary's blood spilled into the cold earth of a shallow grave. The scene replayed in his head endlessly, each time, Radamacher trying desperately to right the course of events. He should have shot Devine and Skeeter and anyone else who insisted on his son's execution. He and Zachary could have escaped to Brazil or Belize or any number of places in the wide world. It would have been worth the risk to the Aryan Nations movement to try. But, try as he might, Radamacher could not alter the course of past events. And, despite his daydreams to the contrary, Zachary was very much as cold as the ground where he lay.

Radamacher came to the courthouse on Monday morning, hoping to lay his eyes on Zeb one last time. He was uncertain if the boy could survive the prison that surely awaited him. But the thought that Zeb might survive it, relatively intact, was the only hope that had kept Radamacher alive through the weekend.

The courtroom was filled with jurors in the morning, and Radamacher was turned away by a deputy. He walked around the courthouse, and outside, on the cold lawn for the entire morning, while a jury was selected to consider Zeb's fate. He had enjoyed the relative solitude, alone with his haunted thoughts. But, as the lunch hour approached, the crowd of supporters began to swell, making Radamacher uncomfortable. He was certain his monstrous guilt, for delivering Zachary to Devine, was manifest upon his face. Any person walking past would surely see him, a demon, pacing the courthouse lawn, and flee screaming from the horror he had become.

He made his way to the steps and into the courthouse. Once inside, away from the crowd, he slipped into Parr's empty courtroom. He took an aisle seat near the bar and rested his head in his hands. He massaged his temples, as Zachary's execution played out again and again inside his mind.

He sat there through the noon hour, unmoving, the silence like a blanket for the wounded. Its comfort was inadequate. He contemplated the levels of hell that were only hours away. Slowly, it dawned on him that he had already arrived. Here, alone in the courthouse. A silent and unchangeable movie playing over and over in his mind. Zachary, repeatedly put down like a rabid dog. Radamacher's skin crawled from his neck down his shoulders, and he shuddered.

As he shook, Jeremy Jefferson entered the courtroom. Jefferson looked at Radamacher for a heartbeat and then looked away. Radamacher's eyes tracked the lawyer as he passed, hoping to engage the young man. Jew or no, Zeb's entire life now rested in his hands, Radamacher thought.

Jefferson sat at the defense table and started unloading his shiny leather briefcase. Books, papers and folders were slowly taken from the case and laid neatly on the table.

"Mr. Jefferson," Radamacher croaked, his voice waking from inactivity.

Jefferson turned and nodded slightly at Radamacher.

"Mr. Jefferson," Radamacher started again, "might I have a moment of your time?"

Jefferson rose and leaned his tall frame down on the bar that separated the men. "What can I do for you, Mr. Radamacher?" he said.

"I know you probably think I hate your kind," Radamacher said.

"My kind?" Jefferson said.

"Look," Radamacher said brusquely, "we can cut through the games. I know Zeb's probably told you how I feel."

"Zeb's mentioned some of your ideas," Jefferson said cautiously.

"Well, I don't care about none of that," Radamacher said. "You're my boy's lawyer, and that's that. And I just wanted to say that Zeb's a good kid. He was always a good kid until his mother got his head screwed on a little backwards. But he's still a good kid."

"I know, Mr. Radamacher," Jeremy said. "I think he's a great kid."

"Just do your best for him, will ya," Radamacher said, pleading.

"Of course," Jeremy said. "I always do."

"Thanks," Radamacher said. "You do your best."

Slowly the court filled up around the two men. Reporters, spectators and the prosecutor all took their places. A deputy led Zeb into the courtroom. Radamacher reached out to his son as the deputy led him past. He touched Zeb on the hand, to the deputy's displeasure, and Zebediah looked up at his father. Radamacher was pleased to see his surviving son smile. It was a smile Radamacher had seen Zeb flash since he was a small boy. It was an easy, disarming smile. The smile was heaven on earth. And then Zeb looked away, shook hands with his lawyer and took his place.

Radamacher knew that his own court date, with a much higher authority, was rapidly approaching. Zeb's smile had lightened his burden slightly. Maybe there was salvation even for the worst of sin, he thought. He rose and set off out of the courtroom, his last mission accomplished. He thought of the shotgun in his cabinet, and of the shower room in the cellar, where he could put an end to the intense pain of his worldly existence. He was ready to meet the Great White maker; to face heaven or hell at the will of the Shepherd.

Jeremy glanced at Zeb out of the corner of his eye. The boy had been a quick study on trial tactics, and he followed Jeremy's advice to the letter. He sat attentively, listening to every word uttered in the courtroom, a mirror to Jeremy's own behavior. The two of them sat side by side, listening to Gray's opening statement without reaction. Occasionally, Zeb would scribble a note on the pad Jeremy had provided for him.

Gray's courtroom demeanor was that of a competent professional. He was never spectacular or theatric. He plodded on, like a tractor, plowing through facts in a straight line. He laid out the state's case with effective simplicity. And, as he stopped speaking, his bony index finger was again pointed at Zeb, asking the jury to convict the boy on all charges. Gray took his seat.

"Mr. Jefferson, will the defense be giving an opening statement?" Parr asked.

"Thank you, Your Honor," Jeremy said. He took his trial book to the lectern and adjusted the microphone to a comfortable level. He looked at each juror with a fluid sweep. Gray had held their attention, and they now eyed Jeremy with a look that asked, "How can you be sitting so close to that young man and not be guilty yourself?" Jeremy thought.

"Good afternoon," Jeremy said softly, nodding to the jurors. "This case is the story of two young men, and the crimes they committed on a

Saturday night, this past October. One of those young men is my client, Zeb Radamacher. Now, this isn't something you are going to hear from many defense lawyers, so you better listen closely. Zeb Radamacher is guilty of malicious destruction of property – one of the crimes he's been charged with. And Zeb is going to tell you in his own words how he carefully planned, and then carried out that crime."

Jeremy was pleased to see the puzzled looks on the faces of the jurors. They hadn't anticipated this opening. Jeremy slipped a peek at Gray, whose face also registered some alarm, though he was struggling to remain blank.

"What makes this case unusual is that while Zeb Radamacher was committing malicious destruction of property, a different person – Jared MacAdam – the State's star witness in this case, showed up at the crime scene and committed two other crimes – arson and terrorism," Jeremy continued. The sheep on the jury nodded slowly, but his two wolves looked at Jeremy with critical eyes. He would have expected no less. "And, when you review all the evidence that will be presented, the fact that Zeb Radamacher and the State's star witness committed different crimes will be as plain as day.

"You see, the evidence in this case will show you quite clearly that Zeb Radamacher is a very intelligent young man. He is an activist, who believes that large corporations are ruining the earth. And his crime in this case was to take what activists call 'direct action.' That is, to go out and try to damage property of a corporation to slow development or make development more expensive.

"Now, I'm not going to stand up here and defend Zeb Radamacher's decisions. I don't expect you to cut him any breaks for the crime he has committed. I understand what he thinks, but this is not a case where anyone is asking you to endorse a particular brand of political thought. What I am going to ask you to do, is to look at Zeb Radamacher, and listen to what he says. And, I think that if you do that, you will be left with no doubt that he is a smart kid, even if you think he is misguided.

"Being a smart kid, Zeb was very cautious in what he planned to do. He will tell you that he researched and planned his 'direct action' against Blue-Mart carefully. And in his research, he will tell you about a resource he came across called *The Monkey Wrencher's Handbook*. Zeb followed *The Handbook* like a road map. And it taught him how to commit his crime and how to avoid getting caught. Because if you are a monkey wrencher – someone who takes direct action – you want to stay out of jail so you can continue to fight for the environment.

"One of the most important lessons in *The Handbook* was that monkey wrenchers should never firebomb heavy equipment. There are a number of reasons for that. It's a very inefficient way of damaging property. It draws greater scrutiny to the crime. And it can result in more severe penalties should the monkey wrencher be caught. Zeb knew these things. And that is why he would have never firebombed the bulldozer in this case. Because, whatever you think of his politics, he is a smart kid.

"Now, on the flip side, you have the State's star witness, Jared MacAdam. Back in October, before these crimes, he was taken in by Zeb's group while they were planning to put grit - a substance called silicon carbide, which Zeb learned about from *The Handbook* - in the oil supply of the vehicles at the Blue-Mart site," Jeremy continued. Some of the sheep were beginning to nod in the affirmative, and even Rose Galbraith, purveyor of environmentally friendly lawn designs, had begun to show interest. "At one meeting, MacAdam stood up and suggested that they firebomb some of the equipment at the Blue-Mart site. But Zeb, knowing that this was a very bad idea, kicked MacAdam out of the group. Zeb said, 'No way.' Because he didn't want to take that risk.

"On the night in question, Zeb led his group to the Blue-Mart site. With him were Melissa Dobbs and Steve Wynn. Each of them wore gloves to avoid leaving fingerprints, and socks over the top of their boots to avoid leaving shoe prints behind. And carefully, they drilled small holes in the oil intake valves of three vehicles. They drilled the holes in locations so they would not be noticeable to the heavy equipment operators," Jeremy said. Kevin Vontom sat up in his chair and took renewed notice. "Then they carefully poured a silicon carbide solution into the oil system. And guess where they got this plan? All of it. Right from *The Handbook*. It was right from the textbook on how to correctly, and secretly, monkey wrench a construction site.

"And as they were finishing their plan, who should show up but Jared MacAdam. He came without being invited by Zeb. And despite being warned not to, MacAdam came armed with a Molotov cocktail - a homemade bomb - that he had made himself. MacAdam spray-painted the letters ELF, for Earth Liberation Front, on a backhoe at the scene. And though Zeb and Steve and Melissa yelled at him to stop, MacAdam lit the Molotov cocktail, and chucked it at one of the bulldozers.

"And guess what? Every single thing MacAdam did was wrong according to *The Monkey Wrencher's Handbook*. Zeb was committing a crime straight by the book, and MacAdam committed crimes in ways exactly warned against in the book, if you wanted to take successful direct action.

"Now in doing these very different activities, Zeb and MacAdam have committed very different crimes. MacAdam actually committed the crime of terrorism - if you want to believe the prosecutor's definition of that law

- and the crime of arson, while Zeb committed the less serious offense of malicious destruction of property."

Jeremy paused to glance at his notebook, carefully turning pages to a new point in his opening argument.

"So how is it that we are here, where Zeb Radamacher faces terrorism and arson charges?" he continued. "I would submit to you, that the reason we are here is because the prosecutor has completely refused to see what will be obvious to you after viewing the evidence. That there were two separate criminal actions by two separate young men. And instead of acknowledging that fact, the prosecutor chose to offer MacAdam a sweetheart deal to get him to testify against Zeb Radamacher.

"Now, in order to buy MacAdam's testimony against Zeb Radamacher, the prosecutor dismissed a life offense and recommended probation for their star witness. And if that wasn't good enough, the prosecutor then bought another witness - Melissa Dobbs - dismissing her life offense charge and recommending a four-year sentence. And these bought witnesses, ladies and gentlemen, are the only evidence that the prosecutor has to suggest that Zeb Radamacher was in any way involved in the crimes of arson or terrorism.

"The problem with relying on this evidence, of course, is as plain to you as it would be to anyone. Wouldn't a young person, like MacAdam or like Dobbs, be happy to tell a fib if they were in hot water? Of course they would. And they were not just in hot water. They literally avoided a potential of life in prison by telling the prosecutor what he wanted to hear. But, the problem is, the evidence they offer is completely unsupported by any of the other evidence in the case.

"I'm going to ask you, in this case, not to be swayed by the terrorism hype that is going to be heaped on you. That has already been heaped on you. I'm not going to be asking that you put any stamp of approval on Zeb Radamacher's conduct. He has done wrong, and he will admit that to you in this trial. But, he is not the worst criminal before you in this case. That honor goes to the State's star witness. And in the end, if you look carefully at the evidence that is presented to you, I think you will understand that the prosecutor is going after the wrong guy for the wrong crime. Thank you."

No one fell asleep. Each juror seemed engaged. And, unlike legal dramas on television, that was a lot to ask for a jury. Jeremy took a seat next to Zeb and prepared to take evidence.

Gray called Trooper Nielsen to the stand. Nielsen gave a crisp twenty-minute rendition about how he caught Zeb red-handed at the construction site. It was a fast start for Gray, and the jury appeared to eat it up. Jeremy rose knowing he needed to put a dent in the officer to avoid a rout.

"Good afternoon, Trooper Nielsen," Jeremy said, establishing a base at the lectern. "You testified here today that your attention was first drawn to a fire? Isn't that correct?"

"Yes, sir," Nielsen said.

Jeremy wanted to establish some control over the trooper early, before reeling off the mostly innocuous points that would confirm Zeb's version of events. "This isn't the first time you've testified in this case, is it?"

"No, sir," Nielsen said. "I testified at the preliminary examination a few months ago."

"And you were under oath then, just as you are here today, correct?"

"Yes, sir."

"At that hearing, you testified that your attention was first drawn to an explosion, didn't you?"

"Yes, sir," Nielsen said. "But you helped me correct myself. My attention was drawn by a fire."

"My question, Trooper Nielsen," Jeremy honed in on the witness, "is whether you testified, under oath, at the preliminary examination that, 'I was traveling southbound on twenty-seven when I noticed an explosion on the east-hand side of the highway.' Did you say that, under oath, at the exam in this case?"

"Yes, I did," Nielsen said.

"Today, your testimony is different, under oath, isn't it? You testified today that you saw a fire on the side of the road, not an explosion, correct?"

"Yes, sir," Nielsen said. "Like I said, you corrected me on that back at the exam."

"So the jury is clear, then, which statement under oath is true? Did you first see a fire or did you first see an explosion?"

"I first saw the fire. It just seemed to me that there had been an explosion, because the fire was so big, but I didn't actually see any explosion," Nielsen said.

"So your statement, under oath, that you first saw a fire is true?"

"Yes."

"And your statement, under oath, that you first saw an explosion is not true?"

"I didn't see–"

"Objection," Gray said, remaining seated. "Argumentative."

"Sustained," Parr said.

"You never saw any explosion, did you?" Jeremy continued on, unrepentant.

"No, sir."

"The only way you even knew there was an explosion was because you were told the cause of the fire, by Chief McGuigan that night, correct?"

"Yes," Nielsen said, some resistance crept into his voice.

"And you have no way of knowing, other than by sheer speculation, what time the fire was started, do you?"

"I know it was started fairly close in time to when I was driving by," Nielsen said, rising to the bait.

"You know that because you have some expertise in fire investigation?"

"I know it because the fire was still burning when I drove past," Nielsen said.

"Do you have any idea how long a fire started by a Molotov cocktail can burn?" Jeremy said.

Nielsen paused. Wheels appeared to spin behind concentrated eyes. "No, sir," Nielsen said.

"So you can't say if the fire was started five minutes before you passed or five hours, can you?"

"Well, I know it wasn't five hours," Nielsen said. "Because the construction site closed down at about six-thirty. So at most it was three hours, maybe."

"Okay," Jeremy said, unwilling to let go of any point. "So you can't say if the fire was started five minutes before you passed or three hours, can you?"

Nielsen thought again before conceding the point.

Having established control, Jeremy led Nielsen quickly through the highlights of his limited investigation, before closing with the main points of his cross.

"Now you've been a trooper for what? Eight years?" Jeremy said.

"Yes, sir. Coming up nine."

"And you've seen a lot of crimes and crime scenes in your experience, correct?"

"Yes, sir. Thousands," Nielsen said, clearly tiring of the cross-examination.

"Let me ask you this," Jeremy said. "When you found Zeb Radamacher at the scene with socks over his boots, what did that indicate to you, in your experience?"

"Well," Nielsen said, "footprint evidence has become very reliable. I mean I've investigated dozens of cases where footprint evidence leads to a conviction. So, my thought at the time was that he was clearly trying to avoid leaving footprints at the scene."

"Have you ever seen any other crimes where this was done to avoid leaving footprints?" Jeremy said.

"Yes, sir," Nielsen said. "I had a B and E last year – breaking and entering – out at a warehouse, where the guy was wearing foot coverings. I think those were surgical boots, though."

"So this is done, at least in your experience, to try and conceal one's identity, correct?"

"Yes, sir."

"And what about the fact that you caught Zeb with gloves on? In your experience, did you think those were worn to help him conceal his identity?"

"Yes," Trooper Nielsen said, "just like with the footprints. Criminals frequently wear gloves to avoid leaving fingerprints."

"So, would it be fair for the jury to understand that, based on your experience, it looked to you like Zeb Radamacher was going to great efforts to conceal his identity in the commission of this crime?"

Nielsen paused and said, "Yes, sir."

"Okay," Jeremy said, checking off a point in the notebook. "Turning to your police report in this matter, you did your best to include all the information you have about this crime in the report, true?"

"Yes," Nielsen said.

"There is nothing important that you omitted from your report, to the best of your knowledge, true?"

"I don't think so."

"And your testimony is complete. I mean, you haven't omitted any information you have about this crime while testifying, have you?"

"No, sir," Nielsen said, smiling. "I think between you and Mr. Gray, we have covered everything."

"So, based on your personal knowledge of this case, you have no evidence to offer which would suggest that Zeb Radamacher started the fire on the bulldozer, do you?"

"Well," Nielsen said, thinking out loud, "I guess there is the fact that I caught him running away from the fire just after it was set."

"You testified earlier that you couldn't tell if the fire was set three hours before or five minutes before, correct?"

"Well, yes. But the fact that he was running away from the fire."

Jeremy thought for a moment, and then asked, "If I understood you correctly, when you pulled into the construction site, the bulldozer that was burning was to the left of your car, true?"

"Yes, kind of up and to the left," Trooper Nielsen said.

"And you also testified that when you first saw Mr. Radamacher, he was running in front of your vehicle, from right to left, if I understood you, correct?"

Trooper Nielsen paused. "Yes, that's right. From my right to left."

"So, if Mr. Radamacher was running from the right of your vehicle, and the burning bulldozer was on the left of your vehicle, he wasn't running away from the burning bulldozer, was he? He was actually running toward it."

"Well, I think he was running away from the entire area. He was headed for the woods."

"But, my question, Trooper Nielsen, is whether he was running away from the burning dozer when you first saw him? He was not, was he?"

"No, sir. Not really."

"In fact, he was actually running toward the burning dozer, from the direction of where the other equipment was parked, wasn't he?"

"Yes, sir. Kind of in the direction of the burning dozer. But he was heading for the woods."

"But, Mr. Radamacher definitely was not running from close proximity to the burning dozer at the time. He was actually running from where the other equipment that had been damaged was, wasn't he?"

"I guess so. Yes."

"So, I'll ask you again," Jeremy said, raising his voice for emphasis. "You personally have no evidence to offer which would suggest that Zeb Radamacher started the fire on the bulldozer, do you?"

"Other than he was at the scene, no."

"And just based on your personal observations and your personal investigation, it is entirely possible that someone else may have actually used the Molotov cocktail to start that bulldozer on fire?"

"I guess that's possible, that someone else in the defendant's group was responsible for starting the fire," Nielsen said, still battling like a hooked fish. "But I'd say the group was responsible for all the damage that they did together."

"Judge, I'd move to strike that answer as non-responsive and drawing a legal conclusion," Jeremy said, looking to Parr.

"If you could just answer the questions," Parr gently prodded the struggling police officer, "things would probably go a lot quicker."

Nielsen nodded.

"Again, is it possible, based on your personal observations, that someone else may have used the Molotov cocktail to start the bulldozer on fire?"

"Yes. Anything's possible."

"You just aren't in a position to tell the jury one way or the other, because you don't personally know the answer to that question, true?"

"No. I don't know."

"Thank you, Trooper Nielsen," Jeremy said. "No further questions."

Jeremy took his notebook back to the defense desk. Zeb let a smile break slightly, and Jeremy sent daggers with his eyes, reminding the boy to stay focused before the jury. Jeremy and Zeb sat again, side by side, as Gray wasted several minutes trying to rehabilitate Nielsen's testimony. Jeremy had what he wanted from the first witness. One down, he thought.

Jeremy figured the trial would be completed by Thursday. Friday at the latest. He was always amazed at the incredible length that high profile cases seemed to take when they were televised. Months and months of witnesses. Jeremy had never had a trial that lasted more than two weeks.

His attention drifted to the camera in the first row of the gallery. He had almost forgotten that his every move was being broadcast. Court TV was featuring the trial, and every network had an affiliate taking tape earlier in the day. This case was going to be his fifteen minutes of fame. Allie was right about that.

When Gray finally stopped flailing around with Nielsen, Parr called the lawyers to the bench.

"It's almost four. Do you have a short witness we can get in today?" Parr said.

"Yeah," Gray said. "I can't imagine the next witness will take an hour."

"All right," Parr said.

Gray called Evan Ondyer to the stand. Gray led the affable construction foreman through his testimony in ten minutes. It was a coherent story of the aftermath of the firebombing. The crew had returned to work on Monday. The burned-out dozer had already been removed from the site. But they had quickly discovered that a backhoe, a loader, and an off-highway truck had been sabotaged, as one by one those vehicles failed. The crew belatedly figured out that the vehicles had been monkey wrenched, and even found the drill that had been used to affect the sabotage.

The jury warmed to Ondyer instantly, and Jeremy made a note at the top of his cross-examination sheet. "GENTLE," he wrote in block letters.

"Good afternoon, Mr. Ondyer," Jeremy said.

Ondyer nodded and smiled. He was tall, even as he sat in the witness stand, and his skin had paled with the winter skies.

"I just have a few questions for you," Jeremy began. "First, let me ask you about the damage that was done to these other pieces of equipment. If I understand your testimony, there were four vehicles in total that were damaged, correct?"

"Uh-huh," he said.

"You have to say yes or no, for the record, okay?" Jeremy reminded him gently.

"Yes," Ondyer said. "Sorry. Yes. Four of 'em. The burned-out dozer. Then a backhoe. And the loader and a 769 – a truck – which all burned up their engines because of the grit in the crankcases."

"Okay," Jeremy said. "So, if I understand you, there was really some very different kinds of damage between the one dozer and the other three pieces of equipment?"

"Yeah," Ondyer said. "Well, the dozer was burned out. And the other three, their engines burned up because someone fouled the oil."

"I'm not very mechanically inclined, Mr. Ondyer. So I apologize if my questions might not seem educated on this stuff."

The witness smiled. "Naw. It's all right."

"Okay," Jeremy said. "So on the three that were, uh, where the oil was fouled, you said."

"Yeah, on the three of them. Basically, they put something in the crankcases like sand, but I think it was some kind of silicon or an industrial abrasive or something. The mechanic said what it was. But they put some of that in with the oil, so that when we ran them for a while, the engines just seized up. The grit scored the engine blocks and pistons and everything. It was a mess."

"Okay," Jeremy said. "So on those three, they put some type of grit into the crankcases. Do you know how this was accomplished?"

"Yeah," Ondyer said. "I should've caught it at first. But it was slick work. You see, when we leave the site at night, we try to park the stuff up on a hill in the light, next to the highway. To deter theft and stuff. And also, we have locking oil caps to make sure that no one can put anything in the oil."

"Okay," Jeremy said. "So what happened? How did the grit get into the heavy equipment?"

"Well, after the loader seized up, I went and checked it out. I found this little hole," Owen held up his thumb and forefinger to show the small width of the hole. "They drilled it in the back of the oil pipe, so you couldn't see it from where we normally stand when we check the oil."

"So why would they drill a hole there, if you have any idea?"

"Uh-huh," Owen said, happily explaining the theory of monkey wrenching. "Well, we check our oil almost every morning. Because we want to be careful about these types of things. So if they just drilled the hole in the front of the pipe, or if they just drilled off the locking cap, we'd know about it in the morning, and then we wouldn't operate the equipment until we got the grit cleaned out."

"So, how do they get the grit into this little hole?" Jeremy asked. He had managed to relax the affable foreman more than Gray had been able to do on his own.

"Well, they probably used a tube and funnel. And they would have suspended the grit in some oil, and then just poured it in once the hole was drilled."

"Okay. I see," Jeremy said, playing the student on a subject he knew more about than most ardent environmentalists and heavy equipment operators combined. "So whoever is drilling these holes, and putting this grit in these machines, is it fair to say that that person is trying really hard to do so without raising any suspicions from anyone?"

Ondyer pondered the confusing question. "Come again," he said.

"Whoever put the grit in these vehicles, that person was doing all they could so that their work would not be seen by the equipment operators, right?"

"Oh. Yes. That's true. Because if the operator sees that the oil's been tampered with, then they're not going to start that machine until they get it checked out and cleaned."

"Okay," Jeremy said, checking off a point in his notebook. "Now, the other bulldozer that was damaged, it was burned out, you said?"

"Yeah," Ondyer said. "The exterior of the dozer was burned right up."

"And there was no attempt to hide that damage, was there?"

"No. I mean they had already removed it from the site when we got in on Monday. But I went and saw it at the shop. And, it was just burned right up."

"Also, on the backhoe, there was a word or a logo painted on it, correct?"

"Yeah," Ondyer said. "Kind of like a bright purple color. It said, um, what was it–?"

"E-L-F?" Jeremy said.

"Uh-huh, yeah. E-L-F, right."

"And nobody tried to hide that graffiti, did they?"

"Nope. It was just there plain as anything when we came in. We thought it went along with the burned-out dozer, you know. Stupid, I guess. We really should have checked the oil better."

"So, would it be fair for the jury to conclude that whoever put grit in the crankcases was trying very hard to hide what they did?"

"Yeah."

"And would it be fair to also say that whoever burned the bulldozer wasn't really trying to hide what was done at all?"

"Uh-huh. Yeah, sure seems that way."

"Fair to say that whoever spray-painted 'ELF' on the backhoe wasn't trying to hide what was done?"

"Yeah. That's fair," Ondyer said.

"No one on your crew was hurt by the grit that was put in the crankcases, were they?"

"Nope."

"And no one on your crew was hurt when the dozer burned."

"Nope. We didn't even get on the site until Monday. And it was already taken to the shop by then."

"Just a couple more questions, Mr. Ondyer," Jeremy said. He glanced at the jury. He could see Rose Galbraith soaking in the import of his testimony. All ahead full, he thought. "You don't know Zeb Radamacher, do you?" Jeremy swept his hand toward Zeb.

"Nope. Never met him."

"You don't have any personal information to say that Zeb Radamacher was the person to set the bulldozer on fire, do you?"

"No. I don't," Ondyer said. "I wasn't really there."

"Is it possible that someone other than Mr. Radamacher set this fire, as far as you're concerned?"

"Yeah. I just don't know, really," Ondyer said.

"Thank you, Mr. Ondyer," Jeremy said. "No further questions."

Testimony was concluded for the day. The jury was instructed not to discuss the case with anyone and not to watch, read or listen to any coverage of the trial. Parr adjourned court until Tuesday morning.

Once the jury was led out, Zeb broke out in smile. "Great job, Mr. J.," the boy said.

"Thanks, kid," Jeremy said. "Let's just keep on an even keel, okay? One day at a time."

"Okay," Zeb said, before being escorted back to the lockup.

Jeremy headed home, exhausted. He scarfed down a bowl of Chunky Beef soup, drank a Mountain Dew, and started reviewing for Tuesday's witnesses.

34

"Ed Gray on one," Bishop's secretary said over the intercom.

"I'll take it," Bishop snapped. He had been waiting for the call all day. Watching the trial on Court TV was no substitute for a report from someone on the front line.

"Hello, Ed," he said.

"Hello, Mr. Bishop," Gray said. The prosecutor's voice sounded tired and distant, Bishop thought. "I was just calling to keep you posted on the trial. Just got back in the office."

"It's about time," Bishop said. "We've been waiting for something all day."

"Well, it's just me up here," the prosecutor sniped back.

"Can't you get that assistant of yours, Fitchett, to relay messages to us to keep us posted?"

"Believe it or not, Mr. Bishop," Gray said, "my office has about two hundred active cases right now, so Pamela doesn't really have time to act as my press secretary. She's handling the other hundred and ninety-nine cases that are going to hell while I'm trying this one."

"Well, do what you can, because–" Bishop was interrupted by an annoying tone coming from his intercom. His secretary knew not to disturb him if he was on the line. "Can you hang on a second, I have to take this." Bishop put Gray on hold, oblivious to any response, and punched the intercom line.

"What is it," he hissed at his secretary. "I'm on the line."

"I know," she said apologetically. "Sorry. But, the governor wants to see you right now. They said to drag you out of a meeting if I had to."

Bishop had an open door to Howell but was unaccustomed to the governor demanding his time. It had been years since Howell had demanded his presence, maybe all the way back to the early congressional campaign days.

"Tell him I'll be right over," Bishop said.

He punched up Gray's line but only got a dial tone. Gray was going to have to learn who he shouldn't hang up on, Bishop seethed, and slammed the phone into the receiver.

Bishop walked in shirt sleeves to the governor's office. Howell was on the phone, and the secretary made him wait in the lobby. Bishop rolled his eyes and paced the reception area.

After two minutes, the secretary showed him in. Howell was seated behind his desk. The governor's eyebrows were knit by some unknown concern.

"Bish, we need to talk," he said sternly.

Bishop was rattled by his tone. Since when was Howell making his own decisions about who he needed to talk with?

"I've been on the phone for the last two hours," Howell said, staring straight into Bishop's eyes. "Just hung up with Xavier, that prick."

Leonard Xavier, III was the attorney general. He was a hip-hop era version of Martin Luther King, Jr., and he was the odds-on favorite to be Howell's opponent in the governor's race in two years and nine months.

"What are you doing taking his call?" Bishop said. "Our contact protocol says all calls are supposed to flow through my office. You shouldn't–"

"Just relax a minute, Bish," Howell said, touching the fingers of his hands together in a contemplative pose. "Artie called this afternoon. My cell. I don't even know how he got the number. But, you know, I'm glad he did."

"Governor, it's just not the proto–" Bishop started, only to be cut off again by his suddenly assertive boss.

"Relax, Bish," Howell said. "Let me finish, okay? Artie called me direct because he wanted to avoid talking to you. He said he shared some bad numbers with you on the whole MEGPAT issue over a month ago, and that you've been blowing him off ever since."

"Oh, Christ, Roger," Bishop said. He made Howell a congressman and a governor, and didn't like taking shit from the ungrateful prick. "You know Artie. A few numbers get out of whack, and he runs around like the sky's falling. I've been meaning to talk with you about it, but things have just been busy. I got Artie's stuff right in my in-box. You want me to get it?"

"No," Howell said, tapping his fingertips together with greater intensity.

"What, then?" Bishop said.

"Artie's the best pollster we got, Bish," Howell continued. "We can't just ignore him. And it's worse than just these numbers. He thinks that we need to make a major overhaul in the way information flows around this place. He thinks you've got too much control."

"Oh, for fuck's sake, Roger. What in the hell are we talking about here?" Bishop was uneasy. He was in uncharted waters. Since Howell had turned to him as his main political operative, Bishop could not remember a single time when Howell had questioned his judgment.

"Have I ever steered you wrong?" Bishop said. "I mean, we've got this far, haven't we? There's nothing wrong with the way information flows. This is just Artie with his undies in a knot, because he's not getting enough attention."

"It's more than that," Howell said, his voice raised. "How come you haven't told me about *ELF v. Howell?* We're getting the shit kicked out of us in federal court, and I've got to hear about it from fucking Artie Fisher a week after it's happened. It wasn't in the daily brief, and I sure as hell haven't heard anything from you."

Bishop suppressed the urge to tell Howell to shut the fuck up and follow the script. The possibility of a run at the White House must have swelled his pea brain. Better to let him vent, though, Bishop thought. Get it over with.

"Do you know that as of this morning my numbers have officially started to slip?" Howell ranted. "My negatives are now higher than they were when we started in with this whole domestic terror bullshit. I'm losing base support for fucking crissakes.

"Artie made me take direct calls from Xavier and from Usterman, because he's afraid that you're isolating me, Bish. He thinks you're fucking up in a big way. So I had to have an impromptu chat with Xavier about how we want to handle the appeal of the MEGPAT case, and I don't know shit about the case - or the goddamn statute. And then Usterman is telling me that there is a whole troop of farmers that are up in arms over this thing. He tells me there's a goddamn revolt brewing up there in Wabeno County. And I don't have a clue."

Bishop sat, waiting for Howell to lose steam. Howell's rage was already starting to seek direction. The governor lacked the skills to lead a hunting party, let alone a state, Bishop thought. But, in an age where the only requirement for high public office was a pretty face and the ability to read a speech, Howell was a star.

Artie Fisher was making some kind of move, Bishop thought. And he wanted the little statistician's head on a plate.

Howell finally wound down.

"Look, Roger," Bishop said, his tone that of a father to a pouting child. "There's a little softness on the MEGPAT numbers. Yes. I didn't think I needed to worry you about it. But I'm sorry you got blind-sided by all this shit. That fucking Artie Fisher is a piece of work.

"Now look. I've gone over his numbers. And they are weakening some. But that's the beauty of this issue. Where are the voters going to go? Even if they start to have questions on this policy, you think they're going to run to Xavier on a matter of security? Life or death, and they're going to turn it over to that guy? No way. These people are going to be with us on this issue. We just need to fight it through. Stay strong. Tough. Stay on message. And this is going to crush Xavier or anybody else in your way. I'm talking about the White House, Governor, and I don't think I'm exaggerating."

Howell shook his head. "That's not the way Artie sees it. He thinks there's some real danger. Wants us to cut and run. Blame an activist judiciary for declaring the law unconstitutional. You know, damn judges are keeping us from protecting you and then just let it blow over."

"No!" Bishop said. "Look. I was just on the phone with that prosecutor up there in Wabeno. Good guy. He's been telling me his case is a slam dunk. We're going to get our first major victory in the war on domestic terror. Probably get a verdict late this week.

"Let me set up another press conference up there," Bishop continued, closing the deal. Howell just needed direction and a little reassurance. "Day of the verdict. We'll go up there, bask in the glow of victory. Announce that Gray has earned his way on as the Domestic Terror Czar. And then we'll let Artie take some more numbers. If I'm wrong about this, we will kill it right there. But I'm not wrong, Roger. This thing is ours for the taking. Right to Pennsylvania Avenue."

Howell sat, dropping his face into his hands for several seconds. "I dunno, Bish," he mumbled through his hands. "I just don't like the sound of it."

"Come on, Roger. Five more days isn't going to change things. Don't be a pussy, now."

"I dunno," the governor said.

"Gray tells me that Pamela Fitchett has been asking if she can follow him down to Lansing if he gets the Domestic Terror Czar gig," Bishop played his final card. "Apparently she would like to talk to you some more about her prospects."

"Really," Howell said, picking his head up out of his hands. A crooked smile loosened his face.

"Scout's honor," Bishop said. Never underestimate the power of vanity, he thought.

"Oh, hell," Howell said, laughing. "I guess four or five more days isn't going to kill anyone. So we'll take one last trip up there. I might see if Usterman wants to go. Maybe he can talk some sense into the damn farmers up there."

"Sounds great," Bishop said. "I'll set things up. Don't worry. I promise this is going to work itself out. This is our issue, Roger."

"I'm getting out of here," Howell said, relief washing over his face. "That was a long afternoon."

"You deserve it, sir," Bishop said, suppressing a growl.

"Oh, and Bish," Howell said, looking back as he headed for the door. "Don't tell Artie about this, okay? I told him I wouldn't tell you. He's getting a little paranoid, I think."

"No problem, Roger," Bishop said. "Good night."

Bishop stalked back to his office. Artie Fisher was not paranoid, Bishop laughed to himself, because someone really was out to get him. Bishop was fantasizing about asking Richard Alarie to assassinate the nosy little pollster, when it occurred to him that the governor didn't really know about Richard Alarie, a.k.a. Colin Green. Had Artie known about that, Bishop might not have been able to reel Howell back in. It might have been curtains. It sucked being number two, Bishop thought. You were always just one step away from the street if you were number two just as soon as number one wanted to cut you loose.

Bishop kicked his feet up on his crowded desk, resting them neatly in the in-box, on top of Artie's report on the political failure of MEGPAT. He lit a cigar and started mapping out the press conference he would be sponsoring at the end of the week. Convicting the state's number one most wanted domestic terrorist would put a stop to all this Monday-morning quarterbacking in a big hurry. And then he could turn his attention to dealing with Artie Fisher, once and for all.

The first day of trial had drained him. But Jeremy still reviewed his notes until midnight before trying to get some rest. He never slept well during trial, and Zeb Radamacher's case was no exception. He tossed and turned, trying to get comfortable, but it was 3:00 a.m. before sleep finally came. And even then, he dreamed of the case and of the cross-examinations to come. The alarm sounded like a slap shot at 6:00 a.m., and Jeremy dragged his weary body out of bed for another day in Parr's courtroom.

While he had worn his best suit for day one of the trial, he dressed down for day two, trying to reach the casual dress of his audience. He wore a grey wool jacket over tan slacks. A light blue tie with diagonal stripes contrasted with a heavy blue shirt.

Jeremy reviewed the prosecution witness list over his morning coffee. The entire day would be devoted to testimony, and Jeremy expected that Gray would be able to get through four or five witnesses. The prosecutor was not forced to follow any specific order, but logically, Jeremy tried to anticipate the witnesses he would be facing down in court on the second day of trial.

It made sense that Gray would finish off with the witnesses related to the damaged equipment in the morning. That would be the owner, Ian Cashman, and the mechanic, John Few. They would be short, necessary witnesses. There would be no bombshells from either of them. From there, who Gray would call was anyone's guess. There were several tangential witnesses yet to come. Amanda Ratielle, from the hardware store. Allen Kryszinski, the shop teacher. Greg Westbrook, the clerk at a rock shop in Lansing who sold Zeb the silicon carbide. All these witnesses would be short and to the point, and Gray might pile them all into the same day.

The case really boiled down to two witnesses, Jeremy thought. Jared MacAdam and Melissa Dobbs. How he handled the cross-examination of Zeb's collaborators would likely seal Zeb's fate. And Gray might want to work one or both of them into today's testimony, just to make sure the jury did not fall asleep.

That would only leave Chief McGuigan and Detective Russell, and Jeremy did not expect their testimony until last. He looked quickly through his notes on all the witnesses one last time before heading out. Whoever Gray sent to the plate, Jeremy felt ready.

A powdery snow had come down overnight, leaving an inch-thick, white blanket across Milton. Jeremy dusted off his car, taking care that he did not soak his suit, and headed off for the courthouse.

The courthouse was considerably more sedate on Tuesday morning, blanketed in a fresh white snow. The absence of the entire jury pool made the courthouse seem larger. Still, the trial had drawn a good crowd. The television cameras were all back for day two, arranged in the front row of the gallery. Joining the television media were Allie and Sam Oster from WHIP. A couple of dozen spectators had filed in. About half, Jeremy recognized from the *Save Zeb* outings, but the other half were just citizens looking for cheap entertainment, Jeremy thought.

Zeb was brought in five minutes before the 8:30 a.m. start time, directly from the holding cell. The jury was sequestered in the assembly room, so there was no need to go through the ruse of acting like Zeb was a free man.

"Morning, Mr. J.," Zeb said, greeting Jeremy at the defense table.

"Good morning. How'd you sleep?"

"Like a baby," Zeb said, and he looked well-rested. "Can't wait to get started again. You did a good job yesterday, Mr. J."

"Thanks, Zeb," Jeremy said.

Deputy Short called the courtroom to order and Parr entered on time for a second straight day.

"Are we ready for the jury?" Parr asked. Jeremy nodded, along with Gray. "All right. Gaylord, you can bring them in."

The jury filed in with Deputy Short's guidance. Though they had not been instructed to do so, Jeremy noticed that they were sitting in their exact same seats. It was a sign of an orderly jury, and Jeremy would have bet money that either Rose Galbraith or Kevin Vontom already had the inside track toward becoming the jury's foreperson.

Parr welcomed the jury back with some brief instructions, and Gray called Ian Cashman to start off the day.

Cashman projected an air of unrefined entitlement that went along with his *nouveau riche* clothing. He was downright annoying, in Jeremy's view, and if the substantive part of his testimony were not so inconsequential, Jeremy would have been inclined to make a run at him on cross-examination. However, it was difficult to cross-examine a man whose only real contribution to the case was to say that he owned the damaged equipment, and that repairs would cost over a hundred thousand dollars.

Unwilling to bash the victim, no matter how arrogant and unsympathetic the man seemed, Jeremy simply confirmed that Cashman had no personal knowledge of Zeb's involvement in damaging the equipment. Gray must have coached Cashman on this point, because he had been far more happy to answer Jeremy's questions at trial than he had been at the exam. Cashman's entire testimony took less than ten minutes.

As Jeremy expected, Gray then called John Few to the stand. The mechanic was short, with hands that had been dyed grey from years of working in grease. He was obviously a knowledgeable mechanic, and, as he had done at the exam, he explained the damage caused to the vehicles.

The burned bulldozer was actually the least damaged of the machines, having suffered mostly superficial burns. Few then explained the damage to the other vehicles with all the authority of a high school auto-shop teacher. The oil systems had been spiked with silicon carbide. The substance was likely mixed with oil and then injected through holes that were drilled in the oil supply tube. The size of the holes was consistent with the hand drill that was found on the scene.

Few explained that the silicon carbide was extremely hard, but floated in the oil, and scored the engines of the backhoe, loader and off-highway truck that had been sabotaged. The engines were totaled. And the repair tab for the four vehicles totaled $108,021, parts and labor included. His testimony was clear and concise, and the jury seemed to accept it all without question, Jeremy thought.

Few was an easygoing man, and he gladly followed Jeremy's lead on cross-examination. He agreed enthusiastically with Jeremy about the odd paradox that was being painted for the jurors since the first day of testimony: Three of the vehicles were destroyed in a stealthy and secret fashion, yet the fourth vehicle was publicly burned in the most open way, and a spray-painted calling card was left, announcing the criminal act. Jeremy watched as Rose Galbraith nodded along with the testimony. She was a good wolf, he thought.

Few spent a total of twenty minutes in the courtroom. When he was released, Gray walked toward Jeremy.

"You said you'd stipulate to a hard copy of the website information?" Gray whispered.

"As long as it is complete, I said."

"Yeah. I'll mark it exhibit two. It's got everything that was on the site," Gray said, offering Jeremy a thick stack of documents. Jeremy browsed through the documents. He made sure that *The Monkey Wrencher's Handbook*, which had been published in full on Zeb's site, was duplicated in the hard copy of the records. He also made sure that the ELF article was included.

"You'll stipulate, then?" Gray said.

Jeremy nodded his agreement.

"Your Honor," Gray announced in a strong voice. "Defense counsel is going to stipulate to the admission of People's Exhibit Number 2. It is a hard copy of the website that was maintained by the defendant from August 26, 2003 through October 18, 2003.

"Mr. Jefferson?" Parr said.

"Yes, we stipulate to the admission of People's Exhibit Number 2." Jeremy thought he might have been able to prevent the admission of parts of the website, but the new theory of the case, based on the truth, had nothing to hide. And getting *The Monkey Wrencher's Handbook* and the ELF article into evidence with no hassles from Gray was a great tradeoff.

"All right," Parr said. "People's Exhibit Number 2 is admitted as a hard copy of the defendant's website maintained from August 26 through October 18, 2003. Another witness, Mr. Gray?"

"Yes, Your Honor," Gray said. "The People will call Melissa Dobbs to the stand."

For the first time in the trial, Zeb veered from Jeremy's instructions. His body jerked slightly when Melissa's name was called. Jeremy didn't think the jury noticed, but he put a hand on Zeb's leg to calm him.

In many ways, Melissa Dobbs was the witness who could completely destroy Zeb's defense. Jeremy thought he could deal with MacAdam's testimony. MacAdam was responsible for the firebombing and was lying to save his own skin. But Jeremy was at a loss to explain why Dobbs would lie.

If Melissa Dobbs came through for the prosecution, Zeb's case became almost untenable. The opening statements were made. And Zeb's defense had been cast in stone by Jeremy. MacAdam was the bad guy. MacAdam made the Molotov cocktail and burned up the bulldozer, over Zeb's protest. But why would Melissa need to lie and dump responsibility on Zeb's doorstep? Jeremy did not have a good answer, and that's why he had talked so little about Melissa in his opening.

He would need to pull a rabbit out of the hat with Melissa Dobbs to get Zeb acquitted on the terrorism charge, he thought. But, it was an extremely tall order. He had no serious ammunition to take her down. And this was not "Matlock."

Detective Russell led the young woman toward the witness stand, and Jeremy could scarcely recognize her as Melissa Dobbs. She was no longer a gothic teenager. She was now a freshly-washed witness for the State. The black tinting in her hair was washed away, leaving a presumably natural brown. The rings that studded her left ear were gone, leaving only holes. She had traded in her black eye liner for a plain face, and her black clothes were missing in action. She wore dress pants and a collared shirt. At five months pregnant, she looked no fatter than the average teenage girl in the American heartland.

She walked to the stand without looking at Jeremy or Zeb. Parr swore her to tell the truth, and Melissa's new version of reality slowly poured out in her nervous, quavering voice. It was a halting confession of how she, Steve and Jared had been led astray by the charming anarchist, Zebediah Radamacher. It tracked completely with the version of reality Jared had shared with the police, after he was apprehended and brought back from New York. Zeb had made the plans. Zeb had provided the necessary equipment. Zeb had scouted the location. Zeb had provided the ideological pep talks when the group wavered. Zeb had made the Molotov cocktail. Zeb had bought the silicon carbide. Zeb had stolen the paint from the hardware store. Zeb had spray- painted the "ELF" calling card on the backhoe. Zeb had drilled the holes. Zeb had poured the silicon into the oil systems. Zeb had firebombed the dozer. Zeb did. Zeb did. Zeb. Zeb. Zeb. Jeremy could not believe her conversion from defense ally to prosecution shill.

Gray took his time in letting Melissa pour out her story, but she never calmed. Before turning her over to Jeremy, he tried to inoculate her from tough questions.

"You pled guilty to attempted terrorism, malicious destruction of property over twenty thousand dollars, and arson over twenty thousand dollars, correct?" Gray asked.

"Yes."

"And, as a part of your plea bargain, the charge of terrorism was dismissed, correct?"

"Yes."

"And the prosecution recommended that you receive not more than four years in prison as a part of this deal, on the minimum end of an indeterminate sentence?"

"Yes."

"And you agreed that you would testify truthfully against all co-defendants?"

"Yes."

"Have you received anything else for your cooperation?"

"No."

"And, Ms. Dobbs, you said earlier in your testimony that you were an acquaintance of the defendant."

"Yes, uh-huh."

"What specifically was your relationship?"

"I am, er, was his girlfriend," Melissa said, still not looking at Zeb.

"No further questions, Your Honor," Gray said.

"Mr. Jefferson. Any questions?" Judge Parr said.

"Thank you, Your Honor," Jeremy said. He looked at his cross-examination notes. There was nothing on the page that could possibly undo her testimony, he thought. The jury had listened and absorbed it as gospel. He considered blasting her right out of the gate with the pregnancy that Gray was obviously not aware of, but he needed a strong point to close on.

"Ms. Dobbs, last Monday, you were at the courthouse, correct?"

"Yes."

"And you were in custody at that time, correct?"

"Yes."

"You were facing the very same charges that Zeb Radamacher is facing in this trial last Monday, weren't you?"

"Yes."

"You were scheduled to start your trial on that day, weren't you?"

"Yes."

"And the prosecuting attorney, Mr. Gray, he offered you a deal last Monday, didn't he?"

"Yes. I just told you."

"So you went from facing potential life in prison, down to facing, at the most, four years on the minimum, correct?"

"Yes."

"And you haven't been sentenced yet, so it could conceivably be less than four years on the minimum, correct?"

"Yes."

"And you're hoping that it is less, aren't you?"

"Yes."

"And you know that if you cooperate with the prosecutor, you have a better chance of him saying nice things about you at your sentencing, don't you?"

"Objection," Gray said. "Calls for speculation."

"Overruled," Parr said.

"You know that the better you cooperate, the better chance you have of the prosecutor saying nice things at your sentencing, don't you?"

"I guess," Melissa said. Her nerves had increased as Jeremy questioned her. "But, I'm only supposed to tell the truth. That was the only thing they want me to say."

"You know what sentencing guidelines are, from being a defendant in this case, don't you?"

"Uh-huh," Melissa said. "Yes."

"And your guidelines on the terrorism charge called for a minimum sentence of somewhere between twelve and nineteen years before you agreed to cooperate with the prosecutor, didn't they?"

"Yes. I think that's right."

"And you're aware that when we're talking about a minimum sentence, we're talking about a date when you would likely be paroled, correct?"

"Yeah. I guess. Uh-huh."

"So, if I understand your deal correctly, when you agreed to testify for the prosecutor, you received a sentence reduction of at least eight years, and perhaps as many as fifteen years, depending on how the judge sentences you under the guidelines."

"I don't understand," Melissa said.

"Well, the best you could have done under the terrorism guidelines was twelve years on the minimum, right?"

"Oh. Yeah. I get it. Yeah, I am getting four at the most now. So I see. Saving eight. Yes."

"And in the worst case scenario, if a judge would have given you nineteen at the high end of the guidelines, you would be saving fifteen years, right?"

"Yes," Melissa said. The lack of emotion she showed in calculating her own freedom annoyed Jeremy.

"So you'd say about anything to save fifteen years of your life, wouldn't you?" Jeremy said, venom in his voice.

"Objection, argumentative," Gray jumped up.

"Sustained," Parr said.

Jeremy made a check in his notes and moved on. The deal was the deal, and browbeating her with it wasn't going to make it any different.

"You testified that Zeb planned this entire operation, correct?"

"Yes."

"You were at these planning sessions, right?"

"Yes."

"How many were there?" Jeremy asked.

"I dunno. Three or four, I guess."

"And you were at all of them?"

"Yeah," Melissa said.

"Was Jared MacAdam at all of them?"

"No, uh, I'm not sure. I think he might have missed a couple. Because I brought him. But it was after we started planning."

"When you say *we* started planning, you mean you and who else?"

"I mean Zeb was planning. Telling Steve and I what to do," Melissa said.

"So when you say we started planning, you mean Zeb, is that your testimony?"

"Yes, uh, I mean, uh, we were all there. Steve and me and Zeb."

"So initially, it was just you, Steve and Zeb, correct?" Jeremy said.

"Yeah. For the first couple of planning sessions."

"And then you brought Jared MacAdam along to the third session, is it?"

"Yes. I think that's it. I'm not positive," Melissa said.

"And while you were at these planning sessions, did Zeb ever show you a copy of *The Monkey Wrencher's Handbook?*"

"I dunno," Melissa said.

"Let me show you what's been marked as People's Exhibit Number 2," Jeremy said, getting permission to approach the witness. "In the back of this exhibit, do you see this handbook?"

"Yeah. Yes. Zeb showed Steve and I this book. Parts of it. He got it off the Internet, he said."

"Okay," Jeremy said. "Now, do you remember Zeb being very concerned with not getting caught?"

"Yeah."

"Do you remember him telling you to wear socks over your shoes and gloves on your hands on the night of the direct action?"

"Objection, hearsay," Gray said.

"I'm not offering it for the truth of the matter, Your Honor. It's for the effect on the listener. I want to know if she got this information or not."

Parr paused. "I'll allow it," he said finally.

"Yeah. Zeb told us all that. But, Jared forgot his."

"So, you and Steve and Zeb all wore gloves and socks over your shoes to avoid leaving behind any evidence?"

"Uh-huh," Melissa said. "Yes."

"But, Jared missed the memo on that, is that correct?"

"No. He just forgot, I guess. Maybe he was nervous. I don't know."

"Okay," Jeremy said. "Now, during this planning did Zeb explain to you the process for putting silicon carbide into the oil systems of the heavy equipment?"

"Yeah," Melissa said. "He was like a teacher kind of. He told us everything about it. Most of it straight out of that book."

"And did he tell you that it was important to put the silicon carbide into the equipment without leaving any sign that the equipment had been tampered with?"

"Yeah," Melissa said. "Because they had to start the machines up or the thing wouldn't work. So if they suspected something, they might drain the oil before starting the things up. So you had to be careful so they wouldn't think someone was messing with their oil."

"Okay," Jeremy said. "Now, did he tell you that the silicon carbide was a far more effective way to damage equipment than, say, using a Molotov cocktail?"

"I, uh, no, I don't think so," Melissa said.

"Did he tell you that you shouldn't spray paint any messages on the sabotaged equipment because it would probably tip off the operators to the silicon carbide in the oil?"

"No. Not that I remember."

Jeremy was almost done. He was pretty sure that she was lying through her teeth, but he didn't know if the jury would see it that way.

"Just a few more questions," Jeremy said. "Ms. Dobbs, you are what, five months pregnant now?"

Melissa's jaw dropped. She looked from Jeremy to Zeb. "You told him," she mouthed, as if no one would notice as long as the words weren't audible. Zeb, to his credit, made no reaction.

"Objection, relevance, Your Honor," Gray said, taking advantage of Melissa's pause.

"Mr. Gray brought up the relationship between the witness and Mr. Radamacher, Your Honor. I'm just following up on his question."

"Well," Parr said, thinking, "as long as it has to do with the relationship between the witness and the defendant, I guess that's relevant. Overruled."

"So, is it five months pregnant?" Jeremy asked again.

Melissa had started to cry silently. "Oh God," she said. "Oh God. I can't believe he told you."

Jeremy took a box of tissues from the defense table and offered them to the melting witness.

"Whenever you're ready, Ms. Dobbs," Parr said.

She blew her nose and did her best to compose herself. After a moment, Jeremy asked again, "Five months pregnant, then, Ms. Dobbs?"

"Yes," she said, crying all over again.

"Five months pregnant and facing twelve to nineteen years in prison. Did that factor into your decision to take the deal you were offered?"

Melissa did not answer. The tears flowed. Jeremy jumped ahead to the question that had been nagging at him, fearing that if he did not, the judge was going to give Dobbs a recess to compose herself.

"Is it Zeb's child or Jared MacAdam's, Ms. Dobbs?"

The look of horror that swept over Melissa's face confirmed Jeremy's suspicions.

"Oh God," she said through streaming tears. "I'm sorry, Zeb. I'm so sorry."

"So, is the baby Zeb's or MacAdam's?" Jeremy pressed on.

"Objection," Gray said, trying to drown out her crying.

"I don't know. I don't know. But, I couldn't go to jail and let the baby have no father. I'm so sorry, Zeb. My attorney made me take this deal. I'm–"

"Objection!" Gray yelled, trying to regain control. "May we approach, Your Honor?"

Parr called the attorneys to the bench.

"Judge, he's badgering this poor girl," Gray whispered. "I'd ask that we excuse the jury and let her regain her composure."

"I did not badger her," Jeremy said. "He brought up their relationship. It's legitimate cross. And I want to finish."

"Settle down, boys," Parr smirked. "I don't see it, Ed. I think this is a legitimate line of inquiry. I don't know what she was about to say, but I don't like the sound of it. I think I'm going to excuse the jury, and we can proceed a bit without them to get a handle on what is and isn't going to be admissible."

The lawyers agreed.

"Ladies and gentlemen," Parr said, his smile fooling no one. "The lawyers need to argue some legal issues now, and they're going to do that on the record. So I'm going to ask you to go with Gaylord to the jury room. Please don't discuss the case, and I'll let you know as soon as we're able to proceed."

"All rise for the jury," Gaylord bellowed, and he whisked the jurors out of the room.

"All right, gentlemen," Parr said. "Let's put this on the record. Mr. Gray, you objected that Mr. Jefferson was badgering the witness. I'm going to overrule that objection. But, I would like to proceed with a few questions outside the presence of the jury, because I don't know if I like where this testimony appears to be headed, and I would like to avoid any mistakes in front of the jury, if possible. Any objection to proceeding in this manner?"

"No, Your Honor," Jeremy and Gray said in chorus.

"All right," Parr said. "Ms. Dobbs. Are you able to continue? Or do you need a break?"

"I'm okay," Dobbs said, sucking back tears.

"Go ahead, then, Mr. Jefferson," Parr said.

"Ms. Dobbs, you are approximately five months pregnant, true?" Jeremy said, trying to calm the girl with a slight smile.

"Yes," she said.

"And who is the father?" Jeremy asked.

"I – I'm not sure," she said. "I'm so sorry, Zeb."

Jeremy tossed a glance toward Zeb, who sat stoically, as if unfazed.

"When you say you're not sure, does that mean you were having relations with more than one man at the time of conception?" Jeremy said.

"Y-y-yes," Dobbs said, crying again.

"And who do you think the father might be?" Jeremy said.

"I think it's Zeb's baby," Melissa cried. "B-but, I was with Jared, too. Just once. B-but it was at about that time. I'm not sure."

"Now you testified, I believe, that you couldn't have your baby without a father? What did you mean when you said that?" Jeremy asked quietly.

"I meant, at least Jared was free. Since he got out of jail by testifying against me and Zeb. And he was going to get probation. I just thought, that at least if Jared was free, then the baby would have a father, even if I was in jail."

"And you said something about your lawyer making you do something?"

"She made me take this deal," Melissa whispered. "She said I had no chance at trial and that my baby would be a teenager before I ever got out."

"So, are you saying that your testimony here today has been false?" Jeremy asked.

"Objection, Judge," Gray was on his feet again. "The witness should be warned of her rights if he's going to ask that question."

Jeremy was ecstatic. It was exactly the response he had hoped for from Gray, but he kept the smile off his face.

"I agree," Jeremy said. "She should be warned before she answers the question."

"Would you like to give the warning, Mr. Prosecutor," Parr said, with a bemused smile. Jeremy was glad someone was enjoying the spectacle.

"I think I'd prefer it if you did the honors, Judge," Gray said.

"Okay," Parr said. "Ms. Dobbs, you have been asked a question about whether you have given false testimony in this proceeding. If you were to answer that question in the affirmative, you could be subjecting yourself to criminal liability for perjury. Therefore, you may have the right to refuse to answer this question by invoking your Fifth Amendment privilege against self-incrimination. If you are not sure whether you want to exercise this right to remain silent, you may wish to consult with an attorney of your own choosing, or if you cannot afford an attorney, I would appoint one for you to consult with at public expense. Do you understand your right to remain silent as I have explained it to you?"

"Yeah," Dobbs said. "I think so. I just have one question."

"What's that?" Parr said.

"If I take the Fifth, what happens to my plea deal?"

"Well, that is something you and your lawyer would have to discuss with the prosecutor."

"Okay," Dobbs said. "I'd like to take the Fifth for now, Your Honor."

"Okay," Parr said.

"Judge, I'd move that the witness' testimony be stricken from the record, and that the jury be so instructed," Jeremy said, rising to his feet. "Since the witness has exercised her privilege, she has denied my client his right to confrontation. I'd further ask that the jury be specifically informed of the reason that the testimony is being stricken. And, I'd like to reserve my right to make a motion for mistrial. I'd like a chance to look at some case law this evening and make my motion first thing in the morning."

"Any response?" Parr said sternly.

Gray looked as if a twenty-five-pound bag of cement had just fallen on his head. "Judge, I'd have no objection to the testimony being stricken. I would oppose the jury being informed that the witness has taken the Fifth. I don't think it's proper."

"Well, I think I have to strike this testimony, then," Parr said. "I will not instruct the jury on the specifics at this point. I'm going to let Mr. Jefferson bring his motion for mistrial in the morning, and you can both suggest an appropriate instruction at that time. Ms. Dobbs, you may step down. You may consult with your attorney about this matter."

Parr brought the jury back in and filled them in on as little as possible. "Sorry about the delay," he said. "As you can see, the witness who had been testifying, Melissa Dobbs, has been excused from the witness stand. She was unable to continue with her testimony. As a result, I'm going to order you to disregard her entire testimony. It is stricken from the record, and you should not consider it as evidence in this case."

Jeremy glanced again at Zeb out of the corner of his eyes. He could see Zeb's clear blue eyes covered with a watery film, but the boy held on to his composure. Parr broke for lunch, and Jeremy turned and exited the courtroom as the happiest lawyer on the face of the earth.

He spoke with Allie on the way out. She was excited for him. He knew he would get good press about his cross-examination from her. He wanted to take her to lunch. There were so few days left before she left for Chicago. But he needed to talk to Charlie and break down the morning court session. She understood and left him to his trial work.

Jeremy found Charlie hunched over his crutches on the frozen steps of the courthouse, smoking a cigarette. A small band of *Save Zeb* protestors were organizing a lunch picket.

"That was regular Perry Mason stuff, champ," Charlie smirked.

"C'mon, let's go over to the diner, and I'll tell you how I did it," Jeremy said, with false bravado. He only had a hunch that Melissa was sleeping with more than one of the Milton anarchists. And he had no idea that she would break down or take the Fifth. Sometimes things just went right. And, it was about time he and Zeb caught a break, he thought.

Jeremy walked slowly, allowing Charlie to hobble along at an easy pace. The snow had died away, but there was a strong wind that dragged the windchill factor well into negative territory. Jeremy's cheeks and fingers stung by the time they walked two blocks to the diner.

They rehashed the morning session, Charlie freely sharing his insights. His boss was pretty certain a mistrial could be had because of the Dobbs fiasco. Jeremy admitted he was flying completely blind when he questioned the girl about her baby. Trials were often about preparation, but sometimes about instinct, Charlie observed.

"You know," Charlie said, polishing off the last of an Ada lunch special, "I wasn't liking the whole 'Zeb committed this crime, but not that one' thing. I just didn't think a jury was going to buy it. But, with her out of the way, I think you might actually have a shot."

"You think?" Jeremy said. "I dunno. I'm just going with the truth and hoping for the best."

"The truth," Charlie spat. "You've got to be kidding me. You've been at this for over a year now and you still think there is some truth? You are a piece of work, Jefferson."

They made their way back to the courthouse after a quick lunch. Jeremy went into the courtroom alone fifteen minutes before the start of the afternoon session. He listened to the near-silence of the room. Old pipes banging gently, trying to heat the giant space. Voices, muffled, from the hallway, like whispers of the cases that had passed through for the last hundred years. He was trying the most publicized case in the history of Wabeno County, but he was insignificant in the constant wave of litigation that rolled through. One courtroom in a sea of a million courtrooms across the country. How much did any of it matter, he thought? And the obvious answer pounded through him, making his throat tight. It mattered a hell of a lot to Zeb, and no amount of rationalizing away his own significance was going to change that. Zeb's life was in his hands.

Gray came into the courtroom, followed shortly by Detective Russell and Jared MacAdam. Detective Russell parked MacAdam in the front row of the gallery. Gray was going to try to recover what he had lost in the morning session right away. The protestors, reporters, cameramen and court watchers trickled back to the show. Deputy Short brought in Zeb. Followed by the judge. And the jury. Cue act two, Jeremy thought.

35

"The People will call Jared MacAdam," Gray said in a commanding voice. He was showing no weakness to the jury over the Dobbs fiasco. They would no doubt be confused about the morning's events, and Gray did not want to answer their questions with a look of defeat, Jeremy surmised.

MacAdam took the stand. He was a tall boy, with tangled red hair and a receding chin. He looked nothing like the villain Jeremy wanted him to be.

As a prosecution witness, MacAdam was everything that Melissa Dobbs was not. He was calm, clear and believable. As Jeremy watched the boy spin out his story, he found himself thinking that it was possible Zeb was the liar here and that MacAdam was the victim of Zeb's revolutionary fervor.

"So, when was it that you first met Zebediah Radamacher?" Gray asked.

"It was on a Saturday night. A few weeks into the school year," MacAdam said.

"Where was it that you met him?"

"It was at his house. He was having, like, a party. At least that's what I thought. In his basement."

"When you say a party, what do you mean?"

"I had been going out with Melissa. Melissa Dobbs," MacAdam looked from the jury to Zeb as he spoke. "She said that she had been going out with Zeb for a long time. But that he was crazy. Like, losing it-"

"Objection, hearsay," Jeremy said.

"Sustained," Parr said.

"Without telling me what Melissa said, how was it that you ended up at this party?" Gray redirected the boy.

"She wanted me to go with her to this party at his house. Because she was scared of Zeb. Only it turns out, it wasn't a party. There were only four of us, and Zeb was just going on and on about how bad the Blue-Mart was, and how we had to stop them from building a store here."

"So who all was at this gathering?" Gray asked.

"There was me and Melissa. And Steve Wynn. And Zeb," MacAdam said.

"How well did you know the defendant?"

"Zeb?" MacAdam said. "Not so well. Just from around school. He was kind of a freak, you know."

"Objection," Jeremy said.

"Sustained," Parr said, turning to the witness. "Son, if you could kindly just answer the questions that are asked, and not give us your editorial comments, things will go a lot smoother. Okay?"

"Yes, sir," MacAdam said.

"So you knew the defendant from around school?" Gray asked. "You had seen him on a number of occasions around school?"

"Yes," MacAdam said.

"And you saw him that night at the gathering at his house, correct?"

"Yes," MacAdam said.

"Do you see Zeb Radamacher in court here today?" Gray said.

"Yes," MacAdam said.

"Could you please point him out for the jury?" Gray said.

"He's right there," MacAdam said, pointing at Zeb. Zeb, having maintained his calm through Melissa's testimony, looked unflappable to Jeremy's eye.

"So you said that the defendant was going on and on about Blue-Mart. Do you remember specifically what he said?" Gray asked.

"Yeah. He was, like, just talking about how we could shut down the construction site if we disabled all the machinery," MacAdam said, a study of earnestness. "And he was talking about how if we put sand in the crankcases, that would make the engines seize up. And how we could make bombs with a bottle of gasoline and detergent."

"What did you do when he was going on about his plans to stop the Blue-Mart development?"

"We were just scared, really," MacAdam said. "I mean, he was kind of crazy. And he said we would all have to swear on our lives that we would never tell anyone about it. So, he was just kind of scary. And I wanted to protect Melissa, so I was, like, just going along with him."

"So, did you agree to help him?" Gray asked.

"Yeah," MacAdam said. "I would have said anything. Because he was, like, serious about killing someone if we weren't in, and if we talked to anyone."

"Did you have any contact with the defendant after that night?"

"Just on the night, like, when all this happened," MacAdam said.

"Could you please describe that night for us?" Gray said.

"We went out there after dark," MacAdam began. "Zeb brought a duffel bag with everything in it. And I forgot, I was supposed to wear socks over my tennis shoes. But I forgot. So Zeb was, like, go without shoes, and I was like, no way–"

"Let me stop you," Gray said. "First, you said *we* went out there. Who is we?"

"Me, Melissa, Steve and Zeb."

"Okay. And how did you get there?" Gray asked.

"I drove. I picked everybody up," MacAdam said.

"Okay. So describe what happens again," Gray said.

"Well, like I said, I forgot my socks, and Zeb was, like, go without shoes, and I was, like, no way. Because we parked over on Morgan Road. And we had to walk through the woods to get to the Blue-Mart place. And I wasn't walking through there without shoes. So I just told him I would get rid of the shoes, and then I didn't.

"So we all hiked over there. Through the woods. It was really dark. And when we got there, Zeb started taking stuff out of his duffel bag. And he was, like, directing us all around, but mostly we ended up just watching him. Because none of us really knew what to do. I held a flashlight for him. It had a red lens so it wouldn't shine bright. And I, like, held it while he was drilling all these holes and pouring in the sand stuff.

"And then he takes out this can of spray paint, and he writes E-L-F on the backhoe. Really big–"

"ELF," Gray interrupted. "Do you know what that stood for?"

"It was, like, the Earth Liberation Front," MacAdam said. "Because that's what Zeb called us. We were like an ELF cell."

"And what happened after he spray-painted the backhoe?"

"That was when he pulled out the bomb. It had a rag in it. And he lit it. And he was, like, laughing, and then he chucked it at one of the big pieces, uh, you know, one of the, uh, I don't know what you call it. One of the trucks, like. And it just went up in flames."

"What happened, next?" Gray said.

"We just started running. I was, like, so scared. I mean the bomb-thing. It, like, made this really loud WHOOSH, and it was really bright, so I was, like, you know we're gonna get caught. So I was just running back to the car."

"So everyone ran away? What about Zeb?" Gray asked.

"I'm not really sure," MacAdam said. "Things were pretty crazy. I was just running as fast as I could. And I got to my car. And then Steve and Melissa made it back. But, there was no Zeb. So we waited for, like, a few seconds. But, we were all really scared. So we just took off."

Gray finished off his questioning with MacAdam's flight to New York and the deal he had struck to testify in the case. The boy's story was solid, and, as Parr took an afternoon break, Jeremy could see that the jury pool had largely bought in to MacAdam's cogent explanation of the evening.

Jeremy paced the hallway for the duration of the five-minute break, trying to focus on his upcoming cross-examination and trying to block out thoughts that Zeb would be going to prison if he failed.

Detective Russell came out of the courtroom and called to Jeremy, snapping him from his thoughts, "The judge is ready."

Jeremy walked directly to the lectern, grabbing his trial notebook as he passed the defense table. MacAdam had resumed the witness stand and sat there, the picture of composure. Parr called for the jury, and Jeremy launched in to try to save Zeb.

"Mr. MacAdam, when you fled the state to New York City, you did that because you were afraid, correct?" Jeremy began.

"Yeah," the boy said.

"You knew your name had been connected to this crime?" Jeremy said.

"Yeah."

"And you knew that Zeb had already been charged with terrorism for this evening's events?"

"Yeah."

"And you knew he was facing possible life in prison, correct?"

"Yeah. That's right."

"And you knew that Melissa had been charged?"

"Yeah."

"And you knew that you had been charged? Or were about to be charged?"

"Yeah. That's what I thought."

"And so you ran to New York City to hide from these charges? Isn't that correct?"

"Yeah. I was scared."

"But it's your testimony here today that you didn't really do anything. That it was really all Zeb's plan. That Zeb did everything to damage all the equipment that night. Is that right?"

"I drove," MacAdam said calmly. "I held the flashlight. So, I figure I was involved, too. I was just scared."

"You were arrested and charged, though, correct?" Jeremy said.

"Yeah. They found me in New York. And I was brought back here."

"And you faced the same charges as Zeb, correct?"

"I dunno," MacAdam shrugged.

"Well, you were charged with terrorism, weren't you?" Jeremy asked.

"Yeah. And arson and mal - uh, and destruction of property, too," MacAdam said.

"And Zeb is charged with those same crimes, correct?" Jeremy asked.

"I dunno," MacAdam said.

"Well, you faced life in prison under those charges, correct?" Jeremy said.

"Yeah. I guess. My lawyer said I'd have never got life, though." MacAdam said.

"But, you faced a maximum possible sentence of life? Correct?"

"Yeah. I guess."

"And do you know what your sentencing guidelines were under the terrorism charge?" Jeremy asked.

"My what?" MacAdam said.

"The sentencing guidelines that would tell you about the amount of prison time a judge could give you for the crime you committed," Jeremy said. "Your lawyer explained those to you, didn't he?"

"I had a couple of different lawyers," MacAdam said. "My dad got them for me. And they didn't say much. They just arranged this deal, where I-"

"So you were not aware of how much time you faced for the terrorism crime?" Jeremy asked.

"No. Not really. I mean they, uh, the judge said the maximum was life in prison, like you said. But my lawyers were, like, you will never get life, and then they worked out this plea, uh, this deal."

"And it was a pretty good deal, wasn't it, Mr. MacAdam?" Jeremy said.

MacAdam studied Jeremy for a moment, then his eyes rolled up and to the left. "I don't think so," he said finally. "I had to plead guilty to two felonies. And I'm going to be on probation for three years. Because your client is an idiot. I don't-"

Jeremy cut him off. "You were facing life in prison on the most serious charge, correct?"

"Yeah. But-"

"And you faced a maximum of twenty years on each of the other charges, correct?"

"I dunno, I guess. But my lawyers were, like–"

"And as a part of your deal, the prosecutor dismissed the terrorism charge? Got rid of the life offense, right?"

"Yeah," MacAdam said, seemingly resigned that he would not be able to out-explain Jeremy.

"And as a part of your deal, the prosecutor recommended that you be given probation instead of jail time, correct?"

"Yeah," MacAdam said.

"And at the time of the deal, you were in jail, correct?"

"Yeah," MacAdam said.

"You were being held on a million-dollar bond, correct?"

"Yeah."

"And you couldn't meet that bond, could you?"

"No," MacAdam said. "I ain't got no million dollars."

"But, as a part of your deal, your bond was reduced so that you could get out of jail, correct?"

"Yeah."

"And as a part of your deal, the prosecutor recommended that you receive HYTA, correct?"

"What?" MacAdam said.

"As a part of your deal with the prosecuting attorney, it was agreed that you'd be sentenced under a provision of the law that allows the felonies to be removed from your record, so long as you complete probation, right?" Jeremy said bitingly.

"Oh. Yeah. The youthful trainee thing. Yeah. But, like, I have to finish the probation first, or–"

"So you had a life offense dismissed," Jeremy cut him off again, "you were guaranteed probation instead of jail, you were let out of jail on bond, and you were given a chance to come out of this situation with no criminal record whatsoever, and you don't think this was a very good deal for you?"

"Objection, argumentative," Gray said.

"Sustained," Parr said. "A little less heat and a little more light, please, Mr. Jefferson."

Jeremy nodded at the judge's admonishment.

"So what did you have to do to get this deal?" Jeremy asked.

"What did I have to do?" MacAdam said.

"It was a deal, wasn't it? A deal implies that each side got something?"

"I didn't have to do anything. My lawyers just worked it out and told me to plead guilty."

"So, it is your testimony that you didn't have to give anything for this deal?" Jeremy said.

"No. My lawyers just worked it out."

"Well, Mr. MacAdam," Jeremy said, "as a part of the deal, you did have to plead guilty to two felonies, correct?"

"Yeah. But that's not giving them anything."

"Did the judge here tell you that you had a right to a trial on all the charges, if you wanted one?" Jeremy felt frustrated. MacAdam was yielding nothing, and Jeremy thought he might be coming out the loser of the entire exchange.

"Yeah."

"And when you took the deal and entered your plea, you gave up that right, didn't you? There wasn't going to be a trial?"

"Yeah," MacAdam said.

"So you gave up your right to a trial to get this plea deal, right?"

"I guess."

"You also made a promise that you would become a witness for the State, correct?"

"Yeah. I guess."

"So you made that promise in order to get this deal, didn't you?"

"Okay. Yeah."

"So you gave the prosecution certain things to get this deal, correct?"

"Yeah," MacAdam said. "Okay."

"And the prosecutor wanted you to testify against Zeb, correct?"

"Yeah," MacAdam said. "And Melissa, too."

"And you were willing to do that so you could get the plea bargain, right?"

"My lawyer told me I'd be a fool not to," MacAdam said.

"My question is, that you were willing to testify against your friends in order to get the plea bargain, weren't you?"

"Yeah. I guess."

Jeremy made a check in his trial notebook. He was beating a dead horse.

"All right," Jeremy said. "Let's go over the night of the crime. You said that you were the driver that night?"

"Yeah," MacAdam said.

"And what kind of car were you driving?"

"I drive a black Trans Am," the boy smiled, obviously proud of his ride. "1982. Vintage. Mint. With the firebird on the hood."

"Great," Jeremy said sarcastically. MacAdam had thoroughly gotten under his skin. "That's a two-door, isn't it?"

"Yeah."

"A little cramped for four people?" Jeremy said.

"No," MacAdam said. "Not really."

"All right," Jeremy said. "You testified that Zeb brought all the equipment that was needed? Is that right?"

"Yeah."

"What, uh, was he carrying these items in his hands, or how?" Jeremy said.

"No. He had a big black duffel bag full of stuff."

"And, it's your testimony that everything – every tool – everything – that was needed for that night was in the bag?"

"Yeah. He brought everything," MacAdam said.

"So, he brought the drill, for instance, in the bag?"

"Yeah."

"And he brought the flashlight you talked about, in the bag?"

"Yeah."

"And he brought the silicon-oil mixture, in the bag?"

"Yeah," MacAdam said. "It was in a plastic gas can."

"The spray paint?" Jeremy asked.

"Yeah. In the bag."

"And he brought the Molotov cocktail – the homemade bomb – in the bag?"

"Yeah," MacAdam said. "Everything."

"And he would just grab these things as he needed them from the bag, is that right?"

"Yeah."

"So when he needed the drill, for instance, he just grabbed it?" Jeremy said.

"Yeah. That's right."

"And when he needed the flashlight, he just grabbed it?" Jeremy said.

"Yeah."

"And you testified that he just pulled the Molotov cocktail out, lit it and chucked it? Right?"

"Yeah," MacAdam said.

"Did you know he had the bomb in the bag?" Jeremy asked.

"No. Not really," MacAdam said. "I mean, like, he said he might do that, but I didn't know about it in advance. No way. I don't know if I could've gone through with it if I would've known that."

"So he just pulled it out and chucked it?" Jeremy said.

"Yeah–"

"Asked and answered," Gray objected.

"Sustained. Can we move it along, Mr. Jefferson?" Parr said.

"So you didn't smell gasoline before he pulled out the bomb?" Jeremy asked.

MacAdam paused. Rolling his eyes. Thinking. "No," he said, after a pause. "I don't think so. Maybe. I mean, like, he had the whole gas can full of oil and sand in there, so I don't know."

"He didn't have to unwrap the bomb or anything, right? You said he just pulled it out and chucked it?"

"Yeah."

"He didn't take it out of a box or a case, did he?" Jeremy said.

"No."

"So it was just loose, rolling around in this duffel bag?" Jeremy asked.

"Yeah. I guess."

"Well, do you guess or do you know, Mr. MacAdam. You testified that he just pulled it out and chucked it, right?"

"Yeah. It was just in there."

"So this was a cloth duffel bag?" Jeremy asked.

"Yeah."

"And though there was a bottle full of gasoline rolling around inside it with just a rag to cap it, you didn't smell anything?" Jeremy asked pointedly.

"No."

"Okay," Jeremy said, making a checkmark in his notebook. "Now Zeb brought this bag when you picked him up? Correct?"

"Yeah."

"And he had the bag in his possession during the whole time? Correct?"

"Pretty much," MacAdam said.

The boy was starting to look somewhat uncomfortable on the stand, and Jeremy chanced a look at the jury. Their eyes were trained as a unit on Jared MacAdam.

"And he had all the equipment inside the bag the whole time? Right?'

"Yeah," the boy said.

"Well, let me ask you this," Jeremy said. "Who had the bag when you left the scene that night?"

MacAdam paused again. "I, uh, I'm not sure."

"Well, did you have the bag?" Jeremy continued.

"No. I never touched it."

"What about Melissa, did she have the bag?"

"No. I don't think so."

"How about Steve? Was he carrying the bag when you left the scene?"

"Uh, no. I didn't see him. I don't know, though."

"So, is it fair for me to say that you don't think any of the three people you had in your car had the bag with them when you left?" Jeremy asked.

"I think so. Yeah. I don't think we did. But, I can't be sure."

"You said you ran right after Zeb threw the bomb on the dozer, right?"

"Yeah," MacAdam said, clearly squirming, now.

"And you said he had just taken the bomb from the bag, before he threw it, right?" Jeremy said.

"Yeah. I think he might have set it down to light the, um, the bottle."

"Okay," Jeremy said slowly. "So did he take it somewhere to set it down before he lit the bomb or did he just set it down beside his feet, Mr. MacAdam?"

"I don't really know," the boy said.

"You don't know?" Jeremy asked.

"No."

"You don't know what happened to the bag, do you, Mr. MacAdam?" Jeremy asked.

"No, sir."

"You've had a chance to read the police reports in this case, haven't you?" Jeremy said.

MacAdam paused. "Yeah."

"So you know what items were recovered from the scene, don't you?"

"I don't know about everything. They found a drill, I think," MacAdam said.

"They didn't find a duffel bag, though, did they?" Jeremy said.

"Objection, lack of foundation," Gray said.

"Sustained," Parr said.

"You don't know who had the duffel bag, because you didn't leave with Melissa or Steve, did you?" Jeremy started again.

"I gave them a ride home that night," MacAdam said.

Jeremy made another checkmark in his notebook.

"Mr. MacAdam, I want to show you People's Exhibit Number 2," Jeremy approached with Parr's permission. "Are you familiar with the ELF website?"

"Yeah. Since this whole thing. Yeah."

"Do you see, here on page 53 of Exhibit Number 2, there is an article on the ELF website about this incident?"

"Yeah."

"It was linked through Zeb's website? Are you familiar with that site? Milton Anarchy?"

"Yeah. He showed it to us," MacAdam said.

"Well, in looking at this article, I want to go over some of the information with you to see if you can help me understand what it means," Jeremy said.

"Objection, relevance, Your Honor," Gray said.

"Mr. Jefferson?" Parr said, a quizzical look creasing his brow.

"This is cross-examination, Your Honor. I'd ask just a bit of leeway to fully test the witness' veracity," Jeremy said. It was code for saying, "I don't want to tell the witness what I'm doing, Judge."

"I'll give you some latitude as long as you connect it up," Parr said.

"Do you see in this article where it refers to the crime you committed at the Blue-Mart development site in Milton?" Jeremy asked.

"Yeah."

"It refers to the crime specifically, by date, time and location, doesn't it?" Jeremy said.

MacAdam reviewed the article for a moment. "Yeah. This is us."

"Do you see in the article where it refers only to a bulldozer being burned?" Jeremy said.

"Only one piece was burned," MacAdam said. "The others were the sand in the crankcase."

"My question is, do you see in the article, that it refers to only to the bulldozer that was burned?" Jeremy repeated.

"Yeah."

"It says the bulldozer was ignited with a gasoline bomb, right?" Jeremy said.

"Yeah."

"It talks about ELF being spray-painted on the backhoe, right?" Jeremy said.

"Right. Yeah. It does," MacAdam said.

"But the article makes no mention of the other three pieces – the ones where the sand was put into the crankcases – does it?"

"No," MacAdam said.

"Would you agree with me that whoever wrote this article for the ELF website does not appear to know that three other pieces of equipment were sabotaged on that same night?" Jeremy said earnestly.

"I dunno," MacAdam said, too fast. "Maybe whoever wrote it just wanted to stick to the highlights."

Jeremy paused, thinking. "So, according to you, the highlights of this crime would be the firebombing and the ELF graffiti, then, correct?"

"Well, I dunno," MacAdam said.

"Well, you just said that the person who wrote this article might have avoided mentioning the sand in the crankcases of three vehicles," Jeremy said, "because that person wanted to stick to the *highlights*, right? That was your word, right? I'm not putting words in your mouth, am I?"

"Yeah," MacAdam acknowledged. "That was my word."

"So, according to you, then, the highlights are the firebombing of one dozer and the spray-painting of the backhoe, right?"

"Well, I'd say at least the bombing," MacAdam said. "Right."

"And you think that explains why the person who wrote this article didn't write about the other three acts of sabotage? Right?"

"Yeah. I dunno," MacAdam said.

"Isn't the truth, Mr. MacAdam, that you are the person who gave this press release to ELF to publish, and the reason you omitted the other acts of sabotage is because you weren't really familiar with what exactly Zeb and the others had done that night?"

MacAdam talked over Jeremy. "No. That's not true," he said, twice.

"Isn't the truth, that you only wrote about the burning of the bulldozer, because that was the crime you committed on your own that night?" Jeremy said louder.

"No. That's not true," MacAdam said, shaking his head.

Jeremy sneaked another peek at the jury. The lambs all concentrated on MacAdam's denial, but Rose Galbraith and Kevin Vontom both turned to gauge Jeremy's reaction as well. Jeremy had no idea what they were thinking. But at least they were thinking.

"Mr. MacAdam, you are aware that Ms. Dobbs is five months pregnant?" Jeremy said.

"Objection," Gray said, "relevance."

"Judge, it goes to relationship, bias, motive and intent."

"I'll allow it," Parr said.

The slack-jawed look on MacAdam's face told the story. He had no idea Melissa was pregnant.

"You didn't know Melissa Dobbs was pregnant?" Jeremy asked.

"No, sir." MacAdam said.

"You were having relations with her in September of 2003, isn't that true?"

"Yeah."

"Sexual relations?" Jeremy asked.

"Uh-huh," MacAdam nodded.

"She never told you she was pregnant?" Jeremy said.

"No, sir."

"You were aware, at the time you were having relations with Ms. Dobbs, that she was also going out with Zeb, isn't that true?" Jeremy asked.

"Yeah," MacAdam said, "but, she said she was, like, scared of him, though."

"You liked Ms. Dobbs a great deal at the time, isn't that true?" Jeremy said.

"I dunno. You know," MacAdam said.

"You were sleeping with her, but you didn't care for her. Is that your testimony?" Jeremy said.

"No. No," MacAdam said defensively. "I liked her. Yeah. I liked her a lot."

"And she returned your affections?" Jeremy said.

"Yeah. I think, like, yeah. She really liked me, too," MacAdam said.

"But she was still going out with Zeb at that time, correct?" Jeremy said.

"I think that she was trying to, you know, like, break it off," MacAdam said.

"Your testimony on direct examination was that she was *going out* with Zeb at the time this crime was being planned, correct?" Jeremy demanded.

"Yeah. She was going out with him," MacAdam said.

"You didn't say on direct that she was trying to break it off, did you?" Jeremy said.

"No."

"Because, the truth is, she was seeing both of you at the same time, right? That's what was going on, isn't it?" Jeremy said.

"Yeah," MacAdam said, almost sighing.

"And the truth is, you were jealous of Zeb Radamacher, weren't you, Mr. MacAdam?"

MacAdam thought for a long moment. "Yeah. I guess so," he said finally.

Jeremy checked off the last item under MacAdam's cross-examination notes. "Nothing further, Your Honor," he said, closing his trial notebook and returning to sit next to Zeb.

36

Both Charlie and Allie thought the cross-examinations went well. But Jeremy was not certain. He had always found it impossible to evaluate his own courtroom performance. There were always mistakes. Always places where he could have been smarter, faster or better. And if the results of a trial were good then the mistakes didn't matter. But, if the trial was lost, then those small changes might have made the difference. Being a lawyer was almost an exercise in masochism, Jeremy thought.

He sat in his recliner, still wearing his slacks and shirt from court. He tuned in to the late night recap of Zeb's trial on Court TV. It was surreal to conduct a trial in the day and watch analysis of that trial by commentators in the evening. But the commentators seemed to side with Charlie and Allie: Jeremy was apparently doing okay. Still, there were only two wolves who mattered, Jeremy thought.

The trial, like all trials, had been exhausting. A full eight hours in the courtroom, and another three researching Melissa's aborted testimony. And if he spent the next nine hours preparing for some aspect of tomorrow, there would still be stones unturned.

Jeremy had been considering going to bed for the past thirty minutes, but could not find the energy to lift himself from the recliner. He nodded repeatedly, then snapped himself awake. The thought that he might nod off for good in the living room and miss his alarm in the morning was finally enough to move him to the bedroom, where he collapsed.

Though he slept for six hours, the exhaustion from Tuesday had carried over to Wednesday morning. When he arrived at court at 8:15 a.m., his eyes were red and underscored by thin, dark circles. He splashed cold water on his face in the men's room and made his way to the defense table for day three of the trial.

Gray had used his heavy artillery on day two, and Jeremy did not believe the prosecutor had any big guns in reserve. Jeremy had little idea where the jury stood, but it was likely that most had already made up their minds. And, until Zeb's testimony, Jeremy doubted they could be swayed much by the details that would float into the record on day three.

Jeremy took his place at the defense table, and Deputy Short was kind enough to bring Zeb out a few minutes early. The two talked quietly, waiting for the courtroom to fill.

"I think we might get through the prosecution case today," Jeremy whispered.

"Really," Zeb said. "That's great, because I don't think I can stand much more. All these people talking about your life. In front of the whole world. I just feel like crawling under a rock, Mr. J."

"It'll be over before you know it," Jeremy said. He was going to miss Zeb Radamacher, whatever the outcome. "I think I'll get by the jail tonight. We can go over your testimony one last time."

"No way, Mr. J.," Zeb said. "Don't sweat it. I got my part down cold."

"Practice makes perfect," Jeremy said. "I'll be at the jail at seven tonight. I hope it won't drag you away from any other engagements."

"My mom thinks you're doing a great job," Zeb said. "I don't see how they could convict me after what you did to MacAdam."

"I don't know, Zeb," Jeremy said. "I don't think I really laid much of a glove on him. It will all be about who the jury believes. You or him. So that's why we're going to practice it one more time."

"Okay. Okay, Mr. J. That's cool," Zeb said.

"I haven't seen your dad at court since Monday," Jeremy said. "I wonder what's going on there?"

"I don't know. Don't care," Zeb said. "Guy is such an ass–"

Judge Parr's law clerk entered from behind the bench, "Mr. Jefferson. The judge would like to see you in chambers."

Jeremy followed the law clerk out the back of the courtroom and into Parr's office suite. He could see the jury bustling about the assembly room to his left, grabbing coffee and homemade cookies, joking with one another. They seemed loose.

Gray was in Parr's reception area, waiting. The law clerk led the two lawyers back into Parr's chambers.

"Morning, gentlemen," Parr said. "Can I have Carolyn get you a cup of coffee?"

"No, thanks," Jeremy murmured.

"No, Judge," Gray said. "I don't think I could sit still in there if I had any more caffeine."

"Well, Dan has been working all night," Parr said, motioning to his law clerk, "looking at the issue with Dobbs taking the Fifth yesterday, and he's a little worried about the state of our trial."

The law clerk reddened at being thrust into the spotlight by his judge. Jeremy remembered his own time as a clerk for a federal district court judge. Being a law clerk was a lot like being someone's dog, he thought. A clerk is loyal, devoted and eager, but is not usually asked to host a dinner party.

"I didn't find anything controlling last night, Judge," Jeremy said, "but I do think you're on very shaky ground. I think her testimony may have been reversible error by itself if my guy gets convicted."

"Oh, come on," Gray said patronizingly. "No court's gonna overturn a terrorism conviction. Not for this, Judge. The most important thing is that we kept it out from in front of the jury."

"Yes," Parr said. "That was good. I think we might really be up the creek if she would have taken the Fifth in front of them. But, even as it is, Dan's got some concerns. He tells me there's a case—"

"*Mobley*," Dan timidly came to the judge's aid when the old jurist fumbled.

"*Mobley*," Parr continued, "that says a co-defendant can't take the Fifth once he starts testifying, right, Dan?"

The clerk nodded assuredly. Jeremy doubted the precedent. He had studied *People v. Mobley* last night, but thought it was easily distinguishable from Zeb's case. Still, if Parr thought it was a problem, Jeremy was not going to step up and disabuse him of the notion. Unfortunately, Gray had been reading case law last night also.

"No, Judge," Gray said. "I read *Mobley*, too. But there's a later case—" Gray shuffled through his notes, "– *Thomas* – that specifically said *Mobley* didn't apply where the witness invokes the Fifth for protection against a different crime. Like here, she invoked the Fifth because of possible perjury, not because of the charged offenses. So *Thomas* says she can do that."

"I read those cases, too, Judge," Jeremy admitted. "But, I still think there are problems."

Parr was deflated and the law clerk looked flattened. "Well, if *Mobley* doesn't keep her from taking the Fifth, what's the problem?" Parr asked Jeremy.

"Well, I didn't see a Michigan case directly on point," Jeremy said. "But, in reading every case I could find, it seems to me that our situation is a definite violation of my client's right to confrontation. I mean, you can't have a prosecution witness testify all day that the defendant did something wrong, and then when it comes time for cross, just take the Fifth."

"You struck the testimony, though, Judge," Gray said. "So if you give a limiting instruction, I think we're going to be okay."

"I'm still moving for a mistrial," Jeremy said. "It's just patently unfair. You heard her. She was about to admit that she perjured herself. You can't let her testimony stand."

"I don't want a mistrial," Parr said. "We're already two days into this. And I don't really want to do it again if we don't have to."

"We don't, Judge," Gray said. "You have been careful. This wasn't a deliberate effort by anyone to make her take the Fifth or to hide some favorable testimony for the defendant. You give a limiting instruction, and there's no way a court would ever overturn it."

Parr looked anxious. Jeremy knew it was going to be a good issue on appeal, regardless of what Parr did, but Gray might be right. The way appellate courts had moved to stymie defendants' rights in the past decades was alarming and clear to anyone who ever researched a criminal issue. If they could find a way to uphold a conviction, they would.

"Well, let's argue it out there. I may take it under advisement and let Dan take a closer look at it," Parr said. The clerk looked pleased to get a second bite at the apple.

The motion was put on the record in the courtroom, Jeremy objecting and moving for a mistrial, Gray opposing him. Parr took the matter under advisement, and the jury was brought in to resume testimony.

Gray started the morning off on a positive note. He called Amanda Ratielle to the stand. She was a short, square girl, who worked part time at the Milton Hardware. She was an enthusiastic witness for the prosecutor, reveling in her opportunity to protect Milton from a terrorist.

She recalled for the jury how she was working the evening shift at the hardware store alone on the night of the crime. She remembered clearly, because there had been a strange young person in the store, at around sunset, who had shoplifted a can of Mauve Krylon paint. She watched the boy as he nervously paced the store. She got a good look at him and was certain that the young man was, in fact, Zebediah Radamacher. She pointed at Zeb with glee when asked to do so. And, she had even picked Zeb out of a line-up, she boasted, to wrap up her direct testimony.

It was a case where Jeremy had violated the Hippocratic Oath – first, do no harm. He had requested the line-up when Zeb adamantly denied that he had ever stolen the paint. And now, that foolhardy denial was coming back to bite Zeb.

Jeremy had no solid information on which to cross-examine Ratielle. In his head, he could hear his old advocacy professor yelling at him to sit down and let the witness leave the stand. She was not the most damaging witness in the world. But Jeremy stubbornly refused to pass on questioning her. He could not let her go unchallenged. He would only ask a few questions, he thought – get her to confirm the good parts of his case – and then they could move on.

"Ms. Ratielle, you were very specific in your testimony about the type of paint that was stolen, correct?"

"Uh-huh," she nodded.

"You'll have to answer yes or no, for the record."

"Yes," she said.

"Yet you testified that you never got any closer than twenty feet to where the young man was pacing, isn't that correct?"

"Yes, that's about right. It's about twenty feet from the till, back to where the paint section is."

"So, if you were twenty feet away, it must have been difficult for you to see the paint cans from that distance, wasn't it?"

"No," Ratielle said. "Not really."

"Well, you couldn't read them, could you?" Jeremy asked.

"No. I couldn't read them from there."

"So how could you be so specific about which paint was taken?" Jeremy asked.

"Well, I saw him take a can and put it under his sweater when he walked out–"

"Yes," Jeremy interrupted, "but how could you be so certain that the can he took was Mauve Krylon spray paint?"

"Because, after he left, I went and looked at the shelf. That is the ugliest color we ever had in the store," Ratielle said. "Mauve 2414 Krylon. We had that can for about two years, and we aren't ordering any more."

The jury laughed. The gallery chuckled. Jeremy's internalized professor taunted him with "I told you so." Jeremy laughed along with the group, trying to save face.

"Ms. Ratielle, you don't have any personal knowledge about the incident that took place out at the Blue-Mart site that night, do you?"

"Personal knowledge? Just what I read in the paper," Ratielle said.

"But you didn't personally witness any part of that incident, did you?" Jeremy said.

"Oh," Ratielle said. "No, I didn't."

"Your only contribution to make is that you saw Zeb take a can of paint, correct?" Jeremy said.

"Mauve 2414 Krylon spray paint," Ratielle said to more muffled laughter.

"You have no information to suggest that Zeb burned a bulldozer that night, do you?"

"Don't really know, nope," Ratielle said.

Jeremy ticked off the only two points in his notebook under Ratielle's name. She had beaten him badly so far, and it would have been prudent to let her go. But, Zeb was adamant that he did not steal the paint, and that was enough for Jeremy to press one more attack on her testimony. He went with his instincts, hoping not to invoke more laughter.

"So how many times have you seen Zeb Radamacher, now?" Jeremy said.

"Total?" Ratielle asked. "Let me see. That would be three. Once that night. And once at the line-up, and today."

"And you have never seen him on any other occasions?" Jeremy said.

"Personally, no," Ratielle said.

"Personally?" Jeremy said. "Has someone else you know seen him and told you about him?"

"No, no," Ratielle said. "I mean in person. The only other time I saw him was in a picture."

"You saw him in a picture?" Jeremy said.

"Yeah. The day before the line-up. Detective Russell came by the store."

"Detective Russell showed you a picture of Zeb Radamacher?" Jeremy said.

"Well, not exactly," Ratielle said. "She had her file open, and I could see his mug shot in her file. I knew that was him right away. I don't even know why we had to do a line-up."

"And this was the day before the line-up?" Jeremy said, incredulity having taken over his voice. "Can we approach, Your Honor?"

The jury was excused, and Jeremy was allowed to rant on the record.

"Judge, I would again ask for a mistrial," Jeremy said. "First, the prosecution has put on a witness who claimed the Fifth before I could complete my cross-examination, and now, after we had made a pretrial motion challenging this witness' identification of my client, the witness takes the stand and admits that she was shown a photograph of the defendant on the day before the court-ordered line-up in this case. It's outrageous. A curative instruction is not going to be sufficient here. We'd ask that you declare a mistrial."

The hiccups in Gray's case were clearly raising Parr's ire. "Mr. Gray? Response?"

Gray rose and took the lectern. "Judge, first off, I've just discussed this with Detective Russell. This was an inadvertent event. Detective Russell did not show the witness that photograph nor intend for her to see it.

"Second, just because the witness saw the photo does not automatically taint her identification. Look at the evidence in the record already, Judge. All the evidence suggests that the defendant did have a can of mauve spray paint in his possession on this night. So I don't think we are running astray from the truth here. You can give the jury whatever instruction you want about her seeing a photo before the line-up, but you don't need to go beyond that to correct this. And it is certainly not grounds to throw this case out and start over."

The crimson that had risen in Parr's cheeks was subsiding. He took a deep breath before speaking. "This case is getting very sloppy, Mr. Gray. Very sloppy. And I think Mr. Jefferson is raising some legitimate issues with regard to the fairness here. I am starting to worry about the cumulative effect.

"Looking at the defendant's motion for a mistrial, I have to decide if the errors that have occurred are going to result in a manifest injustice to the defendant – one that can't be cured by an instruction to the jury.

"I think this was clearly an error by the lead investigator in this case. But I'm not going to bog down the jury now by stopping and having a hearing about Detective Russell's intent, because I am going to give the jury a clear instruction that they are to completely disregard the identification the witness has given.

"Mr. Jefferson, I'm going to deny a mistrial at this point. I believe we can still salvage a fair trial for your client in this case with a limiting instruction. But I am concerned about what happened here. I'm going to direct that you raise this issue in a post-trial motion, where we have time to take testimony about how this picture was shown to the witness. And I'll deal with it at that time. But for now, we're going to go ahead.

"Gaylord, bring the jury back in," Parr concluded.

Jeremy had rarely seen the judge so articulate. Though he disagreed with the ruling, he was starting to think Parr would be a pretty good trial judge if he weren't spending so much of his time trying to settle cases off his docket.

The judge rebuked Gray and Detective Russell before the jury, and instructed the jury to ignore all that Ratielle had said as it related to providing any identification of Zeb as the person stealing spray paint from her store.

Jeremy watched as the lambs nodded reverently at the judge. Rose Galbraith looked angry that she had been deceived by Gray. But, Kevin

Vontom looked like he was reserving judgment. It was another unexpected boost for Zeb, and Jeremy could now almost believe that the boy might escape a terrorism conviction.

Gray spent the rest of the morning trying to regain momentum with small witnesses. Allen Kryszinski, Zeb's shop teacher, identified the drill that had been found at the scene and placed Zeb in position to have lifted it from class. The poor man obviously liked Zeb. But Gray skillfully made him paint Zeb as having a terrorist's ideology, wanting to drive the corporate behemoth, Blue-Mart, out of Milton.

Jeremy's cross was gentle, exposing Kryszinski's sympathy for a likeable student. The shop teacher confirmed that he could not connect Zeb to the arson. The witness did little to get Gray back on track with the jury, Jeremy thought.

Gray closed out the morning with testimony from Greg Westbrook, a clerk at a rock shop in Lansing, Michigan. The clerk remembered a morning in the fall when Melissa and Zeb had come to his store with questions about a rock-cleaning compound, silicon carbide. He sold them a two-pound bag so they could start their new hobby.

Jeremy troubled the man little. He was friendly, and only on the stand long enough to confirm that he could not say Zeb had anything to do with a Molotov cocktail, or firebombing a bulldozer.

Parr broke for lunch after Westbrook was excused. Court TV was really going to love his performance today, Jeremy thought, as he turned to leave the courtroom. He looked for Charlie and Allie. He wanted to be lauded after a brilliant morning in court. But, neither were in the gallery. He headed to the Milton Diner alone, grabbing a seat at the counter, and settling for a warm bowl of Ada's vegetable barley in lieu of adulation.

37

Allie's cell phone vibrated with a call as the lunch hour approached. She had heard about all she could take from the lapidary supplies salesman. Nice guy, but boring. She would have been sleeping if she was on the jury, she laughed to herself.

She walked to the hallway to take the call. It was Stoops. He wanted her back at the office. There had been a call about the Richard Alarie story she was working on. Stoops sounded excited, so she hurried back.

"We got a call from a guy named Art Fisher," Stoops rambled when she barged into his office five minutes later. "Sound familiar?"

"Yeah," Allie said, searching her brain. "Where have I heard that name before?"

"Big-time pollster," Stoops clued her in. "Operative in the governor's office."

"Oh yeah," Allie said. "I've read about him. He's like their top pollster or something, right?"

"Uh-huh," Stoops said. "He called for you. Apparently he has been following your *Save Zeb* series online."

"Cool," Allie said.

"Well, he's all in a rush to talk to someone, so Gladys put him through to me," Stoops said. "He says he knows something big about Alarie. Will only talk to you. Said you could reach him on his cell over the lunch hour."

Allie's spine tingled. This story was going to be monstrous. She ripped the number out of Stoops' hand and ran to her office. Stoops followed along, standing behind her as she dialed. She fished a memo pad and pen out of a drawer as the phone rang.

"Artie here," a voice said.

"Hello, Art Fisher?" Allie said.

"Yes."

"This is Allison Demming from *The Milton Beacon*. I was just returning your call."

"Ah, yes, thanks for calling me back," Artie said. "I've been following your stories about that little movement you have up there in Milton. Very interesting stuff. Great political coverage. You should really consider moving up to a bigger market."

"Thanks," Allie said. "So, my editor tells me that you called about Richard Alarie."

"Uh, yes," Artie said. "I did. I have something you might find very interesting that goes along with that whole story about the lawyer getting arrested under that MEGPAT law. But before I say anything, I'd have to get some assurances from you."

"You want to talk off the record, on background? No problem," Allie said. "I know a little about Alarie already. I am thinking of running a piece on Saturday."

"So we're on background, then," Artie said. "My name is out of it."

"No problem," Allie said. "I won't even use the background without your permission."

"Okay," Artie said. "Do you know who Alarie works for?"

"I'm told he's with the state police," Allie said. "Is that right?"

"Very good, Ms. Demming," Artie said. "Did you ever think about getting out of the private sector? We could really use someone with your skills."

Allie laughed politely.

"He's definitely state police," Artie continued. "But do you know *who* he works for?"

"I haven't been able to come up with a post yet," Allie said.

"Well, he doesn't work for a post," Artie said, obviously liking the Deep Throat ambience of their conversation. "He was on the governor's security detail before getting tasked to the little undercover investigation up your way."

Allie started scribbling notes. "So he is state police, but he worked for the governor?"

"Well, not exactly," Artie said. "The state police have a unit that provides security. The Governor's Security Unit. Top cops. Very elite unit."

"Yes," Allie said, scribbling faster.

"Well, Alarie got transferred to a special assignment, to infiltrate the *Save Zeb* people, by the governor's right-hand man."

"Who's that?" Allie said, wracking her brain but drawing a blank.

"His chief-of-staff," Artie said gleefully. "Kurt Bishop."

Allie wrote the name. She thought she had heard of the man but wasn't entirely sure.

"So Alarie was working for Bishop?" Allie said. "Directly?"

"Yup," Artie said. "He was taken off security by the commander of the state police–"

"That's Colonel Thibodeau, right?" Allie said.

"Right. Very good," Artie said. "And he was assigned to special duty. Reporting directly to Kurt Bishop."

"That's kind of a strange set-up, isn't it?" Allie said. "I mean, that would not be the typical way to conduct an investigation, would it?"

"I've never seen anything like it," Artie said. "And I've been in and out of state government for thirty years."

"So the governor is behind this?" Allie asked.

"No," Artie said sharply, "he doesn't even know about it, I'm afraid. Bishop has just gone off the reservation."

Allie scribbled notes. "So can I attribute this to you? Without a name?"

"That's why I called," Artie said.

"You work directly with the governor, right?" Allie said.

"I sure do," Artie said. "I've known him almost twenty years. And I don't like seeing him ill-used."

"So I can put you down as a source close to the governor?" Allie asked.

"That would be entirely accurate," Artie said.

Stoops was jumping around behind her, reading notes. He held up two fingers and mouthed, "Two sources."

"I'd need another source to go with this, since we're going to use it anonymously," Allie said. "It's my paper's policy."

"Such standards from a small-town weekly," Artie said.

"Well, that's just the way we do things here," Allie said.

"I should think Colonel Thibodeau could confirm parts of it," Artie said. "I can probably make sure he will take your call."

"That would work," Allie said. "When should I call him?"

"I'll try to get through right away," Artie said. "Try him this afternoon and you'll probably get through."

Stoops had leaned in to listen to the phone conversation, jumping like a schoolgirl.

"Just one last thing," Allie said. "Why are you giving me this? Why not go to one of the big guys in Detroit? Or television? It makes me suspicious."

Artie hesitated. "Off the record," he said, "I like your writing. I know you'll do the story justice. And I know the big boys will pick it up the day after you release it Saturday. Plus, Bishop is headed up that way this week, and I want to give him enough rope to hang himself, really."

Allie thought the man sounded as credible as any source in the government could be. "I'll buy that," she said. "Thanks for the call."

"My pleasure," Artie said.

Stoops stood her up from her chair after she hung up the phone. He made her dance a jig with him. "This is the Michigan Press Association Award for political writing," he sang. "Great stuff, Allie."

She smiled at his juvenile brand of joy. It was the biggest story she'd ever had the good fortune to stumble upon. She shooed Stoops from the room and pulled up the Alarie story she had in progress. Gleaning info from her notes, she had Artie Fisher's tale incorporated within thirty minutes and still had time to make it back to court. Not too shabby for a country girl, she thought.

Jeremy arrived back at the courthouse early from lunch. He slipped into the lawyers' lounge, sprawled out on a sofa, and closed his eyes. When the closed-circuit camera to Parr's courtroom began to buzz with activity, he rose wearily and made his way back in for the afternoon session.

Gray put Chief McGuigan on the stand when court reconvened. It was basically a rehash of his preliminary examination testimony. He gave his grandfatherly explanation of the Molotov cocktail that was the cause of the bulldozer fire and his spiel about the danger his men had faced in battling any blaze, let alone one caused by a homemade form of napalm.

Since Jeremy wasn't challenging the cause of the fire, it made McGuigan's testimony largely moot. But Gray had to put him on the stand in an arson case. Jeremy took advantage once more, having the fire chief acknowledge that his investigation gave him no way of knowing who had used the Molotov cocktail to destroy the bulldozer. Jeremy did not bother arguing the danger of the fire with McGuigan, other than to confirm that, in his entire tenure, no firefighter with the Milton Department had ever been injured battling a car fire. Jeremy had his own expert, and there was nothing to be gained wasting time arguing with the chief.

Gray wrapped up his case in classic prosecution style. Detective Russell took the stand to sew up all the loose ends. She chronologically went over her investigation and how she had built the case against Zeb piece by piece. Russell was a solid cop. Jeremy knew it, and when Gray was done with his direct examination, the jury knew it, too.

"You are the lead detective on this case, correct?" Jeremy began his cross.

"I'm the only detective," Russell smiled at him. Jeremy had crossed her a half-dozen times since coming to Milton. She was cute and sharp; a persuasive combination, and Jeremy wanted a clean cross to get her off the stand quickly.

"You were in charge of this investigation, correct?" Jeremy smiled back.

"Yes, sir, I was."

"Being in charge of this investigation, you had access to all the evidence collected by the police in this case, correct?"

"Yes," Detective Russell said.

"Let me review some of that evidence with you," Jeremy said. "Three of the vehicles on the scene were clearly damaged by a silicon carbide mixture, as you've described, correct?"

"Yes, sir. A loader, a backhoe and an off-highway truck. That's correct."

"And through your investigation, you determined that Zeb Radamacher was directly involved in purchasing silicon carbide at a lapidary store in Lansing, correct?"

"Yes, sir. About a week before the terrorist act, sir," Russell smiled at Jeremy again.

"Thank you," Jeremy said. "And, when you searched Zeb Radamacher's home, you found a used bag of silicon carbide in his garage, correct?"

"Yes, sir. That's correct," Detective Russell said. "Admitted as People's Exhibit Number 5, I believe."

"And, you know from your investigation, that a silicon carbide solution was injected into the oil system of the loader, the backhoe and the truck, correct?"

"Yes," Russell said.

"And, you know this was accomplished by drilling a hole in the oil access pipe of each vehicle."

"Yes, sir."

"And, these holes were all drilled on the back of the oil access pipes so they were not easily seen?" Jeremy asked.

"Yes, sir," Detective Russell said. "That's my understanding."

"And, in the course of your investigation, you discovered a drill was found where the off-highway truck had been parked?"

"Yes, sir," Detective Russell said. "It's been entered as People's Exhibit Number 1, I believe."

"And, that drill was marked as the property of Milton High School?"

"Yes," Russell said.

"And, you learned that the drill was taken from a shop class, correct?" Jeremy loved the rhythm of a good cross. His goal was an uninterrupted string of "yes" answers, and, while it never went perfectly, when it went well, the jury would nod with the rhythm. He glanced at them – the arbiters of Zeb's fate. They were properly attentive.

"Yes, that's right, sir." Russell said.

"And, of the four young people who you believe committed this act, Zeb Radamacher was the only one who was enrolled in that class, correct?" Jeremy asked.

"Yes, sir," Russell said.

"And, it would be your contention to this jury, would it not, that you believe Zeb Radamacher took that drill and used it to effect his plan of putting silicon carbide into these machines?"

"Yes, that's right," Russell said. "It's pretty straightforward, really."

"Thank you," Jeremy said. "Now, you understand, from working on this case, how the silicon carbide would work to destroy these engines, don't you?"

"Well, yes," Russell said. "I think the mechanic, John Few, told us. Once the engine is running, the hard particles of the carbide get suspended in the oil and groove the metal of the motors. They wreck it."

"Thank you," Jeremy said. "So it's true that you understand this process now, from working on this case, isn't it?"

"Yes, I do," Russell said.

"And you understand that this process starts to work, not when the silicon carbide is first put in the oil, but only after the machines are started and the substance is worked through the engines, isn't that correct?"

"Yes. That's my understanding," Detective Russell said.

"And that's why the perpetrator of this crime went to great lengths to drill holes in the back of the oil intake pipes, isn't it? To make sure that the equipment operators wouldn't see that the engines were tampered with? Right?"

"Yes. That's my belief."

"That's your belief from working on this case, and from understanding how the acts of sabotage were carried out, right?"

"Yes, sir," Detective Russell said.

"And, the reason for that is because, if the equipment operator sees that someone's tampered with his oil supply, he might check it out before starting the machine, correct?"

"Yes, sir," Russell said. "That is possible."

"And that would defeat the whole purpose, right?" Jeremy said. "If the operator doesn't start the machine, the engine is not going to get destroyed, right?"

"That's possible, sir," Russell said.

"So it would be important to the perpetrator of such a crime not to broadcast the fact that he had sabotaged equipment, wouldn't it?" Jeremy said.

"I don't know what would be important to the perpetrator, sir," Russell said.

"Would it be fair for me to tell this jury, Detective Russell, that all the evidence connected with the injection of silicon carbide into the oil systems of the three vehicles you described is connected directly to Zeb Radamacher?"

"Yes. I don't think there's any doubt about that," Russell smiled.

"Thank you," Jeremy said. "Now let me ask you about the other act of sabotage that occurred on the site that night. You know from your investigation that a Molotov cocktail was used to ignite a bulldozer, correct?"

"Yes, sir." Detective Russell said. "But I wouldn't call the bulldozer a *separate* act of sabotage, sir. There were four vehicles damaged on the site. All at the same time, as best we can determine."

"Three vehicles that you described were sabotaged with silicon carbide, correct?" Jeremy said.

"Yes, sir."

"That was a rather stealthy way, a quiet way, of sabotaging those vehicles, correct?"

"I, uh, yes, sir. I guess you could say that," Detective Russell said.

"Now, the bulldozer that was sabotaged was blown up with a Molotov cocktail, correct?"

"Yes, sir," Detective Russell said.

"That's kind of like a homemade napalm bomb, we learned from your investigation, correct?"

"Yes, sir," Detective Russell said. "That's the way Chief McGuigan described it."

"You haven't learned anything different in your investigation, have you? You wouldn't describe it differently, would you?"

"No, sir," Detective Russell said.

"Okay," Jeremy said. "Now, that is a very loud way of sabotaging a vehicle, isn't it?"

"I don't know, sir," Detective Russell said.

"Well you took a statement from Jared MacAdam in your investigation, didn't you?" Jeremy said.

"Yes, sir." Detective Russell said.

"And he described – you don't have any reason to doubt that he was telling you the truth, do you? You relied on what he said in bringing this case, didn't you?"

"Yes, sir," Detective Russell said.

"Well, he described the sound as loud, right? Like a – WHOOOSH – he said, right?"

"Yes, sir," Detective Russell said.

"So, in the course of your investigation, is it fair for me to tell the jury, that you would conclude that using a Molotov cocktail to ignite a vehicle is a very loud way to sabotage a piece of equipment?"

"Yes, sir," Detective Russell said. "I guess that's true."

"It is also a very visible way to sabotage a vehicle, correct?" Jeremy said.

"Yes, sir," Detective Russell said.

"Trooper Nielsen saw the aftermath all the way from the highway, right? A quarter mile away, correct?"

"Yes, sir."

"And, it's a very immediate way, correct? I mean, when you throw it, it ignites on contact, according to Chief McGuigan, right?"

"Yes, sir."

"Objection," Gray stood. "He's got her testifying about other witness' testimony, Judge."

"I'll allow it," Parr ruled.

"So, my question is, Detective Russell," Jeremy said, "these are two very different acts of sabotage – the bombing and the silicon carbide – aren't they?"

"They all accomplished the same thing," Detective Russell smiled at Jeremy.

Detective Russell had given him all she would, Jeremy thought. The rest would have to be done by Zeb. And by Jeremy, himself, in closing argument.

"No further questions, Your Honor," Jeremy said.

Gray rested his case when Detective Russell was excused from the stand. Jeremy told Parr that he would need a full day to put on his case. Parr let the jury go home early for the afternoon, and court was adjourned.

Jeremy had seen Charlie pop into the courtroom in the afternoon, but, as he looked back now, his old friend was nowhere to be found. Jeremy was dying to hear Charlie's commentary on the case. He found him far more helpful than the anchor on Court TV.

Allie came up to the bar as he was packing his briefcase.

"Got a second?" she said.

"No interviews until after the trial," Jeremy smiled.

The two walked out of the courtroom together.

"You look like crap," she said, "You need someone to take care of you during these trial weeks, I think."

Jeremy was completely drained. Too many stressful hours. Not eating right. He had no doubt that it showed in his appearance, but he did not really want to look in the mirror.

"Thanks a lot," he said. "You look like dirt, too." Allie laughed. She didn't look like dirt, though, Jeremy thought. She was thriving on the story and the new job, riding a wave of energy.

"I didn't mean – you just look like you could use a home-cooked meal," Allie said. "That's all."

"I know," he said, smiling at her. "Not tonight, though. I have to get over and see Zeb at the jail. Tomorrow's our big day."

"So he's taking the stand?" she said.

"Never a doubt. We're just telling them the truth," Jeremy said.

"Well, then why do you need to practice? If it's just the truth," Allie said.

"My, my. Becoming quite the cynic, aren't we, Ms. Big-Time Reporter," he said.

"C'mon," Allie said. "I need to talk to you. Let me make you dinner tonight? Your place. You can relax. Do nothing. Just listen. I have a huge story I have to tell you about."

Jeremy was afraid of the distraction, but looking into her brown eyes, he melted. "All right. All right," he said. "But it will have to be a late one. How about nine?"

"All right," she said. "Let me get there early. I'll have something waiting for you."

"So '50s," he smiled. "It's unlocked. We live in Milton."

38

Jeremy pulled up next to Allie's jeep in the driveway. A soft glow of yellow light seeped from the picture window onto his porch. He dragged himself out of the car. The trial had taken almost every ounce of energy from him, but the sight of Allie in his kitchen when he walked in the door kept him conscious.

"Perfect timing," she said, setting a pan in the middle of the table. It was modest, but the setting could have been ripped from the cover of *Fine Cooking*. A romantic table for two. She had found the cloth napkins. A fresh salad was the backdrop for a main dish that looked like lasagna. Two glasses of Merlot were bathed in candlelight, all inviting him to his seat.

"Wow," he said.

"Come on in," she said. "The lasagna just came out."

He sat in the chair, relaxed by the ambience. "To Milton's best trial lawyer," she said, raising her glass.

"Well," Jeremy said, raising his glass to hers, "maybe we should wait until we see what the verdict is?"

The wine cleared his mind, refreshing him.

"You're doing great," she said.

Jeremy still did not have a sense for how the jury might go. He couldn't even tell if Allie was sincere. And what did it matter? It would be over in a day or two, and that was all Jeremy's exhausted mind really wanted.

The lasagna was heavenly, bested only by Allie's service. He had never felt like such a prince.

"So, you're not going to believe who called me today," Allie said, candlelight falling softly on her expectant smile.

"Jimmy Hoffa?" Jeremy said, deadpan.

She laughed, and, mixed with the Merlot coursing though his veins, it felt like morphine. He laughed, too.

"No," she said. "Better."

"I dunno," Jeremy said, unable to think anymore.

"Someone connected to Governor Howell," she said. "Do you know Art Fisher?"

Jeremy had never heard the name.

"Stoops says he's a big-time political operative in the governor's machine," Allie said. "He calls me out of the blue today, and guess what he says?"

Jeremy thought again. "He knows where Jimmy Hoffa is buried?" They laughed again together, Allie rocking forward. Jeremy could smell her hair; apple blossoms, reminding him of a tree he had climbed daily as a boy.

He looked at her, laughing, and realized that he felt closer to Allie Demming than any human being on the planet.

"No," she said. "He knows who Richard Alarie was working for. The guy was from the governor's security detail. He was working directly for the governor's chief-of-staff when he was infiltrating *Save Zeb*. Stoops says I'm going to win a Michigan Press Academy award for this story."

"Wow," Jeremy said. "That's gonna make a great story. That means you'll have to stay here, then. I mean, you can't move to Chicago if you've got a Michigan Press award, can you?"

Allie stared at her salad.

"No," he said earnestly. "That's great. Really. That will be a great story. I can't even imagine what in the hell the governor is doing trying to spy on *Save Zeb*. I mean, that is just kooky. Do they honestly think we're terrorists?"

"It's not the governor," Allie said. "It's his chief-of-staff. Guy named Bishop. Kurt Bishop."

Jeremy thought for a moment. The name sounded vaguely familiar, but he couldn't place it.

"It's just too much," Jeremy said. "I wish my jury could hear about it. I mean it sounds like the goddamned Gestapo or something."

Allie was quiet again. Jeremy finished his Merlot and refilled their glasses. He knew he was going to have to fight the wine to wake up the next morning.

"You really think it would help?" Allie said.

"What?" Jeremy said. "You mean hearing a story about how fascist the governor's office is getting about terrorism? Yeah. Something like that might sway a few minds. Heck, you never know what a jury is going to base a decision on. Every little bit helps."

"But, the judge tells them every night not to watch the news or read anything about the case," Allie said. "They wouldn't even see it, would they?"

"They're not sequestered," Jeremy said. "You honestly think they're not watching their case on Court TV tonight? They're hearing everything that happens outside of court. It'd be naive to think otherwise."

"Really?" Allie said.

"I'd bet on it," Jeremy said.

"Oh, God," Allie said. "I almost forgot. Charlie called while I was cooking. You have to meet him at the office at seven tomorrow. Mandatory."

"God," Jeremy said. "I don't know what that guy is doing. I was so happy to see him at the courthouse on Sunday, but you know, he's not supposed to be working."

"I know," Allie smiled. "He probably just wants to help, you know? You're very - help-able." She wiped a small spot of sauce from his cheek with her napkin and laughed again.

Jeremy pushed his chair back, feeling warm and sated. "That was so good, Allie," he said. "It hit the spot."

"You needed it," she said. "Sorry I didn't have time to make dessert."

"No, no way," he said.

"Let me just clean up, and I'll get out of your hair," she said.

"No. Just leave it," he said. "Really. I'll get it. I'm done for tonight anyway."

"Are you sure?"

"Yes. Don't worry," he said.

Allie grabbed her coat, and he walked her to the door. "Thanks, again," he said, reaching out to her. She hugged him good-bye, and Jeremy felt as if his heart were breaking. She felt so good in his arms, and again, the sense that she was the closest person to him on the planet washed over him.

"Allie," Jeremy heard himself saying, as if in a dream. "Don't go. I - I have something–"

She drew back, looking at him, concern clouded her eyes for a moment and then faded as she understood.

"I think I'm falling in love with you," he said, letting it go, at once relieved and regretful.

She stared at him, and he could see the feeling mirrored back in her eyes. She hugged him again. "Looking in your eyes," she whispered in his ear. "If you'd have told me this over the phone, I think I would have left for Chicago tonight, but looking at you–"

Jeremy searched for her lips. He could feel her warm tears on his cheek. He wanted to feel everything that could not be said or thought. Their kiss lingered like the wine. It told him what she did not say. His flesh ached for her, whether he could hold her for one night, or all the nights. And, in her eager kiss, he knew she felt the same human longing. Zeb's case was in another universe; a universe that would only reclaim Jeremy with the dawn.

Jeremy awoke like a drowning man breaking the surface of a calm lake. His consciousness returned not in increments but at once. Allie's arm was light across his chest, and the evening they shared flooded back to him in the darkness. A red glow from his alarm clock was the room's only light. 4:32 a.m.

He did not move, not wanting her to wake. He lay still, enjoying the soft rhythm of her breath, the faint smell of apple blossoms from her hair, and the smooth touch of her thigh against his leg. He could never remember feeling so vulnerable with a woman. He had given every emotional ounce of himself to her, and the sleep that had followed was a hibernation. He felt fresh and alive. He could not wait for the sun to rise and a grey winter light to fill his room, so that he could look on her again. There had been more tears – joyful, he thought – than words, but she had given so freely of herself, that Jeremy could only imagine that the consuming love he felt for her would be mirrored back to him in her eyes when the light came.

As he lay beside her, dawn approaching, minute by minute, the drug-like passion he felt for her was slowly balanced by the reality of the coming day. Their time together was measured in days. She was leaving to chase her big-city dreams, a stage in life that had come and gone for Jeremy already. She was beautiful and talented and much too large for Milton. She might give away her ambition if he asked; he knew this without words. But he could not ask it of her, any more than he could ever return to a life of defending soulless corporations.

The satisfaction that his body felt, lying there with a woman he truly loved, was betrayed by his sense that he had been right to avoid giving in to this moment. Life would have been so much easier if he had let her go. And now there would be pain and struggle.

Jeremy felt trapped between emotion and reason, and he knew that by the time the light of day touched Milton, he would need to regain his sensible self. Zeb needed that part of him, today of all days. There would be time to struggle with Allie, and the overwhelming love he felt for her, later.

39

Charlie got to the office early. He loved the look of the place. His building. It was a small office in a small town, doing a thankless job. But, it was something he built from scratch. It was the product of eight years of hard work. And, he was happy to be the first person in again; to see the Sage Law Office asleep on a dark winter morning.

He crutched carefully up the stairs, clutching his prize, to the employee door and let himself in. He laid the document on the library table and started a pot of coffee before picking up a shovel and awkwardly maneuvering out the door.

He shoveled the stairs clean of ice and snow, with difficulty, balancing on the crutches while he worked step by step. He then scattered a cup full of rock salt and went into the warmth of the library. He poured himself a cup of strong coffee and sat holding it, letting the steaming mug warm his fingers.

It was the routine that gave his life meaning, he thought, and he had missed it. Doctors be damned. He wasn't waiting another two weeks to come back to work. He'd rehab the leg on the job. He had already started cutting back on the Vicodin.

Charlie slid the document closer and reviewed it once more. He was more angry than pleased. He had kicked himself all night for not realizing there would have been an incident report before yesterday morning. But here it was, and it was dynamite. Parr would have to admit it, Charlie knew.

In reviewing Zeb's case file, Charlie had always thought Amanda Ratielle was one of the most damning witnesses against the boy. She put the spray paint in his hand on the night of the crime. It was a fact that pierced

314

through Jeremy's "two crimes" theory. How could a jury believe Zeb was committing a secret crime if he was the guy who stole the spray paint on that night? Spray-painting ELF on the backhoe was not the way to commit a stealthy crime.

Jeremy had sought to exclude Ratielle from the start, to keep the jury from learning that she identified Zeb with the paint, using every artifice the law would allow. And, in the end, it had worked. The judge struck her identification, not that the jury could really forget what she'd said. But Jeremy had done a great job with a troubling piece of evidence.

But what really bothered Charlie, as he watched the clerk testify, was that she just did not sound credible. He had read her statement a dozen times, and always assumed it to be a true blow against Zeb. But, seeing her live made him reconsider the underlying reality. What if it really wasn't Zeb who stole the paint? And as he finally considered that possibility, sitting in court yesterday, it dawned on him that there may be evidence that would get to the heart of that question.

He remembered defending a shoplifting case two years before, where a juvenile had tried to steal a hammer and nails from the Milton Hardware for a tree fort the young man was building. While investigating the case, Charlie had found that the Milton Hardware filled out a property loss incident report on every theft from the store. It was something that most of the local police officers did not know or ignored.

It took him half the day Wednesday to track down the store owner and to convince her to dig through last year's records. But she did it. And gave him a copy of the loss report that sat before him on the library table.

It was a homemade form. One created on a word processor, the owner had said, to satisfy her insurance company. It listed basic information about property crimes that occurred at the store. The information on the form, filled out in Amanda Ratielle's own handwriting on the night of the crime, was nothing short of stunning, Charlie thought. It listed the date and time the mauve paint was stolen, and then gave a handwritten description of the suspect and his car:

Description: *He was about 16 maybe 6 foot. Red curley hair and black shirt*

Vehicle Description: *He left an got in a black trans am with an eagle on the hood*

MacAdam stole the paint. And the document before him solidified Jeremy's theory. It would still all hinge on Zeb's testimony, really. But this was a bombshell, and Gray's case couldn't afford to take any more hits. Charlie crutched out of the library and over to the copier, where he burned off three additional copies of the document. Then he returned to his seat at the conference table, sat back, sipped coffee and admired his handiwork until Jeremy finally made it into the office.

"Happy Birthday," Charlie yelled, as Jeremy stomped his feet on the mat inside the door.

"Huh?" Jeremy said.

"Happy Birthday," Charlie said again, and started to sing. "I've got a present for you. You're going to stuff it up Gray's ass."

"You really gotta cut back on that Vicodin, pal," Jeremy said, taking off his coat and throwing it on a spare chair. He sat next to his boss.

"Check this out," Charlie said, sliding him a copy of the document. Charlie grinned as he watched Jeremy take in the new evidence. Slowly, Jeremy's face lit up.

"Where did you get this?" Jeremy said. "You've got to be shitting me. What the-"

"They fill them out for every property loss at the Milton Hardware. I dug it up yesterday."

"You're kidding." Jeremy said. "You made this yourself?"

"Nope," Charlie said. "It's the real deal. I got a subpoena served on Ratielle yesterday. She should be there first thing this morning so you can put her back on. MacAdam stole the paint. Even if she doesn't admit it, the form's coming into evidence."

"You're kidding," Jeremy laughed.

"Happy birthday," Charlie said, slapping his young lawyer on the back. It was always fun cross-examining witnesses when you had ammunition, Charlie thought, but he couldn't ever remember such a bombshell on any big case he had ever worked. It was good to see Jeremy smiling.

"So what did I miss yesterday afternoon," Charlie said, "while I was off saving your case?"

Jeremy smiled, and they rehashed the case for forty minutes.

"Well, it sounds like you've got 'em on the run," Charlie said, checking his watch. "It's about time to get to court, Counselor." He balanced himself on his crutches and picked up a stack of files from the credenza.

"What are you doing going to court?" Jeremy said, putting on his coat. "You're not supposed to be back in here for another couple of weeks."

"Well," Charlie said, holding up his files. "Someone's got to argue this motion you filed on Wilma's case. That was nice work by the way, thanks."

316

"I told Dena to get that adjourned," Jeremy said. "Damn. I swear, it's bad enough being in trial, and then she isn't-"

"I told her not to. Don't sweat it. Everything's zen. You just go and take care of business. Okay? And don't forget your impeachment material," Charlie said, pointing a crutch at the documents Jeremy had left on the conference table. "You better get those in that silly notebook of yours. I can't wait to see the look on Gray's face."

Charlie headed out on his short trip to the courthouse. He hated being idle. Lying in the hospital bed had been enough to kill him. It wasn't like lawyering was all that exciting, he thought, but it was a hell of a lot more fun than lying in bed, popping pills.

He paused at the courthouse steps and smoked a quick Marlboro in the cold. The media trucks hummed off to the side of the building, and people were already streaming in to see the defense case. Charlie had been watching the coverage on Court TV at night, and Jeremy was becoming something of an instant legal star. It made him proud, because, in almost everything his protégé did, Charlie could see his own fingerprints. They were surely different lawyers. Everyone had their own style. But Charlie took some pride in molding Jeremy from a silk-stocking attorney into a street-brawling defense guerilla.

He stamped the butt out with his crutch and headed for the basement courtroom, knowing he could set his watch by the time that Welch took the bench. He walked in and greeted Pamela Fitchett, who was handling the motions for the prosecutor's case.

"This is all we got this morning, Charlie," she said. "Good to see you back. I thought you were out until March."

"Can't keep a good man down," Charlie smiled.

Charlie looked again at the motions Jeremy had filed on behalf of Professor Quinn and Mike Pearson after they had been arrested at the candlelight vigil outside the jail, and again at the Blue-Mart. His motion was straightforward and powerful. The disturbing the peace and permit violation statutes were unconstitutional as applied, because they violated the protestors' right to free speech and assembly under the First Amendment of the United States Constitution and Article One, Sections 3 and 5 of the Michigan Constitution.

It was a motion that would normally have no chance in front of a judge like Welch. He would never think of invalidating a state law in the name of civil liberties. But, given his outburst at Gray the week before, Charlie believed the tide might have changed.

His suspicions were confirmed at 8:30 a.m. when Welch took the bench.

"I've read your motions, Mr. Sage," Welch said, after taking the appearances of the lawyers, "and the response filed by the People, Ms. Fitchett. Is there any need for oral argument on these issues?" Charlie sensed Welch had hostility for Fitchett's position by the way he looked at the young prosecutor when he addressed her.

"I think our position is well laid out in our motion and brief, Your Honor," Charlie said. "Unless the Court has some specific questions, the defense would waive oral argument."

"Ms. Fitchett?" Welch turned on her again, his large head looking almost like that of a bull dog. Gray had really fired the old judge up when he charged Jeremy as a terrorist, Charlie smiled to himself.

"W-well, Your Honor, just briefly," Fitchett stammered. "As we pointed out in our brief, the United States Supreme Court has specifically, and continually, acknowledged the right of the state to put reasonable conditions on the exercise of First Amendment rights. Restrictions on the time, place and manner of protest."

"I see that in your brief," Welch growled. "Do you have anything additional that you need to tell me that is not in your brief?"

"N-no," Fitchett said. "Just that the People believe this is a very clear case, and that the defense motion is without merit."

"Well, thank you, Ms. Fitchett," Welch said. "I, on the other hand, do not think the defense position is without merit. In applying the statutes in question, the State has effectively silenced the right of the defendants to assemble and peaceably redress their grievances with their government. The defendants were neither disorderly nor violent in their protest, and they were assembled on public lands. There was no legitimate public interest served in regulating the time, place or manner of their free exercise of political expression, other than an attempt to silence them in their criticism of government officials.

"I take note of the recent decision in *ELF v. Howell, Slip Opinion 04-1678-A* in the Federal District Court of the Eastern District. By Judge Ball. A man I went to school with, and served in Korea with, by the way. There he uses a similar analysis to strike down this new MEGPAT legislation on its face under both the First and Fourteenth Amendments. You can tell your boss, Ms. Fitchett, that we are not going to trample the constitution here in Wabeno County.

"Therefore, finding that the statutes at issue in this case are unconstitutional as applied, under both the state and federal constitutions, I dismiss the cases against the defendants, with prejudice. Bond is cancelled. You will prepare an order, Mr. Sage?"

"Yes, Your Honor," Charlie said. "Thank you. Judge, if I might inquire with the court about a separate case? We have Mr. Jefferson's exam set for tomorrow, Your Honor. But he is currently in trial upstairs and likely won't be available tomorrow."

"You need an adjournment?" Welch said. "That's no problem, Mr. Sage. Submit a stipulated order along with the order on this case. Take as much time as you need. You may want to take a close look at this new case – this *ELF* case – before we get to the merits of Mr. Jefferson's case anyway. Ms. Fitchett, you will stipulate to the adjournment, won't you?"

Fitchett looked shell-shocked. She nodded her agreement to the judge.

"You should have seen him last week, Pamela," Charlie whispered, gathering his files. "I think you guys may be in for a bit of a rough ride in the next few weeks."

Charlie whistled to himself as he made his way up to Parr's courtroom. He could not remember a better day in court. Inside Parr's courtroom, a group of *Save Zeb* supporters scrunched together to allow Charlie to sit in one of the back pews. Jeremy already had Amanda Ratielle on the stand as Charlie leaned his crutches against the wall and settled into his seat.

"So is there any reason you didn't tell Detective Russell about this, Defense Exhibit Number 1 – what did you call it?" Jeremy asked.

"It's a property loss form," Ratielle said defensively.

"Is there any reason you didn't tell Detective Russell about the property loss form?" Jeremy said.

"She didn't ask," came Ratielle's glib reply. Charlie looked at the jury, who did not seem to take to the young woman's answer well.

"Were you trying to be cooperative with Detective Russell?" Jeremy asked innocently.

"She described the guy they had arrested when she talked to me," Ratielle said, burying herself deeper. "They caught him at the scene. And I told her that the description matched."

"Did you tell her that you could identify Zeb Radamacher?" Jeremy said.

"I told her I could definitely identify the person who took the paint."

"And all this – this conversation with Detective Russell – took place on," Jeremy paused to look into the trial notebook, "the Wednesday following the theft."

"Yeah," Ratielle said. "About then."

"So it was four days after the paint was stolen when you talked to the detective?"

"Yeah," she said. "That sounds about right."

"And you didn't give Detective Russell your property loss form?"

"Nope," Ratielle said.

"And you didn't tell her about the property loss form?" Jeremy said.

"She didn't ask," Ratielle said again, becoming annoyed.

"And, in fact, until I just handed you that form today, you haven't reviewed it since it was written?"

"No," Ratielle said.

"You didn't review it four days after the paint was stolen, before you talked to Detective Russell?"

"Nope," the obstinate witness said.

"Now, when you talked with Detective Russell, you told her that the person who had stolen the paint had blond hair, correct?" Jeremy said.

"Well," Ratielle said, "it was more like she asked me if he could have had blond hair, and I thought about it, and said, yeah."

"Okay," Jeremy said. "And you didn't tell Detective Russell about what kind of car the person who stole the paint was driving, did you?"

"Nope," Ratielle said.

"And, though the judge had stricken that testimony, you did identify my client, in a line-up, as the person who stole the paint?" Jeremy said.

"Yes," Ratielle said.

"And you did that after you had seen his picture in the detective's file the day before the line-up, correct?"

"That's true," Ratielle said.

"And you made that identification after the detective had described Zeb Radamacher before to you?" Jeremy said.

"I, uh, the detective, uh. She didn't describe him before the line-up," Ratielle said.

"I thought you said that four days after the theft Detective Russell was in your store?"

"Yes," Ratielle said.

"And, at that time, she suggested to you that they had already captured someone?"

"Oh," Ratielle said. "Yes, that's true."

"And that the person they captured had blond hair?" Jeremy asked.

"Yeah."

"And all that came *before* the line-up, didn't it?"

"Oh," Ratielle said. "Yeah. A long time before, though."

"Okay," Jeremy said. "Now I'd like to direct your attention to Defense Exhibit 1. That's a property loss form from your store, correct?"

"Yes, it is," Ratielle said.

"And if you look down at the bottom of that form, that is your signature on the form, isn't it?" Jeremy said.

320

"Uh-huh," Ratielle said.

"Yes or no, for the record, ma'am," Jeremy corrected her.

"Yes. That's my signature."

"And at the top. The date of the theft that this report deals with was Saturday, October 11, 2003, correct?" Jeremy said.

"Yes," Ratielle said.

"And the property taken line, it says Krylon Mauve spray paint, in your handwriting, right?"

"Yeah."

"And do you see the line there, next to description?" Jeremy asked. "Could you please read that line for the jury?"

"It says he was about sixteen, maybe six-foot, red, curly hair and black shirt," Ratielle read the document in monotone.

"You wrote that, correct?" Jeremy emphasized.

"Yeah."

"And when you wrote it, you were saying that the person who stole the paint from your store had red, curly hair, correct?"

"Yes, sir."

"And, under vehicle description on the same form, you also wrote something there, correct?" Jeremy said.

"Yeah."

"Could you please read what you wrote, Amanda?" Jeremy said.

"It says he left and got in a black Trans Am with an eagle on the hood," she read again, in monotone.

"Again, you wrote that, true?"

"Yes," she admitted.

"And when you wrote it, you were describing the type of car the person who stole the paint drove off in, correct?"

"Yeah."

"Nothing further, Your Honor," Jeremy said. He had used the document to perfection, Charlie thought. Ratielle sat in ruins on the witness stand. She had already been a bad witness, but now she had completely nuked the prosecutor's credibility. Some on the jury were shaking their heads; others clearly uncomfortable that they had been temporarily deceived.

"Mr. Gray?" Parr said.

Gray rose and buttoned his jacket. "No questions," he said. He had apparently thought it best to let Ratielle sink away in disgrace, quickly.

"You may be excused, Ms. Ratielle," Parr said sharply. She rose and slowly slunk from the courtroom.

Charlie crutched to the door and held it open for the witness to exit behind him. He watched as she trudged down the hallway and out into the cold. He felt like running up and shaking her hand on Zeb's behalf but refrained. He went to the side door of the courthouse and stepped out into the Milton winter.

He cupped his hands around his lighter to fire up a Marlboro and smiled into the teeth of a growing wind. The sky was ominous. A low, heavy bank of grey-black clouds was moving in from the northwest.

A rush of adrenaline and nicotine was mixing in Charlie's veins, overcoming the residual Vicodin, and coursing to his brain. Jeremy had come as close to completely knocking out the prosecution's case as he could. One witness forced to take the Fifth or admit to perjury, and a second made a liar with her own handwriting. Gray was going to have a hard time even looking the jury in the eye. Jeremy's theory about two crimes might actually fly.

As Charlie finished his cigarette, he half-thought he should rush in and advise his protégé not to put Zeb on the stand. A defendant could always go down in flames under cross-examination. Gray was no slouch. Zeb might undo all of Jeremy's good work.

But, as he thought for a moment about his friend, he knew what Jeremy would say to such advice. For someone who worked for corporate America for four years, and then as a public defender for another year and a half, the guy sure had maintained a streak of naive idealism. Jeremy was going to put Zeb on the stand, whether he was ahead or not, because he believed the boy was telling the truth. And maybe that's what made him a special lawyer.

Maybe Jeremy had grown past his mentoring, Charlie thought. Maybe it was now time for the master to learn from the pupil. He squinted hard into the sun. The onrushing storm clouds overcame it, darkening it to a grey disk in the sky and then swallowing it altogether. Charlie wheeled on his crutches and made his way back to his seat on a back bench of the antebellum courtroom where he had learned much of his trade, and where he would listen to the testimony of Zebediah Radamacher.

40

Jeremy studied his witness list as Amanda Ratielle exited the courtroom. He could feel the jury's eyes upon him, and he glanced up. Rose Galbraith and Kevin Vontom, the prospective leaders, looked to him for guidance. Their faces seemed to be screaming, who can we trust now?

Jeremy had Dr. Wendell Myer in the hallway. He was a forensic expert in arson. By putting him on the stand, Jeremy intended to show that the fire was a poor way to destroy equipment, and that the fire was not an inherently dangerous one for the firefighters to deal with. It was his back-up argument. Even if the jury did not believe Zeb, they could still find him not guilty of terrorism if they found that the fire was not such that Zeb would have known it was substantially likely to cause death or serious injury.

It was a technical smokescreen given where the case was now. He looked again at Galbraith and Vontom. Would they believe MacAdam or Zeb? That is all that really mattered. And they were looking to Jeremy for the answer right now.

"The defense calls Zebediah Radamacher to the stand, Your Honor," Jeremy said, the decision coming from his gut rather than his brain. Dr. Myer could wait.

Zeb looked at Jeremy and stood. He walked to the stand smoothly, took the oath, and made himself comfortable. He smiled slightly, greeting the jury. Zeb was a natural, Jeremy thought.

He spent a few minutes warming Zeb's engines. Taking direct testimony was far more difficult than cross-examination, in Jeremy's mind. The witness was really in charge, rather than the examiner. And before a witness was ready to fly solo, they needed to be warmed up with soft, short questions.

Jeremy had Zeb give his biography. It was a short story, but a humanizing one. And by the end, Zeb was clearly relaxed. Better still, the jury was entranced with Jeremy's witness. And that was good.

Once Zeb was ready, Jeremy shifted gears to tackle some of the difficult ground the pair would have to cover. The jury needed to understand what would possess a charming young man to take direct action to protect the environment. The truth was the only explanation, and Jeremy knew the truth was not going to be popular with many of the sheep on the jury. But it had to be done.

Zeb explained, in as friendly a manner as was possible, how he became interested in anarchy. He described his philosophy and his dreams. He described his concern for the environment and the impact of global trade, and the role Zeb personally believed Blue-Mart played in the dismantling of the American Dream.

He was very much like a young professor, and, to Jeremy's astonishment, some on the jury seemed to be taking in the content of what the boy was saying, as much for their own edification, as for an explanation of why Zeb did what he was about to describe. It was so engrossing that Gray was forced to object at one point just to break Zeb's rhythm.

"So feeling as you did about these issues," Jeremy continued after the objection, "did there ever come a point in time where you decided to act?"

"Yes, sir," Zeb said. "About the beginning of the school year, I guess. Stevie – Steve Wynn helped me put together the Milton Anarchy website. So we had that going. And I was going to try and start a school anarchy club, if I could. I went to Mr. Kryszinski and a couple of other teachers, but couldn't really get anyone to sponsor us.

"So then, in about the middle of September, I was reading on the Internet about the Earth Liberation Front. E-L-F, they're called. They are kind of like a loosely-knit group of people who feel like I feel about the environment. And from there I got this book off the Internet called *The Monkey Wrencher's Handbook*. And it gave me some ideas about how regular people could fight back with what is called direct action."

"All right," Jeremy said. "Let me stop you there and ask you a few more questions about ELF, okay?"

Zeb nodded.

"As I understand it, there are principles that go along with ELF direct action, correct? Kind of like rules you have to follow?"

"Yes, sir," Zeb said. "There are rules you have to follow in order for your direct actions to qualify as ELF actions. ELF is nonviolent toward any life. So any ELF direct action has to be completely nonviolent."

"Okay," Jeremy said. "Now, you had mentioned that you found a book called *The Monkey Wrencher's Handbook*, correct? Could you tell the jury about that book?"

"Yes, sir," Zeb said. "*The Monkey Wrencher's Handbook* is kind of like a blueprint for people who want to stop environmental destruction. Basically, it tells you how to fight back effectively against corporate interests who are ruining your land, air, and water quality, and the quality of your life."

"I'm going to object again to relevance, Your Honor," Gray said, irritated and jumping to his feet. "This isn't a platform for the defendant to spew his radical political beliefs."

Parr looked to Jeremy.

"Judge, this goes directly to Zeb's motives in this case, for committing one type of crime, and not committing another. It is the heart of my defense."

"I'll allow it," Parr said. "Objection overruled."

"So you were saying, this book, it is like a handbook for people who want to protect the environment with direct action, correct?"

"Yes, sir," Zeb said. He looked back and forth between Jeremy and the jury as he explained his answers in careful, even sentences. "It is like a tactics manual to stop these corporate polluters."

"And did you find anything in this book that you thought you might be able to apply?" Jeremy asked.

"Yes," Zeb said. "I mean, the book is really great. Very informative. But, as for direct action against the Blue-Mart development, there was a whole chapter that talked about the best ways to monkey wrench a construction site. They explain about the equipment you find there, and how best to damage it, and how to avoid involvement with the authorities. Everything, really."

"And, what is the goal here, in what you call direct action? Is it just malicious destruction or is there some purpose?" Jeremy asked.

"Oh, there's definitely a purpose," Zeb said. "Basically, the idea is to make it less profitable for corporations to destroy your environment. So the more damage you can do in monetary terms, the less profit they make. 'Hit them where it counts' kind of thing, really."

"Okay," Jeremy said. "I understand. Now, what did you do once you had this information?"

"Well, one of the things *The Handbook* talks about is having a small group of people you can trust to help you. You know, the job is easier with a few people helping. So I brought Stevie, uh, Steve Wynn and Melissa Dobbs together. And I told them about it."

"Do you remember what you told them?" Jeremy asked.

"Sure," Zeb said. "I kind of laid out my plan for how we could try to stop the Blue-Mart construction."

"And what was your plan, Zeb?" Jeremy said.

"Well, *The Handbook* said that the most expensive thing you could damage on a construction site was the heavy equipment. And the best way to do it was to put silicon carbide into the oil system. So I explained to them how we could do that, and how it would basically destroy the engines of these really expensive machines."

"How did they react?" Jeremy said. He felt like he was dreaming. It was strange taking his client's full confession in front of a jury. But, Jeremy relaxed as best he could. It was like cutting off a hand to save the entire arm from gangrene. It had to be done.

"They liked the idea," Zeb said proudly. "They pretty much hated Blue-Mart and corporate capitalism as much as me, so they thought it was great. As long as we didn't get caught."

"So what happened after that meeting?"

"Well," Zeb said, "I think it was about a week before we got together for another meeting. I made some really detailed plans about how we were going to do it and not get caught. And then we met again, at my house. But, this time, Melissa brought Jared MacAdam with her."

"All right," Jeremy said. "Now, I think we've heard a bit about this in the State's case, but could you describe for the jury what your relationship was with Melissa Dobbs."

"Yes, sir," Zeb said, straightening up, some concern slipping over his boyish face. "I mean, Melissa and I, uh, we were really, uh, close, I guess you'd say. We were like, I dunno, boyfriend and girlfriend."

"Were you aware she was pregnant, Zeb?" Jeremy asked.

"Yes," Zeb said. "She told me about, uh, about the baby at the time all this was going on."

"And, to your knowledge, was the baby yours?" Jeremy asked.

"Uh-huh," Zeb said. "Yes, sir. I didn't know about her and, uh, not until just the other day."

"All right," Jeremy said. "Who was Jared MacAdam?"

"Uh, he was a new kid in school," Zeb said. "He moved here last summer. Just started school last fall. I guess his parents were getting divorced or something and he moved here."

"How did he end up at this last planning session, I guess you'd call it?" Jeremy said.

"Melissa brought him," Zeb started. His eyes had a noticeable haze, and Jeremy did not think it was hurting him with the jury. "She was just – she said he was always following–"

"Objection, hearsay," Gray said.

"Sustained," Parr said.

"Who brought MacAdam to the meeting, Zeb," Jeremy said, "if anyone?"

"Melissa brought him," Zeb said.

"And how did you react to that?" Jeremy said.

"I was really mad," Zeb said. "*The Handbook* says that you should really keep the number of people involved down. And you should only use people you really trust. Like Melissa and Stevie - they were the closest friends I had, really. But I didn't know MacAdam. So, I was just really mad when she brought him."

"Were you jealous at all?" Jeremy said.

"I dunno. Kinda, I guess," Zeb said. "I knew he was hanging around her a lot. So, I guess I might have been."

"So what did you do?"

"Well," Zeb said, "at first I told him to leave, and I yelled at Melissa for bringing him. And then she said he really wanted to be a part of it. She had already told him kind of. And I was mad, but Melissa kind of insisted. So I let him stay."

"So you continue to have this planning meeting, then, the four of you?" Jeremy said.

"Yes, sir," Zeb said.

"And what happens?"

"Well, I started going over my plan. Which was pretty simple. I was going to go and investigate security at the site to make sure we could get in and out without any problems. And then Melissa and I were going to go and get some of the silicon carbide and mix it with oil. And, then we would all go to the site and destroy as many of the machines as we could."

"And, so you just went through your planning session with no problems?" Jeremy asked, to bring Zeb to the point.

"No, sir," Zeb said. "As I was explaining about the silicon carbide, Jared started saying how he knew how to make a firebomb. He said he could make one out of just about any bottle and some gasoline. And he was-"

"Objection, hearsay," Gray interjected.

"It's a prior inconsistent statement, Your Honor," Jeremy said before Parr could rule.

Parr thought for a moment. "I'll allow it," he said.

"So, you were saying Mr. MacAdam was bragging about a firebomb?" Jeremy said.

"Yes, sir," Zeb said. "I think he was trying to impress Melissa with how gung-ho he was for direct action or something. But he was explaining how he could make a homemade bomb and blow up some of the equipment. And how we should definitely spray-paint ELF at the site, so that the developers knew who they were up against."

"And how did you react to that?" Jeremy said.

"Well, I got pretty angry again," Zeb said. "He was just kind of a loudmouth. And kind of a jerk, really. I could tell he was going to get us busted. You could just tell. So I tried explaining at first how I had read about all this stuff. And how, first of all, firebombing the machines wasn't going to necessarily destroy them like messing up their engines with the silicon carbide. And I was also telling him how it was important not to do stupid things to get caught, like spray-painting messages, and that.

"So he got kind of hot, and I just kicked him out. I thought we were gonna fight, but Melissa got him to calm down and leave. So then, I told Stevie and her that we would have to call the whole thing off, because he knew too much."

"So, why didn't you call it off, Zeb?" Jeremy said.

"Well," he said. "Melissa kind of calmed me down. She really wanted to do this. And so did I. So she said that she could talk to Jared. And that he would understand. And wouldn't say anything."

"And you took her word for that?" Jeremy said.

"Yeah," Zeb said. "Kind of stupid, I guess." It was the boy's most human moment on the stand.

"So you went ahead with your plan, then?" Jeremy said.

"Yeah. Yes, sir," Zeb said. "Me and Melissa and Stevie – Steve."

"And could you describe for the jury what you did?"

"Well," Zeb said. "Me and Melissa went to that store in Lansing and got the silicon carbide, like that guy said. And the three of us mixed it up with some oil in an old gas can at my place.

"Mr. Kryszinski was right, too. I borrowed the hand drill from shop class on the Friday before, because none of us had one. I wasn't gonna steal it, though. And we had everything else. Steve had an old duffel bag and a military flashlight – the kind with a red lens, so you can use it without it being seen from far off.

"I took a bunch of stuff from our garage. A wrench, and some WD-40 and rags. And a funnel we had, too. And we put all that stuff in the old duffel bag. I made sure that we all wore big socks over our shoes and work gloves – because *The Handbook* said that was the biggest way to get caught – you know, fingerprints and shoe prints.

"I went and scouted out the site the night before by myself. There was no security. No fence or cameras or security guards. The dozer and stuff were just parked on a hill, so you could kind of see them from the highway, but that was all. It looked really easy."

"And could you describe for the jury what happened on that night, October 11, 2003?" Jeremy said.

"Well," Zeb said. "I waited until after dark and borrowed my mom's car. I went and picked up Melissa first. And we drove over to Steve's house. His house was the closest to the construction site.

"We were all dressed in dark clothes, so we were hard to see. And we took the duffel bag and hiked over to the highway. We didn't want to take a car, because we figured it would be too easy for someone to see it parked.

"We walked across the overpass to get closer to the site, and then we circled around those woods that are to the west of the site, and came up from that side so we wouldn't be seen. We stopped on the rise that comes out of the woods. Just to check and make sure there was no one there. Which there wasn't, of course.

"Then we went down and just started taking each big piece of equipment, one at a time. They all had locks on the oil caps, like I had seen the night before, so we took turns drilling the oil pipes."

"Let me stop you for a second there," Jeremy said. "You have heard the testimony that it appeared that the drill holes were in the back of oil intake pipes, to try to conceal them from inspection. Is that true? Is that where you drilled the holes?"

"Yes, sir," Zeb said. "It kind of gives you a blueprint in *The Handbook*, Mr., uh, it is right there in *The Handbook*. You know, the idea is that these heavy equipment operators are sometimes pretty smart about what is going on with direct action against their machines. I don't know about here in Milton, because I don't think this has been going on around here much, but there are places in the country where monkey wrenching has been going on for a long time. So these operators supposedly check their oil supplies very carefully. So you don't want to alert them that you've put something in the oil or they might not ever start the machine, which is what gets the gunk into the engine to cause the breakdown."

"I understand," Jeremy said. "Thank you. Now, you were saying you started doing every machine. Could you please describe that again?"

"Yes, sir," Zeb said. "We just started in a line. The first one was a backhoe. And I drilled that one, and Melissa and Stevie poured in the oil mixture. And we cleaned it up and moved down the line. The next one was a loader. And Stevie drilled it, and I poured in the stuff. And then we went down, and Melissa drilled the next one – the off-highway truck – only she couldn't get it. So I finished up that one, and then we heard something.

And we got pretty freaked out. So we all dove under the truck and just listened for a while."

"And did you learn who or what had been making the noise?" Jeremy asked.

"Yes, sir," Zeb said. "We were there for a few minutes, listening, and then we could hear it was the sound of spray paint. Someone spray painting. And I knew right away. So I crawled out. And it was Jared. He was spray-painting the backhoe we had already drilled.

"So I cussed him out. I mean, he was going to get us arrested. So I was freaking out. And Melissa and Steve were trying to get me to shut up. And then, he was carrying something. And I knew right away. He had made one of his firebombs. So, I told Melissa and Stevie to just run. And I grabbed the duffel bag and we started running for the woods, and you could hear it when he threw it. He hit the bulldozer that was right across from the line of stuff we were working on."

"So you didn't actually stay to watch him throw the Molotov cocktail?" Jeremy asked.

"No," Zeb said. "I mean, I looked back. But, we were just hauling. We just wanted to get out of there."

"Did he say anything to you while you were at the scene?" Jeremy asked.

"Oh, yeah," Zeb said. "He was kind of yelling and baiting us. He called us a bunch of puss–" Zeb stopped and looked at Judge Parr. "Can I say that?"

"Just tell the truth, son," Parr said, and Jeremy could have kissed the judge for his imprimatur.

"He called us a bunch of pussies," Zeb finished.

"So what happened as you were running away?" Jeremy asked, spurring Zeb on to the finish.

"Well," he said, "we were running and were almost at the woods when I realized I had left the drill back under the truck. He scared me, when we heard him, and I just dropped it under the truck where we had been working. I double-checked the bag and knew I left it under there. So I gave the bag to Steve and told him to take Melissa and get out of there, and that we would meet up at his place later. And I went back."

"And what happened?" Jeremy said.

"I was running back, and about three-quarters of the way across the lot, I could see the sirens coming. From that officer's car. I didn't know if he could see me, but I was just out in the open. So I figured I would try to get the drill. Because I knew we were gonna get caught if they found it there.

"So I am running up as fast as I can, and his car is pulling in the lot. And, I couldn't make it to the truck. I mean, he was driving right up on me. So, I kind of dove - slid like - under the backhoe to try to get out of sight. And he was just kind of rolling up between the bulldozer and the backhoe. He was going to roll right past me. And I figured the only way I was going to get away was to make it back to the woods. I couldn't get the drill. So I tried making a run for it. But he kind of chased me down pretty easy. I'm sorry to the officer, for making him have to tackle me, but he was telling the truth about how it happened."

"Now, you talked to the trooper after he caught you, correct?" Jeremy said.

"Yes, sir," Zeb said.

"And when he asked you why you were running, what did you tell him?" Jeremy said.

"I told him I had just been walking by and that I saw the fire," Zeb said. "And then he asked why I was running, and I said because the police didn't like my family."

"That wasn't true, was it?" Jeremy said.

"No, sir. That wasn't true. Except the part about my family. That might be true, but I lied to him."

"Why did you lie, Zeb," Jeremy asked, again feeling strange. But the jury was going to hear it either with Jeremy doing the questioning or from Gray's cross.

"I was scared, Mr. J., uh, Mr. Jefferson. I'm sorry for lying about that, but I was just scared at the time."

"Just a few more questions, Zeb," Jeremy said. "Is it your testimony that you did not have any involvement with the burning of the bulldozer?"

"No, sir," Zeb said. "I didn't."

"And, you didn't have any knowledge that Jared MacAdam was going to come to the site that evening and commit any act of arson?"

"No-"

"Objection," Gray stood. "Leading."

"I'll take it," Parr said, ignoring the prosecutor.

"You didn't know Jared MacAdam was going to come to the site that night?"

"No, sir," Zeb said.

"And you didn't know he was going to use a firebomb to burn any equipment that night?"

"No, sir," Zeb said.

"You weren't in any way involved in the planning of that act?" Jeremy said.

"No, sir," Zeb said. "I wasn't."

"And, in fact, you had told Jared MacAdam specifically that firebombing a vehicle would be a bad idea, correct?"

"Yes, sir," Zeb said.

"Zeb," Jeremy said finally. "Did you have any intent either to commit arson or to put anyone's life in danger that night?"

"No, sir," Zeb said. "The direct action Melissa and Steve and I were taking that night was an ELF action. We would never want to harm any people. We support people. It's corporations we don't like. And corporate property."

"Were you ever in the Milton Hardware that night? Did you steal that paint?"

"No, sir," Zeb said.

"Finally, Zeb," Jeremy said, "you realize that in the testimony you have given here today that you have basically given a plea of guilty to the crime of malicious destruction of property over twenty thousand dollars, don't you?"

"Yes, sir," Zeb said. "That is what you told me."

"And you realize that I am not going to oppose the jury finding you guilty of that crime, correct?

"Yes, sir."

"But, you deny being involved with the arson or with the crime of terrorism, isn't that correct?"

"Yes, sir. I did not do those things," Zeb said. Jeremy checked the last box on his papers. He closed his notebook.

"It's getting close to the lunch hour," Parr said. "Mr. Gray, I think we will come back and start your cross in the afternoon."

Parr instructed the jury and recessed for lunch.

41

Allie had not felt her feet touch the ground all day. She floated, unable to put Jeremy out of her mind for a second. Everything she felt for him swirled inside her, so that she could not separate out any individual feeling. Most of what she felt was very good. Love, was it? Attraction, certainly. Desire. Satisfaction. But it was all tinged with sadness. She could not let herself imagine where they would go from last night.

Her feelings were complicated by the fact that he was the lead in the biggest story of her life. And she knew any objectivity she might have ever had for Jeremy Jefferson had long since departed. That is why, as the court recessed for lunch and the press corps clamored toward him, she could only wonder if they all saw what she saw.

He was brilliant, standing there in the center of the old courtroom. Every eye was drawn to him as he spoke, his voice rising and falling like a conductor's baton. He owned the room with a personal presence that was intoxicating. But was this person she saw only some illusion brought on by her own emotion? She didn't know.

She let the television and radio crews crowd each other in search of their seconds of "no comment" from Jeremy, because she knew she would have full access. She caught up to him in the hallway where he was talking with Charlie.

"Nice job in there, Jefferson," she said, touching his shoulder. She wanted to kiss him again but was completely unsure of herself.

"Allie," he said, his face lighting up as he turned to her. He hugged her, completely unashamed to be seen with a reporter, she thought. "Charlie, you don't mind if Allie joins us, do you?"

"Heck no," Charlie said with a wide grin. "Beats the hell out of looking at you the entire time."

"Charlie dug up that incident report that hung Ratielle," Jeremy said.

"That was great," Allie said. "I almost felt bad for Ed, you know."

They were dusted with snow on their way to the Milton Diner. She had heard the morning forecast on the way in to the courthouse. Cold air was moving down from Canada under a southern warm front. Early predictions were for four to six inches.

Though she tried, Allie just couldn't keep her hands off Jeremy at lunch. She contented herself with listening to him and Charlie talk about technical aspects of the trial while she found subtle ways to touch him. A hand on his strong back when they laughed. Her forearm against his as she reached for the salt. Her lower leg brushing his under the table. She wanted to hold him again. Or maybe she needed to, she thought.

"Allie's found herself a major story," Jeremy said to Charlie. She had been quiet, and she loved him for trying to include her. He was a kind man.

"I guess so," Charlie said. "This is going to be the biggest defense win this county's seen in, well, at least in about eight years."

"No," Jeremy said. "She's got something major, don't you, Lois Lane?"

"My editor seems to think so," Allie said.

"What could be bigger than our office winning a major trial?" Charlie said with feigned indignity.

"She found out who Richard Alarie was working for," Jeremy said. "He was on the governor's security team. Attached directly to the governor's office, doing surveillance on *Save Zeb*."

"Holy smokes," Charlie said. "That's huge. Man, if that don't top it all off. These lunatics passing crazy anti-terror laws that roll back our civil rights, and then infiltrating peaceful groups like the friggin' Gestapo. I wish the jury could hear that. Show them how goddamned crazy all this terrorism crap has gotten. No way they would convict Zeb if they knew what these lunatics were up to."

"Yeah," Allie said. "It's a good story. I'm sorry it's not running until Saturday." She was consumed with thoughts of Jeremy and had almost forgotten the story. But Charlie's comment prodded her to think. Both Jeremy and Charlie had given some indication that her story might have an impact on the jury if they heard about it.

Though she knew him little, she had grown to like Zeb Radamacher since she had been covering this story. He seemed like a humble but inspirational young man. And the movement he had inspired was intriguing, if nothing else. Though she sensed things at the trial were going very well, she might be deluding herself, because she had lost any objective detachment from the case. It was possible that the case could still be lost, and that would be a tragedy, Allie thought.

She had been sitting by like a witness to the series of events for months. As a journalist, that was what she was supposed to do. Give an unbiased account of things. But at what point was the Fourth Estate supposed to rise up and point fingers at an obviously flawed policy? The entire anti-terror effort was certainly taking on the undertones of a modern-day Red Scare. And Allie might have a chance to get off the sidelines and contribute to a just result, if she could only think of a way to let the jury know about her story before they started their deliberations.

Charlie grabbed the check when it came. The trio walked back to the courthouse, Charlie's crutches slowing their progress, on sidewalks that were fast filling with snow. She gave Jeremy a kiss on the cheek when he and Charlie broke away for the lawyers' lounge. Allie went to Parr's courtroom. The press corps was beginning to return for the afternoon session. Allie saw Sam Oster from WHIP.

"Got a second," she whispered to Sam, pulling him aside. "If I gave you the story of your life, do you think you could get it on the air by five o'clock?"

Gray went after Zeb in a fury, his questions alternating between bitter sarcasm and saccharine superiority. It was no less than Jeremy had expected. Unless Gray just wanted to give up, it was the prosecutor's only chance to get the terrorism conviction he wanted.

"Just so we're all clear here," Gray said. "You have, in essence, pleaded guilty to committing malicious destruction of property over twenty thousand dollars, correct?"

"Yes, sir," Zeb said, looking Gray straight in the eye.

"But your contention is that you didn't commit the act of arson or terrorism, correct?" Gray said.

"I didn't commit those crimes, sir," Zeb said.

"And that is your contention to the jury, isn't it? That you did not commit those crimes."

"That's right," Zeb said.

"So, you're asking the jury to believe that you did willfully and maliciously destroy three of those pieces of equipment out there that night?" Gray said in feigned astonishment.

"Yes, sir."

"With silicon carbide?" Gray said.

"Yes, sir."

"The way you read about it in a book?" Gray said.

"Yes, sir."

"And that book's sole purpose was to instruct you on destroying property, or taking direct action, as you called it?" Gray said.

"Yes, sir," Zeb said. "That's what the book's about."

"And you did this because of your political beliefs that capitalism is wrong, and that Blue-Mart is bad for people, correct?" Gray said.

"Yes, sir," Zeb said.

"You knew when you were planning and executing this crime of yours, that malicious destruction of property was illegal, didn't you?" Gray said.

"I didn't know the name of the crime, really," Zeb said. "But, yeah, I knew it was illegal to put the silicon into those engines."

"You knew it was a crime to destroy other people's property?" Gray said.

"Yes, sir," Zeb said.

"But, you thought about it, and came to a decision that your political beliefs were more important than obeying the law, correct?" Gray said.

"I didn't think that," Zeb said.

"Well," Gray said, "you knew it was a crime to destroy other people's property, right? You just testified to that."

"Yes," Zeb said.

"But you wanted to destroy other people's property because it furthered your political agenda, right?" Gray said.

"Yes, sir," Zeb said.

"And you did take a lot of time to think about doing this, right? Planning sessions and scouting out the scene?" Gray said.

"Yes," Zeb said.

"So you were thinking about whether to commit the crime, right?" Gray said.

"Yeah. I guess."

"And you made a decision to go ahead with the plan, right?" Gray said.

"Yes, sir."

"So, isn't it fair to say, then, that you made a decision, and that your decision placed your political beliefs ahead of obeying the law?" Gray said.

"I don't know if it's fair to say it that way," Zeb said, "but I see your point."

Zeb had performed well on the stand. He had followed Jeremy's instructions to the letter, and he had the jury in the palm of his hand on direct. But, he looked like he was growing tired, and he was starting to argue with Gray's points. Jeremy was troubled. He looked over to the wolves

336

on the panel and could see that they were reconsidering their commitment to Zeb's testimony.

"Isn't it a fact that your decision to commit this crime did put your beliefs ahead of obeying the law, then?" Gray didn't let up.

"I guess so," Zeb said. "I don't really know, but I can see your point."

"You admitted that you stole a drill from shop class to commit this crime, correct?" Gray continued.

"I didn't steal it," Zeb said. "I was going to take it back."

"You took a drill from shop class without permission, in order to commit a felony to further your political beliefs, right" Gray said.

"I wasn't stealing it," Zeb said, showing modest irritation.

"You took it without permission, correct?"

"Yeah," Zeb said, "I guess so."

"Well, I don't want you to guess, Mr. Radamacher," Gray said. "Either you took it without permission or you didn't, which is it?"

"I took it."

"You lied to a police officer when you were caught at the scene of your crime, correct?"

"Yes, sir."

"So, isn't it true that you were both a liar and a thief in order to further your political agenda?" Gray said.

"Objection," Jeremy said. "Argumentative." He had not wanted to object. He didn't want to give the appearance to the jury that he was standing in the way of the truth. But Zeb was on the ropes.

"Sustained," Parr said.

"You would agree with me that there was an arson committed out there on the scene of your crime, correct?" Gray immediately started down a new line, giving Zeb no break.

"Yes, sir."

"You saw it being committed? That was your testimony, at least, correct?" Gray said.

"Yes, sir," Zeb said. "By Jared."

"That was your testimony. That Jared MacAdam committed an arson, right?" Gray said.

"Yes."

"And this arson that was committed, that was – it was committed at the same time and when you were out there committing the crime that you have confessed to the jury, correct?"

"Yes, sir."

"And it was committed at the – it was committed against the same construction site. The same corporate target, correct?" Gray said.

"Yes, sir."

"And the man you say committed the arson, you admit that he was at one of the planning sessions for your crime? Correct?" Gray said.

"Yes," Zeb said. "He was, but only for a short time. He–"

"And you would agree with me, would you not, that the Molotov cocktail that was used was an incendiary device, correct?" Gray said.

"A what?" Zeb said.

"An incendiary device – a device that explodes or causes a fire to start, correct?" Gray said.

"Yes, sir."

"Mr. Radamacher," Gray continued peppering Zeb. "You would agree with me, that what you say Jared MacAdam did, in throwing a firebomb at a bulldozer, created a dangerous situation, wouldn't you?"

"Yes, sir."

"You say you didn't want to start a fire at the scene, correct?" Gray said.

"No, sir," Zeb said. "I thought that was stupid."

"Is a part of the reason for your thinking that, that you recognized the inherent risk such a fire might cause to responders at the scene?"

"Yeah," Zeb said. "I guess so. I mean, I wanted this to be an ELF action. And that means no person gets hurt, so I didn't like the idea of using a firebomb."

"Because, someone could get hurt in a fire, right?" Gray said.

"Yes, sir."

"If I understand your philosophy correctly, Mr. Radamacher," Gray started yet another line. He was obviously confusing Zeb with the rapidity of his questions. "You hoped to keep people away from Blue-Mart, because you believe Blue-Mart is bad for our community."

"Yeah," Zeb said. "I would have liked it if we could have stopped the development, but realistically, I knew that was a long shot."

"You were jealous of Melissa's relationship with Jared MacAdam, weren't you, Mr. Radamacher?" Gray said.

"Wh– no," Zeb said. "I didn't even know they had a relationship until the other day."

"But you knew he was hanging around her a lot, back in the fall, when you were planning your crime, correct?" Gray said.

"Yes, sir."

"And that bothered you, didn't it?" Gray said.

"I guess so," Zeb said. "Yeah."

"And you testified on direct that you were jealous because he was hanging around her a lot, didn't you?" Gray said.

338

"I suppose," Zeb said. "But, I didn't really know that they – about their relationship – until the other day."

"So were you jealous when you learned?" Gray said.

"Yes, sir."

Gray paused, flipping through his yellow legal pad. He walked to the prosecution desk and whispered to Detective Russell.

"No further questions, Your Honor," Gray said, sitting back down. It had been a rapid fire cross, but Jeremy was fairly certain it had taken hold with some of the jury. They all looked to him, seated at the defense table, alone.

"Any redirect?" Parr said to Jeremy. He had no questions of any import. He did not take a single note of a factual error that should be corrected, or of an impression that could be dispelled with further questioning. But, because of the jury's expectation, he found himself rising involuntarily.

"Very briefly, Your Honor," Jeremy said, approaching the lectern. "Did you have any involvement with making that Molotov cocktail, Zeb?"

"No, sir," Zeb said quietly.

"Did you have any involvement with firebombing the bulldozer?"

"No, sir."

"Did you in any way encourage or assist Jared MacAdam in firebombing that bulldozer?" Jeremy asked.

"No, sir."

"Did you, in fact, try to discourage him from taking that action?"

"Yes, sir," Zeb said.

"No other questions, Your Honor," Jeremy said, uncertain if he had done enough.

Zeb was excused.

Jeremy called in Dr. Myers for his expert analysis of the arson and for his opinion that the fire did not pose a substantial likelihood of death or serious injury to the firefighters or anyone else. His testimony was slow and anti-climactic. If it had any benefit, Jeremy thought, it may have distracted the jury from Gray's blistering cross-examination. As a technical matter, Gray had been sharp, but it didn't lessen Jeremy's palpable dislike of the prosecutor.

Jeremy rested the defense with a whimper not a bang. The jury had turned their attention from him to the judge, and Jeremy was completely uncertain about where Zeb's case stood.

"–clerk tells me that the roads are getting slick out there," Parr said to the jury. "So, we're going to stop the proceeding here today. I'm going to meet with the lawyers, and I'm going to send you home. We will be back here at eight-thirty sharp, tomorrow, to listen to closing arguments. And then I will submit the case to you for deliberation.

"Now," Parr continued, "it is so close to the end of the case. And, we don't want to have to *ever* go back and do this again-" the jury laughed nervously, "-so I'm going to instruct you again. Do not read or watch any reports regarding this case. Do not discuss the case amongst yourselves or with anyone. If your spouse wants to hear about how interesting jury service was tonight, when you're having dinner, you just tell them you can't talk about it - and you can blame it on me, okay?"

The jury nodded and laughed nervously. Parr had won fourteen votes for re-election with his friendly style, Jeremy thought. The jury was excused. Jeremy and Gray accompanied Parr to his chambers where they hashed out the jury instructions in the remains of the afternoon. Jeremy was distracted. He was tired and more than a little troubled by Gray's cross.

He turned and looked out Parr's windows. A heavy snow was falling from blackened skies. He only had his closing statement now, and then the case would be out of his hands. And that would be good, Jeremy thought.

42

Allie brought a pizza from Fatty's and ended up staying the night again. She had forced him to listen to the hourly news updates on WHIP, and Jeremy was wide-eyed as he listened. She had given up her scoop on the Richard Alarie story. Sam Oster told Milton how the governor's office had been involved with putting an undercover agent inside the peaceful *Save Zeb* coalition, and how it had resulted in the arrest of a well-respected local attorney on questionable charges. It was a hatchet job on Gray's office, and the governor, and Jeremy could hear Allie's authorship in the lines of the story.

She explained why she did it; she wanted to help Zeb, even if the help was remote. Any potential award was far less important than doing the right thing, she'd said. He loved her even more for her small sacrifice to the cause. He hoped that at least one of the jurors would hear the story before court tomorrow, because if one heard it, chances are all would learn of it.

They watched the highlights of Zeb's testimony on Court TV and drank wine. The commentators panned Jeremy for putting Zeb's partial confession on the stand, and lauded Gray's crisp cross-examination.

They watched the snow pound down outside and listened as the wind howled about Jeremy's little house. They made love again; their warmth, fending off the cold. Jeremy couldn't sleep afterwards. He worried about his jury and who they would believe. He got out of bed near midnight and updated his closing argument to reflect the evidence as it came in at trial. Nothing ever worked out exactly as planned, he thought, but the twists in Zeb's case were bizarre to say the least. He returned to bed at 1:30 a.m., and lay next to Allie. Sleep did not come until nearly 3:00 a.m.

341

*

Wabeno County was hit with over a foot of icy snow throughout the night, and the roads were treacherous. But Jeremy made it to court on time. Parr called the lawyers into chambers before the start of the session.

"We ready to go, boys?" he asked, putting his robe on over a freshly pressed shirt and tie.

They were.

"I just wanted to let you know," Parr said. "One of the juror's husband's phoned in. Apparently she went in a ditch on the way in this morning. She's way out near Whitfield, so I excused her. We're going to move up one of the alternates."

"Not number eighty-six?" Jeremy said. He knew without being told. Murphy's Law dictated the answer to his question.

Parr checked with his clerk. It was juror number eighty-six. Rose Galbraith was off his jury. Jeremy did not like the way the morning was starting out.

Gray made a compelling case to the jury. He railed against Zeb as an admitted felon and an admitted liar. He went through the evidence – the overwhelming evidence – of Zeb's involvement. He closed out with a line of reasoning that sounded good, even to Jeremy.

"Let me just close with this, folks," Gray said, pointing a long finger again at Zeb. "He got on that stand, and he told you he was a felon. He admitted one of the charges – malicious destruction. And he told you he lied to the police about his involvement. And he did those things because he held his misguided political beliefs to be higher than the law.

"If you think about that, folks, you'll see why you have no choice but to disregard his entire testimony. The judge will tell you that is your role – that you have the power to believe what you think is true – and completely reject what you think is false. And there is no way on the good earth that you can trust him. And here's why.

"He knows he's charged with a serious offense. And, is there any doubt in your mind that he's a true believer in his cause? He would be out there trying to tear down Blue-Mart, or whatever other target he desired, tomorrow, if he could. You know that from his testimony. So I ask you, if he is willing to break the law for his beliefs, how hard is it for him to perjure himself – to get on this stand and tell you the only silly story he can – to try to get out of a crime where he was caught red-handed?

"You should reject his testimony, folks. And if you do so, this case is very simple. I'd ask that you bring back a verdict of guilty on all three counts. Thank you."

Gray walked back to his table and sat, Detective Russell giving him a smile.

Jeremy made his way to the lectern for the last time. Rose Galbraith had been replaced with an alternate sheep. Jeremy was almost certain that Kevin Vontom would be leading this jury. So he addressed himself directly to Vontom as much as possible.

He took his time, and slowly went through the evidence. It was plain, Jeremy told them, that there really were two separate crimes committed on the Blue-Mart site that night. All the evidence fit with that theory, except for the testimony of Jared MacAdam. And he had been paid handsomely for his lies. Not in dollars but in freedom.

Some of the sheep nodded, satisfied that what Jeremy said may have well been true. But, Vontom held a poker face that would have made "Amarillo Slim" fold good cards. Jeremy had no idea what the young man was thinking.

Jeremy took a detour into the legal elements of terrorism, to explain how Dr. Myers' testimony prevented a conviction on that charge, due to the fact that no reasonable person would have thought the fire would have caused a substantial likelihood of death or serious injury.

It was a highly technical argument, and the sheep were obviously lost. It occurred to Jeremy that the argument distracted them from their central role - to decide who was being truthful between MacAdam and Zeb. And, he cut the explanation short, returning to the main point.

"Now, if this were a civil case - where you only have to decide by a preponderance of the evidence - which side's evidence is more believable," Jeremy said, his hands pantomiming the scales of justice, "I think I would still be up here telling you that the defense presented the more convincing case. And that you ought to find in our favor.

"I'm not going to go over it all again. But, you just take People's Exhibit Number 2 back in the jury room, and take a look at *The Monkey Wrencher's Handbook* that Zeb told you was his blueprint. This isn't a story he could have made up after the fact. He committed the crime his conscience told him to commit. And he did it by the book. You run down what that book tells you and you will see it lines up exactly with what Zeb did in committing the crime of malicious destruction.

"And then you look at that book, and what it says about using a Molotov cocktail, and about remaining anonymous, and about the importance of not letting the equipment operators know that you've tampered with the oil supplies, and you can see clear as day that Zeb Radamacher did not both try to commit a covert crime - one that required secrecy - and at the same time commit a crime that screams out to all the world, 'We were here!' Because one crime would completely work against the other.

"And that's all in *The Handbook,* ladies and gentlemen. And it fits with Zeb's testimony completely. And it fits with all the physical evidence completely.

"And then you look at MacAdam's testimony, and you know it was not true. It was bought and paid for. He implicated Zeb, because he committed the crime of terrorism, and he would have been subjected to life in prison if he didn't find a way to save his hide. But he bought his freedom. He's getting probation, ladies and gentlemen.

"But, you compare his testimony with the other evidence – the physical evidence – and you see it's just not true. He stole that paint, ladies and gentlemen. Amanda Ratielle's notes on the night of the crime tell you that. And he wanted to firebomb the equipment, and tell the world ELF committed the crime. That was his plan. Zeb told you that. And it explains why there were two such drastically different crimes committed that night.

"So, even if it were a civil case, I'm sure I would be up here saying the evidence is on our side. We should prevail. But you know, ladies and gentlemen, this is not a civil case. It's a criminal case. And when the State charges someone with a crime, there are some time-honored rules that are put in place – protections – to make all of us safe from the State. They can't just throw out a charge and then try to stand it up with evidence – evidence that is bought with a plea bargain – and then expect you to convict.

"They bear the burden of proving their case beyond a reasonable doubt. If you have a reason to doubt why the State's charge might be true, and it's based on the evidence, or lack of evidence, then you have a duty not to convict in this case. The judge is going to explain that to you. You cannot convict Zeb Radamacher if there's a reasonable doubt based in the evidence that was presented."

Jeremy honed in on Kevin Vontom. "And, ladies and gentlemen, I'd tell you that we have actually proven our case. And that we're right. And that the evidence tells you that what Zeb told you is the truth. But, I don't need to go that far. If you can say to yourself, the evidence on the whole leaves me with a question as to who is telling the truth – maybe MacAdam is telling it right – or maybe it is Zeb, that's a doubt based on the evidence. And if you're there, then it's your duty to bring back a verdict of not guilty. And I'm confident that you're going to do your duty in this case and acquit Zeb Radamacher."

Vontom did not break his stoic stare one time during Jeremy's presentation, and this concerned Jeremy a good deal. He had to put on his own poker face and sit down next to Zeb with a false confidence that they had won the case.

Gray rehashed his points in his last run at the jury, but there was nothing new under the sun. Vontom gave Gray the same vacant stare. It was a jump ball, Jeremy thought, but the ball was in the air. There was nothing more to do than sit back and prepare for the result.

Parr read the jury their charge. It was a painfully boring process, taking twenty minutes, and Jeremy was certain most of the jurors understood little of what they were told. Fortunately, Jeremy thought, Parr was one of the enlightened judges in the state who gave the jurors a written copy of the instructions, so they might actually follow the law in their deliberations.

The jury went out just before 10:00 a.m. Jeremy went to the lawyers' lounge and collapsed on the Naugahyde sofa. Charlie popped in with *pro forma* encouragement, and left Jeremy to wait alone. Exhaustion was knocking on Jeremy's door, and he closed his eyes and let his head rest on the arm of the sofa. In minutes, he had drifted off to a well-deserved slumber.

43

Bishop scowled as he walked through the empty hallway. He had to trudge through a foot of snow to get to the little courthouse. Some of the snow had fallen in his pant cuff and was now melting on his silk socks and leather shoes. The Milton press conference had gotten off to a horrible start.

The itinerary for the day had the governor's party scheduled for an early morning departure on the King Air turbo-prop. But, when Capital City shut down all outgoing flights, Bishop had to scramble just to keep the media event on. He reassured Howell about the importance of the press conference and ordered the governor's fleet car and a back-up car for a convoy to Milton.

The highways were awful. Bishop was irritated that Usterman had taken his seat with the governor, while Bishop was forced to ride in the back-up vehicle with Artie Fisher, of all people. The back-up driver ended up losing the governor's car, and Bishop did not get to the courthouse until 11:30 a.m. He had wanted to see the closings but had missed them by a wide margin.

As he headed for the stairs to Gray's office, Bishop chanced a glance to a room on his left. He saw Jeremy Jefferson, alone, sprawled out on a couch like a hobo at a bus station. How the mighty had fallen, Bishop thought. He could not resist gloating over his dispirited rival.

Bishop turned up the volume on his cell phone and pushed the automatic ring. He then answered the phone and had a short, loud conversation designed only to wake the sleeping lawyer. It worked. When Jefferson awoke, Bishop hung up on the imaginary caller and moved to greet the fallen attorney.

"Jeremy Jefferson," Bishop said, offering a hand. "Long time. I haven't seen you since – law review, I think."

Jefferson looked dazed and disoriented as he righted himself on the couch. He ran one hand through his disheveled hair, and shook Bishop's hand with the other. After a moment, he said, "Law review?"

"Class of '97," Bishop said, "at DCL, right? I never forget a face."

"Oh yeah," Jefferson said, but his eyes showed no recognition.

"I'm Kurt Bishop. I was an associate editor."

Much to Bishop's dismay, Jefferson still didn't seem to recognize him. "I'm chief-of-staff to Governor Howell, now," Bishop said. "We were on the *Studs Nolan* show a few months back."

"Oh, yes," Jefferson said, recognition suddenly filling his eyes. "I remember now. Nice to meet you again."

"You've become quite a star," Bishop said. "I've been watching you all week."

"Oh, yeah," Jefferson said, checking his watch. "It's kind of weird, all this press. What brings you to Milton?"

"The governor's having a little press conference," Bishop said. "As soon as the jury convicts your client. Pretty tough fighting against that much evidence, huh?"

Jefferson shifted on the couch and stared at Bishop for an instant.

"You're not the Kurt–" he started. "You're the Kurt Bishop who was running that undercover operation against *Save Zeb* out of the governor's office?"

Bishop froze, wondering how Jefferson could possibly know this. Did Gray tell him? Was his own name in Alarie's reports. "What?" Bishop said, playing dumb.

"You were running that undercover state cop. From the governor's security team. Aldrich. Or Alarie," Jefferson said. "You must not listen to the radio much?"

"What are you talking about?" Bishop snapped.

"I heard about it all night and this morning," Jefferson snapped back. "You were running an undercover operation from the governor's office – Kurt Bishop, yup – you goddamn fascist. Spying on innocent people. It's on our local radio station."

Bishop was stunned. He said nothing.

"You were using the governor's security detail," Jefferson went on. "Man, that sounds a lot like a secret police force or something. Is that even legal?"

"I don't know what you're talking about," Bishop growled. "I think you've been defending terrorists too long. Hell, providing material support to terrorists from what I hear – I think you've cracked."

Jefferson rose up off the couch and stood nose to nose with Bishop, forcing Bishop into the uncomfortable position of looking up at his rival. "You can shove all that terrorist shit straight up your ass," the angry lawyer said. "If I wasn't on bond right now, I would personally kick your ass."

Before Bishop responded, he took small steps backwards, out of Jefferson's range. He had no desire to make a bad morning worse by getting punched in the nose.

"Is that how you backwoods lawyers settle things," Bishop smiled through his sneer. "We're a little more calculating down in Lansing. I guess it's lucky for you that you are on bond. We'll see you after the verdict, I suppose. Oh, and maybe at your trial. When is that coming up? Maybe the governor could make a stop up here on that day, too?"

"Oh, I'll see you after the verdict, all right," Jefferson glared at him. Bishop left the lawyers' lounge. He was going to have to stay close to the security team. Jefferson was about to snap under the strain of losing the case, he thought.

"What are you doing?" Artie Fisher said, the little pollster's feet chopping down the stairs. "The boss wants to see you ASAP."

Bishop would be glad to see the end of Artie Fisher. He had talked Bishop's ear off on the way up about how the governor was concerned about the MEGPAT issue. The small man was enjoying his moment near the top, and Bishop had not yet hatched a plan to dispatch him. But, it would come. When this trial was over, and Bishop's political instincts on the domestic terror issue proved right, Artie would be ripe for a fall.

As he followed Fisher up the wooden stairway, Bishop considered what Jefferson had said about Alarie. The cute reporter from the local paper had been on the story about Alarie since Jefferson's arrest. So that part was in the open. But, where on earth had they gotten the information about Alarie's connection to the governor's office? Bishop had specifically told Alarie to keep mention of the governor, and Bishop, out of the reports. The story was supposed to be that he was working directly with Gray. Was it the prosecutor who had leaked it? But why? Gray was about to get a powerful appointment to a state cabinet post in return for his efforts. Why would Gray shoot the governor, and himself, in the foot?

Fisher led Bishop into Gray's office. It was just as he remembered it. Squalid. It was even more cluttered than their last visit. Howell, Gray and Usterman were having a heated exchange from the looks of things, but they grew silent when Bishop entered. Howell fixed angry eyes on him.

"Could you gentlemen excuse us?" Howell said. "I need to talk to my chief-of-staff."

The office emptied, and as Bishop eased into one of Gray's guest chairs, Howell lit into him. "What in the fuck is going on, Bish? You drag me up here to get ambushed by the local press? I want to know what in the fuck's going on?"

Bishop took a deep breath. He had never seen Howell in a rage before – at least not one pointed in his direction.

"I just heard about it, too," Bishop said calmly. "I was talking to the kid's lawyer downstairs. He told me about the local report."

"You were running an undercover operation out of my office, and I don't even know about it?" Howell ranted.

"I wasn't run–"

"Don't lie to me, Bish," Howell screamed. "Gray just told me how he was working with you and the trooper – he was on my security detail for crying out loud – this is not going to play well."

"I wasn't running the show," Bishop said, scrambling to regain the high ground. "I was definitely in the loop, but I wasn't running anything. Gray wanted some help on cracking this group, and I gave him some assistance. That's all."

"That's not what he says, Bish," Howell said. Some of the fire was subsiding. "Why would he lie about that?"

"He's on the hot seat, Roger," Bishop said. "This trial is – well I've been watching it – and it's kind of touch and go."

"Touch and go?" Howell was yelling again. "Why in the fuck do you have me traipsing around in a fucking blizzard to the middle of nowhere if this is touch and go? You said this was a sure winner – that we needed to be here to stay on top of this whole MEGPAT thing. What in the fuck is touch and go?"

"Settle down, Roger," Bishop said calmly. "Just settle down a minute and think. This trial is a winner, no matter what. Yesterday, the kid admitted on the stand that he was sabotaging bulldozers with sand in the crankcase. He admitted it. He was proud. I was watching.

"Now, their whole argument comes down to this. They say the kid didn't have a part in firebombing the bulldozer. So, therefore he's not guilty of terrorism. Either way, whether the jury convicts him of terrorism or not, we win. Because under the new law you passed, he would be guilty of terrorism for what he has admitted doing. So it is win-win for you, Roger.

"But, Gray, now he's got some other problems. If he loses this terrorism case, he's got to explain to the local electorate why he has wasted all this time and effort just to get a destruction of property conviction. I think he might have leaked this to the press to take some heat off himself. He's kind of been getting his ass kicked in this trial."

349

Howell put his head in his hands. "Why would he do that, Bish?" the governor said. "He's getting appointed MEGPAT czar today, right? Why would he attack you, or me, for that matter, in the press?"

"Just trying to save face, maybe?" Bishop pinwheeled from one lie to the next, pulling out all stops in an effort to remain in Howell's good graces. "Maybe he's got his eyes on a higher prize, later. You were an agent in the field once, right? Maybe he's just trying to take the sting out of any potential loss by distracting the media right when the verdict is going to come out."

"I dunno, Bish," Howell said. "This is just getting so fucking messy. Maybe Artie is right. We ought to get out of this issue right now."

"Roger," Bishop said, feeling back on top of the situation. "We had a plan. We're going to make one more major announcement, today. Bask in the glory of a win, or rail about how we need this new law because of the loss. And then we'll check the numbers again. I guarantee this is a winner. I'd stake my job on it."

Howell sat, thinking for a moment. "I don't care about this issue. Winner or loser. We're just going to dump it if it doesn't work," he said finally. "But, I swear to God, Bish, if this traces back to you, your job *is* on the line. I can't have an office where I don't trust the people around me."

Bishop nodded. He had to talk to Colonel Thibodeau as soon as he got back to Lansing to clear this mess up. They would pin this story on Gray or somebody and business would go on as usual. "I'm going to go down and wait for some word from the jury," Bishop said. "You having lunch with that assistant – what's her name?"

"Pamela. Yeah," Howell said, brightening. "That sounds like a good idea."

Jeremy returned to court in the afternoon with two case files in hand. It was sit and wait on Zeb's case, which did not bother Jeremy in the slightest. He always thought that the longer they were out, the better it was for a defendant. He also had Nuccio's file. Parr's docket was backlogged thanks to the trial, and the judge wanted to clear off as many cases as he could on Friday afternoon.

Jeremy read the pre-sentence report on Nuccio while sitting in the lawyers' lounge. It was basically a rehash of the PDI from a month before, only this time it included Nuccio's perjured testimony from the trial. The recommendation was for the top of the guidelines. Twenty-three years and five months. Nuccio should be so lucky, Jeremy thought. Though it was a rare occurrence, Parr was not afraid to deviate upward from the guidelines, and Nuccio's pointless trial had probably yanked the judge's chain enough to invoke his wrath.

Jeremy looked around for Deputy Short for some time, before finding him jogging down the stairs to Welch's courtroom.

"Can I get back and see Doug Nuccio?" Jeremy asked.

"Oh, sure," Deputy Short said. "You're gonna have to hang on one second, okay? It's just me covering both courts today. Storm's got everybody else on the road."

"No problem," Jeremy said. "Whenever you get a chance. I'm not really in any rush to see him."

"Yeah," Deputy Short said. "He's a surly little cuss, isn't he? Maybe they'll get that straightened out for him where he's going."

Deputy Short hustled off but was back in a minute to let Jeremy into the lock-up.

Jeremy called Nuccio forward from the back where he and Zeb sat facing one another.

"Mr. Nuccio," Jeremy said. "Did you read over the PSI we dropped off for you yesterday?" He doubted very sincerely that Nuccio could read.

"Yeah, I read it," Nuccio said. "Just tell me how much they're giving me."

"It's up to the judge," Jeremy said, "but the report recommends twenty-three years, five months on the low end."

"He can't give me that much time for this," Nuccio said confidently. "Nobody even got hurt."

"I'm concerned that he may give you more," Jeremy said. "I've seen Judge Parr depart upward from the guidelines before, and it wouldn't surprise me if he does on your case."

"Bullshit," Nuccio spat the word in Jeremy's face. "You're just trying to scare me. That's what all you public defenders do."

"I told you before the trial, Mr. Nuccio," Jeremy said. "Fifteen years was a very reasonable cap, given the evidence against you. I will do everything I can to get him to adopt the recommendation, but I frankly think he's probably going to hit you a little harder than that."

"Adopt the recommendation," Nuccio steamed. "You listen to me. If you don't get him to give me ten, I swear to the fucking Lord I'm gonna get outta here and hunt you and your family down, you no-good son of a bitch. You didn't do a goddamn thing for-"

"Back off," Jeremy said firmly. "You're not going to stand there and threaten me over your decision to go to trial. Now, I'll do the best I can-"

"You cock-sucker," Nuccio growled. "You don't know what they do to a guy like me in there, do you? You ain't got a goddamn clue. I can't go into the joint serving twenty-five on a crime where I didn't even hurt no one. They're gonna eat me alive."

"I'll do the best I can," Jeremy said, regaining his composure. "I'll do the best I can for you. I'm sorry it's not a better situation, but I'll do the best I can."

"You fucking better," Nuccio said, and turned away from Jeremy.

Zeb nodded cautiously from the back of the cell and shrugged.

"Don't know anything yet," Jeremy said. "I'll let you know as soon as I know."

Jeremy left the lock-up. He would argue his best for Nuccio, that was true. But Jeremy knew the world would be a safer place for every extra year Parr gave the young man. Nuccio was a monster, and not the kind that would ever turn into a prince.

Jeremy peeked in the judge's office as he walked by. He raised his eyebrows at Carolyn, Parr's secretary.

"He's meeting with civil attorneys," she said in response. "Nothing from the jury yet."

"I'll just be in the lawyers' lounge. Let him know we are ready on Nuccio whenever he's ready."

Jeremy paced the hallway for a time. The courthouse was oddly silent. The snow had driven off the casual court watchers. The media types had made themselves scarce. Even Allie must have went back to the *Beacon* to work. He stared out at the front doors of the courthouse, feeling February's breath as it leaked in the cracks. The snow was constant and driven diagonal by a strong north wind. It blanketed everything outside – the grey granite of the war memorial, the majestic oak trees, the snow banks stained with car exhaust, and the little shops in downtown Milton – swaddled in a blanket of pure white. Jeremy, still very tired, lost himself as he stared. It was silent and beautiful.

"Mr. Jefferson," Jeremy was startled by Parr's law clerk, peering out of the judge's office suite. "The judge is ready on the Nuccio case."

"Thank you," Jeremy said. He dragged himself into the courtroom and took a seat at the defense table. Deputy Short brought Nuccio out, Pamela Fitchett materialized, and Judge Parr took the bench.

The judge ran through the sentencing like a rote recital of the pledge of allegiance. Make sure the defendant understands his rights, make sure he has read the reports, take any corrections necessary. Yada, yada, yada, Jeremy thought. He hoped that Zeb's jury would not be out through the weekend. He was never going to get any rest until they gave up their answer.

Jeremy spoke on behalf of Nuccio. The young man had no redeeming qualities, and Jeremy had difficulty finding true words. He was a troubled boy. He almost never had a chance. He hoped to rehabilitate himself, and to start a new life once he repaid his debt. It all meant nothing, Jeremy knew. It was just a ritual, like someone smacking a champagne bottle across the bow of a ship before its maiden voyage. While he spoke, Parr's law clerk entered the back of the court quietly. He slipped Parr a note. The judge scribbled something and handed the note back to his clerk, who exited. Jeremy spoke because Nuccio needed someone to say something before he was launched into the prison system. When Jeremy finished, Nuccio took his turn.

As Nuccio spoke, projecting the hatred and anger in his heart at every person in the system but himself, the courtroom began to come to life. One reporter, and then another, drifted into the courtroom. Then Allie. And Gray. And Bishop. And Professor Quinn and a band of hardcore Zeb supporters. Even Charlie had gotten the word. The jury had either reached a verdict or had a question, Jeremy knew. He prayed that the case would be over, whatever the result.

Pamela Fitchett did her part, after Nuccio's pointless whining. She stood up for society. She asked the judge to protect everyone. She asked Parr to depart upward from the paltry guidelines to keep Nuccio from hurting future victims. Jeremy remembered the small twine noose that Parr had swung on his finger when they were discussing a plea bargain for Nuccio. He saw little pity in the judge's eyes.

Parr carefully recited the law as it applied to sentencing. There would be no reversing his decision, Jeremy thought. And when he had laid the legal groundwork, he then addressed Nuccio directly.

"You stand there and blame everyone, Mr. Nuccio. Your parents. The criminal justice system. And, you are right, in some ways. I know it's not a level playing field out there. I don't have any doubt that you had some awful breaks growing up. And that is too bad. But let me tell you something. There are a lot of people who have it hard growing up. A lot of people who have been through what you've been through, and worse. And they don't all grow up to be thugs. And that's what you are, Mr. Nuccio. Killing animals. Stabbing people. Stealing. When you racked a round into that pistol and pointed it at that poor woman, she was terrified. I bet you didn't ever stop to think about that, did you? Because you've become less than human. And that's your fault, Mr. Nuccio. No one else's.

"You stand up here, and you ask me for mercy. Well, mercy does not equal justice, Mr. Nuccio. You didn't show a lot of mercy when you pistol-whipped these people. Came into their homes and beat them. Scared that woman until she urinated. And then had the gall to lie about it under oath.

"No, Mr. Nuccio, mercy has nothing to do with justice in this case. For the reasons I stated on the record, which are outside the considerations in the sentencing guidelines, I'm going to depart upward from the guidelines in this case.

"On Count One, Armed Robbery, Habitual Second, it is the sentence of this court that you serve a minimum of thirty years and a maximum of sixty years in the Michigan Department of Corrections, credit for two hundred and eleven days served."

Jeremy scribbled the sentence in the file. Mercy did not equal justice, Jeremy thought. He had heard Parr say it many times, but it never dawned on him before that the judge was right. Mercy was the province of God and religion and fantasy. And justice was that human thing that Parr and Jeremy and Charlie and Gray waded through every day in the beautiful circuit court in Milton, Michigan.

Parr finished the sentence and passed the appeal papers to Jeremy. Jeremy gave Nuccio his pen to sign the papers, giving him the right to appeal the conviction and sentence – fat lot of good that would do him, Jeremy thought. Nuccio was sedate, which was far more than Jeremy had hoped. He was expecting a mild outburst at the least. Deputy Short led Nuccio out of the courtroom, while Parr asked Jeremy and Gray to approach.

"They've reached a verdict," Parr said, when the attorneys approached the bench. "Let's get them in here and get it on the record. I want to get home. It's such a mess out there."

Deputy Short returned with Zeb. The boy looked much as he did when Jeremy had first seen him in Welch's jury box. A little taller, maybe. A bit paler. In the khakis and dress shirt, he could have been one of Professor Quinn's students. But he was the same boy.

"What's up, Mr. J?" he whispered nervously.

"They've got a verdict, Zeb," Jeremy said, patting him on the shoulder like a coach sending a player into the game.

"Thank God," Zeb said. "I was going crazy back there. That little cell is enough to make you nuts. I couldn't spend the rest of my life in a place like that."

Jeremy was thinking that the prison cells he had seen were not much bigger. What if the jury didn't buy Zeb's defense? Zeb admitted to one felony, committed for political reasons. He admitted lying and stealing. Was it really such a stretch to believe he would lie to try and save his own skin? And, what if Parr decided mercy didn't equal justice for Zeb's case either? Zeb could be spending a good part of his life in a cell just like the lock-up.

Jeremy felt slightly sick. His stomach growled low, and Detective Russell leaned back to smile at him. They all rose for the jury to come in the room. Jeremy was not a huge believer in courtroom legends – so when the jury did not look at him or Zeb when they came in, he didn't take it for a sign that they had necessarily convicted his client.

Jeremy looked to the stone-faced juror at the bottom right of the front row. Juror one-forty. Kevin Vontom. His eyes betrayed nothing – his mouth was as level as any human mouth could be. But Jeremy was right about one thing: Vontom carried the verdict form. He was the wolf.

Deputy Short passed the verdict form to the judge, who read it, and had it returned to Vontom. Parr asked him to rise and read the verdict. Jeremy stood with Zeb, and they looked at Vontom. The moment before the verdict was read lasted forever, Jeremy thought. It was a moment that he had experienced twenty-five times before. And whether a case dealt with corporations hurting people, or land disputes, or bank transactions, or the life of a boy, it was always an important moment. In that moment, Jeremy knew a decision had been made. He knew the course of events had been forever cast in one direction. There was no chance or chaos that could intervene in that moment that could come between the parties assembled in the courtroom and their fate. A fate that would remain a mystery to them for only fleeting fractions of a second.

"We, the jury, in the case of the People of the State of Michigan versus Zebediah Radamacher find as follows: as to count one, malicious destruction of property over twenty thousand dollars, we find the defendant guilty; as to count two, arson of property over twenty thousand dollars, we find the defendant not guilty," Jeremy let out a breath he hadn't realized he was holding. It seemed to him that the courtroom exhaled with him, "–count three, terrorism, we find the defendant not guilty."

Vontom looked at Jeremy, and Jeremy nodded in appreciation. Zeb rocked forward slightly, and Jeremy put an arm on his back. There were no hugs or cheers. Gray stubbornly asked Parr to poll the jury, and individually they confirmed their verdicts. Most of the sheep nodded to Jeremy, as their leader had, and he accepted their small gestures with gratitude.

Parr thanked the jury profusely and sent them out into the snowstorm. He then returned to housekeeping matters.

"Mr. Jefferson," Parr said. "I assume you would like to address bond."

Parr lowered Zeb's bond to five thousand, personal recognizance, again over Gray's stubborn objection. The prosecutor was like a petulant child who had just been deprived of a favorite toy.

"Does that mean I can go?" Zeb asked Parr.

"You're going to have to go with Gaylord, and they will process your paperwork back at the jail," Parr explained. "You just sign your bond and you can go. But you'll have to show up at the probation department for an interview, and then back at sentencing, or you'll owe me five thousand dollars."

"No problem, sir," Zeb said, still his good-natured self. "I'll be here."

Parr set a sentencing date that Jeremy could not write down - he had misplaced his pen while experiencing the rush of the acquittal, he thought. He did his best to commit it to memory.

"Thanks, Mr. J.," Zeb said, as Gaylord started him back to the holding cell. "I knew it was going to be all right."

"We've still got a sentencing on a serious charge," Jeremy said, suppressing the triumph that swelled in his chest. "You call my office and set up an appointment as soon as you get out, okay?"

Zeb nodded and was gone.

Jeremy turned to a small crowd that had gathered at the bar behind him. Most of the media crews were hustling out the doorway - to file their 6:00 p.m. stories, Jeremy thought - but Charlie, Allie, Professor Quinn and the *Save Zeb* faithful were there to pat him on the back. Winning a trial at Barnes & Honeycutt had never felt this good, he thought.

44

Bishop moved out of the courtroom and passed the press corps as they gathered near the base of the main staircase. The governor would come down, make a brief statement, and then get the hell out of this snake-bitten town, Bishop thought.

He shook his head in disgust at the jury's verdict. An all-white, red-blooded jury of rural Americans was going to let that pompous little Marxist walk away with a slap on the wrist. He was baffled. Bishop would have staked his reputation on a guilty verdict on the terrorism charge. But juries were baffling, he thought, remembering the much-publicized McDonald's hot coffee case. There was really no telling what a given jury might do. At least he had a good back-up plan. Bishop could hear the governor delivering the line – "This young man would have been convicted under the new domestic terrorism law that we passed, and our state would be a safer place tonight because of it."

He wound his way up the stairwell to the second-floor office of Ed Gray. Artie was just coming out as Bishop arrived.

"They acquitted him on the terror charge," Bishop said.

"I know," Artie said. "I was in the balcony."

"So, we're going to have to go with Plan B. Does Roger know?"

"He wants to see you," Artie said.

Roger Howell was seated behind Gray's desk. He was just finishing a phone call. "-for calling, Colonel," the governor said. "Okay. I will. Good-bye."

Howell pivoted in the swivel chair. "Sit down, Bish," he said.

"We're going to have to go with Plan B," Bishop said, taking a seat in one of the uncomfortable chairs. "I can't-"

"There's not going to be a Plan B, Bish," Howell said. His tone was flat and his eyes were dead, as they stared right through Bishop's head. "Artie has worked up some talking points for me. We're getting out of this whole MEGPAT debacle, starting today."

"But, Governor-"

"You know, Bish, I remember the day you showed up at my congressional campaign headquarters," Howell said, the chair rotating and his eyes starting to drift around the dark office.

"I remember that day, too," Bishop smiled. "You were six points down when I got there."

"You know, I knew that day. My gut told me," Howell continued, as if talking to himself. He paused, rotating the chair back, and refocused his stare on Bishop. "I just didn't like you, Bish."

Something inside Bishop bristled. He couldn't identify it. Pride, maybe? But, he kept a stoic facade.

"I just didn't trust all the crap you were saying. About the campaign, and about how we could hone my message, and come back and win that race," Howell said. "You know, I never really wanted to be a politician, Bish?"

"Really, sir?" Bishop said.

"After I burned out at the Bureau, I was just drifting, and Dad kind of pushed me," the governor continued. "But I really didn't know what I was doing. We had the money, you know. And I guess I craved the power, too. But, I never wanted to craft my image. I don't even know who I am anymore, Bish."

"Well, sir," Bishop said, trying to seize an opportunity provided by Howell's angst, "you have been a good-"

"That was Colonel Thibodeau on the phone, Bish," Howell said.

There was a long silence. Bishop's mind calculated like an old mainframe computer but could not come up with a political calculus that would allow him to escape.

"He said you ordered Alarie off the security detail to investigate this *Save Zeb* group," Howell continued. "You told him I wanted them checked out. And, he was pissed because you blew the guy's cover rushing to get a warrant against that lawyer - what's his name - Jefferson. Says you gave the entire department a black eye."

"We needed to know about this group, sir," Bishop said. "They are like some kind of insurgent group, and we needed-"

"We nothing," Howell said, waiving Bishop off. His voice was calm but steadfast. "I didn't order that. You never even talked to me about it. I think you forgot a long time ago who is supposed to be running this show, Bish."

"Governor, I know it's your show," Bishop said, holding back all the rage that was building in him. The idiot deserved a smack in the head, instead of an obedient servant, Bishop thought.

"I'm going to go with my instincts for once, Bish," Howell sighed. "Artie says we should get out of this MEGPAT thing, and my gut tells me he's right."

"What Artie doesn't know about politics could fill up a library, Roger," Bishop said. "He's a great numbers guy, sure. But he's no advisor."

"That's where you're wrong, Bish," Howell said, trying to smile. "I'm giving him your spot. I just can't trust you now. I should have went with my gut on it a long time ago."

Bishop stifled an urge to dive across the table and seize the politician by the throat. It would have given him satisfaction. But Howell was a fit old FBI agent. The governor probably would have kicked his ass even before the security team could have made it inside to finish the job, Bishop thought. Violence would be a backwoods way of dealing with the problem. That's not the way it was done in Lansing.

Bishop smirked. "You know, you stupid son of a bitch," he said, a quiet fury building in his voice. "I could have taken you to the fucking White House in six years if you would have had just enough sense to sit there and do what you're told.

"But, instead, you go off on some witch hunt, looking for the truth about some insignificant story. Do you know, Roger, that politics is the art of lying? You can't begin to imagine the shit you don't know about that gets done in your name every day. It's why you are where you are, you ignorant-

"You can take my job and shove it up Artie Fisher's ass, because you know what - I am going to bury you in two years' time, you ignorant fuck."

Bishop rose, turned his back on the sputtering governor, and left Gray's office. If Roger Howell didn't want to go to the White House with him, then he would just have to find another half-wit who looked good on camera.

Bishop saw Usterman pacing in the prosecutor's lobby.

"How's he taking it?" the senator asked.

"He's gone round the bend," Bishop said bitterly.

"Really?" Usterman said, "He said you had a plan to spin this thing even if it was a loss."

"I do," Bishop said. "I did. But, he's packing it in. Apparently Artie's got him convinced to give up on MEGPAT altogether. He's bailing out. Getting ready to talk to the press right now."

"I'm not sure I want to stand in on this conference, Bishop," the nervous senator said. "It's beginning to look bad."

"Look bad," Bishop said. "No shit. I quit on the spot. If this guy hasn't got the guts to stand up for the right thing – I'm just not wasting my time."

"You quit?" Usterman said. "You didn't?"

"Told him I was resigning," Bishop said. "This is too important an issue to be flip-flopping all over. I think what he's about to do is a disaster."

Bishop looked Usterman over. He was old. But he was the salt of the earth. And since when had age stopped anyone from becoming president. He could do a lot worse than Usterman. He'd have to get him elected governor first. But, that would just be payback at this point. And, from there, the sky was the limit.

"I don't think he can hold the party together," Bishop leaned in and whispered to Usterman. "I swear he's been losing it lately. Slacking at work. Chasing women. I just don't think his heart's in it."

Usterman's eyebrows raised. "I'd heard rumors," he whispered.

"Senator," Bishop said, "you wouldn't have any room for me on the legislative staff, would you? Just until I can land on my feet. I assume I'll be working for someone when the governor's race rolls around, but I need a place to keep me inside until then."

"I might," Usterman said, interested. "Call my office on Monday, and we'll have lunch."

Bishop shook Usterman's hand and patted the old man on the back. He headed down the stairway to the gathered press corps and slipped past them unnoticed. He spotted Jefferson in the hall chasing after a deputy.

Jefferson grinned at him. "You like that verdict?" the arrogant lawyer said.

"I hope you have as much luck with your case," Bishop sneered. He walked out the courthouse doors and into the snow. It was good to be rid of Howell, really. He felt free as the cold air swept across the open lawn and onto his face. All he needed was someone who looked good on camera and who was smart enough to follow directions, and he would be back on top, he thought.

"Gaylord," Jeremy yelled after Deputy Short, who had just started down toward Welch's courtroom. The deputy stopped and waited for Jeremy.

"Sorry to bug you," Jeremy said. "I just wanted to get an idea of when you think you might get back to the jail. The kid's mom wants to know when to pick him up."

"No problem," Deputy Short said, glancing at his watch. "I think I'll be on the road in about twenty minutes. So, that will put me back there about four-twenty. He oughta be processed and ready to go by four-thirty or five."

"Thanks–" Jeremy said, cut short by a loud crackle from the deputy's radio.

The words were muffled, like listening to cops talk on an old police scanner, but Jeremy made out enough. "Parr's emergency alarm," Gaylord said. "Oh, shit."

The gangly, old deputy broke into a sprint toward Parr's suite, with Jeremy flying behind him. A cameraman from TV-23, oblivious to the onrushing deputy, stepped back in Gaylord's way and was plowed to the floor. Jeremy sprinted through the hole like a halfback following a lead blocker.

Deputy Short swiped through the security door and ran in.

"The lock-up! The lock-up!" Carolyn hollered, over a confused mix of screams and curses that thundered from the small, closed-off cell.

Jeremy was right behind Gaylord as the deputy fumbled for the large brass key. The security door opened to reveal Nuccio sprawled on top of, and across, Zeb Radamacher. Their bodies were a knot of arms and legs, swinging wildly. The predominant orange of Nuccio's jumpsuit was broken by the pale blue of Jeremy's dress shirt, and the tan of the boy's pants, and all the colors were over-laden with thick splashes of red that seemed to be multiplying with every gyration.

Jeremy found himself screaming as the door opened. It was not the calm, rational voice of a closing argument. His message was simple and repeated itself over and over. "Get off him!" Jeremy screamed. "Get off him!"

Deputy Short unlocked the inner cell door and bolted directly at Nuccio. He speared the attacker like a free safety and drove his orange-clad body six feet into the aluminum toilet. Zeb's body, wrenched free, fell limp. Deputy Short somehow managed to land on top of Nuccio and was bashing something from the boy's right hand. Jeremy saw a bloodied pen fall to the floor.

Jeremy stopped screaming and ran toward Zeb. Zeb's eyes were open and clear. They moved to meet Jeremy's face. His lips moved silently, revealing an ugly smear of bright red blood covering his teeth. Jeremy involuntarily scanned Zeb's body. Blood leaked everywhere on the boy's left side, from his abdomen up through his chest, to his neck.

He dropped down close to Zeb, wanting to hear what the boy was saying. As he drew close to Zeb's face, he could hear a sucking sound from the boy's chest cavity. Blood appeared to bubble out of a jagged hole in Zeb's dress shirt.

"Try to stop the bleeding," Deputy Short gasped, his breath coming in short bursts, as he struggled to get handcuffs on Nuccio.

The words "sucking chest wound" exploded in Jeremy's mind, as when they were first told to him by a scrawny drill sergeant in the heat of a Missouri summer, fifteen years past. Jeremy needed to stop the air flowing into the chest cavity. He needed something plastic.

He stumbled up and out of the cell and started toward Carolyn's desk, then whirled back toward the empty jury room. There was a large Ziploc bag of cookies on the juror's table. He sprinted to the table, grabbed the bag and emptied its contents in the hall as he ran back to Zeb.

The boy's blue eyes had rolled back up into his head. He ripped Zeb's shirt open and plastered the bag onto the chest wound with one hand, as he tried to get his own suit coat off with the other.

Deputy Short had cuffed Nuccio to one of the aluminum benches and came to the rescue. The deputy ripped Jeremy's coat off and started shredding it in strips. They worked as a team, first securing the bag, and then trying to stop every hole they could.

"Hang on, son," Deputy Short whispered. "Help's on the way."

Blood pooled on the cream floor around them. At some point during the emergency bandaging, Nuccio had begun to cry out like a trapped animal: "I CAN'T GO FUCKING BACK THERE FOR ROBBERY! YOU DON'T KNOW WHAT THE FUCK THEY'RE GONNA DO TO ME! NOT IN MAXIMUM! FUCK NO!"

Zeb was still breathing, and his eyes came back for a moment. Jeremy held onto to his hand, hovering over Zeb's blood-smeared face.

"Hang on, buddy," Jeremy said, fighting back tears. "Hang on, man. They're gonna be here in a minute. It's okay."

Zeb tried to speak again but only made a clicking sound. He then moved his right hand down, with a jerk, toward his pant pocket. Jeremy followed Zeb's hand. Zeb touched something there, and nodded, his eyes rolling back again.

Jeremy pulled a paperback book from Zeb's pocket. His old copy of *To Kill a Mockingbird*. The blood had somehow spared the book, and Jeremy held it.

"It was good, huh?" Jeremy croaked, though only Deputy Short could hear. Tears ripped loose from Jeremy's eyes and poured down his face. Zeb continued to breathe until the ambulance arrived.

45

It was a full week before Jeremy returned to the old courthouse. If it had not been for his own preliminary examination, which he was compelled to attend, he wasn't sure how long he would have stayed away.

He and Charlie walked to the courthouse together. As February neared its close, the arctic mass of air that had frozen Milton receded, and the distant promise of spring could be smelled on the southerly breeze. Charlie had graduated from crutches to an ornately carved wooden cane – a gift from Professor Quinn. Charlie said he enjoyed the walk because it was better than doing his home rehab exercises, but from his grimaced expressions, Jeremy wasn't sure if he believed his boss.

They took the back elevator down to Welch's empty courtroom and were seated at the defense table five minutes early.

"Thanks for the break," Jeremy said. Charlie had insisted he take the week off after the trial, and Jeremy was grateful for the respite.

"No problem," Charlie said, opening a file. "It was good to get back into the swing of things. But, what in the hell did you do to my desk? I couldn't find anything. Don't mess with the system, man."

"You have a desk?" Jeremy gave Charlie a droll smile. "I didn't see one while you were gone. There was just that big stack of papers in the middle of your office."

Jeremy's one-week vacation was a blur. Allie comforted him through the weekend with mixed moments of sorrow and joy. But when she left on Monday to drive her parents to Florida, Jeremy was left alone to wrestle with what had happened.

He couldn't help but feel responsible for what had happened to Zeb. His own pen was used to stab the boy thirty-two times. Jeremy had helped free Zeb but had almost killed him in the process. While Zeb struggled for his life, Jeremy was almost overcome by the role he had played in the tragedy.

When word came in mid-week that the boy was going to survive the attack, Jeremy felt like the luckiest man in the world. He really didn't know how he would have gone on, had his most notorious client died.

Pamela Fitchett showed up for the prosecution, with Detective Russell in tow, followed moments later by Judge Welch – at 8:30 a.m. sharp.

"I see you've filed a motion to dismiss this charge, Mr. Sage," Welch began, after the lawyers identified themselves on the record. "Why don't we start there, so we don't take any unnecessary testimony."

It was a clear hint at where he was headed in his thinking, and no surprise to Jeremy. Welch had clearly become an ally of the defense in the Milton County battle over terrorism and civil liberties.

"I've read your motions and briefs," Welch continued. "Any need for oral argument?"

Charlie and Pamela stood pat. They too were unsurprised by Welch's inclination.

"Very, well," Welch said. "This issue seems very cut and dried to me, and I won't belabor the point. I think this so-called war against domestic terror has used about enough time in our courthouse. Mr. Sage contends in his motion that the statute at issue is unconstitutional on its face because it is vague and overbroad, among other arguments.

"Mr. Sage sites the case of *ELF v. Howell, Slip Opinion 04-1678-A* in the Federal District Court of the Eastern District of Michigan. That case finds that the MEGPAT statute is vague and overbroad on its face, in that its language prohibits almost any act of innocent, peaceful political protest at the discretion of the governor. It is a violation of the due process clauses of the state and federal constitutions. I will therefore grant the defendant's motion to dismiss.

"Any questions about my ruling?" Welch asked. The lawyers facing him were silent. "Very well. Mr. Sage, you will prepare an order?"

"Yes, Your Honor," Charlie said.

"Bond is discharged," Welch said. "Unless we have any other matters, court is adjourned."

"Thank you, Your Honor," Charlie and Jeremy said in unison.

"Thank you, Mr. Jefferson," Welch said. "How is that client of yours? The Radamacher boy?"

"He's going to make it, Judge," Jeremy said. "He's a tough kid. He's gonna be okay."

*

Allie fought back tears as Jeremy loaded the last box into the back of her Jeep. She had made it home from Florida on Friday just in time for the good news; the case against Jeremy had been dismissed. They shared a magical weekend, and she wore a smile to cover her pain the entire time. But now, the weight of everything was preying on her emotion. The sale sign in the yard of the only home she had ever known, her father's demented pleas to return to his home, the new job that awaited her, and saying good-bye to this man: it overwhelmed her all at once, and she cried.

He held her, there in the street, his embrace like a down comforter on a cold winter night. She let herself cry on his shoulder, unashamed. She did not regret that they had become lovers in the short days before she was to depart. She told herself by day that they were adults – that these affairs of the heart happened, and then people moved on. But late at night, lying in his arms she recognized her childhood fantasy creeping over her like sleep. She kept waiting for him to become a prince – to ask her to stay, or to tell her he would follow her to the four corners of the earth. She knew it was a silly fantasy, but it never left her on those nights they shared.

"You're gonna call me when you get there, right?" he said, leaning back to look at her.

She dried her eyes on her coat sleeve and nodded.

"Maybe I can come down next weekend?" he said.

"Okay," Allie smiled at him and his dark eyes. "Let me see how work goes, and I'll let you know."

He kissed her again. Enchanted, she thought. She let her hand slip from his and climbed into the old Jeep. He waved as she looked in the rearview mirror, a gnawing ache growing inside her as she drove away.

46

Monday settled into a normal routine. The biggest trial he was ever likely to have in Milton was behind him, Charlie was back, and Jeremy tried to slide back into his weekly paces. He showed up at Parr's courtroom to argue a search and seizure motion with Fitchett, but somehow quibbling about a quarter-ounce of marijuana did not seem earth-moving.

The clerks, lawyers and secretaries he bumped into at the courthouse all slapped him on the back or shook his hand, with a "congratulations," or a "great job," or a "heard about your case" comment. He was suddenly everyone's hero and did not like the feeling. He ran into Allie's replacement – a short, young man, who was eager to interview the Wabeno County Bar Association's newest star. Jeremy politely declined.

When he got back to the office for lunch, Charlie had a large Fatty's Pizza with everything waiting on the conference room table.

"Game on," Charlie said, reaching for the chessboard.

Charlie opened with the classic King's Gambit, and Jeremy laughed at his own luck. When sleep wouldn't come last night, in Allie's absence, he had randomly opened *Chess for Dummies* and studied the King's Gambit opening. He matched Charlie move for move, forcing his boss to take long pauses.

"I'm thinking of running for prosecutor," Charlie said, as he calmly pondered the chessboard before him.

"What?" Jeremy said. Charlie would say anything to throw him off a winning game, he thought. "You are not."

"Yeah," Charlie said. "Wilma suggested it the other day. I could run on the Green Party ticket."

"You're not seriously considering it, are you?" Jeremy asked. "That would be like Luke Skywalker joining Darth Vader to conquer the universe. Who's gonna protect all these guys' rights?"

"You?" Charlie said. "Besides, you can do more good from the inside, man."

Charlie finally moved. It took Jeremy a moment to see it, but the old chess master had made a mistake. Jeremy plotted out several moves, and thought he could see the endgame.

"You know anything about the Illinois Bar?" Jeremy asked. Allie had not left his mind for a moment.

"What, you thinking of changing venue on some of my cases?" Charlie smiled.

"No," Jeremy said, moving his bishop into an attacking position. "Check."

"She is something special," Charlie said, moving a pawn to block the check. "I don't think you should let her get away."

"Yeah," Jeremy said, moving his queen to dominate the center of the board. "I've been thinking that. Check."

"I think Illinois is a reciprocity state," Charlie said. "They just swear you in. Check the Internet."

Charlie started toward his rook and paused. "I think you've got me mated in four," he said, studying the board.

Charlie tipped over his king and took a dollar out of his wallet.

Epilogue

Jeremy managed to escape by 2:00 p.m. Life in the Cook County Public Defender's Office was hectic, but Jeremy liked it. It combined the big city pace of his job at Barnes & Honeycutt with the ability to fight for justice, as he had in Milton. A win-win situation. When it came right down to it, he would have liked any job – or any place – where he got to go home and see Allie at the end of the day.

He called ahead on the cell, and she had the bags packed, dutifully waiting on the curb outside their apartment building. They were on the highway by 3:00 p.m., fighting Chicago traffic on the long trek south and east around the shore of Lake Michigan.

It was election day, and Jeremy had promised Charlie and Zeb that he would return to see the results in person, if at all possible. It didn't look like he was going to get in until late, but Jeremy was happy to be on the road.

He drove east on I-94 across the southern farmland of his old state, then northeast on I-69 to the capital, and finally onto US-27 north toward Milton. Allie helped the time go by reading *Slaughterhouse Five* by daylight, and then by flashlight. War, Jeremy thought, listening to the words of Kurt Vonnegut, was a miserable human preoccupation. He hoped desperately that his country would take a new direction on this day of renewal – this voting day.

The blue light from the Blue-Mart sign off the highway exit was the first sight to welcome them home. Jeremy took the exit and headed up to Adams Road for the gathering of the Wabeno County Greens at the old barn. Charlie had been giving Jeremy weekly updates of the campaign by e-mail, and it sounded like they might actually make some headway in the election.

The barn was surrounded by a sea of cars. Jeremy parked in the first spot he could find, in a grassy field not far from the farmhouse. He and Allie walked to the barn to find it a hive of activity.

Long tables lined half the hall, with an open area and a makeshift stage at the far end of the barn. Someone had run a cable wire from the residence into the barn, and a big screen television played election night news coverage, complete with stereo sound. The crowd inside the barn was awash with green. Green Party hats, signs, stickers and shirts were everywhere Jeremy looked. Speckled in amongst the Green Party propaganda, Jeremy saw a number of the old *Save Zeb* T-shirts.

Jeremy and Allie plowed through the crowded hall and found Charlie and Professor Quinn standing near the head table, on camera, talking with a television reporter from TV-23 in Mount Pleasant.

When the lights from the camera died away, Charlie came over.

"Glad you could make it," he said, throwing an arm around both Jeremy and Allie.

"Wouldn't have missed it for the world," Jeremy said, patting his old friend on the back.

"There's a reporter here from the *Detroit Free Press*," Professor Quinn said, stealing Allie away. "I would really like you to speak with him. Maybe some of your journalistic talent will rub off, and we'll end up with a good story."

"How've you been?" Jeremy asked Charlie.

"It's been hectic," he said. "Running for office is like being on a treadmill. But I'm pretty charged up."

"How's it looking? Do you know anything yet?" Jeremy asked. The room was buzzing with energy.

"We've got a couple of people calling results back from the courthouse," Charlie said. "It's actually looking pretty good so far, but there are still votes to count."

They walked to a buffet line, and Charlie grabbed two bottles of beer from a cooler.

"Where's Zeb?" Jeremy said.

"Oh, he's around here," Charlie said. "That guy's living the life of Riley, I swear."

"How's that?" Jeremy said over a rising din.

"Well, you remember," Charlie said, "the old man offed himself. And, his brother is nowhere to be found. Well, Zeb is the only heir. So, you know, it wouldn't have been much. Just a house and some land. I mean, not bad.

"But then, Tommy Hughes filed a civil suit for the old man's estate. For when they shot him. Just settled it for policy limits, I guess. A quarter of a million. Zeb's gonna have a nice Christmas."

"Unbelievable," Jeremy said, smiling. "No one deserves it more. What about his appeal on the malicious destruction?"

"Well," Charlie said, grinning, "if I can pull this out tonight, that will take Gray off the case at least. I won't be able to handle the prosecution end of his appeal. But I have been talking with the prosecutor over in Gladwin. We might do some case swapping when I get elected, because I'll have so many cases I've worked on as a defense lawyer, you know, that I'll have to recuse myself in."

"So, this guy in Gladwin might prosecute Zeb's appeal, then?" Jeremy said.

"Yeah," Charlie said. "And he's pretty laid back. I think, from talking to him, that he might be amenable to settling on a plea bargain and dismissing the appeal. Maybe we can still get Zeb HYTA."

"Life of Riley is right," Jeremy said.

"Yeah," Charlie said. "It's all good."

A voice over the public address system interrupted them. "We've got final results in two precincts!" the voice said, quieting the low hum of conversation in the hall. "Precincts two and six. In two, the winner is Mike Pearson of the Green Party–" a loud roar from the crowd drowned out the public address announcer, "–six, the winner is Frank Wenzlick of the Green Party." A louder roar erupted in the hall. Jeremy cheered with Charlie.

"We didn't even register voters in precinct six," Charlie yelled over the crowd. "Wenzlick's just a farmer who signed up to run as a Green."

"That means a great night," Jeremy yelled back.

The results rolled in to repeated cheers as the votes were tabulated at the courthouse and relayed to the hall. It looked like a wave of green was rolling through Wabeno County. Five out of seven commission seats were won. And, in the last election result announced, Charlie Sage ousted incumbent Prosecutor Ed Gray in a landslide.

Jeremy was able to give Charlie a high-five before his old friend was swept to the stage for a victory speech.

"Mr. J.," a voice called, and Jeremy turned. It was the first time he had ever seen Zeb as a free man.

"How are you, Zeb?" he said, giving his ex-client a bear hug.

"I'm great," the boy said, smiling, the peak of a scar visible above the collar of his jean jacket. "Isn't this amazing?"

"You made this happen, Zeb."

"Not without you, Mr. J.," the boy said.

Jeremy looked around at the jubilant hall. He breathed in the cool air of the barn. His eyes found Allie near the stage with Professor Quinn, and they exchanged a wave. He didn't want to hear the speeches. He only wanted to remember the exuberance of the eclectic crowd around him. He hoped the storm that started with Zeb might roll out of his old state and spread like a snowy blanket across his new home and beyond.

About the Author

Terry Olson has spent the majority of his ten-year legal career practicing in small towns in Michigan as both a prosecutor and a criminal defense attorney. He graduated with honors from Michigan State University and Thomas M. Cooley Law School. He went on to serve as an adjunct professor at Cooley. As a freelance journalist he has written for The Grand Rapids Press, The Williamston Enterprise, The Towne Courier, and The Escanaba Daily Press. He lives in East Lansing, Michigan with his wife Bryna and their two children. *Direct Actions* is his first novel.

Printed in the United States
38585LVS00004B/79-153